Cille

LARRY ANTONE LUDWIG

Publishing Coordinator – Sharon Kizziah-Holmes

INDIE PUB PRESS
Springfield, MO

ISBN -13: 978-1-956806-13-7

CHARACTER'S NAME

Cille [syll. cil-le ci-lle] (or See-lee). The name Cille is an infrequent name used for a girl. Out of the group of girl names directly linked to Cille, Cecillia was the most commonly used. Cille's language or origin is Latin, and it is predominately used in the Scandinavian language. Cille is a pet form of the English, Finnish, German, Italian, Scandinavian and Spanish Cecilla.

During the course of writing this story, Cille is given the Indian name Rides ~ Alone.

Shirley Earnestine and Larry Antone Ludwig
We hope our labor of love will become your enjoyable read.

AUTHOR'S NOTE

The story of 'Cille' began, when I listened to the wind. She was known as Cille by the whites, when she arrived in the Dakota Territory. She was also known as Rides~Alone by the Indians. Her life should have been forgotten, after the fire that burned down the newspaper office of the Bad Lands Cowboy, owned and published by Arthur T. Packard. Her story should have lost importance over time, brushed aside, by the many dust storms that whipped across the Dakota Bad Lands. But if you stand still on the North Dakota prairie, near the land called the Scoria, and listen long enough, the story is in the wind. The rustle of the leaves, as the wind passes through the cottonwood trees may sound like a soft whisper of 'see lee'. But if you truly listen, you can hear the words more clearly 'Cille...Cille.' I was there, I stood, listened, and then I felt compelled to put it down in print.

Medora, North Dakota is a short distance off interstate 94, and thrives on the bustling tourist trade. The Scoria is part of the Theodore Roosevelt Park, and the chateau where Medora and Marquis De Mores once lived draws many a tourist. The mark that Theodore Roosevelt and the De Mores family left behind made Medora the city it is today. But if you stand and listen ... you may also hear the story that has been written in time, hidden within the gusts of wind, caused by the storm clouds that thunder out the excitement of the past. The heads of the cheat grass, and the swaying limbs of the cottonwood trees bend to make an eerie sound of 'Cille.' Could it have been? Take time and listen to the wind, when you stand near the Scoria, and judge for yourself. Then you can understand why, the story you are about to read, is an important part of the past of North Dakota.

CHAPTER 1

Monroe, New York 1868

The sounds within the town square reflected the robust rhythmic pattern of shod horses and the screeching noise of tempered metal rims used on sturdy wagons to haul commerce about the community. The carriages with crafted springs for comfort and their hardwood wheels rendered a softer muffled sound during their travel up and down the busy cobbled street. Today the sidewalks were filled with numerous shoppers chatting amongst themselves. When they recognized a friend, a cordial tip of the derby was made by the men or a slight curtsey from the women along with a brief comment in passing. They casually went about doing their shopping on this beautiful summer day. The sky was a soft blue without a cloud in sight, a perfect day to be out of doors and to have the carriage tops down. It appeared that most of those with leisure time on their hands were looking for the highest quality in fashion. The latest unrivaled apparel had arrived in some of the more exclusive shops in Monroe over the previous weekend.

The country was beginning to recover from most of the scars left behind from the Civil War. The bitter memories over the slave issue had virtually been swept aside as the town struggled to become prosperous once more. Most of the Negroes in the north who chose to remain beholden became domestics, drivers, butlers, maids and gardeners receiving a small salary and the ability to travel. It was far more than they had in the past.

The most attractive and fashion conscious of them all was Esther Morgan. She was tall and slender while nearing her middle thirties, she considered herself a leading figure within the social structure of the community. She gracefully displayed her stature upon stepping from the family carriage, under the watchful eye of her carriage driver Corbi. He offered his hand, allowing her to check her balance. He bowed ever so slightly to provide proper protocol in her passing, a form of respect carried on from his many years of servitude. Her intentions on any given day were to keep tabs on the latest fashions from Europe and the markets in New York City. She didn't want the best to arrive without her knowledge, then have her face the social elite ill prepared and lacking in fashionable dress. It made no difference if it was a dress, hat, purse, gloves or accessories, Esther made it her duty to have the latest in fashion. She walked away from the carriage with the extended feather from her hat slightly bouncing with every step she took.

Her daughter Elizabeth and niece Cille Hodges were momentarily left alone in the topless carriage to continue their youthful conversation. They were busy discussing and giggling over what girls of their age found entertaining. Esther Morgan wouldn’t be but just a couple of moments in her favorite shop before she would return to her carriage. She had chosen to let the girls talk while being alone for a very short time.

At sixteen, Cille was a shy refined young lady whose complexion was smooth, but lightly touched with a helping of freckles. A set of auburn ringlets dangled in front of her ears with the remaining cascading over her shoulders and resting on her back near shoulder-blade length. She remained properly seated in the carriage across from her cousin with her white-gloved hands resting in her lap. Her composure reflected the schooling and discipline her parents required of her. She was comfortable in the role society and her parents expected while she was out in public.

Elizabeth Morgan, a couple of months older, was the complete opposite. She sat bright-eyed, taking in all of life that surrounded her. She was fair-skinned, her lengthy naturally-wavy auburn hair pulled back by a fashionable wide yellow ribbon. She was often outspoken with an uncommon exuberance that caused her to get into more trouble for one who had yet to have her debutante. She did her best to converse about fashion, but with the absence of her mother, the subject quickly switched to the excitement of young men.

Sometimes Elizabeth's flirting ways embarrassed Cille. Her

cousin was very vocal, and definitely not a bit shy when it came to expressing herself outside her mother's presence. Nothing about boys dare be discussed in front of her dear Aunt Esther. Any unguarded talk about them would provoke a reprimanding frown or a wrath of indignation upon both girls. She enjoyed being with her cousin, but she also respected her favorite aunt.

Suddenly, a loud commotion filled the street as a wagon full of cheerful upperclassmen from West Point rolled to a thunderous stop in the town square. At first, Cille gave little thought to their reason for being in Monroe.

Elizabeth, being older, became excited saying, "Cille, wouldn't you like to have one of them over for dinner sometime?"

Shocked at the sudden question, she replied, "Not without a proper meeting, I wouldn't!"

Elizabeth squirmed and brought her feet up under her body on the plush seat, the adjustment allowed her to turn, and face the new arrivals. "Look at them Cille, they look so handsome. I sort of like the looks of that tall heavy one, I bet he gets a lot of respect. I would just simply melt in his arms if I had a fleeting moment to do so."

"Your mother would just die," Cille teased, "if she knew what you were thinking. And if he did appear at your house, she would probably run him off the instant he showed up."

"It doesn't hurt to dream of meeting a man like that. Now don't sit there acting so prim and proper to tell me you can't find a one of them the least bit fascinating."

Cille looked, and at the same moment, one of the cadets getting down from the wagon looked in her direction. He was tall with a slender build. Noticing her glance, he smiled, reached up to the rim of his forage cap and made a slight gesture in her direction. She suddenly felt flushed for the first time, but in a pleasing way. In an attempt to answer Beth's question, while restraining her unguarded emotions, she shyly conceded, "That one appears most interesting."

Her cousin leaned forward with an expression of excitement on her face, "He sure does; looks well-mannered and polished, nice choice cousin. Wouldn't you simply love to have him attend your coming out?"

"Elizabeth!" Cille looked back at her cousin in disbelief. "I don't even know his name. Besides, I'm not interested in a man unless we meet properly. That would be brash. I cannot imagine seeing my parents sending an invitation to him." She felt a strange warm feeling come over her. "You're just being silly."

With a face full of excitement and her eyes open wide, she declared, "I am not. If I knew of such a way, I would see that you two met. I have half a mind to…"

Corbi deliberately cleared his throat forcefully, interrupting the girls and getting their attention. Esther was making her way back to the carriage.

"Girls, come-come," she called out, "you must see these latest fashions. They just arrived from Paris and they're simply stunning. Come-come, we mustn't take all day. Corbi, we shan't take too ghastly long."

"Yes'm."

When the girls stepped from the carriage, Corbi offered his hand, allowing the girls to check their balance as he bowed slightly in their passing. They followed Mrs. Morgan, disappearing into the fashionable shop one following the other. Corbi was left on his own near the carriage amongst the rowdy, boisterous cadets who went about their antics.

◇◇◇

When the women returned to the carriage, Corbi in his fashionable driver's attire was hustling back after venturing up the street a short distance. Esther gave him an inquisitive, reprimanding look, but did not say a word to him.

Corbi had a self-satisfying smile upon his face. He opened the coach door, bowing slightly, as he offered a hand to each of the three women as they stepped up into the carriage. After seeing that they were seated, he stepped up into the driver's position.

The ride back to the Morgan estate was a somber affair. Esther simply insisted that the girls, while out in public, behave like Victorian young ladies should. Elizabeth's unbridled behavior was being held in check by her strong-willed mother. Cille took her aunt's comments as good advice rather than a form of admonishment.

CHAPTER 2

Morgan Estate 1868

When the carriage returned to the Morgan estate, Corbi offered a hand to each as they stepped down from the carriage interior. Esther went directly into the house and began giving instructions to the household staff. Then she rushed to her room where she would prepare herself for an evening of receiving guests.

The girls bounded from the carriage, circled the house bordered by a large, manicured lawn and strolled over to the gazebo located in the center of a large flower and shrubbery garden. The small, wooden structure rested on the back part of the estate surrounded by a variety of green shrubs and various flowers, each casting off a splendid fragrance. When they arrived, Elizabeth began chatting about the cadets they saw in town. She began to express her growing impatience of having to wait for her coming out. "Cille, I find it might near impossible to wait for my debutante next month. I'm ready to bust at the seams right now." She smiled while giving a stargazed look before slowly running her hands down the side of her breasts to her hips.

Laughing at such behavior, Cille asked, "What's the hurry?"

"I just don't think it's right that I have to wait for some delicate declaration at a formal function to declare my stae of readiness. I'm ready to meet one of those strong eligible young men from the Point, or anywhere else, and the sooner the better."

"Heavens, Beth! I do declare, you would have others think it's an eternity to your coming out. If the truth be known, your knight in shining armor won't even be in attendance that night."

"I don't plan on being bored to tears, if that's what you're implying. I just think, I'm ready right now."

"Silly, you're so anxious to grow up and face the world. The time will come soon enough when you'll probably complain of too many suitors calling."

Rebecca the maid descended the steps from the veranda on her way to the gazebo. "Miss Elizabeth, yo' mama say, et time fo' ya an' Cille, ta come in an' fres'en up fo' dinnah."

"Thank you, Rebecca, we shan't be long." Turning to Cille, she said in a dreaded tone, "Come, let's not keep mother waiting."

On their way across the lawn, she added, "When I have my party, just think, yours will be the next one in the neighborhood. I'm sorry you can't come to mine. I hope it doesn't cost me a golden chance of being invited to yours."

"Beth, didn't that finishing school in Paris teach you anything? Of course, you'll be invited. I don't have any problems waiting for my coming out, least ways not like you do. Social restrictions keep me from attending yours. I won't hold that against you."

◇◇◇

That evening, Cille sat next to Elizabeth at the supper table. The male head of the house said grace before the main course made its initial round. She did her best to maintain the Victorian image throughout dinner. Elizabeth, on the other hand, had to be reminded several times about her actions not being proper.

Oddly enough, the topic at the dinner table happened to focus on the status of academia at the Military Academy at West Point. Cille's uncle Horace, still in his brown business suit, said, "Those young men going through the academy should realize they're attending a mighty institution. The war may be over, but the west will hold challenging engagements in the years to come against the Indians. I hear tell, the latest points of military tactics are now being taught to those studying a variety of skills, including the cavalry."

"Daddy, are you going to be inviting any of the cadets from the Academy to my coming out?"

"Elizabeth!" Esther snapped condescendingly, "The discussion of who will and will not be invited will be discussed between your father and me at a proper time and not across the dinner table!"

"Mother! Not in front of Cille, please."

Mr. Morgan spoke up softly, saying, "Mind your manners, Beth. Your mother has made herself very clear on this matter. Cille won't be able to attend and there's no need to discuss the subject while she's here visiting. Is that understood?"

"But Daddy…"

Esther tossed her napkin near her plate and bristled when she looked at Elizabeth. "That is enough and the end of the subject, Beth, is that clear?"

Elizabeth sat with a flushed face, knowing she had pushed the issue too far.

After witnessing the altercation, Cille for the first time felt uneasy while sitting next to her outspoken cousin. She felt sorry for her, yet realized she was sitting at the table of her favorite aunt and uncle. As she witnessed the altercation at the table, Cille felt troubled, possibly more than the others realized.

◇◇◇

There was a rap at the front door. Cecil, the butler, responded quickly to answer it. When the door was opened, Randu, the carriage driver for the Hodges Estate stepped inside. In a raspy voice, he said, "Ah is heah ta geet Miss Cille an' takes 'er home."

Hearing the news from where she sat at the dinner table, Cille nearly lost her composure and almost leapt to her feet. Then she caught herself and tried to remain composed.

Cecil quietly approached the head of the table. Bending at the waist, he spoke softly into Mr. Morgan's ear before leaving the dining area.

The domestic disappeared from the dining room before Horace spoke. "Cille, it has been our pleasure to have you visit with us. Your carriage is waiting to take you home when you have finished."

Speaking softly, Cille said, "It has been a rather long day. I believe I'll pass on dessert. Uncle Horace, Aunt Esther, I have truly enjoyed the visit. I should be getting along…"

Before she could finish, Horace spoke up, "You're excused,

Cille. Give our regards to your family when you arrive."

Aunt Esther was nodding with an approving smile on her face, after seeing Cille acting gracious and proper before saying, "Take care, my dear."

Cille removed herself from the table. In doing so, she rested her hand on her cousin's shoulder, "Come by when you can. Maybe we can carry on the discussion we had outside."

Elizabeth patted her hand before it left her shoulder, "I'd like that very much. Give my best to your mother and father."

After nodding in the direction of her uncle and then her aunt, she softly said, "I shall." She removed herself from the dining area to join her driver near the front door.

"Miss Cille, is yah ready?"

"That I am, Randu. I'll be with you in a moment. I need to pick up a small package I bought today."

With the door partially ajar, a figure opened it wider and stepped inside. Corbi the carriage driver for the Morgans was big eyed as if he had been goosed and was smiling. "Randu, et good ah cotched yah, befo' yah lef'. Heah is dis papah fo' Mastah Hodges. An' wha' evah yah do, no let Miss Cille see et."

"Corbi, wha' no good yah been up ta dis time?"

"Ifn ya promise not to tell Miss Cille I…"

Cille suddenly appeared in the hall, ending their conversation.

"I'm ready, Randu," she said.

Cecil attended the door and held it open. Randu quickly made his way to the carriage. As Cille stepped into the night, Cecil bowed before her passing. Randu was at the carriage ready to offer a hand up as she stepped into the carriage. With a smile on his face, he uttered softly, "Miss Cille." He waited until she was seated before he stepped up into the driver's seat. With a slight ripple of the reins, the horse responded and Cille was heading home.

CHAPTER 3

Hodges Estate 1868

The short ride home for Cille in the horse-drawn carriage was quiet with the exception of the rhythmic sound of the hoof-beats against the country road. Absent tonight was the usual humming or a softly-sung Negro spiritual in a low voice, as if Randu would be singing to himself. It was quiet.

She sat back but remained erect as most girls her age had been trained to do. Her mind began to wander as she thought about the argument at the dinner table. The training at the finishing school came easy for her. She had always remained rather refined, where Beth had challenged authority, more so of late. Her cousin's actions troubled her. She knew Beth had an itch to be with the boys and could hardly wait for her coming out. But she fell short in understanding her cousin's behavior and actions. She couldn't figure out why Beth was so willing to step out of character, making such an issue before her parents.

When Cille arrived at home, the carriage rolled to a stop near the front entrance. Randu hopped down from his seat and at the carriage door, he offered his hand to Cille. She needed the momentary check in her balance while holding a small parcel in her other hand.

"Thank you, Randu," she commented, "I missed your humming or singing tonight." She slowly turned and made her way into the house.

Randu gave a polite bow, saying, "Yes, Miss Cille," in her passing. He was feeling troubled by the note, why he had to keep it from her and only to give it to Master Hodges. He slowly turned and hopped up into the driver's seat before driving the team to the carriage house.

She sat across from her mother in the sitting room as they enjoyed tea. Talk of her future debutante ball crept into the conversation.

"Cille, the time is nearing when plans for your coming out will be put in place," Constance softly mentioned.

"Yes Mother, I know. Will you and Father be making all the plans or will I be allowed to help in the preparation?"

"Your father and I will be making most of the proper social arrangements for the event. However, I don't see why you can't take part in some of the planning. After all, it will be your party. Why do you ask?"

"Mother, I don't want to talk out of turn, but Elizabeth…"

Constance held up her right hand, almost shoulder high with fingers extended but together, palm facing her daughter, as if to shut off any further comment. "Cille, you must not talk of something that is not of your concern. I'm sure her mother and father know what is required of them, in their home and socially."

"I'm not questioning that, Mother," as she leaned forward slightly with a sincere look on her face. "I dearly love Aunt Esther, Uncle Horace and Elizabeth as well. It's just when I'm visiting, I seem to be standing in the middle of a tug-of-war where my emotions get pulled different ways at the same time."

"You will rest easier if you put that subject aside."

"I'll try."

"Mind what I tell you, Cille. By being neutral when you're visiting, it will simply not offend your aunt or uncle. It will give Elizabeth a message that you're not going to get involved or be put in the middle. Regardless of how you feel, that is how things must be done. I realize that both of you are close. But when you're alone together, let her know you can't go against her parents, even if you understand her situation."

"I hope she'll understand."

"She will if you make yourself clear. It needn't disrupt your friendship, if you handle it properly.

◇◇◇

Randu casually entered the house through the servant's entrance. Meeting the butler in the kitchen area, he whispered, "Albon, wha' way ah go ta' find Mastah Hodges?"

With an inquisitive tone, Albon asked, "Wha' yah nee' heem fo' dis time o' nigh'?"

"Ah has dis frum da Morgan house." He waved the note in Albon's face, close enough to show it was a note, but not close enough that he could read it.

"Las' ah sees o' heem, mastah wa' lightin' up in da library."

With a nod, Randu hustled toward the library. He found Master Hodges leaning back in a plush high-back leather chair relaxing while casually drawing on the end of an imported pipe from Germany. In one hand, he held a book with his thumb separating the pages as he read.

Randu cleared his throat lightly before tapping on the rich mahogany doorframe as he said, "Mastah?"

Casually looking up from his position, he replied, "Yes, Randu, what is it?"

Still somewhat troubled about the note, he said, "Ah gotch a papah frum da Morgan house. Ah's tol' no' let Miss Cille 'no' 'bout et, but ta see dat yah gotch et firs'." He handed the small note over to Mister Hodges.

The note read: CADET PATRICK WOODBURY

CLASS OF 1870.

Augustus looked surprised, and with concern asked, "Randu, who gave you this note?"

Nervously he explained, "Corbi, da carriage drivah fo' da Morgans. Heem took Miss Cille an' da Morgan women fo' some shoppin'. Heem nab me at door, all out of bref, say' et good thing heem fin' me. Den han's papah to me an' say ta give ta yah."

"That will be all, Randu."

The driver quickly turned on his heels and removed himself from the library, thankful there was no further questioning about the note.

When Randu left the library, Augustus settled back in his chair and pulled several times on the new pipe. He was satisfied he would have to smoke a few more bowls full before it became broken in. He began to wonder if his daughter had stepped out of character by talking with an unknown while in the company of her cousin, Elizabeth. He knew the Morgans were having problems with her. One thing for sure, he best not mention a word of this to Constance or she would get upset and have a very abrupt tongue lashing for their daughter. He began to ponder what actions he needed to take without causing unnecessary concern. He knew a trip to the Morgan's in the morning would be in order. While there, he could check with Corbi on his daughter's behavior to determine how the note came into being.

CHAPTER 4

A Note Of Interest 1868

It was near noon when Augustus Hodges reined up his favorite chestnut after enjoying a short ride to the Morgan estate. Dismounting, he made a quick loop in the ring post near the front entrance. He walked to the front door and proceeded to knock lightly.

Ellen, the Morgan's nanny, answered the door. "My my, Mastah Hodges, come in out o' da heat o' da day. Ah fetch Mrs. Morgan fo' yah," she said as she darted from the room.

Augustus had no more stepped into the house when his sister entered the room. She was wearing a stunning, intricately-detailed long calico polonaise jacket, bustled at the sides and back with a faux vested look in the center front and lace-covered lapels. It was an egg-shell white with miniature ivory floral patterns in the material, undoubtedly one of the dresses she had purchased the day before. "Augustus, what brings you calling at this time of the day?"

"You look great in that dress. Don't let Constance see it or she'll have to have one just like it. I need to talk to your carriage driver Corbi."

She smiled from the compliment and replied to his reason for being there, "What on earth for?"

"I'm not sure. I got some mixed signals from my driver, so I thought I'd clarify them before I made something out of possibly nothing."

Esther turned and called out, "Ellen, get a hold of Cecil. Tell him to get Corbi and have him report to the house. Mr. Hodges will be in the library." She turned to her brother, asking, "You will have tea with me out in the garden once you're finished, won't you?"

"I can't stay long, but I will join you and spend a couple of moments."

"Good, then you'll beat the crowd. I'm having the Garden Society by for tea and pastries a little later on in the day. It's my turn to host."

"I will join you as soon as I speak to Corbi," he replied.

Catching the maid before she was out of earshot, she called out, "And, Ellen, make that tea for two in the garden. Mr. Hodges will be joining me later."

There was a faded, "Yesum."

◇◇◇

Several uninterrupted moments had passed while Augustus casually strolled about in the large library. He was admiring his brother-in-law's enormous collection of books. He stood near a selection of Shakespeare's work, when Corbi tapped on the mahogany doorframe. Augustus turned to utter, "Corbi!"

Bright-eyed, Corbi answered, "Yes sah."

"My driver Randu said you gave him a note to give to me yesterday evening."

"Ah dah one dat gives heem dat papah, yes sah."

"What I want to know is, how Cille came to meet this cadet?"

"No sah, she not know him sah."

"What do you mean? How did the name of the cadet come about?"

"Dat be wha' da note say, but Miss Cille no' 'no' heem. Miss Cille an' Miss Elizabeth was in da carriage, fun they-z a haven'. Den dis wagon full o' cadets frum Wes' Point comes inta da square jus' a racin'. Dem girls go ta gigglin' an' talkin' 'bout 'em boys. Miss Elizabeth did mos' o' da talkin', an' teasin'. When Mrs. Morgan take da girls inta a dress shop, ah look up dat stree'. Ah see dis cadet comin' an' heem wave arm for me to come. Ah goes up de wa'k a bit an' him ask fo' Miss Cille's name. All ah say is, she call' Miss Cille. Den he ask is older woman her mama? Ah say no sah. Den heem give me papah, an' say fo' me ta see dat her papa gets et. Heem say heem would like ta properly meet Miss Cille. Heem sho' looks like gentleman, an' ah think maybe Mastah Hodges be prou' ta see heem at Miss Cille's party."

Angered somewhat by the action taken outside the family circle, he held his tongue only giving a mild reprimanding comment. "The responsibility of who gets invited is at the discretion of her mother and me, no one else. Is that clear!"

"Yes sah. Ah jus' pass papah alon' dat heem give me."

Unsure if his daughter had stepped out of character in public to draw such attention, he asked, "How did he come to wanting to meet Cille?"

"When heem get dow' frum dat wagon, heem look at da carriage. Cille see heem, before heem smile an' tip da brim o' hees cap, lik' dis." Corbi snapped to attention, straightening himself properly before showing how the cadet smiled and tipped his cap.

Understanding that a cadet may take a fancy to a pretty young lass and how it could have taken place was one thing, but for the first time, he was beginning to realize his daughter was no longer a little girl. He looked at Corbi for a long moment, then said, "You're excused."

The Negro wasted little time departing the library, leaving Augustus to ponder the information he had just received.

Moments later, Augustus joined his sister in the garden for a cup of tea. She spoke first. "Well, that didn't take long. Come over here, my dear brother and join me for a couple of moments at least. The tea should be out shortly where you'll be able to sample some hot pastries straight from the oven."

He adjusted the chair before he sat at the small wire table while glancing into Esther's face and seeing that she was extremely inquisitive.

"Are you going to share with me the 'Why' you had to talk with Corbi?"

Augustus knew his sister was one to dig for information unless her appetite for the news could be averted. He didn't want to cause any problems in their household by putting Elizabeth in a bad situation. He knew he may not have all the facts. "Nothing from what I can determine. Apparently it's just a misunderstanding between our two drivers. One sees or does one thing one way, then when the other gets around to talking about it, the whole thing gets lost in the way they talk."

"I can understand Corbi. I can't help it if you can't understand your hired help. It's a weak excuse, but I'll not press the issue any further. The way I see it, if you wanted me to know, you would have said so."

"Thanks Sis, you're so understanding."

Ellen arrived with the tea and pastries interrupting the current conversation. When she left, their conversation settled in on the dress Esther was wearing, "I saw this dress yesterday knowing in my heart I simply just had to have it."

Augustus smiled and said, "It looks stunning on you."

"Thank you, dear brother." With the fashion brushed to the side for a moment, they talked of the weather and the threatening clouds. But Esther found a way to return to the main topic, about the latest fashions she and the girls had an opportunity to see the day before. During their talk, nothing from his sister reflected negatively upon the girls' behavior while in town.

After a short visit with his sister, Augustus excused himself and each conveyed their best to each other's family. He saw his way out while Esther remained in the garden fussing over the smallest of details for her expected society group.

CHAPTER 5

A Visit To West Point 1868

Two weeks had passed and Augustus was busy receiving textile shipments from Europe. With most of the dispersing orders completed, he placed the rest of his work on hold for a day so he could resolve an issue that had been bothering him. It was time he made a side journey to West Point to check on cadet Woodbury, a matter of importance that had been bothering him. Maybe he could determine why the cadet showed an interest in his daughter. Could it be the young cadet's interest alone, or would he discover his trusted daughter had stepped out of character while in Elizabeth's company? The weather was clear with a slight breeze blowing in from the west before heading out over the Atlantic. There was a crisp clean freshness in the air, making it a perfect day to be out of doors.

◇ ◇ ◇

Upon his arrival at the Academy, he glanced at the parade field, often referred to as 'the plain' by cadets. Many of the classmates were mounted and going through cavalry drills. They would charge in lines of eight, then suddenly rein up before forming skirmish lines in front of their mounts. Every fourth man would dismount and tend to the horses. It almost looked as if it were choreographed, the riders like fluid moved in unison with a given purpose. He glanced beyond 'the plain' where he could see the distant tops of the trees growing below the bluff. Far beyond them was the picturesque Hudson River. He paused momentarily to enjoy the view.

Augustus had Randu pull the carriage to a stop near the Administration building. The towering walls of gray granite stone seemed to stretch to the heavens. Several young cadets could be seen hustling from one building to another. Stepping down from the carriage, he said, “Randu, I’ll be but a short time. I’ll be right back.”

“Yes sah, ah wait fo’ ya.”

Upon entering the building, Augustus was struck by the length of the long corridors and hallways. He could see young cadets in uniform hustle briskly through the halls going from one class to the other. As one cadet approached, he asked for and received directions to the superintendent's office.

When he stepped into an outer office, he was greeted by one of the cadets, “Sir, may I help you?”

“If you would, I’m Augustus Hodges from Monroe. I’d like to speak to the Superintendent, if he is in.”

“Please have a seat. I’ll have one of the senior officers speak with you.”

Moments later, Major Robert Adams explained, “The superintendent has been called to New York City for an engagement. He is meeting with several congressional leaders concerning additional funding for this Institution. Is there something I can do for you after making such a trip?”

“Yes, there is,” Augustus replied. “My wife and I will be extending invitations in the near future to those we would like to attend our daughter's debutante ball. The purpose of my visit is to seek the background on one of your cadets.”

“I see and which one of our young men are you seeking information on?”

“The name is Patrick Woodbury.”

Major Adams asked one of the cadets to get Woodbury's file. Then he ushered Augustus into the superintendent's office where they could discuss the cadet’s file in privacy. There was a rap on the door moments later and the young cadet handed the file to the officer.

As Major Adams looked through the folder, he read several portions before commenting. “Well, Mr. Hodges, it appears that Cadet Woodbury is in the top five percent of his class. His major role and potential assignments after graduation will be with the cavalry. His promotional potential is above average, but you must consider the officers who fought in the war will have somewhat of an edge for the first few years. He is an outstanding cadet, and if he keeps this up, he'll be in line for several awards upon graduation."

"What kind of stock does he come from?"

The major flipped through several pages, paused and read for a moment before saying, "Mother and father are both Londoners, they married in Boston, two children Patrick and Molly. Let's see, she is two years younger than Patrick. Oh, here we go, father knows shipbuilding and works in the timber industry. Impressive. He has worked his way up to become quite influential in the northeast. Now here is something interesting: Patrick worked after school at the local armory, caring for and repairing military weaponry for the Union forces stationed nearby. There is a commendation and West Point recommendation made by the commander stationed there." Augustus had been sitting in a high back chair, mostly of wood with very little cushion. He got to his feet, pleased with the information he had acquired. Augustus felt the senior Woodbury would extend his contacts that were influential in business and industry and felt an acquaintance would be in his best interest. "Tell me, can I get his parents' address? I would like to extend an invitation to Cadet Woodberry and his parents as well."

"That shouldn't be a problem."

"How should I address the invitation to Cadet Woodbury?"

"Send it here to the administrative building. We will see that it gets to the cadet. I might add, it is recommended the invitation arrive a couple of weeks in advance where the cadet can bring it to our attention. That way we can suspend any institutional duties he may have, so that he may honor the invitation."

Augustus thanked Major Adams for the senior Woodbury's address and chose not to speak to Cadet Woodbury before he headed back to Monroe in an attempt to get there before nightfall.

It was dusk when the carriage returned to the outskirts of Monroe. The gaslights for the street had already been lighted. The streets were nearly deserted, with most of the crowd apparently remaining inside after calling it a day. Augustus called out, "Randu, it has been a rather long day. I don't need to go by the office, just head for home."

"Yes sah, it be a long day fo' sure."

They passed through the quiet community where several of the shops were beginning to close. A short time later, they were headed down the country road leading to his estate.

His estate was not large, but showed a mark of distinction, resting southwest of Monroe nestled up against a densely wooded hillside. A small stream bordered the front part of his property. A looping drive in front of the seventeen-room house allowed numerous guests to park their carriages and come inside for entertainment. To the west of the house was a carriage barn where a variety of five different carriages were stored out of the weather, until ready for use. Beyond the carriage barn was the stable, where the best of stock was housed and cared for. To the rear of the stables, the pastureland followed the contour of the hillside.

Crossing the wooden bridge, he was glad to be home. He was tired, but happy knowing he had acquired a great deal of information about the Woodbury family worth cultivating in the future. Now he could rest and enjoy the evening with his family.

When Augustus stepped down from the carriage, he headed for the front door. Randu rippled the reins, as horse and carriage headed for the barn.

CHAPTER 6

Plans For Debutant 1869

Months had passed since Elizabeth Morgan was allowed to have her debutante ball. The festivity had finally unshackled her and the world was a newer place to explore. Her knight in shining armor did not appear at her ball.

It was not until she had attended the debutante ball of Mary Becky Banister that she discovered the light of her life. After several dances throughout the night, she realized his wry humor and outlook on life was captivating. From that very evening, they had seen each other on a regular basis. Leon was the son of a legislator from the State of Tennessee. He was well educated, had done a considerable amount of foreign travel and knew a great number of people in diplomatic circles.

◊ ◊ ◊

Elizabeth was willing to admit her good fortune when she dropped by the Hodges'. She wanted to visit and gossip with her cousin. She found Cille near the flower garden talking with her mother. "Good morning. I see the both of you enjoy nature early in the morning."

Constance looked up to see Elizabeth bounding along the narrow path that bordered the flowerbeds. "Good morning, Beth. What brings you by this time of day and don't you look stunning?"

Beth wore a vintage dress with matching skirt and horizontally shirred solid center front. The hem had a deep cotton flounce with an overlay of lace ruffles. The skirt formed a train in the back, but

Elizabeth had it bustled up with the tie-ups. It fit her figure and showed a touch of sophistication. "Thank you. Mother bought it for me last week. She has plans to visit New York City sometime next week and was wondering if you would be interested in making the trip with her?"

"Thank you, Beth. I think I'd like that very much. We have almost completed all the plans for Cille. I'm about as worn to a frazzle over putting the whole thing together, as one can be."

Cille spoke up, "Mother, I told you, you're making such a fret over too many things."

"Child, you know there isn't a thing in this world me or your father wouldn't do for you. It's simply a hectic responsibility and one that I take great pride in. This trip will give me an excuse to see some of the latest fashions that never seem to make their way out of the city to Monroe."

Beth said, "Aunt Constance, I'm sure everything will simply fall into place as you have planned. I know Mother had a fit and later said she had worried over nothing."

"Just the same," Constance replied, "if your mother isn't too ungodly busy tomorrow, ask her to drop by for tea and we can make plans. I'll be putting the finishing touches on the guest list and all that goes with the dance. If you two will excuse me, I must tend to some things inside. I imagine you girls will find plenty to talk about."

As Cille watched her mother walk off, she looked at Beth before she teased, "How's the sweet life with you and Leon these days?"

"Cousin, I think he is the funniest man I ever come across. Just to listen to him talk makes my heart skip. He has big plans to return to Tennessee and run for some sort of political office."

"What's in Tennessee that we don't have the best of right here in Monroe?"

Beth thought for a moment, "I'm not sure, but if he goes there, I guess it would be him."

Cille got inquisitive, "You two are not getting sugar-coated serious on us, are you?"

"Don't I wish? Oh, if you only knew how I truly feel. Anyhow that's enough about me. How are the plans going for your dance?"

"Most of it is done, I guess. There's a large guest list that I haven't seen. I got to invite a few friends, but the total list still remains a secret. You're invited and you should get your invitation in a few days."

"Thanks, Cille, you're true blue. Have you gone shopping for your gown yet?"

"We picked it up yesterday. I have it up in my room, ready to be fussed over. I'll show it to you later."

"Are there any boys on the list that you know?"

"No, the only one I knew that I would like to have invited was Harry Belford. But he can't be here, because he'll be two days at sea. He's headed for France to do some studies his parents had managed to arrange."

"Too bad. I hope there are a few eligible young men in attendance for your sake. That way, they will keep you from having to dance with the older set."

"That's okay. I just hope it all goes well. Mother and father have put a lot into the whole thing. If there aren't that many young gentlemen that show up, I'll be happy, as long as my parents are."

"Cille, I can't stay long. Can we go take a look at that dress? Then I'll have to scoot along."

When they darted into the house, Corbi was visiting with Cora the cook, hoping get a taste of some of her cookies. He was as sweet on her as he was on the cookies she made. He looked up in time to catch their passing. "Is ya ready, Miss Elizabeth? Yo' mama be waiting fo' the carriage, soons we get there."

"Go to the carriage Corbi, I'll join you in a moment."

They took the stairs on a young girl run, hurrying, but making sure they stepped on every step.

When they arrived in Cille's room, she held the dress up to her front before turning around for Beth's remarks.

Beth was spellbound, "Oh, Cille, it's simply gorgeous. Where in the world did you find such a lovely gown?"

"Remember that fashion shop we went into the last time we were in Monroe?"

"Don't tell me that is where you found it."

"No, the lady at the shop got with mother. When she went to New York on a buying spree, she had an idea what mother was looking for. She bought it and brought it back for our approval."

"Well, if the dress is any indication, your parents are not holding back on any expense for your ball."

"Beth, I'll be the first to admit my parents have always lavished me with the best that money can buy and I love them for it. I guess that is what I get for being an only child."

Still struck by the beauty of the dress, Beth shook her head slightly before saying, "I've got to run. Mother wants to have Corbi take her to Monroe soon as I get back."

A short time later, the pair bounded down the stairs and Elizabeth was gone.

CHAPTER 7

Nearing Cille's Debutant 1869

Nearly every day, Cille discovered something new about the dance that caused her to run about trying to help where she could. But it was her parents who made the final preparations for the long-awaited evening. Additional cooks, maids and butlers had to be contacted and brought in to fulfill the needs of the anticipated crowd.

The furnishings in one of the largest rooms in the house had been removed. An elegant display of fabric panels with sashes of soft colors and lace decorated the lavish interior in preparation for the dance. The large, high-ceilinged room had six glass-paneled shutter doors that opened onto a huge stone veranda two steps above an extensive flower garden area. The veranda and garden were decorated and furnished to meet the needs of a sophisticated crowd.

◇ ◇ ◇

It was mid-afternoon on the day of the ball when the first of the entertainment arrived. They had journeyed from New York City and without question, were considered the best the big city had to offer. Upon their arrival, they were formally seated and fed.

The added help hustled back and forth with trays of sampler foods prepared in bite-sized pieces. Two long tables in the garden had been set up to accommodate several trays of food. At the end of each long table were several large punch bowls. After the placement of the food, the bowls were filled with refreshments over large blocks of ice.

Cille had eaten sparingly. She went to her room and began preparing for the evening events. The European styled velvet sash to her window was drawn early, as was the custom. She was fussed over by two maids who assisted her after bathing. Her hair was touched up while she sat in her camisole before a large imported dresser and mirror. The gown and accessories were laid across the latest silk velvet coverlet from France that adorned her large feather tick bed.

Constance appeared at the bedroom door, checking on her daughter's progress.

"Mother, have any of the guests started to arrive?"

"There were a handful arriving before I journeyed upstairs. I must get back down in a few moments and assume my proper role. I dearly wanted to check and see that everything was going well with you."

When she turned at the doorway, Elizabeth and Esther met her. Constance asked, "Beth, would you help Cille?"

"I'd love to."

Esther said, "Come-come Connie, there isn't any need to get all worked up now. From the looks of things, it will simply be a charming event. Take up your place with Augustus and enjoy the evening. I'll check on the girls to assure Cille is ready before the time is announced."

The guests had been greeted at the front door and ushered across the large foyer. They were then introduced to those gathered near the huge double doorway leading into the garden. They were then allowed to mingle among the other guests while the refreshments were served. For Constance, she was overjoyed and nervous at the same time. It appeared, if the trend continued, that most or maybe all of those invited would be in attendance.

She observed that a considerable number of young ladies were in attendance. They had accompanied their parents and all seemed to be in a festive mood.

Constance fanned her face to beat back the nervous perspiration. She took time to brush her hands at her dress, as if to place the layers of material in their proper position over the bustles.

The Hodges stood at the main entrance to witness three wagons full of cadets pulling up in the front. They were representatives from West Point, Cadet Patrick Woodbury and several of his classmates ready to accommodate the expected number of girls that would attend.

Every cadet was dressed sharply in black shako with pom pom, cadet gray short jacket with "frogging" in black, white gloves and white cross belt, red sash, gray pants with a single black stripe centered and running down the outside of the leg. The cross belt had a gold-colored buckle, as did the buttons and their ranking on their upper sleeves. An academy sword was held in place at their side.

In a snappy military fashion, each cadet was introduced to the guests in the garden. They were ushered into a small room where they removed and placed their swords and shakoes for safe keeping before joining the crowd in the garden.

As the evening grew, additional guests arriving were those associated with Mr. Hodges in the textile and shipping industry. Friends and associates of Mr. Morgan came with their families. There was a handful of legal buffs and legislators who managed the trip from Washington, each representing their State. Joseph D. Woodbury, wife Mattie and daughter Molly travelled from Boston to be in attendance. They arrived shortly after the group of cadets had been introduced.

When the crowd had ample time to take part in the refreshments, Augustus gave instructions to the musicians. They were dressed in their tuxedos and took their places on stage. They began playing a medley of music that drew the crowd from the garden into the large room for the formal announcement and dancing.

The guests from the garden filtered into the large room and took up positions around the edge of the floor. The women were afforded the chairs, while the men stood, as was the custom. Augustus turned to his wife, "Well, the dance is about to begin. Shall we bring on our daughter?"

Constance replied, "Let me rush upstairs to get her. I just hope that girl is ready. I'd certainly be mortified if we had to keep our guests waiting for her appearance."

Augustus stepped up on the risers the band was playing on and the room slowly quieted. Augustus said, "Ladies and distinguished guests, you have indeed honored my wife and I with your presence this evening. My daughter will join us shortly. I trust that you will enjoy the dance. Please feel free to partake in the food and refreshments from time to time. They are there for your enjoyment, as well as our splendid music." Turning to the band he said, "Gentlemen, let there be music."

While the beat of a medley filled the room, additional couples from the garden stood near the door, a few just outside and on the veranda. Augustus made his way to the bottom of the stairs in the foyer in his tailored dark brown pin-striped suite. Looking up, he saw Constance making her way down the stairs. She held onto and lifted the outer portion of her plum-colored vintage taffeta gown with embroidered black lace overlay on the bodice. The full taffeta elbow length sleeves were gathered at the cuff with lace and the full skirt had triangular bands of black silk velvet. Her movements were slow and measured, allowing the gown to flow smoothly as she descended the stairs. "Well, where is Cille?"

"She's coming. Beth is putting the final touches on her."

CHAPTER 8

Cille's Debutant 1869

Cille and Beth appeared at the top of the stairs and slowly began walking down the slightly curved staircase. Beth was bouncing with a spring in her step as she descended the stairs. Cille was more careful as her hair was lifted upon her head, held in place with a rhinestone tiara and supported with a wide bright yellow bow, the ends of the ribbon protruding only inches beyond her dangling auburn ringlets. She gracefully glided downward showing a touch of nervousness. Cille wore a pale gold taffeta gown with embroidered black lace overlaying the bodice. The full- length sleeves gathered to a cuffed lace at her slender wrists. The full skirt had triangular bands of pale gold. She descended the stairs with the tips of her golden-colored shoes peeking out from beneath her gown as she made slow measured steps. Beth's gown was lovely, though purposely not as stunning to allow her cousin to shine on this special occasion. At the bottom of the stairs, Beth left Cille's side and joined her parents while Cille and her parents prepare for the grand entrance.

The musical conductor caught sight of the three at the entrance to the ballroom. The music faded and then stopped. He raised his musical baton and the musical group played an entrance number recognized by all. The Hodges entered with Constance on the left of Cille and Augustus on the right. They stepped in time to the music provided and went to the slightly raised platform. They stepped up on the riser, turned and faced the crowd, as the music faded.

Augustus raised his voice in order to be heard by all, "My wife Constance and I now have the privilege of introducing to you, our daughter, Cille." The announcement was met with a soft applause.

Then he said, “As her father, I insist on the first dance.”

Stepping down from the platform, he held out his arm and Cille joined him. Waltz music filled the room, but the only ones on the floor were Cille and her father. She looked up into his eyes, to hear him say, “Sweetheart, you have grown up so fast. I hope you're happy.”

“Daddy, you know I am and I'm very loved by you and mother.” She looked into his face and saw his soft smile bordered by well-trimmed sideburns. She hadn't notice until now, being this close, how tall and sturdy he really was.

Midway through the dance, Mr. Morgan tapped Augustus on the shoulder. Horace took Cille’s hand and danced with her as Augustus left the middle of the floor to get his wife and join them on the floor. In doing so, the guests began filtering onto the dance floor.

Looking into Uncle Horace's face as they glided across the floor, she noticed his bushy sideburns and a well-shaped mustache that was twisted. It reached out from the side of his face. Beneath the mustache, a smile reflected pure pleasure.

With a tap on his shoulder, he was gone and another dancer took his place. A big barrel- chested gentleman with heavy puffy mutton chops held her at a distance, but she noticed he was light as a feather on his feet. “It's indeed a pleasure, Miss Cille.”

“And who might I ask is such an elegant dancer?”

“Joseph D. Woodbury. Your father saw fit to invite me and the misses down from Boston.”

“I am deeply honored to dance with such a distinguished gentleman who has traveled such a distance.” Before the conversation could continue, he was tapped on the shoulder and Cille was off dancing with another. The initial waltz was extended several times to accommodate the crowd and eventually came to an end.

The dancing continued through the evening. When the musicians took a break, some of the guests moved into the garden area for refreshments. Cille followed them and mingled in the crowd of well-wishers. She remained very proper and showed a spark of congeniality in her conversations.

With a tap on her shoulder, she turned to see the cadet that she had seen in Monroe some time back. She was nearly speechless as a flash of excitement suddenly consumed her body. His face and smile had been etched in her mind since that day. "Cadet Patrick Woodbury, Ma'am. May I have the honor of a dance with you when the music resumes?"

"Most certainly, and please call me Cille. Ma'am makes me feel older than I want to be right now. Haven't I seen you before in Monroe?"

"It has been a way back, but I sure remember you. You were sitting in a carriage with another who was full of giggles if I recall."

"Such a memory you have, that was my cousin Elizabeth."

"May I get you a refreshment?"

"Thank you, yes. I'm rather thirsty after dancing so much."

Helping himself to the refreshments, he returned and handed her a cup of punch. As thirsty as she was, she held back the urge to gulp it down. After taking several sips, she placed the cup down.

"Tell me, Mr. Woodbury, have you been at West Point very long?"

With an unshaken voice, he replied, "Please, call me Patrick. I've been there two years, starting my third. I'll graduate in two years and receive my commission at that time."

"What happens after that?"

"I'll be assigned to a unit somewhere. I hope it's out west."

"Why out west?"

"My main emphasis is cavalry tactics and my skills can be put to better use out there. Word back at the Point is that Custer led a handful of troops against a large Indian encampment at Washita. He came out victorious and is making a name for himself. The war has ended here. It's the west that holds the future for one in the military."

"Your convictions sound rather impressive. I admire that."

Most of the guests were making their way back inside for more dancing. Patrick and Cille joined them. Shortly after stepping inside, the fluid beat of a waltz filled the air. They stepped out onto the floor and Cille felt herself being swept off her feet for the first time. As they glided across the floor, their eyes seemed to lock upon the other's and a flurry of unbridled comfort raged within her tiny frame and remained constant. She felt totally protected within his arms.

When the dance ended, Patrick said, "Cille, you're as graceful off the dance floor as on. I hope you will reserve another dance for me before the evening is out."

"It will be my pleasure, Patrick, and thank you for asking."

As the evening passed, the music changed from waltzes to the Virginia Reel and other favorites. The guests were enjoying themselves and so was Cille. The cadets talking and dancing kept Elizabeth, Mary Becky Banister and several other girls busy. The young men attending were kept busy catering to a handful of girls invited in from an all-girl's school. They would run for refreshments and dance with the girls again.

Augustus and Constance were kept busy socializing with the many distinguished guests and trying to keep up with the demands of directing the hired help. They took it upon themselves to see that the Woodburys were introduced to as many of the influential guests as possible. If they were not busy supervising, Horace and Esther helped in making the Woodbury's evening most enjoyable and rewarding.

Cille noticed how Patrick seemed to stand out from the others for some reason.

Between several numbers, she deliberately walked near him. When the music started, he would hold out his hand and remark, "You did say this was our dance."

As she held her eyes upon his, the world beyond them became a blur. Her body felt fluttery the instant she placed her hand in his. They glided across the floor swaying to the music, captivated by the mere presence of the other, exchanging small talk where they could.

When the dance ended, he said, "Cille, the honor is truly mine. By the way, I ran into my parents here tonight. Have you had a chance to meet them?"

Cille said, "I had the pleasure of dancing with your father earlier. But I haven't met your mother." She followed him willingly through the crowd, finding both parents talking on the veranda.

"Mom and Dad, I would like you to meet Cille."

"I have already had the pleasure, Son. Cille let me introduce my wife, Mattie, and this over here is our daughter Molly."

The women exchanged gestures, as Molly held out her hand saying, "Patrick, is there any law that says I can't have a dance with you?"

Mattie added, "Patrick, your mother would enjoy a dance later on, too."

Patrick winked at his mother and nodded to her saying, "Cille, if you will excuse me."

Cille nodded as Patrick and Molly headed for the dance floor. Turning to carry on a brief conversation with the Woodburys, her mother and father appeared.

Constance said, "Are you having a fun time, my dear?"

Directing her comments to both of her parents, she said, "I sure am and I love you both." She felt compelled to introduce her parents to the Woodburys who traveled so far.

A voice from behind her gathered Cille's attention. She excused herself and was off dancing once more. This time, a number of cadets tapped into the dance for just a moment with her. She was nearly spellbound with all the attention from each cadet, but the experience she had while dancing with Patrick was missing. She moved gracefully between each cadet as they stepped forward to dance with her for a few moments. They were a lively group and enjoyed what precious little time they had with her on the dance floor.

While the music played, she danced with cadets, young men from Monroe to Washington, and their fathers. She was truly having a delightful time. But in the waning hours, the last dance was announced.

From across the hall, she saw Patrick standing so sharply and gesturing with his right hand held out for the last dance. They both moved toward each other and met on the floor. The gentle waltz allowed them to gaze upon each other once more.

He found her eyes sparkling with excitement.

She found a gentle softness in his eyes, a softness she would never forget. When they left the dance floor, she asked, "Would you stand by my side as I bid good evening to the guests?"

He nodded and said, "The pleasure will be mine."

Cille held his hand and ushered him to the front door.

There she thanked the guests upon their departure. Nearly all the guests were gone when Patrick's father stepped up, "Miss Cille, you're a charming young lady. Son, the Hodges' have extended an invitation for the family to spend the night. Must you be going back to the academy, or can you spend the night?"

"I'm sorry, duty calls early in the morning. I have duty on the square and I haven't made arrangements in advance for someone to stand in for me. I didn't realize I'd be seeing you here."

"Patrick, I understand. Go back and give it your all."

Mattie spoke, saying, "Son, Boston is not the same without you."

"I miss you all, too," Patrick said. "Mr. and Mrs. Hodges, it has been an honor. And Cille, I was honored to share several dances with you tonight and would like very much to have the opportunity to call upon you, if I may?"

Cille blushed, her body felt warmer than usual, as she lowered her head just a little, smiled and softly replied, "I would like that very much, Patrick."

Augustus spoke up, "Patrick, we look forward to seeing you when you call, and you're most welcome."

Constance interrupted, "There is additional room and you're welcome to spend the night when you visit if it is too late for you to make the journey back to the academy."

A call from one of the cadets in the wagon broke into their conversation, "Hey, Woodbury, are you coming?"

Patrick smiled and said, "Good evening, folks, the wagon awaits me." With a dash, he ran, holding the academy sword in one hand and his shako in the other. Moments later, the wagons were across the bridge and gone from sight.

Turning to go back inside, Elizabeth was standing in the doorway. She was spending the night with Cille. Everyone entered the house and the Hodges took the Woodburys to their sleeping quarters. The maids and butlers scurried around picking up and collecting what needed to be done that night. Some of the cleanup had to wait until the daylight hours.

The girls made their way upstairs, with Beth saying, "Cille, the ball was simply divine. You simply have got to tell me all about your soldier," They both giggled as they climbed the stairs and entered Cille's room.

CHAPTER 9

A Family Trip to West Point 1870

Cille and Patrick realized it had been nearly two full years since they had first met at her debutante ball. After the dance, she saw him as often as his classes at the academy would allow. He continued to excel in his studies and duties as a senior cadet. They knew his remaining days at the academy as a cadet were numbered. Beyond his graduation, they didn't know what lie in store for either of them. Would his future assignment separate them before they had a chance to grow close?

◇◇◇

The temperature was in the lower seventies and the sky was a soft blue. The heavens were filled with small white clouds, absent of the gray bottoms that would indicate any possibility of rain. One could not ask for a better day. The country seemed to come alive as the Hodges family made their yearly journey to the military academy to watch the cadets pass in review parade as the senior class graduated.

Today was a special day for Cille. Patrick would be graduating and would later depart from the academic side of the academy for an as yet undisclosed assignment.

On this day, Cille rode in the same carriage with her parents. Her father had a business suit on and would be seated near the speakers' platform because of his legislative duties. He would be a spectator this year and would not be called upon to speak.

Cille wore a long gray skirt with a jacket of taffeta blend with black braid decorating the skirt and the sleeves of the jacket. A gray hat with a small plume complemented the attire she wore. Her parasol was of a matching gray with black ruffles. Her mother sat across from her next to her father. She wore a burgundy satin dress with several layers of white lace at the throat and ruffles at the wrists. Her attire was more fitting the image required of a freshman legislator's wife.

They had left their modest estate on the outskirts of Monroe early that morning. This allowed them to make the journey to the academy in time to join others for refreshments with the superintendent before the graduation ceremonies in the afternoon.

Randu was sitting atop the carriage wearing a distinguished garment Mr. Hodges had picked up for him in New York, including white gloves. The carriage had been cleaned very meticulously and given a light coat of wax to bring out the shine and polish on the wood. The set of chestnuts was a matching pair and very well groomed. Their harness equipment was well cared for with the metal well-polished reflecting the sun's rays and the leather lightly oiled then rubbed dry, leaving a slight sheen.

They headed north through Monroe to a junction road that linked Goshen to the west and the Military Academy at West Point to the east. The parade of carriages was a traditional yearly event that drew the best from nearby communities. The halfway point was at the West Point Academy for the gathering of carriages and the graduation of cadets. Everyone knew there would be no finer display of carriages than on this day. After all, the academy is one of the finest educational institutions that has produced some of the nation's greatest leaders, thus causing reason to celebrate.

When they arrived at the junction, Randu found his place in a long line of carriages. There were wagons and carriages as far as the eye could see in either direction.

Constance reached into her drawstring purse, produced a handkerchief, wiped at the corners of her eyes and once at her nose. She complained, "This dust and pollen simply gives me fits every time we make this journey. My nose looks a fright by the time we arrive. Then, to make matters even worse, the Academy has a shortcoming in having adequate facilities for the softer gender to freshen up."

Augustus said, "I'll speak to Superintendent Pitcher about the situation. You have made the same complaint over the last three years. You have also reminded me more than once before his graduation this year. I intend to mention it, in my position as a legislator, on your behalf."

"Well, I certainly wish you would!" said Constance. "It should be pointed out that we make up more than half of the crowd when we come out to see the cadets going through their ceremonies."

"Daddy, she's right. The facilities are primitive at best. Don't do anything on my account because Patrick is graduating. I doubt if I will be returning to another graduation. But please do something for mother. It gets terribly embarrassing to ask another to hold your parasol while you freshen up."

"You will speak to him, won't you?" Constance asked. She sneezed once more, complaining, "I must look a fright. I'm afraid by the time we get there…"

Augustus replied, "I said I would and I shall."

Randu kept the carriage going at a good pace, keeping up with the others. The road was dusty and a fine mist of dust had been kicked up from their carriage as well. It was noticeable shortly after they had entered the road at the junction.

He felt proud of the special outfit Mr. Hodges had purchased for him, just for this very day. From Randu's view, he couldn't see any other driver that came close to the classy look he projected.

The parade of carriages finally made their way to the academy property. They went directly to the north side of the parade field where the gigantic field stretched from the administrative area to the bluffs near the banks of the Hudson River. The view overlooking the academy grounds, to include the extended beauty of the Hudson River, was simply picturesque and breathtaking this time of year.

After sneezing several times, Constance brushed at her dress, and complained, "Must they neglect the roads around here? My dress looks a fright from it! Come Cille, let us try to freshen up. I feel as if my nose has reddened some from sneezing so much."

Randu overheard the complaining while stepping down from his seat and opening the carriage door. "Yes sah, dus' all ovah dis carriage. Sho done made a mess, ah wipe it dow' an' hoppin' et don' go an' rain some." Augustus stepped from the carriage followed by Constance and then Cille. The women walked off to freshen up while Augustus found an acquaintance and began talking.

Randu opened a small box that contained additional cleaning material and began humming as he worked. He went about removing the dust from the seat and wood frame around the passengers' compartment.

The Hodges' carriage arrived early, allowing a few minutes of leisure and relaxation. They could look to the east and see the steady stream of carriages still making their way to the academy. There was going to be a larger than usual crowd this year.

Augustus said, "Randu, if the ladies wonder where I am, tell them I will be in Superintendent Pitcher's office addressing the very complaint they have burned my ears about."

"Yesah, Mr. Hodges. They ta meet yah in his office or go to de reviewin' stan'?"

"Tell them I shall join them on the reviewing stand. There is reserved seating and I shouldn't be long. I may even be back before they complete freshening up."

"Yesah, I tell 'em, soon as ol' Randu sets eyes on 'em."

As if on a mission, Augustus walked smartly to the Administration building looking for the superintendents' office. Cadet Johnson, a lowerclassman, said, "Yes sir, may I help you?"

"Yes, I'm Representative Hodges from Monroe and I am in hopes of getting to speak to Superintendent Pitcher. Is he in?"

"No sir, you just missed him, I'm surprised you didn't see him in the hall. He just left for the stable area, then he was to go to the reviewing stand for the commencement and the pass in review ceremony."

"Thank you, young man," Augustus replied. "I'll try to catch him there, before the ceremony."

When Augustus returned, Cille was approaching the carriage in a leisurely fashion, swirling the parasol ever so slightly as she walked. "Mother said she would be along directly. She ran into Mrs. Mary Pitcher and they're discussing the changes the academy has made this year for the women. Mrs. Pitcher was pleased the changes were made in time for those who journeyed this far to see the ceremony."

When he returned near the carriage, he said, "Then the walk to the administration building was for nothing."

Cille replied, "Why did you walk way over there?"

"I was going to address the deplorable conditions for you women you two have been complaining about."

"Oh father, I told you not to bother on my part, and as for mother, she's simply struck in awe with the personality of Mary Pitcher. She is simply the most charming person I have seen in a long time. She and mother will be sitting next to each other on the reviewing stand. Mother is simply fascinated with her. And she adores the dress mother is wearing. Both of them are talking of doing some shopping in New York City when they can find the time."

After gearing himself up to face the superintendent, making his way across campus and back, only to hear a rosy situation existed after all, Augustus was momentarily frustrated. He gathered his thoughts and said, "I'm glad your mother is happy and as for you, young lady, is this one of your happier days?"

She simply began to melt knowing her father was so genuinely concerned about how she felt and realizing she had been looking forward to this day for so long. "Father, this graduation is our beginning."

He cleared his throat, then asked, "Cille, is there something you and Patrick have been keeping from your mother and me?"

Feeling flushed over the prospects of Patrick popping the all-important question and talking with her father sent a warm feeling up her neck and across her cheeks,

"Father, Patrick is a gentleman and I'm sure if he has something to say to you, he would."

He looked at her and smiled saying, "That's nice."

The graduation ceremony of 1870 at West Point began and would become a special moment that would always live within Cille. She sat upright and attentive, collecting all the events that began to unfold with a collective interest.

CHAPTER 10

Cadet Woodbury's Graduation 1870

The academy had all the cadets turned out, with the exception of those with duties throughout the military campus. The lengthy parade field had several marching companies in formation. At the far end of those units, the cavalry companies were the last to pass in review. The band played ruffles and flourishes before Superintendent Colonel Thomas Gamble Pitcher announced the names of the fifty-eight who would graduate.

Shortly after the announcement, a lone trumpeter played 'Adjutant's Call'. The adjutant called out several commands and later ordered the units to pass in review. The band began to play a number of military marches as the units on the parade field made maneuvers to march to the far end of the field and prepare to pass in review. The first marching unit was the West Point Academy Band. After passing the reviewing stand, they took up a position center field in front of the platform seating the dignitaries. They were followed by large units of cadets resembling a long gray line, before they passed the reviewing stand, executing the command of, "Eyes right!" As they passed in review, the senior cadets were followed by lower class cadets. The units would march to the far end of the parade field and were later dismissed. The four-year program at the academy not only taught the latest in the classrooms but added polish to those cadets passing in review. Then came the cavalry unit, the first being an ammunition wagon pulled by a team of six mules. The academy logo printed on the canvas above the notation read "Class of 1870". A lone cadet rode one of the mules in the near pole position. Behind the wagon came the graduating mounted cavalry unit, followed by lower cavalry classmen on their mounts. The cadets on their horses gave a display of precision riding.

Cille scooted forward in her chair in hopes of getting an early glimpse of her favorite cadet. Her heart nearly exploded with pride when she saw Patrick sitting so erect. When the unit passed in review, a cadet gave the command, “Eyes right!” and looked into the stands as they rode past. Cille couldn't hold back; she waved her arms in hopes that Patrick would see her and possibly smile back. She was disappointed as he rode past with a sober expression on his face. She hoped, oh, how she hoped that he had seen her and he knew she was so excited of his presence within the unit and his graduation.

Distinguished guests on the reviewing stand began to stand in front of Cille where she began to lose sight of the departing cavalry unit. She sighed and turned to her mother saying, “How disappointing, I don't think Patrick had much of a chance to see me. I do so hope he knows where we will be so I can talk to him after he puts up his horse.”

Constance was getting to her feet while listening to a comment from Mary Pitcher in the other ear as she appeared to disregard her daughter's remark. They were moments away from enjoying refreshments with Superintendent Colonel Thomas G. Pitcher.

Cille sat baffled, as if being shunned by those around her. They just didn't care how she felt as a young girl. She was the youngest on the reviewing stand, and apparently the only one unmarried or without a companion near her side. The frustration overtook her and she didn't like it. She blew out a puff of air, as if to blow at a lock of hair in front of her face, except the lock wasn't there. Forced to stand, she tried to make herself feel comfortable among those around her. Stepping from the reviewing stand, she glanced momentarily at the parade field stripped of cadets who moments ago had adorned its vast surface in large numbers.

She had no sooner stepped from the reviewing stand when she saw Molly Woodberry leaving the bleachers reserved for parents and guests of the graduates. “Molly, my goodness girl, I’m glad to see you. Did you make the trip down with your parents?”

Molly smiled and said, “Cille, it's so good to see you. Mother and father will simply be so pleased to see you. They will be down shortly.”

"Did you get to see Patrick when he rode by the stands?" Cille asked.

"Yes, and as is typical of my brother, he looked so stiff and proper, not even a smile on his lips."

"Oh, so you noticed that, too."

"Is there a place nearby where I can freshen up? I simply will not last very long once the socializing starts. We arrived just in time to get a seat before the ceremony began."

"Follow me, Molly, maybe we can beat the crowd. Then you can be at my side when I greet your parents."

They lifted their hooped dresses slightly, to allow them to move across the huge lawn and arrive at the facility that was set aside for them, ahead of the crowd. Moments later, they stepped from the stone-gray structure laughing at the urgency they had placed on getting there. They returned to the reviewing stand and mingled with the large crowd looking for the older Woodburys.

"There you are, my dear," both girls turned to see Mattie walking toward them. "Cille, it is such a pleasure to see you. My you look so refreshing; that dress simply looks stunning on you."

"Thank you, Mrs. Woodbury, you're so kind. I'm so pleased that you were able to make it to Patrick's graduation. I know he'll be happy to see you."

"Girls, you may join me along with the others that are gathered around Mary Pitcher, the superintendent's wife. We'll wait with them until Patrick and the others finish doing what has to be done."

The rest of the afternoon was spent walking and talking with friends. They joined new acquaintances partaking of refreshments that were provided by the faculty and staff of the academy.

Graduating cadets made their way to their quarters to retrieve their belongings, as most were leaving the academy for assignments beyond the limits of the campus grounds. Patrick, however, would be returning to the academy in three days. He would assist part of the cavalry department in preparing for the upcoming course of instructions while waiting for his orders out West.

During the early part of the afternoon, the Woodburys were convinced to return to Monroe for a short visit. When it came time to leave the academy, the Woodburys were invited to ride in the Hodges carriage, while Cille, Patrick and Molly were allowed to ride in a separate carriage the Woodburys had made arrangements for.

The Woodburys had given Molly added funds to spend while on the trip. She pleaded, "Patrick and Cille, can we depart ahead of the others? I would so much like to spend a dash of time in Monroe at one or two of their shops before we have to venture on."

With little resistance, they were on their way back to Monroe ahead of the older set. When the carriage pulled from the academy grounds, it was clear the ride back would be at a leisurely pace, as the road had already been filled with those leaving early.

Patrick called to the driver, "Turn left up here and turn right at the curve later on. It is a shortcut to Monroe where we will beat a good number of these folks there." Turning to Cille, he said, "I would like to show you some of the scenery up this way."

Molly said, "With the time saved, big brother, does this give me a bit more time in Monroe, to enjoy my shopping?"

He glanced across the carriage, and said, "We'll let you shop as you wish. There is something I wish to share with Cille when we get there."

Cille was content and remained joyously quiet. While sitting next to Patrick, she was wondering what he had on his mind, only to hear his sister say, "Is it a big secret? Is little sister included, or excluded?"

Patrick asked, "I thought you had some shopping you wanted to do? We are not going to just sit and wait for you. Do what shopping you need to do and we'll be close by when you're ready to leave." His answer seemed to quell any further inquisitive remarks from Molly. The carriage passed farms and pastureland as the road snaked through densely-wooded areas that added to the romantic texture of the luscious countryside.

Molly was restless and shifted in the seat often, while Patrick and Cille remained proper, even though the carriage was the only one traveling the road. Cille asked, "How did you come by knowing about this lovely stretch of road?"

Without being defensive in his reply, Patrick said, "When we got the wagon at the academy and had to make a run to Monroe, this is the shortcut we used."

Cille looked at him while smiling, accepting his answer without question. She settled in to enjoy the scenery. The trip was short lived as they soon reached the outskirts of Monroe. When the wagon rolled to a stop in the square, Molly grabbed at her drawstring purse and made an effort to be the first out of the carriage.

When Patrick stepped down from the carriage, he offered his hand to Cille. When she stepped through the small door, she looked at him and asked, “I have been sitting very patiently wondering about your remark. When will I get to know what you have on your mind?”

Patrick held on to her hand while they walked to the opposite side of the square. He teased, “You're about as inquisitive as my sister.” When they had crossed the square, he stopped her short of the sidewalk. “Cille, it was here that I first laid eyes on you some time back. I feel it is the only appropriate place to ask you to share a part of my life and become my wife?”

As warm as the day had been, she was feeling a cool splash hit her. She gasped in surprise at the sudden question. He just up and said it and didn't him-haw around, allowing her to prepare for the ultimate. She responded without thinking, “Patrick, I think the proper thing to do is to ask my father, I mean for my hand. But, oh, you sure know how to get a girl’s attention. And yes, oh, yes, I would be so pleased. I'm sure my father won't…” She suddenly felt flush, as a series of strange feelings crashed over her, similar to how she felt while dancing with him, at her debutante ball. It made her unsure how she should respond to a thunderous series of questions tossed out by Patrick. She desperately tried to regain her composure. While the magic of the moment left her without words, Patrick’s light kiss upon her lips added to the emotional excitement.

He softly whispered close to her face, “Good, then we’ll keep the news from Molly until after I have the opportunity to properly talk to your father tonight.”

Cille smiled and allowed him to make the decision on when the announcement would be made to family members. Her heart was ready to burst with excitement; she found it hard to restrain herself. They waited for Molly’s return to the carriage after her shopping.

CHAPTER 11

The Proposal 1870

When the trio arrived at the Hodges estate, Cille and Molly ran ahead and found Constance and Mattie having tea in the drawing room. Patrick casually entered the house closing the door behind him. He turned to see Albon entering the foyer, and asked, “Where might I find Mr. Hodges and my father?”

Albon replied, “Dey-z en de library.”

When Patrick entered the library, he saw them both standing near a selection of French writings. He heard his father say, “Well, Son, what took the three of you so long?”

“Molly had some shopping to do and she decided to do it all at one time when we were in Monroe.”

“Looks to me like she has the same traits her mother has. I tell you Augustus, Mattie loves to shop, and having Molly with her, their shopping endeavors are twofold. They can spend more time looking over the finer things to wear than a dozen women.”

Augustus smiled and motioned for them to have a seat in one of the leather chairs.

Joseph had a seat in one of the overstuffed chairs followed by Augustus in another, while Patrick remained standing.

Both men adjusted themselves as a slight pause began to set in. Not wanting to put off the inevitable, Patrick spoke up, “Mr. Hodges, I love your daughter very much and I am asking your permission for her hand in marriage.” He felt he had said what was necessary to either get a yes or a no and there was little need to waste words.

Not surprised by the short statement, Augustus raised his eyebrows over the small box that had previously sat on the corner of his desk containing imported barrels of long-rolled tobacco. He offered the open box to Joseph. There was a deliberate stall in the answer. Joseph picked up a cigar from the box and prepared to light it.

Taking a cigar for himself, Augustus took his time and lit it. Pulling on the tobacco, he sent a mouthful of smoke loose before answering. “Patrick, let me be the first to say, welcome to the family. You certainly have my blessings and I'm sure Constance will be happy as well.” Turning his attention to Joseph, he added, “You have an outstanding son here and it is my pleasure to welcome you and Mattie into the extended family circle.”

Joseph was leaning back enjoying the fine taste of the cigar and nodded his acceptance of the families joining. “Augustus, I thank you for those kind words. Let me say this of your daughter Cille: she is a gem and a delight. Mattie and I have been extremely pleased that Patrick has been showing an interest in her.” He turned his attention to Patrick and said, “Son, it is nice to know they taught you how to make proper decisions at the academy.”

“You might just as well pull up a chair,” Augustus added, “I don't reckon you'll grow much taller by standing.” He held out the cigar box when Patrick made himself comfortable.

“No thank you, sir, I'm not an avid smoker of cigars, yet.”

Moments later, Augustus reached out and knocked a long ash off the end of his cigar. “Well, Joseph, shall we finish our smoke and join your son as he tells the rest of the household the latest news?”

Joseph's barrel chest was poking out past the jacket he was wearing. He smiled, rolled the tasty cigar in his fingers and slowly leaned forward to remove the initial extended ash from his cigar in a tray. “Do you reckon he's nervous enough to leave here and face the women?” He smiled, finding an opportunity for some light humor.

Augustus winked and said, “I reckon he has felt uneasy long enough.” Turning to Patrick, he said, “You ready to face the wrath of the women?”

With a smile, he replied, “I would be most happy to have it done with.”

When the men arrived in the sitting room where the women were chatting, they fell silent when Augustus cleared his throat.

“Excuse us for intruding, but there is something young Patrick would like to say.”

Constance, Mattie and Molly looked on in anticipation, while Patrick held out his hand for Cille. She rose from her chair and joined him at his side.

Patrick looked briefly at his sister then gave his mother a longer look before his eyes rested on Constance. He spoke clearly saying, “I have had the honor of asking for your daughter’s hand in marriage from your husband, and I am honored to convey my intentions to you as well.”

Cille held on to his arm tightly with tears of happiness in her eyes and a smile on her face. She was so proud of him. He wasn't a bit bashful about stating his intentions to her, or to her parents.

A smile appeared on her face as Constance asked, “Did my husband give his best wishes?”

Patrick couldn't hold back any longer, “He sure did.”

“Then you have mine as well. This gives us all a reason to celebrate. Oh, by the way, have either of you set a date yet?”

Cille gasped, “Mother, he just asked. We haven't had time to talk of that, yet.”

The rest of the evening was spent in cheerful conversation between both families.

CHAPTER 12

Woodbury Home Near West Point 1870

Patrick and Cille made arrangements to use a house located on a small estate near the academy where he was assigned for temporary duty for six months awaiting orders. The arrangements for possession would be made after they were wed. The house was a modest seven-room home and would be lightly furnished, knowing a move would be in their future. There was a lot to do in a short period of time.

Invitations for the wedding of Patrick Woodbury and Cille Hodges had been sent out for some time. The rehearsal for the wedding was scheduled to take place on the 14th of August 1870. When the wedding rehearsal took place, they were both pleased. It was a brief affair; Patrick and Cille had worked together to keep the event small, short and simple. It was to be a simple wedding at the point in the town square where they first laid eyes on each other and the same spot where he had proposed to her. He would wear his military attire and she would be in her wedding dress with a brief reception to follow at the Hodges' estate.

Cille was full of excitement and at the end of the rehearsal said, "Patrick, I do hope the wedding goes well tomorrow. I'd simply be mortified if anything went wrong."

"I don't think we have too much to worry about. It is about as short and sweet as we're going to get it."

Before returning to the Hodges estate, Patrick looked into Cille's face, and said, "Cille, my love, in a few moments we will part company, but I'll see you in the morning at this very spot."

"I'll be here my dear. Oh, I'm just about to explode with excitement."

When they journeyed to the Hodge's Estate and stepped through the door, Joseph and Augustus were passing in the foyer on their way to the library. Augustus said, "If it isn't the happy couple. Patrick, would you care to join us, and Cille, your mother and Mattie are both wanting to talk to you." At that point, they were separated for the rest of the evening.

◇◇◇

Morning came early, not only for those in the Hodges estate, but throughout the countryside. There would be a rush to get things in order for the wedding at 10:00. At the Morgan estate, Esther had Elizabeth up early, fed and assisted into her gown. "Oh, Mother, Cille is going to be so surprised. Neither of them have any idea."

"Beth, are you sure you didn't give anything away?"

"Goodness no, Mother! I want to see the looks on their faces as much as anyone else."

Downstairs, Superintendent Colonel Thomas Gamble Pitcher and his wife Mrs. Mary J. Pitcher from the Military Academy at West Point visited with Horace, while the military escort was preparing their mounts and the academy carriage.

◇◇◇

At the Hodges', Patrick ate before he rode into Monroe for the early meeting with his best man, Lieutenant Daniel Winters, the Cavalry instructor from the academy and the academy chaplain Captain Jacob Meyers. They were tasked with making arrangements for the small wedding before the others arrived. They would only use a small portion of the square, allowing the community to conduct business around their preparations.

◇◇◇

Constance, Mattie and Molly joined the maids as they fussed over Cille and the wedding gown. Cille wore a soft white imported velvet bridal gown of vintage design with lace trimmed satin, off-the-shoulder collar and trios of satin rosettes on the collar and skirt. The over skirt she wore was a matching velvet with a ruffled underskirt of satin, to give it flair. Adding to the true Victorian look, a boned hoop beneath the skirt added volume. Upon her head, a beautiful tiara supported the wedding veil that rested upon her auburn hair. Ringlets cascaded down the side of her face with the length of her hair reaching to the bottom of her shoulder blades. Satisfied with how her daughter looked, Constance said, "My dear child, you're about ready. Goodness, please don't grab too much air!"

"Mother, please! I'll be fine. Thanks to all of you for the fussing, but I'll be okay."

The women were coming down the stairs, when a knock on the front door sent Albon into action. When he opened the door, a cadet captain from the academy stood there.

"I have been dispatched by Colonel Pitcher, the Superintendent of West Point to escort Miss Hodges to the carriage."

Albon was surprised, turned and called out, "Mastah Hodges." There was no need, because Augustus was right behind him.

"She will be right with you," her father said. He called out to his daughter about the time the women made it to the bottom of the stairs. "Cille, it looks as if you'll be escorted."

Cille looked on in surprise. This certainly wasn't in the plans. Her first thoughts were that Patrick had something to do with it.

Augustus added, "The rest of us will have to get to the carriages if we don't want to be late.

The household emptied as they made their way to the carriages. They would leave the estate before the bride and her escorted carriage. Cille was escorted to the academy carriage where Colonel Thomas Pitcher and Mary Pitcher were seated across from Elizabeth.

The cadet stepped forward and opened the door for the bride before he returned to his mount and took up his position in front of the carriage team. He ordered, "Cadets, post!"

Hearing the command, six mounted cadets in full dress rode up near the side of the academy carriage.

While Cille made herself comfortable in the plush carriage, she looked at Elizabeth and asked, "Did you know anything about this?"

"Cousin, I had nothing to do with this. I was just sworn to secrecy and you know me, I had to work at that."

When Cille turned her attention from her cousin, she said, "Colonel, it is nice to see you and Mrs. Pitcher again. Now I don't suppose either of you will admit to knowing anything of this fanfare?"

Mrs. Pitcher smiled and said, "Cille, you look simply stunning and I might add the wedding gown looks exquisite on you. We were just invited. Heavens, Cille, if I were you, I'd relax and enjoy all the attention."

"Beth, this is sure a heap of attention. Wow, I'm impressed."

Colonel Pitcher, a stoic figure of a man, was in full military dress with his mustache and goatee neatly trimmed. He simply nodded and smiled, as if he knew more than he was letting on.

A stream of carriages left the estate before the escorted carriage began to move. The entourage formed an even pace as they all made their way to the square in the center of Monroe.

In the town square at the very spot where Patrick first laid eyes on Cille, and where he proposed to her, a religious altar had recently been placed. Chaplain Captain Jacob Meyers from the military academy stood nearby ready to officiate.

As time drew near for the wedding, the men stood near the altar waiting for the Hodges' family carriage. Suddenly, the route in from the estate appeared to be congested with early morning travelers. Patrick was beginning to wonder, why all the commotion, because there were carriages and activity as far as the eye could see.

Without warning, the square seemed to clear and all at once become busy with added wedding preparations. Patrick was about ready to leave his position near the wedding altar to find out what was going on, when he saw Augustus and Constance stepping from their carriage without Cille.

Mr. Hodges looked at Patrick and gestured by touching the tip of his hat with his forefinger like a modified salute. He offered his arm to Constance and escorted her to her reserved chair near the wedding altar. He looked toward the confused Patrick and said, "I'm on the way to lend an arm for my daughter."

Patrick knew there was some added fanfare that was not in the original plans for the wedding. Not knowing who was responsible, he looked at his best man, Lieutenant Winters.

Daniel shrugged his shoulders and rendered a vacant expression.

Beyond the Hodges carriage, the street was filled with an eight-man honor guard from a Boston armory: an officer in charge of the unit, a guidon bearer and six riflemen. The local armory of Monroe furnished the same. Beyond them, the carriage from the academy came to a stop.

Sidewalks bordering the streets of Monroe were fast beginning to fill with spectators to witness the event that was about to unfold. Inquisitive, they gathered quietly and looked on in silence.

The West Point cadet opened the carriage door and Colonel Pitcher stepped down. Mrs. Pitcher was to follow her husband, Elizabeth and then Cille, each getting a helping hand from a cadet as they stepped down to the street.

Colonel Pitcher held out his arm for Cille. Mrs. Pitcher and Elizabeth walked closely behind the pair. The Academy honor guard had dismounted, and with the senior cadet in front, the others marched in two columns, one on each side of the Superintendent, Cille, Mary and Elizabeth.

When they reached Cille's waiting father, the escort halted. The bride was handed over to Augustus. Colonel and Mrs. Pitcher walked past them and took their seats near the wedding altar. Elizabeth remained behind with Cille and Mr. Hodges until it was her turn to move to her position.

The wedding ceremony was short and sweet with the small group that was invited. Off to the side, the curious onlookers from the community looked on in silence. At the end of their vows, Mr. and Mrs. Patrick Woodbury were introduced to those closely gathered.

While close friends gave congratulations, Colonel Pitcher notified Patrick that the academy carriage was available and would be their transportation back to the Hodges.

When Patrick and Cille left the wedding altar, as they walked down the street toward the academy carriage, they first met with the eight-man honor guard from the unit he had worked with in Boston during the Civil War. As they came near the unit, the rifle salute was ordered. Patrick was surprised to see his old commander, the one responsible for recommending him to the academy. After exchanging a couple of words, the officer assured Patrick they would talk later at the Hodges.

The next unit Patrick and Cille met was from the local armory. They rendered the same military courtesy. When Patrick and Cille passed, the Commander ordered, "Rifle salute!" The officer in charge was at attention in front of his unit and gave a snappy hand salute as they passed. Patrick returned a salute. From that point on, they were escorted by the two columns of cadets to the academy carriage.

Upon their arrival at the carriage, so nicely provided by the academy, the senior officer stepped forward and opened the carriage door. Cille entered first, followed by Patrick. When the door was closed, the officer commanded, "Escorts post!" The cadets went to their horses and mounted. The cavalry escort quickly rode up near the carriage. They waited for the senior cadet to get to his position and for his command.

Cille looked at Patrick with questioning eyes, only to hear him say, "I didn't have anything to do with this, honest."

She smiled and said, "I'm so overwhelmed with all the attention, I don't know what to say."

"We may find out who put this all together when we get to your parents' estate."

As the carriage began to roll forward, it began a leisurely tour through several streets in Monroe. They would slowly make their way to the countryside estate a short time later. This would allow the others to get to the Hodges' before the bride and groom arrived.

◇ ◇ ◇

Hired help from the Morgan household was due to arrive at the Hodges estate shortly after those involved in the wedding had left. When they arrived, they were to assist in getting the garden prepared for the huge reception that was anticipated.

The first to arrive were the same musicians from New York who had played at Cille's Debutante Ball nearly three years earlier. The hired help scurried about as the musicians set up their equipment and took their instruments out of their cases.

Carriages began to arrive and the front of the estate soon filled with a variety of horses, horse-drawn wagons and various carriages. Most of those who came early waited out front for the arrival of the bride and groom.

When the academy carriage pulled to a stop in front of the Hodges' estate, the senior cadet dismounted. The cadet handling the carriage quickly secured the reins and scurried from his position to join the honor guard escort team. The escort team quickly formed two lines on each side of the carriage door, and as the senior cadet opened the door, he commanded, "Cross saber … salute!"

Patrick stepped from the carriage and helped Cille down. They walked between the line of cadets who had their sabers raised in the air, reflecting the sunlight and crossed at the tip, just above the heads of Patrick and Cille.

The afternoon was filled with an array of relaxing music by the musicians, while guests visited with each other. It wasn't until late in the day when the music from within the large room of the house was playing for the evening dance. Food and refreshing beverages were abundantly available in the garden area. As with any dance, local girls were invited to be available for the guests during the dance.

After the musicians had played a few dance numbers, the old Commander, Major Gordon Sanders from Boston, drew the attention of the crowd. "Excuse me, ladies and gentlemen, I have an important presentation to make, and I thought now was as good of time as any. Patrick and Cille, it does my heart good to see such a happy couple. Patrick, on behalf of the Boston Armory, we wish to present to you the original guidon that marked the unit you were assigned to when you worked for us."

Patrick came forward, rendered a salute and had it returned before he received the neatly folded cloth flag. "I'm very much honored sir and I thank you from the bottom of my heart."

Major Sanders said, "There is yet another gift." One of the men from the Boston guard came forward with a long box and gave it to his commander. "As the records show, you were assigned a musket numbered 327." He opened the box and pulled the musket from its wrapping.

"I'm overwhelmed. Thank you, sir."

"It took some doing, but the approval came just hours before our leaving to get here. I am proud of you for representing us while you were in the academy and I'm glad I had the foresight to recommend such a fine lad to the academy years ago. I salute you."

With that, the commander rendered a salute and Patrick returned it.

As Patrick went to put the presents aside, Colonel Pitcher caught his attention. “Patrick, I have it on reliable authority that you will be affiliated with the academy for the next six months. Beyond that, I believe you can anticipate an assignment in the Dakota Territory, where you can use the skills for which you were trained.”

“That is great news. I'll be able to get Cille settled in before I have to leave.”

“Have you found a place to live?”

“We have a house a short distance from the academy. I believe it is less than two miles.”

“Congratulations on that and your wedding to Cille. Let neither of you be a stranger in our home.”

“Thank you, Sir. We're both honored by the invitation.”

When the musicians took one of their breaks, the presentations of wedding gifts were made. The first and most important gift was a new Family Bible presented by the Hodges. The other gifts were opened and recognized and remained at a table where all the gifts were placed.

Late in the evening, the dance came to an end. Most of the invited guests that lived nearby went home. Those guests who had traveled far were accommodated at the Hodges or Morgan estates.

Patrick and Cille remained at the Hodges estate for the night. They would make preparations to travel to their first home the following day.

Later that fall, Cille had the privilege of being invited to the Change of Command Ceremony at West Point where she would sit near Mrs. Pitcher and was introduced to Diane Ruger, the new superintendent’s wife.

Mary said, “Diane, Cille is having the next gathering at her home for tea and cookies. Most of the ladies connected to the academy get together once a month to chat and share common interests. I hope you will carry on when I leave. It will give you a great opportunity to meet the wives of the husbands that are on staff. The tea is tea, but you simply can’t miss out on Lizzie’s tasty secret cookies.”

Cille added, “I’ll miss you Mary, and Diane I hope you’ll attend. I know the other ladies and I would like to know you better."

Diane smiled and replied, "I accept your invitation and I wouldn't miss it for the world. I look forward to meeting with you and the others."

Patrick had his assignment as a staff officer. Colonel Pitcher and his wife Mary would head out for another assignment, and to take their place was Colonel Thomas Howard Ruger and his lovely wife, Diane.

The Change of Command Ceremony was brief but colorful and Cille felt honored to be so close to the heart of the academy.

CHAPTER 13

A Dakota Assignment 1872

For the next year and a half, the younger Woodburys enjoyed their home near the academy. The house was adequate for their social affairs. With the dowry given to them by her parents, it was put to good use by employing Lester and Lizzie as a butler and maid, allowing their lives to be quite comfortable.

Lieutenant Woodbury continued with his duties at the academy. During the day, he would assist in teaching cavalry tactics to the young cadets of the freshman class. There were times when the saddle would slide to one side or the other, losing the young cadet when he had failed to follow proper instructions. The set of instructions varied little and could be adjusted at times, especially when word from the frontier dictated some form of modification in tactics.

In the evening hours, he and Cille would enjoy horseback riding. They went to the stables and used a pair of the horses that had yet to be assigned to a cadet. Patrick taught Cille how to properly care for her mount. He was patient and took his time, knowing she might need to pull from her experience if she ever ventured out west to be with him. He showed her how to saddle up. Then he removed the saddle and talked her through the steps as she did the saddling. After a couple of times, they left the saddles on and he showed her how to mount.

Cille watched Patrick swing into the saddle with little effort. She tried to do what he had done, but when it came time to move her body upward, she didn't have the strength in her arms to go about it smoothly. "Oooh, I can't," she cried out as she could barely see Patrick over her saddle before she dropped back down to the ground.

Patrick dismounted and showed her again as he mounted. With the reins in his left hand, gripping the forward part of the saddle, the right hand on the mantle, left foot in the stirrup, he swung his weight upward using the motion and strength of his arms along with the strength in his left leg. It was one fluid movement throwing his right leg over the back of the mantle as he removed his hand from the mantle before he sat down. "Cille, once you get your weight moving, don't pause or stop until you're on top."

She said, "I'll try." Failing to make a good mount the first night was set aside once she had managed to mount up. They went riding about the academy grounds at a leisurely pace. However, Cille would struggle with the mounting more as time went on. But in the end, she would win over her gentile ways and was soon mounting with ease. In time, she also learned how to ride without having to hang on to the saddle with her hands.

The first night was a gentle ride over some of the terrain that the cadets used during the day. She said, "Patrick, I have enjoyed the ride and find the tour of the training area most interesting."

As the weeks passed, Patrick taught her how to mount in a hurry, and to get her mount at a high gallop, as if caught in a tight situation, such as being pursued. She needed to learn how to ride hard and get away. Cille enjoyed the exhilarating feeling of riding at high speed.

A month later, Patrick showed her how to ride at top speed and lower her body in the saddle to make a smaller target, as well as how to ride off to each side a bit, without losing control of her mount. When she rode with her body on the left side, she had the reins in her left hand, her right hand held onto the saddle and her right leg hugged the shelter roll behind the saddle. When her body was on the right side, it was the opposite. When the lessons were over, they would go on a leisurely ride across campus. At the end of each day, there was the care of the mount before they returned to their home. "How did I do today?" she called out while caring for her horse.

"Cille, I'm right proud of you as to how fast you have been catching on. Take your time and build your confidence. Things of this nature can't be learned overnight."

◇ ◇ ◇

He talked to her about various situations and how she should react. Cille was becoming a good listener and over the following months, she learned from doing. When they were horseback riding, their talks afterward pointed out different aspects of proper riding. In time, Cille learned as much as, if not more than, some of the freshmen cadets at the Point.

◇ ◇ ◇

One afternoon Patrick was summoned to the Superintendent's office. When he arrived, Colonel Ruger said, "Patrick, I regret that I'll be losing you and your skills here at the academy. Your orders came in today. You will proceed to Fargo, Dakota Territory and report to General Thomas L. Rosser."

Patrick smiled and asked, "When do I report, sir?"

"According to the information I have, the first of July."

"Is there any indication of the duties I'll be doing?"

"It looks as though you'll be in charge of a unit of troops. You will escort and provide protection against the Sioux for the railroad workers. They will make the right-of-way and lay track for the Northern Pacific through the territory."

"When will my duties here at the Academy end?"

"We would like you to remain on staff until the graduation class of 1872 finishes up. Then you can have some time off to prepare Cille for your departure."

"She will sure be surprised."

"I'll see that Diane keeps in touch with her from time to time, in your absence."

"Thank you, sir."

◇ ◇ ◇

Cille met Patrick at the door, and they embraced for a short time, as had been the custom every night. When she pulled away, she said, "What's wrong, Patrick?"

"I've got orders for out west."

"When and where, may I ask?"

"I have to be there the first of July and it's in the Dakota Territory, a place called Fargo."

"Well, I can't say I'm surprised. I wasn't sure how much longer the academy could justify keeping you here."

A moment of silence fell between them, before Cille broke the spell. "Patrick, if that is where you need to be, and according to the Army it is, I'll support you because it's your life, and it's in your blood.

"Thank you, my dear."

"My love, I married you for who you are, and what you stand for, then as a cadet and now as an officer. I believed in you then and I always will. Go and do your best. I'll be here waiting for you, but the first chance we get, I want to join you, even if it is in the Wild West.

"That would be nice." He reached out and pulled her close to him for a soft hug.

She momentarily fussed, by saying, "Don't mess the hair or the dress, we could still have company…" She gave in and enjoyed his affection.

Patrick set aside her remarks and continued as he intended.

Moments later she said, "You're persistent," as she looked into his face and smiled. When they separated, she added, "Who knows? Maybe it will offer you some of the challenges you have been missing by being on staff at the academy."

He smiled, and said, "You're so understanding about my military duties. You can say the darndest things at times and make a man like what you're saying. I love you for that and so much more." Patrick reached out, cradled her face in his hands and gave her a soft kiss.

Cille responded, "I love your touch and I'll miss being mussed."

◇ ◇ ◇

After the short visit with her parents, she returned to her home near the academy. She had found some comfort by being there after seeing Patrick off for his assignment. Arriving on the veranda, she was met at the door by Lester her butler, "Lizzie sho gonna be glad ta see ya back. She done made plans fo' special dinnah for ya, once ya gotched here."

"Thank you, Lester, please take the luggage up to my room.

When you see Lizzie, tell her I'll be in my room freshening up and I need to see her."

"Yes Um." Lester took the luggage upstairs before he went about the house looking for the maid. He found her cleaning the sills behind the long lengthy curtains in the library.

"Lizzie, Mrs. Woodbury is back and wants ta see ya in her room."

She left the library with her cleaning supplies and dropped them off in the utility room, before darting across the foyer and up the stairs.

Cille had entered her room, and to her surprise, a letter had been placed on her dresser. It was from Patrick.

Before she had time to open it, Lizzie rapped on the door and entered. "I'z glad ta see ya back, I'z a fixin' ta make ya a special dish for dinnah, if ya like."

"I'd like that very much, Lizzie. Tell me, when did this letter get here?"

"Tadee, I put on dat dressah knowin' it be the firs' place ya would look, when ya gotched home."

"I will be having tea in the garden tomorrow at precisely two o'clock with Mrs. Ruger and a couple of the wives from the academy. Please have the tea ready by then and some of those wonderful cookies you do so well with."

"Yes um."

The maid left the room and Cille sat at the dresser, opened the letter and began to read:

My Dearest Cille,

I arrived a day earlier than expected. I met General Rosser when I reported in and was told it will be a day or so before the troop contingent is formed and ready for duty.

There is a Captain Nelson Cobb who has his patrol across the river and in Sioux territory. The railroad workers are busy stringing wire for communications. He can't protect all the men on the eastern end of the right-of-way where they are laying new track brought in on a work train. That will be part of my responsibility. This is quite a shabby place to be. Most of the men working for the railroad are living in tarpaper shacks close to the river.

My dear, I love you very much and miss you more and more every day. I won't say, I wish you were here, because the living conditions are lacking at best. I'll write more in a day or so. Just wanted to let you know I got here safely.

Love, Patrick

Cille lowered the letter to her lap, still holding it open with both hands. She spoke softly, "Patrick, I'm so glad you made the trip safely. I truly love you and miss you being here." She closed her eyes momentarily, as if to hold back the tears.

◇ ◇ ◇

Time passed and the letters came sporadically, sometimes in pairs. Cille entertained with a social tea once a month to keep up her end of the social calendar. Returning home from a tea with Diane Ruger, a letter was waiting for her. She rushed to her room and sat near her dresser to read it.

My Dearest Cille,

It has taken four months of seemingly trivial duties, when the Sioux Nation suddenly took a dislike to us being in their neighborhood. The work train was at the end of the track and the crew was busy off-loading rails. Early that morning, the Indians came from the hills in a huge attack. There were several times more Indians than we had troops and railroad workers combined. The best we could do was to use the engine and rail cars for some protection. I managed to come out of this situation in one piece, and without so much as a scratch, but a number of my troops and a good number of railroad workers were not so lucky. We lost four railroad workers and a total of 27 others wounded Six of the injured were from my troop.

My dear, I found out how hard it is to command in a situation like this. Even if we could have gotten to our horses and mounted in time, we were vastly outnumbered.

I understand now when they say, "Expect the unexpected" I think this may be what they meant. I miss you more and more every day. My love for you grows with a deeper meaning of importance and I long to be with you. There isn't much to do at night but to reread your loving letters. I'll be so glad to see you and set these letters aside for a time.

After talking with General Rosser, my duties will be to see the railroad to the Missouri River. He will be making a recommendation for my next assignment. If all goes well, we will make the Missouri before long. I may be on my way home for the holidays.

With Love, Patrick

The first part of December 1873 was one of joy and a reason to look upon the upcoming holidays with great anticipation. Cille hadn't received a letter for some time and was in hopes, one day, there would be news of when Patrick would be home.

Lester the butler was busy spreading the decorations around the house where they could be hung in their proper place. In one corner of the foyer was a freshly cut tree waiting for the holiday decorations. A box of ornaments sat near the tree, as Cille anxiously awaited Patrick's return home before decorating it. He would be home before Christmas. "Lester, are these all of the decorations we have?"

"Yes um, not no mo,' to get out a da box an' put out."

Lizzie found herself in the kitchen after seeing that fresh linen was placed upon the beds upstairs and fresh towels in their proper place. She wanted to make a double batch of her favorite secret cookies today for the household and any guests that may drop by. "No way," she softly whispered, "no one gonna get dat list of the makin's. They want, but alls they gonna get is the cookie."

Cille heard the rap on the door, "Lester, get the door, the decorations will have to wait."

When the butler returned, he was holding out the latest news from Patrick. Cille took the letter and went to her room upstairs. At the dresser, she nervously opened the letter hoping for some great news.

My Dearest Cille,

There is little track to be laid before we reach the banks of the

Missouri River. I haven't seen General Rosser for a few days. We have had nothing but trouble out of the Sioux Nation. They hit early in the morning to disrupt the work and then seem to disappear over the hills. When the men lay down their guns to begin work, here they come again. There are so many of them, they can't be ignored, certainly too many for me to lead an attack against. But somehow the rail gets laid and pushes the track further into their homeland. We may make the river sometime this week. I'll let you know when we do. No news on when I'll be released and no word on any reassignment. My love, I can't count the number of times I think of you during the day. I look forward to the day when I can hold you in my arms once more and stare into your beautiful eyes. I miss you and hope to see you before the holidays pass. Until then keep the home fires burning.

I send my love.

Patrick

She held the letter close to her breast. Within her tiny frame she yearned for his return. She gazed without purpose into the mirror to see her butler at the top of the stairs and coming toward her room. "What is it, Lester?"

"Theyz a man at the door, wantin' ta see ya."

Cille left the letter on the dresser and left the room passing the butler in the hallway. "Who on earth is it and why didn't you invite him in?"

Lester did not respond. He followed and made a dash for the kitchen, knowing he should stay out of sight for the moment.

At the bottom of the stairs she crossed the foyer and opened the front door. Momentarily stunned, she stood in shock at who stood before her.

"May I come in?" Patrick asked with a smile upon his face.

With a squeal, she jumped into his waiting arms. They stepped back into the house and held each other in a warm embrace. Following several kisses, she managed to say, "Oh, am I glad your home. I was upstairs reading your letter where you hadn't quite gotten to the Missouri."

"We made it there a couple of days later. The Sioux seemed to leave us alone for a spell and a lot of work got done. When I left, General Rosser was busy drawing up plans for a bridge to cross the river. I didn't know it until just before I left. General Rosser told me that he had graduated from West Point and General Custer was one of his classmates. When the war was on, Rosser chose to serve on the side of the Confederacy. They met on opposite sides at Shenandoah and in a couple of other instances. Now he's wearing union blue and on good terms with Custer. I should be getting my new assignment and orders in a week or so."

"Well, you're just in time to help us hang some of the green."

"We can do that, can't we?" he said with a smile.

"After that, there's this tree that needs decorating. I tried really hard not to touch it, hoping to see you soon so we could do the honors together."

"I'll place the bulbs and you can handle the garland," he replied.

"That sounds fair," she said with a smile.

They spent the rest of the day decorating the house and enjoying the festivities. Many of the neighbors dropped by to check on her only to find Patrick had returned from the Dakota Territory. There was much to talk about between old friends and new acquaintances.

CHAPTER 14

A Period of Separation 1873

A blanket of winter snow was blowing in from the west, heavy for late Februrary. Cille had ventured from her home near the academy and was returning to the Hodges estate. She bundled up in a hooded heavy coat and used a comforting overstuffed blanket to protect her from the elements. Around her neck she had a knitted scarf, partially pulled up to protect her face. In her lap, she had her mitten-covered hands inside a muff to keep them warm. It was not a long trip but venturing out in this type of weather was not advisable without preparation.

She enjoyed the landscape covered with a blanket of fresh snow. The open carriage gave her a wonderful feeling of being exposed to the brutal raw nature of winter this time of year. There was a crisp stillness in the air. Snow on small limbs fell softly to the ground when birds flew from one tree branch to the other. The fence posts of nearby fences seemed to reflect the depth of the snowfall with a white cap resting on each post. The carriage wheels rolled along without a sound. Equally muffled were the sound of the hoof beats from the horse. The driver was quiet as well because he was bundled up, trying to stay warm, while handling the horse and carriage.

For the second time in less than a year she had seen Patrick off to do his duty with the Army. In her heart she was saddened, but deep down she was challenged, knowing she had to prepare for a lengthy journey in order to be with him. That challenge seemed to take on a greater importance. She busied herself thinking of things to put together before her journey would begin. Her extended stay in Monroe was for an extensive shopping trip with her mother. She wanted to buy a trunk for future use before she returned to her home near the military academy. Her thoughts raced through her head and before long, the carriage had left the city of Monroe behind. Beyond the front of the carriage was the familiar road that stirred her emotions before she could see the outline of the bridge that marked the estate of her childhood home, barely seen through the windswept snow.

◊ ◊ ◊

Cille's visit was a welcome change for the family and her mother was excited about going shopping with her. The largest part of the day included her getting there. That evening, they would make preparations for the following day.

◊ ◊ ◊

"Now, Cille," her mother said as they made their way to the carriage, "There is nothing better than a shopping trip to take one's mind off the unpleasant chore of seeing Patrick off." Their trip to Monroe was a quick one and they enjoyed each other's company. The snowstorm had passed and the sun illuminated all that was covered in freshly fallen snow.

They ventured from one fashion shop to the next until it happened. "Oh, Mother, look at this."

Constance looked on and replied, "Where on earth do you suppose they've been hiding that?"

"I don't know," Cille gasped, "but this dress is simply something I'll have to have."

"It is beautiful," Constance replied.

"I'll have to get the hat as well and a pair of shoes to finish things off."

"From the looks of things, you have found what you need. Let me browse and see if they have anything for me in my size."

Cille paid for her outfit and waited patiently in the front of the store. Then she saw her mother making her way to the cashier with an arm full of the latest fashions. "Mother, did you find what you were looking for?"

"Heavens no, but this dress just caught my eye and I knew in an instant I had to have it." Holding it up she asked, "What do you think, my dear?"

"It's simply exquisite," Cille said with a smile. "You'll look great in it."

Their goal was to buy something nice for themselves and a trunk Cille would use at a later date to make her trip out West.

Before the day was gone, Cille and Constance managed to purchase one of the latest fashions, in their size, recently released from the New York area. The ensemble consisted of a hat with plume to match the dress and gloves, not to mention a pair of shoes to finish off the elegant look.

The hardest decision was making the proper trunk selection. There was a variety of wood and some with leather strapping. The function of the trunk was important, but they had to consider the use of the trunk in the home once she had joined Patrick.

After making the selection, they placed it in the carriage. They returned to the Hodges estate where Cille would visit a couple of days longer before returning to her home.

◇◇◇

Patrick arrived in Yankton, Dakota Territory on the noon stagecoach. Upon his arrival, he reported for duty and had the pleasure of meeting Colonel Sturgis and Lieutenant Colonel Custer. He was assigned his mount by the quartermaster and given his equipment for the march.

"Best be sending a note back home," the quartermaster said, "if you're of a mind to. We're mounting up and heading out early day after tomorrow."

"I thought there would be more time before the march would take place."

"Our General has other plans. Around here, the only plans you can count on, to any great degree, is to be prepared to change your plans to fit those of the General's."

That evening, Patrick sat down to write a letter to Cille and inform her of his safe arrival and early departure for a place called Fort Lincoln, somewhere in the Dakota Territory.

◇◇◇

Moments after the sun had cleared the horizon on May 7, 1873, the infantry units and units of the 7th Cavalry Regiment lined up on the parade field. Leaving Yankton was done with an enormous amount of military fanfare.

A handful of civilians living this far west joined in with those who would remain behind, decorating the buildings with red, white and blue buntings.

Custer's band played marching music before the companies would gradually make their way from Yankton.

The companies passed in review, then marched around the parade field one last time before Colonel Sturgis and Lieutenant Colonel Custer led them into the dusty countryside. Custer took an active role in commanding the 7th Regiment and was referred to as ‘General’ by his men. Colonel Samuel Davis Sturgis agreed to this turn of events.

They descended the gentle slope to the river valley below Yankton to a bridge that spanned the James River. The lead military unit stretched out some distance before the second unit of troops began leaving the post. Patrick and another officer led the second contingent of troops.

It wasn't long before the long column of men and equipment disappeared from view. The march would follow the contour of the James River northward over the gentle rolling landscape. The long and dusty trek north was just beginning.

◇◇◇

Cille sat in a stuffed, high wing-back chair as her fingers nervously opened the letter from Patrick. She had waited a long time to get this letter. She began to read as her heart pounded with excitement.

05 May 1873
Dearest Cille,
I safely arrived on the noon stage here in Yankton, Dakota Ter-

ritory. I was assigned my mount and equipment from the quartermaster. Tomorrow, we leave on a two-month march and should arrive at Fort Lincoln deep in the territory close to the Missouri River. I have had the pleasure of meeting Colonel Samuel D. Sturgis and Brevetted General George Armstrong Custer. He is actually a Lieutenant Colonel, but the troops address him as 'General' because of the highest rank he held during the Civil War. Custer will be in charge of this march. I have missed you from the moment we parted. I knew there would come a day we would face a separation, but I wasn't expecting it to be this soon. I have no idea what living conditions are waiting for me at Fort Lincoln. We plan to stop off at Fort Rice before we get to the end of the march. Should it be possible for you to come out this way, I will send for you. With all my heart, I want you to know I love you from the deepest part of my soul.

Love,
Patrick

She folded the letter and placed it on the desk where she could reread it before leaving her room later. She knew that her place was with her husband and found little comfort knowing that his service in the military had caused the separation between them. She loved him and knew the moment she could find a way to be near him, she would be there.

CHAPTER 15

Cille Plans to Go Out West 1873

Cille felt the need to read the last letter she received from Patrick one more time. She sat upon a small, wire-back chair with a pastel-colored soft cushion with decorative fringe. The seat was in front of her dressing table and mirror where she would normally sit while Lizzie was tending to her hair. As she read the letter, she could almost hear him speaking from the pages. Oh, how she wanted to be near him. The glass-blown lamp on the dressing table wasn't needed to light up the room. There was an abundance of sunlight cascading through the lace curtains she had hung to adorn the eastern window in her bedroom. It seemed to place a warm comfortable spell over the interior. After reading the letter, she placed it on top of a box at the back of the dressing table that contained all his other letters. She left her room and slowly descended the stairs.

At the base of the stairs, she heard the familiar knock at the front door. She didn't wait for Lester to get it as she rushed across the foyer and pulled the door open. "Mother, what a pleasant surprise. Did Daddy make the trip with you?"

Constance replied, "He'll be along shortly, my dear. He's up the street doing a bit of calling on one of his constituents."

"I'm so happy to see you."

"My goodness, don't you look bubbly."

"Thank you. I feel pretty good."

"Don't tell me that you have received word from that wandering husband of yours?"

"How did you know?"

"It's written all over your face. Good news, or is he still riding all over the west?"

"He arrived safely at Yankton on the fifth of May and now he's wandering the countryside with General Custer and his regiment somewhere in the Dakota Territory. He wrote the sweetest letter. I have it upstairs." She was beaming with excitement.

"I'm not going to ask you to fetch it, Cille," Constance said.

"I know. Patrick said, he's going on some kind of a march from Yankton to a place called Fort Rice and Fort Lincoln. General Custer is in charge of the march and it should only take him a month to get to where he's going."

"That long? I thought he rode a horse to wherever he goes."

"He does, Mother. It's a military term. He never has explained too much about what some of the terms mean. He's in the cavalry, but there are infantry units making the trip. I guess they will be doing all the marching. He gets to ride a horse and the infantry people have to walk. Maybe that's where the term comes from. He also said if there are proper living quarters at Fort Lincoln, he plans to send for me."

"What? Has he lost all the sensibility I thought he once had?"

"Mother!"

"Why, I'd no more want you to live out that way amongst a batch of those wild Indians and outlaws than..."

"Living at Fort Lincoln isn't living with them, Mother."

"Mark my words, that is no place for a proper young lady to be. You best think this over before acting hastily."

"You love Daddy, don't you?"

"Of course I do, I married him. What a foolish question to ask."

"And you stand by Daddy, don't you?"

"Cille, of course I do. What brings all this on?"

"I love Patrick. I married him and I plan to be at his side, if not here, then I'll join him there."

"But child, your father's decisions were more sensible than asking one to venture out to some forsaken place that isn't settled yet."

"I'll have the whole Army to protect me if there's a problem."

"Well! If you think a subtle statement of that nature is going to reassure your mother, you're dreadfully wrong. I hear those savages are fierce and have overcome some units of the Army. And they just don't kill, they try to send back a message. They deserve the term savages by the way they brutalize the people they kill. They're dangerous for man, woman or child, and you don't have to be in the military for the savages to get all hostile and cut you up in little pieces when they raise havoc."

"Mother! Sometimes, I think your imagination is running away with you after reading some of those nickel novels that sensationalize some parts of the West."

At that moment, Augustus' frame filled the door and Cille called out, "Daddy, come in." The conversation with her mother was temporarily halted as she rushed to the waiting arms of her father.

They embraced for a moment, and when she pulled back, he inquired, "Any word from Patrick?"

"Yes, there is. I was just telling Mother he had written."

"That's good."

"He'll be on a march for some time. He's being assigned to a place called Fort Lincoln. If everything is okay at the fort, then he'll send for me. I was trying to reassure Mother I would have the whole Army to protect me if there were any Indian problems."

"Your mother has every right to be concerned. After all, you're our only child and we would both hate to see anything happen to you."

"I know you both feel that way, but…"

"But nothing, Cille. Your mother and I realize you're married and there will be a proper time when you will need to be by his side. We realize you want to be with the man you love. It makes no difference if he was stationed here at the academy or out West. I'm sure your mother's concern is for your safety, so for the moment, let's consider her side also."

Cille called out, "Lizzie, please see that there are two additional place settings at the table. My parents will be dining with me."

"Thank you, dear," Constance said, "we didn't intentionally come by just to eat."

Augustus added, "No we didn't, but it is very nice of you."

"Lizzie, I hope we have some of the cookies left over. If not, would you make a few so that we may enjoy them at the table?" Cille asked.

"Iz jus' made a short batch this mornin' an' theyz on the counter an' still hot. I jus' do my best ta keep Lester's hands out of 'em."

"Thank you, Lizzie."

Concerns of Cille going out west were brushed aside and the family settled in for a more pleasant time of chatting.

The visit from her parents lasted long enough to get an update on the latest news and they enjoyed a fine meal. But they wanted to be home before nightfall as Augustus had obligations in Monroe early in the morning.

Lizzie smiled. She had her favorite cookies baked and knew they would be a special treat for the visiting pair before they headed home.

◇ ◇ ◇

In the waning hours of the evening, Lizzie cleaned the kitchen and dining area. Lester secured the house and turned down the lights. Cille retreated to her room where she picked up the letter once more and began to reread it. Oh, how she longed to be with Patrick. The mere prospect of going out west to be with him brought comfort to her. She loved him and longed for the day she would find comfort in his arms.

As the evening grew into darkness, Cille snuffed the lights in her bedroom and went to bed early. She tossed and turned in the overstuffed feather bed. Thoughts of Patrick and the journey to join him wove in and out of her mind. She didn't care what the living conditions were like. All she knew was she wanted to be with him and fulfill the proper role of a wife by being near and supporting him. Sometime deep into the night, she found rest.

CHAPTER 16

Lieutenant Woodbury at Fort Rice 1873

The long march from Yankton was nearing an end and the outline of Fort Rice could be seen off in the distance, on a dry dusty tenth of June. It was a welcome site located on a high point a short distance from the Missouri River.

Patrick turned to Captain Mark Collins and commented, "She sure looks good. I wonder if Fort Lincoln will look about the same."

"Most places look good from a distance. I believe I'll reserve my military assessment for when I see the fort up close."

The old Fort Rice had been built under the direction of Colonel Daniel J. Dills of the 30th Wisconsin Infantry. The original post consisted of crude barracks made from cottonwood logs with sod roofs inside a wall. But over time, the walls came down and the garrison became an open post. It was rebuilt in 1868 to a more substantial form. The four original lookout towers remained in use as they stood above the two-story barracks made of cut lumber from the old post. No longer were there any high walls protecting the interior of the fort. The Indian threat had been largely removed with few savages remaining close by. The main entrances to and from the post remained at their original location, one on the south and the other on the north. Housing covered the western and eastern sides of the garrison. The open fort was located on a bluff a short distance above the western bank of the Missouri River. Near the river's edge was a large shed where stores of food and equipment were kept. Hugging the river to the south, a few cottonwood trees lined the banks and became thinner toward the post.

Prior to reaching the southern entrance, there was a corral that held livestock. Off toward the river, a gentle slope left the rugged bluff and approached the river. There was the stable area and additional buildings outside the fort where some trappers had erected makeshift housing.

Located inside the boundaries of the fort to the west was officer's row and a house for Commandant Colonel Thomas Leonadis Crittenden. On the opposite side was a large canteen, enlisted barracks and munitions storage. In the middle of the fort was a large parade field. What few trees that once stood on the ridge now made up the old post, including the walls for the barracks and cabins within the fort.

Patrick said, "Looks as if we'll be able to bed down in some comfort for the night."

"I'll be glad for that," Captain Collins replied, "Last night was nothing but a bed of rocks, I found them very uncomfortable. I tossed and turned all night looking for a comfortable position and found none."

"You weren't alone. This whole trip has stretched my patience."

◇◇◇

As the units passed through the southern entrance, they circled the perimeter of the parade field and formed company size units. They waited for the others to enter from the open land to the south. When all who had made the trip from Yankton with the 7th Cavalry Regiment were in formation, a bugler sounded Officer's call. Colonel Crittenden welcomed Colonel Sturgis and Lieutenant Colonel Custer to Fort Rice. Custer informed Crittenden that he and Sturgis along with the men from the 7th would remain at Fort Rice overnight and proceed to Fort Lincoln in the early morning hours. The Commandant said, "'General', you and Colonel Sturgis along with your wives are invited to be our honored guests at supper. Our son John, a 2nd Lieutenant in L Company which you command, will also dine with us, as his mother would love to see him once again. I'm sure Catherine would enjoy meeting Elizabeth and Jerusha." After a few announcements, the troops were dismissed. The Infantry were shown their barracks and the cavalry the stables where enlisted troops took care of the horses.

◇ ◇ ◇

After enjoying a fine meal, 'General' Custer and Colonel Sturgis and the officers congregated at the headquarters building where socializing, drinking and a briefing of the fort came to pass. Later in the evening, Colonel Crittenden called Patrick to the side and said, "Lieutenant Woodbury, your expertise has reached the General's ears and as we talked, I expressed a dire need for a man like you here at this fort. I guess my argument carried some weight, because he has agreed to allow you to be stationed here for a period of time while still remaining with the 7th. Your adjutant will fill out the necessary papers tonight."

"Thank you, sir, for the compliment," Patrick said in surprise. "What is it here that I will do?"

"I have several members in a mounted infantry unit. Then there are a good number of galvanized troops that know the rebel ways but are not too proficient in cavalry tactics. I'll need you to be my training officer. Teach them the latest. I'll have you take them on patrol later on to see how they perform."

"I'll do my best, Sir."

"That's all I ask of any of my men or officers stationed here. Just remain behind in the morning when they mount up. I'll have someone from the staff get you settled in. Now let's both enjoy the rest of the evening."

Later that evening Patrick entered the small room that would be his quarters as an unaccompanied officer during his stay at Fort Rice. The room was rather small with every bit of space being used for some function; cramped but adequate. He went to the desk and began composing a letter to his wife.

◇ ◇ ◇

Cille bounded up the stairs and went to her room to read the latest letter from Patrick. It had been nearly two and a half months and the long wait for some news had been difficult to endure. She sat at her small dressing table where the sunlight cascaded through the lace curtains that covered the window. She opened the letter and began reading:

Fort Rice, Dakota Territory
10 June 1873
Dearest Cille,

The long march from Yankton to Fort Rice has been completed. We arrived about three hours ago. Our arrival was filled with considerable ceremony and fanfare, officer's call and the assignment of quarters for the troops, if only for the night. The rest of the 7th will continue their march upriver to Fort Lincoln. Yes dear, I'll be assigned to Fort Rice, at least temporarily, as a training officer under the Garrison's Commandant Colonel Thomas Leonadis Crittenden instead of going on to Fort Lincoln with the 7th. I will be training all the mounted units on the most recent cavalry tactics that I taught back at the academy. I will have all the galvanized troops and mounted infantry as my responsibility. Most of them have had little to no training in cavalry tactics.

Tomorrow General Custer and Colonel Sturgis will be leaving with the troops of the 7th for their trip upriver to Fort Lincoln. It has been a hard trip for the men; they look mighty weary at this point. I believe after they arrive at Fort Lincoln, there is a possibility that some of the 7th will be returning to be stationed here. It is only talk at this point.

The quarters I have been assigned are simple, cramped but adequate. They are made of cut cottonwood and some of pine lumber. Most of the men I have talked with say it is an improvement over how the fort looked a few years back. Most of the buildings had sod roofs to keep the winter snow out. The buildings now are of cut lumber with windows and a tapered roof to shed the snow in the winter months. The fort is considered rather modern for this far west.

I talked with Colonel Crittenden and told him of my intentions to send for you. He took it upon himself to show me the quarters for married officers. They are what you may call primitive at best compared to our house outside the academy. But they can be made into acceptable living quarters with a good bit of work. I love and miss you, more than I could have imagined. I will be dispatching a sum of monies to you so that you may start making arrangements to join me.

Your best route would be going to St. Louis and catching a steamer headed up the Missouri River. If you catch a large one, you may have to switch to a smaller steamer with a smaller draft at Council Bluffs for the rest of the journey. The Fort Rice docks on the river are not very far from the post.

Please do not waste time in getting here. Bring what you can and make arrangements to have the remaining sent to your parents in Monroe for safekeeping. I hold you in my every thought. With loving thoughts, I will close for now and make arrangements for the transfer of funds in the morning.

Loving you,
Patrick

Upon receiving the money draft, Cille made a trip to Monroe to visit her parents seeking advice and assistance in preparing for the move. The discussion continued through the afternoon and during the evening meal.

"What do you recommend I do with Lizzie and Lester?" she asked.

Constance said, "Lizzie will go with you of course. To leave her behind would be simply out of the question. Lester can work here with the others. After you arrive out west, you may not find a need for him because of the cramped living conditions."

Augustus said, "Cille, here is your best chance to be with Patrick. The trip would be safer for you if you took Lizzie with you. She will also make a great travel companion and help with the domestics when you arrive at Fort Rice."

"Are you sure it won't be any trouble storing our belongings here?"

"My sweet child," her mother said, "Leave the rest of your belongings here. It took a considerable amount of convincing on his part, but I agree with your father. It's simply too far to travel alone, so please take Lizzie."

"We'll return to your home with you tomorrow and help you make the final arrangements. Then you two can be on your way."

"Thank you both. I would appreciate all the help I can get. I am having problems limiting myself to the essential items I need. I have discovered that what you grow accustomed to is what you would like to take along."

◇◇◇

Several wagons and the carriage left the Hodges estate on their way to Cille's home near the military academy. The added wagons would carry the remaining furniture and clothing not going west back to the estate. The wagon drivers would do the lifting and Augustus would supervise how to load and secure each item on which wagon.

When they arrived, her father began to take charge. Cille and her mother decided what items would make the trip. Lester would return to the Hodges estate for an extended period. Friends and neighbors of the Hodges had joined in to make the move a smooth and quick one. Colonel Ruger and his wife Diana were notified and had a young lieutenant and his family interested in the house. The new couple joined in and helped where they could.

Cille and Lizzie made do with what few items remained and allowed the new tenants, Lieutenant Douglas Hoot and his bride Christina, to begin moving in their furniture. It was crowded at times, but also allowed them to eat with the young couple since Cille's pots, pans and dishes had been packed for the trip.

◇◇◇

They left by stagecoach two days later. Her household belongings were hauled in a wagon by a teamster for hire. He would follow the stage as it made its journey westward. Cille would deal with her household belongings when she and Lizzie arrived in St. Louis, Missouri.

CHAPTER 17

St Louis to Fort Rice 1873

Cille and Lizzie stood near the trunks that had been dropped to the ground in St Louis by the teamsters. His wagon had been towed behind a paddle wheeler on a barge while crossing the Mississippi River. Before her now on the ground were trunks, boxes and furniture; all her current possessions. These were the items she so desperately wanted to take with her into the Dakota Territory. She was beginning to feel frustrated and exhausted from the long trip on the stage. Now she was dealing with a teamster who wanted to quit his responsibility, long before she could make arrangements to get all of her and Lizzie's belongings aboard a steamer headed up the Missouri River.

"I'll need to book passage," she said to the teamster. "Could you watch over them for a moment longer and allow me to do that much?"

"Can't your maid watch them?"

"She could, but she's coming with me!"

"Don't go taking all day. I agreed to haul it all here and that's what I did."

"I realize that!"

"Then be quick about making them arrangements. I don't have all day. Got plans to have this here wagon back across the Mississippi and headed back east before the sun goes down."

Lizzie followed, not saying a word as Cille went about finding the right boat and finally paid for their passage on a steamer called the Josephine. She rushed back to her luggage and asked the teamster, "I'll be boarding the Josephine over on that dock. Could I get you to help me with the luggage or do you need additional pay?"

"Like I told ya lady, I need to be headed back across this here river. You took so long, any further delay on my part, might keep me from getting back across the 'Muddy' today. I'm sure one of the dockhands working around here would be willing to do that for a small price."

She wanted to say something further but realized he had delivered the personal items and had a good reason for leaving early. She said, "Very well, you're excused, go. Just go! If you can't help, I don't need you around!"

The teamster frowned at the way he was dismissed and said, "Well, I'm on my way, good day to ya!"

They watched as the teamster slapped the reins down across the back of the horses as they began pulling the wagon off the wharf and onto the street. Moments later, the empty wagon was gone from sight.

Lizzie looked on as Cille made arrangements with a dockworker to have their luggage placed aboard the Josephine. It was a rather dingy shallow draft steamer in need of a scrubbing and fresh paint and was headed upriver as far as Bismarck, Dakota Territory. Her passage was for Fort Rice, two stops short of the final destination.

They remained near the luggage. The whistle blew and the lines securing the boat to the dock were released. They watched the boat slowly drift away from the dock and head out to deeper water.

"No need to stay out here," a woman's voice was heard above the sound of the water splashing against the hull.

Cille turned to see a woman, not too many years her senior, smiling at her and saying, "Hi, I'm Mary McIntosh."

"I'm Cille and this is Lizzie. I'm pleased to see we're not the only ones making this journey."

"It's nice to meet the both of you. Are you going very far upriver?"

"My husband Patrick is stationed in the Dakota Territory at a place called Fort Rice."

"We just might get to know each other pretty well before we get there. We're headed to Fort Lincoln. Come with me and I'll introduce you to my dear friend."

Mrs. McIntosh turned and walked off, Cille and Lizzie followed, as they made their way to a room directly below the wheelhouse. Mary held the door open while Cille and Lizzie stepped into a large room. “I'd like you all to meet Cille,” she said. Turning to Cille, she asked, “I didn't get your last name.”

“Woodbury, Cille Woodbury and this is Lizzie, my maid.”

Mary continued, “This is Kate Gibson, my sister-in-law and Lizzie, this is Rehema. She’ll be working in the laundry at Fort Rice.”

“Pleased to meet you,” Kate responded.

“Our friendship goes back a few years,” Mary added. “Now we’re headed in the same direction once more.”

Kate got to her feet during the introduction and said, “Welcome aboard, Cille, nice to make your acquaintance. Do make yourself comfortable. Tell us about your husband.” as she gestured to a chair.

She made herself comfortable visiting when the Josephine blew its whistle and swung into the Missouri River. “I married Patrick right after he graduated from West Point. Now he’s stationed at Fort Rice.”

With a soft gentle look, Kate replied, “My Francis is a captain with Colonel Stanley and his Yellowstone Expedition, escorting the Northern Pacific railroad survey crews in the Yellowstone valley, wherever that is. I have to make do at Fort Lincoln for now, fending for myself until he gets back.”

Mary said, “That man of mine is a first Lieutenant in G Company under Major Reno. I’m not sure if his troops are at Fort Lincoln or down at Fort Rice. If he is at Rice, we’ll get to visit quite often.”

“If I get lonesome at Fort Lincoln, I’ll head south and give you two a visit until Francis gets back from the Yellowstone,” Kate added.

Their conversations covered several topics before they began laughing about their childhoods and how they met their husbands. They talked at length and before long Cille felt comfortable conversing with the talkative pair. She was getting to know them about as well as they her.

Rehema said, “Lizzie, fetch yaself ovah here where we can do some talkin'.”

Lizzie joined Rehema and allowed the others to visit.

During the day, the steamer would make its way to St. Charles where it would remain for the night before heading upriver early in the morning. The women made themselves comfortable in the small rooms provided onboard.

Upon their arrival, Rehema and Lizzie stayed on the steamer. Lizzie said, “Howz come ya gonna work in a laundry?”

With a smile, Rehema answered, “I onced was hired as a maid for the Mayor in Baltimore, but he ups and died shortly afta loosin’ his misses. I had ta go somewhere, an’ I gotched me some help, and they say I gots a job doin’ laundry, ifn I want.”

“Whoz britches ya gonna be washin’?”

“They say it be the troopers, I be doin’ the washin’ for. They say pack for a trip, and they gonna pay for the travelin’, so here I iz. Whatca doin’ with the misses?” Rehema asked.

“Been her maid and cook since she up an’ married a cadet,” Lizzie replied as she smiled and shook her head a bit.

Rahema asked, “Where he be now?”

“Got no knowin’ about that, I jus’ stay with Miss Cille. She knows.”

As they continued with their conversation, they became better acquainted talking of things that they both had in common.

The others planned to shop in St. Charles to see what fashions were available this far west.

A short distance from the docks they began visiting several shops. Suddenly, Kate said, “Wow, would you look at this.” She held up a dress with an abundance of lace around the throat and cuffs.

Cille said, “It looks very nice.”

Mary added, “It certainly has some flair about it.”

“On second thought,” Kate frowned before she returned the garment back to its original rack, and said, “I don't think it's for me.”

They laughed and giggled about Kate's sincerity or lack thereof. They purchased several small items before they considered returning to the steamer. They had supper at one of the boarding houses in town that hugged the riverfront. Lizzie and Rehema had a plate carried onboard for them. Upon their return to the Josephine, they spent the evening in small, cramped quarters that provided very little privacy.

◇ ◇ ◇

The second day on the river was spent going upstream. The scenery along the riverbanks were of lush foliage and limestone bluffs. Fewer farms dotted the landscape as they rode further northwest. They spotted a few small towns along the banks before the steamer tied up to a dock on the north side of the Missouri River, directly across the channel from the community of Boonville, Missouri. The dock hugged a mud bank and was the captain's preference to the dock near the boulders below the community hovering above on a bluff.

In a surprise visit, the captain of the Josephine came down from the wheelhouse and spoke to them. "To the north across that flat fertile valley you can see the community of New Franklin high on the hills. The original community of Franklin that once lined the northern bank had not been so lucky. In 1826, the raging Missouri flooded and washed away much of the town. Most of the town's residents moved to higher ground, up yonder. Joseph Kinney is a riverboat captain, like me," he continued. "He had his house built near the bank of the Mighty Missouri. After the big flood, he dubbed it the 'River Scene', completed a couple of years back, in the spring of 1869. I've known Joseph and his wife for a long time. They should be home this time of year. You're invited to pay them a visit, courtesy of the Josephine. If you do, I'll join up with you later, as I'm a fixin' to dock here for the night. We'll continue upstream in the morning."

Transportation was available to travel into New Franklin, or a short ferry ride across the channel to Boonville. The women decided to remain near the boat and made their way to the 'River Scene' to visit with the Kinney family.

Mrs. Kinney was an exceptional hostess and explained that the 16-room home was their summer place. During the winter months, they lived near the French Quarter in New Orleans. They were made welcome for the dinner meal, and in the late hours, Captain Kinney made a toast to those venturing north. "Here's a toast to the fine passengers and crew of the Josephine. May it be a safe trip, all the way to Bismarck." They later returned to the boat for a night's sleep.

The cry of the boat's whistle tore through the air and awoke those passengers who slept in. They were now on their way upriver. Eventually they would dock at Council Bluffs and Yankton, a town on the border of the Dakota Territory, before heading upstream to Fort Rice, Fort Lincoln and Bismarck.

◇◇◇

Colonel Crittenden spoke with Patrick after Officer's Call. "Lieutenant Woodbury, I need you to take our new detachment on patrol. You are to go south to the waters of the Cannon Ball and ride west two days. On the third day, head due north until you come in contact with the Heart tributary, then return to Post with the most direct route."

"Yes Sir, when do I leave?"

"You will leave within the hour. I will have Sergeant Capper assigned to ride with you. He is one of our more experienced sergeants. He's familiar with the terrain and has trained a good number of raw troops in the past. You can trust him, he's good."

"Can we expect any Indian contact in that area, Sir?"

"I won't say no, but from the information we have, they're further west. There may be some renegades here and there, enough to give the men some experience and confidence in a hostile situation."

"Are there any further instructions, Sir?"

"Aside from the training of the troops, I need you to collect intelligence. Anything of interest needs to be reported when you return. Sergeant Capper knows the routine and will assist you."

When Patrick left the headquarters building, he saw Sergeant Capper forming the troops and the wagons necessary for the journey.

The burly sergeant turned to address Lieutenant Woodbury.

"Sir, we're about ready to mount up?"

"In a moment. Sergeant, do we have the mounts and supplies necessary for the assignment?"

"We have everything right down to the limited amount of ammo for each trooper, Sir."

"That's great."

"No Sir, we got three who have never ridden a horse before."

"Three?"

“That's enough. A bit ago, I had to fight hard to keep from laughing when they went to saddle their mounts. They’re a green bunch, I’m telling you, Sir. We're in for an experience of a lifetime getting this bunch ready for any big fight.”

With a smile of confidence, Patrick said, “Riders up, Sergeant.”

They rode two abreast and headed out of Fort Rice to the south and down river. Sergeant Capper rode alongside of Lieutenant Woodbury at the head of the column for a time. He rode back to check on the troops and the supplies before returning to the head of the column.

“How does it look back there?” Patrick inquired.

“Not too bad so far, Sir. But before the day is over, I'll bet we have at least two of the three green troops down with a case of saddle sores. Lieutenant, they bounce more than anyone I've ever seen. They won't be able to walk none too good when they dismount later on. Those saddles won't treat them none too kindly.”

“Sergeant, ride back and have those three men report to me.”

Capper rode back and pulled the men from the column and they reported to Lieutenant Woodbury.

“Take over for a spell, Sergeant, while I talk with these men.”

The column continued downriver while Patrick rode off to the side with the three green troops. When they pulled up, he said, “I understand this is the first time for you three to be riding.”

One of the troopers said, “Yes Sir and I hurt something fierce.”

“Dismount,” Patrick ordered. The men dismounted and tried to find some relief on the ground, but the damage had already set in.

Patrick did his best to give some instruction in the art of riding that might be helpful to them. The advice varied from mounting, to riding properly, to avoiding the problems they had experienced thus far. They were under his command and he felt responsible for and had to look after them as much as the rest of the men.

He ordered, “Mount up and return to your position in the column.” As they returned to their positions, he could tell his instructions were a little late and some of the pain inflicted earlier would be with two of them for a day or so. He returned to the head of the column.

CHAPTER 18

A Home At Fort Rice 1873

On the 10th of June, the steamer Josephine managed to make its way upriver to the docks servicing the Dakota outpost of Fort Rice. In addition to the many Army supplies to be off-loaded, Cille had several trunks, a small handful of furniture belonging to her and Lizzie and things she simply refused to leave behind. These household bundles were lined up inside the railing next to those of Mrs. Mary McIntosh and Mrs. Kate Gibson. Their household belongings would go upriver beyond Fort Rice and be off-loaded for their homes at Fort Lincoln.

Mary said, "Cille, it was such a pleasure to visit with you. Surely the short distance between forts shouldn't be that great of a barrier to keep us from visiting now and again."

"I would like that very much," Cille said, "and the pleasure was mine. I have lived in Monroe for so long, it's going to be an adjustment for me to get used to this lifestyle."

"Welcome to the world of gossip, knitting, cribbage and hanging onto your sanity," Mary added. "Every time Donald goes out, I know he is winding up chasing hostiles down and giving them their dues. You watch, your Patrick is going to be doing the same. It doesn't make it any easier on you, seeing him ride out, not knowing if he'll be coming back in one piece. Be patient with him because sometimes he will appear to be as hard as whang-leather to deal with. Surely Lizzie and the wives of the post will keep you busy while he is away on patrol."

Kate said, "Cille, take care my dear, until we get together again."

"I've enjoyed visiting with the both of you. I look forward to the day we can chat again." Cille added "I best get off, or they will keep me onboard until the next stop."

Cille turned to make her way to the gangboard and departed the Josephine. She lifted her long skirt as she stepped up from the main deck and began walking down the bouncing length of a wooden slat plank. Lizzie walked a few steps behind, followed by Rahema.

At the end of the gangplank was the only physician at Fort Rice. Doctor Slaughter was eager to welcome Cille to the fort. "Well, well .... I take it this is the Misses of a young lieutenant and by chance, does she go by the name of Cille?"

"It is. This is my help, Lizzie and this young lady is Rahema. She is supposed to have a job at the laundry on post. And might I ask, with whom do I have the pleasure of meeting?"

"Doc Slaughter, some call me Franklin, but close friends call me Frank. I'm the doctor for this outfit. Your husband is out on a short patrol and won't be in for a day or so. He asked me to meet the boat by chance his lovely wife should be onboard."

"I guess I can wait a bit longer to see him. This trip has sure been a long one."

"Don't imagine it was none too pleasant. No trip out this far provides the better side of life. I just hope you and Patrick will enjoy the facilities, such as they are."

"What do you mean by that?"

"You just have to look at them from a primitive standpoint, then the fool thing looks good. But if you're expecting the finer things in life, I'm afraid those things were left behind as far back as St. Louis. But don't let me scare you off none."

"I've come this far and that isn't one of the things I'll let bother me today. I'm just anxious to see Patrick."

Doctor Slaughter turned to a sergeant and said, "Get a detail down here and see that her belongings are brought up to the fort and to the quarters for Lieutenant Woodbury and his Misses. And see to it that Rahema's belongings are taken by the laundry. The staff over there will see that she gets settled."

A young sergeant nearby went about gathering up a detail.

The doctor turned to Cille and said, "Let me escort you three to the fort. My wife Linda is up there and will show you most of what needs to be done and where you and Patrick will quarter."

Prior to leaving the dock, Cille turned slightly and gave a small hand gesture to Mary and Kate. They smiled and returned a gesture as well.

Turning her attention to Frank, she asked, “How long have you and Linda been out this way?”

“We arrived here in 1870 aboard the steamboat Katie P. Kountz. I can remember it as if it was yesterday. But the fort has changed a whole lot since then. Linda does her best to call it home, between our quarters and the infirmary. She helps me out a lot when my job gets overwhelming with sick and wounded. But from time to time, I can see the toll it is taking on her. The love we have between us carries us through the rough times and the rough winters.”

“I'm anxious to meet her.”

“I take it she will be fussing over something and later she can introduce you to Catherine Benteen. She answers to Katie and most likely a good thing because the Commandant’s wife is named Catherine.”

“That sounds nice. How many women are here with their husbands?”

“The 7th Regiment sent Major Reno, Captain Benteen and a handful of troops down this way on a temporary basis. They arrived earlier today. What few wives were with their husbands came along also. They will join those stationed here. I’d say a small handful of wives can't adjust and they soon pack up and head back to civilization. Then a short time later, their husbands either get an arrow or orders for back East. One thing for sure, you'll have some adjusting to do. I just hope to blazes you like it, for the both of your sakes.”

“I'll do my best to give Patrick all the support he needs to make things comfortable.”

Arriving at the south entrance to the open fort, they walked across the compound with not so much as a word between them. They headed to a small cabin at the far side. Just before reaching the structure, Frank said, “This is where me and the Misses call home. You will get to see your quarters a little bit later. They still need to put some furnishings in place.”

Opening the door, Frank yelled out, “Linda, she got here in one piece. Cille, please excuse me, I need to get over to the infirmary and check on those two that came down with the 'corn juice flu'."

Linda made her presence known just inside the doorway and called out, "My goodness, come in. I'm Linda and you're Cille, goodness just like the photographs Patrick showed us. I'm so glad to see you and to have you out this way."

"Thank you. The trip has been a long one that's for sure. Linda, this is my help, Lizzie and this is Rahema."

"Lizzie and Rahema, it's nice to meet the both of you., Come in and make yourself comfortable."

Frank spoke up, "I'll let you and Cille chat. I'll drop back later, come with me Rahema, and I'll walk you over to the laundry area."

"Cille and Lizzie, let's sit on the sofa and you can tell me all about your trip. As you can see, I don't have any additional help."

They joined Linda on the sofa next to the knitting she had been working on. "Your home looks lovely. There isn't a whole lot to tell. Lizzie and I caught the stage in Monroe, New York, and the journey was uneventful until we got to St Louis in Missouri. The teamster we hired was rather troublesome after we crossed the Mississippi. He abandoned any semblance of proper behavior before I dismissed him. When we were dockside, we had to make arrangements for our belongings. Then after we boarded the boat, we met Mary McIntosh and Kate Gibson. Mary and Kate are sisters-in-law. Both of their husbands are assigned to the 7th. Goodness, we chatted about everything under the sun during the trip. They're sweet and each so interesting to be around. Mary will be staying at Fort Lincoln for now, because he's out on some expedition and Kate is trying to track down her husband to see if she'll be staying at Fort Lincoln or maybe having to return here at Fort Rice. I guess it is still some distance upriver before they get there."

Linda smiled, "Fort Lincoln isn't so far. It's the next stop upriver. Sometimes we make the trip and do some shopping in Bismarck. I usually accompany Frank and the troops. When we women ride north, we have to wait for a trooper to escort us up that direction."

"Great, then there's an opportunity to visit with Mary and Kate and some of the other wives at Fort Lincoln in the months to come?"

"Sure, sometimes we make a trip that direction, and then there's times General Custer comes this direction and some of the women accompany him this far. Elizabeth Custer, Libby as we know her, sometimes comes along to visit. But the General keeps a pretty close eye on her. I think he's afraid we might influence her."

"Is there more than a handful of us that have ventured out this way to be with our husbands?"

"Heavens yes. Most of them are at Fort Lincoln because the amenities are much better there. The General sees to that. And a few of us here at Fort Rice know the difference. When we get you settled in, I'll see that you get to meet Katie. She's married to a Captain better known as "Ol' Pipe Smoking" Frederick Benteen. He's assigned here under Major Reno."

Small talk filled the air among them and the hours began to pass away. From beyond the cabin walls, there was such a clatter of commotion, they both went to the window to see what was going on.

There was a lot of racket going on across the compound in the direction of the western approach to the fort. A short distance away, they could see a column of troopers returning from the field.

As the column rode closer, Linda turned to Cille, "That's your Patrick and his troops. It appears to me they're bringing back a handful of ponies and the Indians for the brig."

Cille must have looked bewildered for a moment as Linda explained, "Looks like a handful of Indian ponies and two or three Indians as well."

Brimming with excitement from not only seeing her husband, but being in the mere presence of the savages, Cille could hardly contain herself. She shook from fear and excitement at the same time.

Sensing how her new friend felt, Linda said, "Come, let's go outside and watch them ride in."

When they arrived on post, Patrick turned in his saddle and said, "Sergeant Capper, take it from here. See that the Indians are secured in the guardhouse. Then dismiss the troops." As he dismounted, one of the troopers took the reins of his mount.

Before crossing the compound, the commandant stepped off the walkway near the headquarters building to greet him. Crittenden called out, "I'll expect your report later, but for now there's a lovely young lady over at Doc Slaughter's in need of your attention."

Turning, he could see his Cille standing next to Linda. He gave a quick salute to Crittenden and said, "Yes sir!" before dashing off toward his wife.

She stepped down from the walkway and met him a short distance from there. They embraced for a quick moment and then returned to the walkway in time to see Doc approaching.

"Patrick, the quartermaster has assigned you and Cille to the quarters at the end of this row. Do you two want to go take a look at what's there and what's needed? Lizzie, you might want to tag along."

Linda grabbed her husband's arm and Cille did likewise with Patrick. Lizzie followed the two couples a short distance to their rear. They walked to the end of the row of quarters and went into the dark interior. Patrick turned to Cille and commented, "It isn't much."

Although somewhat disappointed, Cille responded with as much enthusiasm as she could muster, "But it's home, our home."

Frank turned to Patrick and said, "I told the orderly to have all the belongings the Misses and Lizzie had with them brought down this way soon as you got in. They should be arriving before too long. You're lucky this set of quarters has two bedrooms. It's one of the last few vacancies available. Now there is nothing but one bedrooms left."

"Great. We'll light these lamps and get the stove going to knock down the chill."

Doc said, after a quick observation, "There's enough wood to last the night and into the day. You're lucky."

Linda joined in saying, "Cille, you two and Lizzie are welcome to have supper with us. That way you won't have to worry about that while you two get settled."

Frank said, "Colonel Crittenden is expecting the four of us over later in the evening so his wife Catherine can meet Cille."

◇◇◇

With the evening meal behind them, they made their way to Colonel Thomas L. Crittenden's quarters. Lizzie stayed behind to clean up Linda's kitchen and would find her way back to the Woodbury quarters later.

Fort Rice's Commandant met the arrivals at the door to his quarters and announced, "Come in, we've been expecting you."

As they stepped into his quarters, Thomas called out, "Catherine, company's here."

The men quickly gathered and went into the colonel's library. He said, "Major Reno and Captain Benteen will be along shortly."

Catherine arrived and said, "Cille, welcome to Fort Rice. You two are most welcome in our home."

"I'm so glad to meet you," Cille said. "What a lovely home you have."

Smiling graciously, Catherine said, "Let's go in the other room where the men can visit and do their share of chatting."

When they arrived in the sitting room, Catherine asked Linda, "Have you told her about what is going to happen tomorrow?"

"Goodness, no!"

A look of surprise crossed her face as Cille asked, "What about tomorrow?"

"Most times when the patrols come back," Catherine said, "we get to go beyond the garrison a way and do some shooting."

Linda smiled and said, "Sure hope you know a bit about guns."

Cille said, "I've never held one in my hands. It just wasn't called for back in Monroe."

"Sometimes," Catherine added, "the unit sergeant or one of his detail men take us out, where we can learn to shoot to protect ourselves. And then there will be a time later in the fall when we might get to go hunting."

"I have never killed anything with or without a gun," Cille replied.

Linda laughed, "Out here, you set aside some of the finer things in life and do what is natural, even enjoyable. It doesn't stop us from acting like a lady when the time comes."

Following a rap on the door, Major Reno, Captain Benteen and his wife Katie entered and were introduced to Cille. The men went into the library to visit and the women remained in the sitting room where they enjoyed refreshments and pastries.

With the conversation centered on what the women had to do on or off post, Cille was caught up in the discussion with her new acquaintances. She said, "I guess we can look forward to having Mary McIntosh and Kate Gibson arrive from Fort Lincoln in a day or so. They were so sweet on the trip upriver. I know you all will enjoy them."

Katie added, "Maybe we can have tea and cookies when they arrive. I know it is important to feel wanted and comfortable when you make a move and first arrive."

"Let's plan on having a get-together at my quarters," Cille suggested. "The day after their arrival would be a perfect time. The day they get here they will need to settle in first, but we can surprise them on the following day."

There was laughter and they agreed to have the social at 2:00 PM the day following their arrival.

Cille smiled and added, "Lizzie has the best cookies I have ever eaten. I'll have her make up a batch or two"

Catherine said, "Thomas and I have often wondered why we haven't hired a domestic or cook with all the meal preparations we have to come up with sometimes."

"I've had the pleasure," Cille said, "of meeting a young lady who traveled from St. Louis and arrived on the boat with us today. She has been hired to work in the laundry. But from our talks, she said that she had worked as a maid and cook, I think for the Mayor of Baltimore before he died. She was left without work and somehow got the job of working here in the laundry."

Being inquisitive, Catherine asked, "By chance do you know her name?"

"Sure do," Cille replied, "her name is Rahema. , As for a last name, I don't have a clue."

The conversation often bounced from one subject to the next. The evening was enjoyable and Cille felt comfortable even this far from her childhood home.

It was late in the evening when the visit with the Crittentens ended. The last words came from the colonel, "Patrick, I will need to see you and Sergeant Capper in my office in the morning, right after Officer's Call." Doc and Linda, Frederick and Katie returned to their quarters and Major Reno returned to his bachelor quarters, leaving Cille and Patrick alone for their journey to their new home.

When they arrived, they found that Lizzie had kept the fire going and the house was warm. They were pleased to discover that she had prepared both bedrooms with fresh linens. She waited in a rocker for instructions as to which bedroom was hers.

"Lizzie," Patrick said, "I'm sure glad you accompanied Cille on the trip. I didn't get a chance to welcome you earlier in the day."

"Yes um, dat was sho some trip, a long one." Turning to Cille she said, "I'z not sure what bed you wantin' me to bed down in."

Cille turned to Patrick and asked, "Do you have a preference?"

"You're the lady of the house," he said with a smile. "Take your pick."

She chose their room and said, "Lizzie, the other is yours."

Lizzie went to her room as Patrick and Cille remained in the living room a while longer embracing and exchanging small talk before they went to bed.

Awakened by the sound of a trumpeter blasting away in the early morning hours, Cille sat up in bed as Patrick explained, "That is reveille, my dear."

"It's a whole lot of unnecessary noise, if you ask me."

He smiled as the household began its first routine the day after her arrival. Cille and Lizzie stayed behind and started unpacking. Patrick was out the door shortly after breakfast on his way to do his duties.

After Officer's Call, he found Sergeant Capper, and said, "Colonel Crittenden is expecting us in his office."

Capper replied, "Yes Sir, it's the report he wants to hear."

When they arrived in the headquarters building, Sergeant Capper was called into the Colonel's office first.

"Sergeant, what is your report?" the Commandant asked.

"Colonel, we left here with the greenest batch of troops I have ever seen. We had an officer who was out on his first assignment. All I can say is that Lieutenant Woodbury is top notch. He looks after his men in every detail. I don't recall ever having an officer of his caliber lead a batch of green troops and come out on top. He knows his stuff, and as far as tactics, those Indians and those ponies, it was his idea on how to make the operation successful."

"What has happened to the Indians that were brought in yesterday?"

"They are in the guard house and their ponies in the corral until such time as they can all be turned over to an Indian Agent and placed on a reservation."

"Is there anything else, Sergeant?"

"That's about it, but there is one other thing I promised myself I would let the lieutenant report on. All I can say is he has a keen eye and a good sense of judgment."

The sergeant was dismissed and Lieutenant Woodbury was next to report. On his way out of the headquarters building, Sergeant Capper smiled at Patrick in passing.

"Lieutenant, what do you have to say in your report?" the colonel asked.

Patrick smiled and said, "Sir, it was an experience. I thank you for sending Sergeant Capper along to help with the detachment. I can see where you're proud of him and his ability. We headed south to the mouth of the Cannonball and then followed the tributary west for two days. During that time, I spotted a suspicious area on the north bend of the Cannonball across from the mouth of the Cedar River. It looked as if someone in a wagon, some horses shod and others unshod, had met to exchange items for booze."

"Was it possible to follow the tracks?"

"No, the windblown sand in the tracks gave evidence that this had happened a week or so ago. The tracks faded without any sense of direction. We headed due north after the second day west. Near the grassland of the Heart River, Sergeant Capper was in the lead and had spotted the three Indians and five ponies we brought back."

"Did you receive any resistance from the Indians?"

"There could have been, but I divided my troop in half with Sergeant Capper taking some of the men to the north of the Indians. We both formed extended lines and came at them with a charge. They virtually had no place to ride."

"How did the men react on the patrol and during the charge?"

"Colonel, they are inexperienced, but I find them willing to learn and ready to respond without asking questions. Give them a little time and they will be a detachment you'll be proud of."

Lieutenant Woodbury was dismissed and went about his added garrison duties for the day. As he left the headquarters building, he saw several women, including Cille, ride out the south gate with a detail of troopers.

Cille did not see Patrick. She was caught up in happy conversation with Catherine, Linda and Katie. The detail took the women about a mile from the post on the west bank of the Missouri River.

When the detail halted, the troopers held the horses while the women dismounted. A trooper was assigned to each woman and they spaced themselves down the bank of the river.

Today they would be instructed in the use of a rifle and the target would be a sawyer midway out in the river. A tree was lodged with its limbs upriver and the current was causing the limb's action to bob up and down. Cille was the first to shoot because she was the first to arrive. Linda said, "Katie, I bet she misses bigger than the both of us."

Listening to the teasing for a moment, Cille set it aside and concentrated on the instructions from the trooper. She was surprised at the weight of the rifle and the end of it began to sway.

A nearby trooper said, "Mrs. Woodbury, hold it."

She lowered the rifle to hear the trooper say, "Aim high and as you come down on the target, squeeze the trigger."

On her second attempt, she pulled the trigger as the sawyer came into view. The splash was at the sawyer, while Cille rocked back from the recoil. She was so surprised; she nearly dropped the rifle.

"That's the way," the trooper yelled.

As she turned, Cille said, "Ok, let's see how you three do."

The shooting and instructions lasted until nearly noon before they saddled up and headed back to the post. Cille was quite proud of her accomplishments for the first day. Linda, however, was the one who was getting the ribbing on the way back. Cille looked forward to the next time they would be shooting.

It was late in the day when a steamer heading south pulled into the landing at Fort Rice. Getting off the shabby boat was none other than Kate Gibson and Mary McIntosh. They were met by Mary's husband and escorted to the garrison. Cille knew she had best notify Lizzie early so that the cookies would be available for the surprise.

CHAPTER 19

Cille's First Hunt 1873

The garrison commander, Colonel Crittenden, stepped forward and solemnly read the latest report as Major Reno and Captain Benteen stood near his side. "Officers and men of this command, it is my sad duty to inform you that Red Cloud and his band of hostiles have massacred Lieutenant Fetterman and 81 of his men. This action took place near the mouth of the Tongue River on the 4th of August 1873.

Future patrols will take on a heightened alert, gather any information that may indicate hostile problems and report it to the proper chain of command with haste." The news struck hard at those assembled. They realized the land beyond the perimeter of the fort was not theirs, but belonged to the Indians until such time as they all could be gathered up and placed on reservations.

Upon receiving word of the massacre, Patrick felt the impact hard in his stomach. Within the hour, he was to take his men on patrol deeper into hostile territory than he had taken them before. Patrick was called into headquarters shortly after the morning muster. He had no sooner stepped into the building when he was informed that Colonel Crittenden wanted to see him immediately.

After reporting, the Colonel said, "Woodbury, here are your patrol orders. Take heed of any Indian problems. Collect as much information as you can and follow your marching orders without deviation. The only exception is if you meet a large number of hostiles that warrant a return to the fort. Do so as safely as possible. Use your head and good judgment when making contact. Is that understood?"

"Yes sir. Should I meet with a situation where we have to make a stand, I will do my best to get a runner back to you, requesting reinforcements. And I do understand the rules of engagement. With Red Cloud fresh from a victory, it's hard telling what this victory has done for the rest who have not agreed to live on the reservations."

"Do your duty, Lieutenant, but keep in mind the lack of experience of your men. That will be all."

"Thank you, Colonel. We will mount up shortly and be on our way."

Patrick left the headquarters building with haste. Outside the headquarters, he saw Sergeant Capper and called out, "Sergeant, get our men mounted and ready. I'll be with you shortly.

"Yes Sir. The men are with their mounts now. We'll be getting the added ammo and assemble near the south gate."

Patrick rushed to his quarters. "Cille, I'm headed out for a march that will last four to six days."

"Oh, Patrick, do be careful."

"I will. It's a routine march and nothing to worry about." As they embraced and kissed deeply, he reached around behind her slender frame and patted her posterior.

She enjoyed the embrace, the kiss and the love tap on her backside as a way expressing his affection. She had some concerns and said, "I heard a rumor from one of the wives that the Indians are on the war path."

"Cille, I have been on this patrol several times and this one is routine. Red Cloud and his band are further west from where I will be on patrol. They're the ones raising some dust. Most of the Indians close by will be heading for reservations. There may be a few still running wild, but we'll take care of them when we come upon them. I'll be watchful, so don't you fret." With that, they parted after a sweet embrace and Patrick was out the door on his way to join his detachment.

After being fully equipped, Lieutenant Woodbury and Sergeant Capper lead their column south of Fort Rice along the banks of the Missouri River to the mouth of the Cannonball River. The unit was halted, and a briefing from part of the marching orders was read to the troopers, most were green recruits and a handful of galvanized rebels.

Lieutenant Woodbury said, "Men, we have been ordered to take this march a half day's ride further west than we have on previous marches. Be on the lookout for hostiles and anything that may be gathered as information. If we make contact with hostiles large or small, we are to take precautions to avoid a trap. We are charged with gathering information only. That is our primary responsibility. Should the need to dismount and fight become apparent, Sergeant Capper will be on the left and in charge of that skirmish line. I will be with the skirmish line on the right side. A cavalry charge will be at my command, supported by the information I share with Sergeant Capper. Just like the training back at the fort, no change, understood. Sergeant, get the men mounted."

The detachment headed westward riding just north of the banks of the Cannonball River. It was near the opposite bank of where Cedar Creek empties into the Cannonball, where they discovered a second batch of evidence. Shod and unshod hoof prints marked the land along with wagon tracks. It was evident that the wagon arrived heavy laden and departed with a lighter load, leaving behind broken booze bottles and five spent military cartridges. Frustrated, Sergeant Capper said, "Lieutenant, these tracks seem to be about three days old. And from what I see, someone…no, make it two riding shod horses were with a wagon along with a pair pulling the wagon. I reckon a whiskey peddler selling booze for pelts. Dad burn it, them cartridges . . . Nonsense like this points to rifles, military rifles. Shoot fire, I'd hate to think someone is selling booze and rifles for furs. And from the looks of things, the horseshoes sure resemble quartermaster issue. They are either still in the Army or a pair of deserters flat in the middle of this."

"Make your written notes Sergeant. Draw out a map as best you can of all the information and I'll do the same. This is something they'll be interested in when we get back."

The troops spread out to gather additional cartridges and any other evidence they could find.

Their detachment mounted up and rode northeast for about two hours before dismounting and making camp. It had been a long day in the saddle.

On the second day out, the column rode to where the Cannonball banks made a twisted turn to the south. At that point, the column broke from the river and headed due north. It was about three hours from the Cannonball when they discovered a crossing point where an estimated 50 or so unshod ponies had ridden to the west. The tracks were estimated to be less than a week old. Sergeant Capper as well as Lieutenant Woodbury made comments in their individual report.

"Sergeant, ride back and inform the men. Tell them to be on the lookout and stay alert."

Moments later the column rode off in a northerly direction. It was near dusk and an hour's ride past the last set of evidence, before the column pulled up and set camp. Since there was evidence of recent Indian traffic nearby, they doubled night watch duty. The night fell into an eerie silence.

Third day out, the camp was struck and the column moved out shortly after sunrise. It was going to be a hard day. A brisk wind was whipping up the parched sandy soil and the sun began beating down as the temperature rose. It would be a hard ride before the next fresh water would be available. It was near mid-afternoon when the distant outline of the Heart River came into view.

When they arrived at the water's edge, Lieutenant Woodbury said, "Sergeant, order dismount, we'll be making camp early. Have the men water their horses and take care of them before they are picketed. I'll need to see you shortly after supper."

"Any special place you want your tent located, Lieutenant?"

"That flat area over by that cottonwood would be fine." Sergeant Capper departed, barking orders to the men as he made his way to the riverbank to water his horse.

Shortly after supper, Sergeant Capper made his way to Patrick's tent. "Lieutenant, anything special reason you wanted to see me about?"

"Come in, Sergeant, sit on the cot and use the end of the bunk to fill out your report. It's not much of a field desk, but it's the best we can do under these conditions."

"There isn't much more to say, other than what we experienced today." Capper did as he was told and sat down on the cot.

"I'd rather have you fill out your report as you see it, Sergeant. That's something I can't help you with. I'm sure the colonel will appreciate your report and how you see the overall march, without any influence on my part. That way he can compare your report to mine."

"If you have a sheet or so of paper and a pencil, I'll make it short. Not too much to say, other than the information across from Cedar Creek and the unshod a ways back."

"Whatever you like, it's your report," as he handed the sergeant the paper and pencil. "Take your time, I enjoy your company."

"Lieutenant Woodbury, that's what I like about you: no pressure and you know what you're doing. If I may say so, sir, I enjoy riding with you. You're top notch in my book."

"Thank you. I'm glad I have a man of your caliber as my sergeant. There may come a time when I'll have to lay a heap of responsibility on you, and knowing you can handle it brings me much comfort."

"I'll finish the report and get to checking on the men. Do you think we can go without doubling the night watch tonight, Sir?"

"I believe we can do without the double. The men have had a hard day and they need the rest. We'll be breaking camp early and heading back to the fort. I'm in hopes of making it there before nightfall tomorrow night."

Moments later, Sergeant Capper left the tent to do his duties before turning in. Patrick had finished his reports and decided to make a round of the camp before he called it a day. There were several of the troops he wanted to give a word of praise before the day was done.

Morning came with a wonderful reddish glow to the sunrise. Moments later, the sun made its appearance above the horizon and the land soon became a hot box to ride across. The column rode south of the Heart River a safe distance from the willows and cottonwood trees where the riding was much better. The ride was made without incident. Prior to departing the banks of the river and cutting across country, the column watered their horses before the long ride to the fort.

◇ ◇ ◇

Three days after Patrick had left on patrol, Cille was invited to accompany Catherine Crittenden, Linda Slaughter and Katie Benteen and others along with a small military escort on a small game hunt. The troopers had their weapons, but the ladies were issued shot guns and divided into two groups. They hunted for various fowl: quail, grouse, pheasant or prairie chickens. The order of shooting would be determined by their husband's rank.

Katie held the shotgun at the ready, and had no sooner walked a hundred yards when a covey of quail made flight a few feet in front of her. Katie pulled the long-barreled shotgun to her shoulder and pulled the trigger. Feathers filled the air. She looked at the two birds she had killed and said, "They're mighty small and it looks as if I blew away the best part of the birds."

Linda teased, "Katie, it looks as if you skinned both of them in flight. As many as there were, I'm just surprised to see you only managed to get two of them."

Cille giggled at the teasing and the look on Katie's face, as she was left speechless. She could see they were going to have some fun on the hunt.

There was an abundance of laughter as Linda took her turn carrying the heavy shotgun. Some ten yards away, a ring-necked pheasant took flight with such a racket that Linda nearly dropped the gun. When she untied her nerves, she hoisted the gun to her shoulder and fired, only to miss on her first try at bagging a bird.

"You missed it! Goodness, Linda, it was as big as a turkey." Katie roared with laughter. "Maybe you need a covey of smaller targets. You're some shot." Katie laughed as she turned to Cille and said, "I hope you don't miss as big as Linda did." The laughter and teasing continued.

There was a round of razzing that included some comments from the troopers Then it was Cille's turn. She took the shotgun and moved to the lead with one of the troopers.

A few moments later, a ring-neck took flight a few feet in front of Cille. She was ready, knowing the racket they made when first making flight. She wheeled the shotgun to her shoulder and fired as if she had done this many times before. When the pheasant was retrieved, she looked at it and said, "Oh, such a pretty bird. I hope it tastes as good as it looks."

"They're pretty good eating," Linda replied. "Frank and I have a mess of them from time to time."

"Nice shot, Cille," Katie commented. "At least we know who is taking this hunt seriously."

“You’ll miss a whole lot more today than I will,” Linda harped back, “because you squint before you pull the trigger.”

The laughing and teasing continued as the hunt went on throughout the day. Each had a chance to tease, and before long, they would find themselves on the receiving end of the teasing. It made for a fun hunt.

The rest of the day continued in similar fashion with the ladies taking turns with the shotgun. There were plenty of hits and misses with a whole lot of laughter. At the end of the day, there were a variety of birds to bring back to the fort.

On the way back to the fort, Cille said, “This is sure more exciting than playing cribbage and making up gossip to pass the time.”

Linda replied, “Gossip! Heck no. All I told you in secret about Katie was the whole truth.”

“You don’t know the truth from gossip, Linda,” she said with a laugh. “Cille, when Linda arrived, she was here six months and all that time, I was told she was under a doctor’s care. Then I found out she was actually married to him. I thought she was a cut up, and now I know why. She married a Slaughter.” She laughed.

“Who is going to clean all of these birds?” Cille asked.

“Junior hunter,” Linda harped, “your initiation for making the first hunt. By the way save the feathers, they make good pillow stuffing.”

She looked shocked and Katie added, “One bird at a time. It doesn’t take long.”

After a couple of moments of teasing, Katie said, “Some of the men will clean the birds. We give them enough birds so that the mess cook can fry them up special for those who took us out on the hunt today.”

Relieved, Cille settled back to enjoy the ride back to the fort.

When Catherine came by Cille’s quarters to visit, Lizzie and Cille were sitting on the sofa and Catherine took the wingback chair. Mrs. Crittenden said, “Thomas has made arrangements to send passage money for another girl to come work in the laundry and I am so happy to tell you that Rahema, the laundry girl, is now our help. I dropped by to see if I might call upon Lizzie at times for help when many guests are invited, in the event things get too hectic for Rahema?”

“I’m sure Lizzie would be happy to help out,” as Cille turned to look at Lizzie.

"Iz so happy for Rahema, Iz be ready to help, when Cille say I can do for ya. Ya jus' tell Rahema, I 'xpect to see her, as soon as her skinny legs and her cheeks can gets her goin' this way. I might help with the cookies, but even Rahema no get the receipt."

They laughed as they continued the short visit, while enjoying the tea and Lizzie's fresh baked cookies.

◇◇◇

On their return on the fifth day, the silhouette outline of the fort's guard towers and the outline of the garrison came into view. Sergeant Capper looked over at Patrick and said, "Lieutenant, it flat sure does look good. I'm ready for some hot chow and a bunk for the night."

"It has been a long hot ride, hasn't it?"

"I like it better hot than to face the same ride in the winter months. That is when your mind can play some miserable tricks on you, making one wonder why you joined the Army in the first place."

"When we get there, make your last day report and I'll tell the Commandant we will be by in the morning with the final report."

Moments later, the column entered the fort and headed to the stable area. Patrick left his tired mount with one of the troopers to tend to before bedding down for the night.

Patrick went to the headquarters building and reported back. Crittenden met him at the door. "Welcome back. Is there any immediate news I need to be made aware of?"

"Two items, Sir."

"Let's discuss it in my office."

Inside the Colonel's office, Patrick said, "Across from Cedar Creek, there was evidence of booze wagon tracks and loose cartridges," he laid five of them on the colonel's desk. "From a quick assessment, it looks like guns and booze were given to the Indians in trade for furs, is my guess. I will finalize my report tonight and I instructed Sergeant Capper to meet me here in the morning with his report also."

"What is the assessment from Sergeant Capper?"

"Colonel, I am giving him full rein to make his report, as he sees it without my influence. But he did most of the 'in the dirt' assessment and I'm sure our reports on this matter will be about the same."

"You indicated a second problem: what is it?"

Walking behind the colonel's desk, Patrick pointed to the section in the map where approximately 50 unshod horses passed.

"Did you see any hostiles?

"Not a one. Doesn't mean they weren't out there. If they were nearby, they remained concealed in our passing."

"Woodbury, the second item of your report is interesting, but the first is troublesome. There is just too much of a coincidence. Refrain from discussing anything of the first with any officer until I have you all together tomorrow, after Officer's Call. Now get out of here, go to your quarters and take care of Cille."

Patrick wasted little time in leaving the headquarters building. On his way to his quarters, he ran into Sergeant Capper. "Sergeant, the colonel is requesting we not discuss anything about the incident across from Cedar Creek until after our report in the morning."

"My lips are sealed, Sir."

"Good, now go get that hot chow."

He made his way to his quarters and upon opening the door, called out, "Cille, I'm home."

A squeal of excitement filled the quarters and Cille rushed into his arms. In the middle of an embrace, Patrick reached over with his foot and closed the door behind him without turning her loose. After a long embrace, and several lengthy kisses, they sat in the living room discussing his edited casual trip into the field and her trip to the countryside for the big hunt. Lizzie was in the kitchen preparing a pheasant supper and her cookies.

The late evening hours were spent discussing the last few days. At times, both felt the other was stretching the truth and giving an added twist of excitement, just for the fun of it. They were happy for each other's company as the day fell into darkness.

Morning came much too early for either of them. Patrick appeared tired and Cille fussed with her hair that somehow had become mussed during the excitement of the night. Lizzie was all smiles while preparing and serving breakfast, as she had heard muffled noises during the night. Breakfast was served and none too soon. Patrick gave Cille a quick peck on the cheek moments before he rushed out the door.

An hour later, Sergeant Capper and Lieutenant Woodbury were giving their final report to the garrison commandant. Before being excused, Sergeant Capper included his belief that the hoof prints they discovered wore quartermaster issued horseshoes. Patrick remained in the colonel's office until the rest of the officers had a chance to arrive. Officers of the 7th Regiment attached to the fort were also invited into the colonel's office for the morning discussion.

Moments later, Colonel Crittenden spoke harshly about a breach of honor within his command. He said, "There have been a number of marches ordered over the past few months. Every one of you who lead your troops into the field returned with information that was disturbing with the exception of one. A disturbing pattern has befallen one of our own on numerous occasions. I have no other alternative than to have one of you held here in this building and your sergeant will be brought here also. You will be taken under guard to Fort Lincoln while an investigation is launched. You will remain there until Colonel Sturgis, the Commander of the 7th Cavalry Regiment, can review the report.

There was an eerie silence in the room for a moment, then Colonel Crittenden said, "Lieutenant Caleb Masters, step forward and surrender your side arms. Is there anything you have to say?"

The lieutenant was one of the galvanized officers that had joined the garrison sometime after the Civil War. He had taken his oath, but his actions still demonstrated a trace of rebel behavior. The men under his command were from the garrison and were galvanized troops as well.

"I have nothing to say, Colonel, except this is a total embarrassment in front of all my fellow officers. It is inconceivable that I should have to face such outlandish charges."

Colonel Crittenden dismissed the officers and asked that the duty officer find and escort Sergeant Joe Kidding to the headquarters building. Major Reno and Captain Benteen remained behind at the commandant's request.

In the commotion of those leaving the colonel's office, Lieutenant Masters turned to Patrick and said under his breath, but loud enough for Patrick to hear, "You're a dead man. Remember that!"

Returning to his quarters Patrick was free to tell Cille more of what he couldn't discuss the night before. "I'll tell you this much, Cille: I received a threat from Lieutenant Caleb Masters and I don't take his remarks lightly. And I definitely don't trust his sergeant."

CHAPTER 20

Cille Nearing Childbirth 1874

General Custer took a number of troops from the 7th on an expedition. Units from Fort Lincoln and those attached to Fort Rice were dispatched into the field. The march into the Black Hills would cover a short period of time, before they would return.

Fort Rice suddenly felt empty with units under Major Reno and Captain Benteen gone from the fort. Along with them rode McIntosh and Gibson leaving Katie, Kate and Mary behind. They seemed to band together giving each other support while their husbands rode out to face whatever nature and the Indians threw at them.

◇◇◇

Over the past several months, Linda Slaughter's reassuring advice was encouraging for Cille. She was nearing her due date for her first child. Lately, Patrick had been in from patrol for only a couple of days and then he was in the field once more. Linda was her main support for medical advice, information that was passed down from her husband. Lizzie had been a daily comfort showing compassion, seeing that the advice from Linda was carried out.

Aside from the usual sicknesses that accompany a pregnancy, Cille complained, "There is a total lack of fashion for a woman in my state of being."

On the 13th of August, the visit from Libby Custer to Fort Rice with her maid Mary Ann was a welcome sight. They arrived on the steamer Far West as it made its southern journey down the Missouri River. She knew Cille was due any day and wanted to pay her a visit. Mary Ann followed Libby up the small path from the dock area to the fort. Arriving on post following proper protocol, they headed directly to the Crittenden house to let Catherine know that she had arrived safely. Catherine welcomed them graciously and insisted they have dinner later as guests of the Crittenden household. After a short visit, Catherine led them to the Benteen residence where they rapped on the cabin door. "My goodness," Katie said, "What a pleasant surprise. Come in."

Mary Ann and Libby stepped into the house and had a seat. Catherine chose to stand. They exchanged a few casual remarks before Libby asked, "I understand that Cille Woodbury is about to have her baby. Am I too early or too late for the delivery?"

Katie said, "Last word I heard from Linda, the doctor's wife, she is a big as a barrel, out of fashionable clothing and due to pop any day."

"Sounds like we arrived in time. I wanted to see her before the happy event and I brought along Mary Ann with me today. I don't get a chance to come down this way very often anymore. When I found out the Far West was going down river, I made it my priority to board her and ride south for this visit. She is such a refined and sweet thing; our visit a couple of months ago was such a pleasure."

"I haven't a thing to do," Katie remarked. "Let's all go over and visit for a moment to see how she's coming along."

Leaving the Benteen residence, they walked down the wooden walkway until they came to the Woodbury quarters. Katie gave a quick tap on the door and waited.

Lizzie answered the door. Surprised to see who was standing there, she turned and spoke with excitement. "Miss Cille, it be a flock of them women folks dat ya know. It be Catherine, Katie, Libby and Mary Ann dat comes to visit ya."

Cille cried out, "Goodness sakes, have them come in."

She opened the door wide and said, "Come in, the whole lot of ya."

When they stepped into the quarters, Lizzie and Mary Ann went into the kitchen to visit. The others had a seat in the sitting room. "Welcome to my home, such as it is."

"It simply looks stunning," Libby said, "and your quarters look so comfortable with a splash of Victorian style."

"Most of the good pieces I'd like to have are being stored back in Monroe. I don't have a whole lot of nice pieces to furnish the place. I was limited to what I felt I could bring."

Libby became inquisitive, "I thought you were going to go back home to see your folks before you had the baby?"

"Plans have changed. I thought about it for a while, but the further along I was, the less I wanted to travel that far."

"A trip like that would be mighty uncomfortable." Katie quipped, "I'm glad you decided to stay and have the child here. That way we don't have to wait so long to see if it's a boy or a girl."

"What are you hoping for?" Libby asked.

"I just hope it is a healthy baby. I know Patrick would like it to be a boy, but I think it'll be a girl."

"Where is the happy father?" Libby inquired.

"He's out on patrol. I don't look for him to be back until day after tomorrow. Oh! That was a sharp one."

Christine asked, "How often have you been having those pains?"

"They have been getting fairly regular, since early morning."

"Goodie," Libby quipped, "looks as if Mary Ann and I have arrived at the right time."

"Cille, when was the last time Linda was over here?" Katie asked.

"She came over for coffee earlier and said the pains need to be coming closer than what they were. If the pains came closer together, I was to send Lizzie running over to her quarters. She had to go help Frank in the infirmary this morning. I think they were going to be sterilizing some of his equipment and he needed her help."

Libby asked, "Have you been timing the contractions?"

"I hadn't thought of that; the pain doesn't last that long."

"No, I mean have you been timing the distance between the pains?"

"No, I haven't."

"There is no time like the present," Christine said. "That last one was about a minute ago. We'll start from there."

With anticipated excitement, Libby got up and dashed to the

kitchen. "I think you two best be putting on some water and get it boiling. Lizzie, you might get some towels and sheets ready and have them standing by. By chance do you have an oil cloth? I've got a hunch it won't be too long."

Lizzie shot from the room to get the supplies ready.

Mary Ann got all excited and said, "Ya mean ta say, we is goin' ta have a baby fillin' the air cryin' an' markin' the day pretty soon?"

"Give Lizzie a hand," Libby suggested. "I don't know if she has been through this before or not. We don't need to have too many inexperienced gals getting excited over what needs to be done."

When Libby returned to the living room, Katie got to her feet. "I'll go get Linda. The pains are coming fast and she should be here. I'll be right back."

Moments later, Linda and Katie came through the door without knocking. Linda tried to gather her breath before she asked, "Cille, how are you girl?"

Raising her head from the bed, she replied, "I had a really sharp pain a moment ago, and Libby had me lay down."

"Get me three or four pillows, Lizzie!" Linda said with urgency, "We'll need to prop her up a bit."

Lizzie rushed into the room with the pillows and gave them to Katie and Linda. They began placing them behind Cille.

Linda said, "Just draw up your feet a bit, lean back and make yourself as comfortable as you can get, because it won't get any more comfortable than this until it's over."

Christine said, "I'm on my way back to my house to get Rahema. We'll be back shortly.

When Cille went to support her back on the pillows, they adjusted an oil cloth beneath her body. She was suddenly hit with a pain that lasted for a short time. She cried out as another pain hit her hard and her water broke.

"They best have the water boiling in the kitchen," Linda remarked, "It isn't going to be long now."

Libby rushed back into the kitchen to see if the water was boiling and the supplies were at the ready. Upon her return to the bedroom, she delivered a few towels and two sheets. "How is she Linda?"

"I took a peek. It looks as if we'll have a baby squalling before too long."

There was excitement on the garrison when Catherine rushed into her house to get Rahema to help Lizzie. Within moments, they rushed out of the house with Rahema following at a trot. It caught the eyes of Mary McIntosh and Kate Gibson, and they knew without asking what was going on. They followed at a quickened pace. When they arrived at the Woodbury quarters and momentarily knocked on the door, they rushed in without a response. The women gathered near the bedroom door to peek in and try to get the latest news. Rahema dashed into the kitchen area where she saw Lizzie and Mary Ann. She planned to sneak in a visit with Lizzie among all the commotion, in hopes of getting one of them special cookies.

Rahema asked, "Lizzie, what you doin' girl? Why ya needin' my help for? It be your misses that be putting up such a fuss."

There was laughter in the kitchen as the three chided each other and did their best to catch up on the latest news in their corner of the world.

Suddenly the Woodbury quarters filled with the urgent news of a pending delivery, when Cille pushed down as the contractions hit hard and fast. She found it hard to follow Linda's instructions because of the pain. As she cried out through clinched teeth and pushed down one last time, she felt the baby ease into the world.

It was silent for only a moment and then the household filled with the cry of a newborn. Mother leaned back, exhausted and damp from perspiration and the wetness of the damp cloth that had bathed her head.

"It's a girl," Linda called out, "Cille, it's a girl! I'll clean her up and you can hold her in just a moment."

The rest of the evening was filled with laughter and small talk as needed for a woman in the frontier to keep her sanity. It was nice to have close friends nearby at a time like this.

As the day drew to a close, Katie returned to her home to fix her supper and Linda returned to her quarters to do the same for Frank. Libby and Mary Ann accompanied Catherine and Rahema as they returned to the Crittenden home where the honored guests had been invited for supper. Mary and Kate stayed behind for a few moments fussing over the baby before excusing themselves and going to their individual quarters. Lizzie remained behind to cook supper for Cille and did what she could to make the new mother comfortable.

Libby and Mary Ann would stay at Fort Rice overnight and boarded the Far West later the next day on its return trip to Fort Lincoln. They would visit Cille again and check on the new baby in the coming weeks.

◇ ◇ ◇

Libby was busy gathering up her belongings, getting ready to catch the Far West on its return trip to Fort Lincoln when Patrick and his men returned from their latest march deep into hostile territory.

When Patrick entered his quarters, he had already been informed of the birth of his daughter. He had a broad smile on his face. He halted when he saw that they had company.

"Hello, I'm Libby Custer and this is my maid, Mary Ann. I assume you're Patrick, the proud father? We can't stay long as we are about to leave and catch that steamer. Lizzie had let us in, but Cille was sleeping, so we didn't disturb her."

"It's nice to see you again, Libby. Please excuse my manners, but I'd like to see my wife and daughter."

"I can't blame you. She is resting now and the baby is simply a sweet beautiful little girl. Mary Ann and I will have to make our way to the docks in order to catch the steamer. Give my regards to Cille and tell her we had to rush along. You take good care of the family."

"That I will and thank you very much for being here. I heard over at the headquarters building how much all you women had done for her."

"It was nothing. Cille did all the work. We'll be on our way and congratulations again."

"Let me see that your things are taken to the dock."

"You will do no such thing. Go see your lovely wife and baby. I'll go by the headquarters building and have a trooper deliver them to the dock. Tell Cille I'll be back in a month or so."

When Libby Custer and her maid Mary Ann left, Patrick turned and went to his wife's side. Next to her in bed was their first child,

Sadie. The excitement of the day filled him with pride. He leaned across the bed, kissed Cille on the forehead, and then gingerly did the same to their daughter. Now they both have what they wanted for such a long time; a child of their own. He said, "Wow, I'm so happy I'm about to..." He was temporarily at a loss for words.

CHAPTER 21

Lieutenant Woodbury Is Hurt On Patrol 1875

With most of the 7th Cavalry Regiment leaving Fort Lincoln and calling upon the units under Major Reno and Captain Benteen from Fort Rice, they ventured into Montana. They were strategically scattered from Glendive to Billings and points west to protect the survey workers for the Northern Pacific railroad. Some of the 7th remained behind and operated local patrols out of Fort Lincoln.

The protection of Fort Rice fell upon the largely populated galvanized troops that Lieutenant Woodbury was working with. Periodic reports came into the garrison about Indians assaulting haying and logging operations. At times there was the loss of horses and portions of cattle herds with no distinction whether they belonged to the army, civilian traders or the farmers.

◇ ◇ ◇

Being out on patrol during the month of March was an uncomfortable experience for the lieutenant and his troops. The wind was blowing with gusts coming from the north. Heavy snow was on the ground, and in some places, a light thaw had taken place, only to freeze solid during the night. Clusters of sagebrush and prairie grasses dotted the landscape giving the distant terrain a pale blue gray color. The ground in some places was slippery, while in others the soil was still frozen. If the thawing period was upon them, could spring be far behind? Patrick and his unit had been on patrol for three days. Their marching orders were to round up any savages they came in contact with and bring them in where they could be placed on reservations.

Topping a hill with caution, they could see twenty Indians in front of them. Patrick ordered double skirmish lines for the charge. He took the lead and center of those advancing down the hill. Should the Indians begin to flee, the forward line would give chase to the right and if to the left, the rear would give chase. The charge down the hill was at a high gallop, bringing the element of speed and surprise to the dismounted Indians.

The surprising sound of the advancing troops brought fear to the dismounted Indians. The thunderous noise of so many troops descending upon them with their mounts at top speed sent out an eerie message to the unprepared Indians. They ran to their horses and began to scatter across the valley floor. Patrick turned slightly to yell his command for the unit to disperse in different directions. Suddenly his mount hit a piece of slick soil and tumbled forward. Patrick was abruptly thrown to the ground in front of his toppling mount. The hindquarters of his horse slammed hard against the ground and his right hip, pinning him to the ground, caused Patrick to temporarily lapse into unconsciousness from the pain.

Two troopers quickly dismounted to take care of the fallen lieutenant as the rest of the line gave chase to those fleeing. Sergeant Capper and the rear column were giving pursuit of those fleeing in the opposite direction.

Moments later, the Indians were rounded up and brought back to the side of the hill where Lieutenant Woodbury lay. He was conscious, but in pain as he lie next to his horse that had broken its front legs in the fall. Sergeant Capper removed the bridle and saddle of the injured horse and stepped back three paces before he drew his pistol and fired, thus relieving the pain and suffering of the mount.

"Get the supply wagon up here," the sergeant commanded. "Let's get the lieutenant on it and make him comfortable!" The race was on to get the wagon in place while some of the others stood guard over the captured Indians.

Sergeant Capper knelt at the side of his fallen leader. Taking a large handkerchief from his pocket, he dampened it with water from his canteen. He bathed Patrick's head as he barked, "Come on lieutenant, don't you go cashing in on us now."

Patrick let out a groan as his face twisted, conveying the pain. The excess water left his face and soaked the scarf around his neck. “My chest and back hurt something awful and I can’t feel anything in my right leg.”

Capper responded, “Don’t you go frettin’ none, lieutenant. We’ll get the wagon here in a jiffy and load you up. We’ll be headin’ back to the fort before too long.”

“What has happened to the Indians?”

“We got them, lieutenant. They will be going back with us. You just hang tough and we’ll try to get you comfortable.”

The supply wagon pulled up near where the lieutenant lay. Several of the troopers juggled tent poles and canvas tenting to make a comfortable area for Patrick. Part of a tent and two poles was made into a stretcher to lift him onto the wagon.

Sergeant Capper called out to one of the troopers, “Head back to the fort and bring Doc Slaughter. Tell him the lieutenant is hurt and to bring what medical supplies he thinks are necessary. We are due west of the fort, so there will be no problem getting the Doc here. Hurry and bring him back this direction and we’ll be coming in.”

Without delay, the trooper left at a high gallop. Eight troopers working together lifted the lieutenant onto the wagon. Once on top of the wagon, they lowered the stretcher onto a pile of tenting canvas.

As the patrol began to make their way back to the fort, the wagon rolled at a slow pace. The driver was mindful of the lieutenant’s comfort. Ahead of the wagon, several troopers escorted the captured Indians.

◇ ◇ ◇

“Rider coming in,” bellowed a trooper on duty in the southwest tower. The interior of the garrison became alive with several troopers running to the headquarters building to spread the word. The commandant was busy in his office, but several staff officers and the officer of the day waited patiently near the headquarters building. They later heard the excited voice of a young trooper who had come riding in hard and reined up frantically saying, “We need Doc Slaughter in a hurry. Lieutenant Woodbury's horse fell on him during a charge and he's hurt bad. When the Doc is ready, I'll show him the way to where the patrol should be."

The duty officer ordered troopers to get Doc Slaughter from the infirmary and to do what was needed for him to make the trip. The duty office prepared a fresh mount for the trooper. "Where is the troop's position?"

"Sergeant Capper said they're due west of here. We're bringing back about twenty-five Indians we managed to capture, Sir."

"Is there a need for added troops to be sent to the field?" asked the duty officer. Looking down from his tired mount, the trooper added, "I don't reckon there is a need. The patrol is about three hours out and headed this way. I didn't see any signs of trouble on the ride in, Sir." He dismounted and quickly mounted the fresh mount.

One of the troopers went to the Woodbury quarters to tell Cille of the problems in the field. She arrived at the headquarters building escorted by the trooper dispatched to get her. She had left Sadie in the care of Lizzie. She tried to hear and digest what the young man was saying when he met with the Officer of the Day. She caught only the last bit of information of what the excited trooper was saying.

Moments later Doc Slaughter and four troopers arrived from the fort. They rode at a high gallop with the medical supply bag bouncing. The group soon disappeared from view.

Mrs. Slaughter arrived in time to see her husband fade in the distance. She said, "Cille, why don't you come home with me. We'll get Lizzie and Sadie on our way. We can do the waiting there."

The remainder of the day went by agonizingly slow for Cille. She knew Patrick was hurt and she had no idea how badly. Her mind raced as she imagined all sorts of injuries.

Linda put on the coffee pot and did her best to maintain soft conversation, reassuring Cille that things would be ok.

Sometime later, there was a rap on the door and one of the troopers called out, "The patrol is coming in."

Leaving the quarters, Cille and Linda went to stand in front of the headquarters building. They could see the arriving patrol off in the distance across the vast open prairie ground. The wait would be a little bit longer.

When the patrol entered the garrison grounds to the south, the Indians were escorted to the stockade and the wagon rolled toward the infirmary. Sergeant Capper rode over to the headquarters building to make his report. Seeing Cille, he called out, "Mrs. Woodbury, he's hurt bad. His horse nearly fell on top of him. I think his hip and leg is busted up."

Cille responded a quick, "Thank you," as she and Linda hustled to the infirmary. She was thankful that she had left Sadie in the care of Lizzie. Right now, she needed to see her husband and know firsthand how bad he was hurt.

Upon their arrival at the infirmary, Linda called to her husband, "Frank, how bad is he?"

Lieutenant Woodbury was being lowered from the wagon as Frank turned to see the women arriving. "He's busted up some and complains of some loss of sensation in his right leg. I'll check him over in a minute or so and try to get a handle on the extent of his injuries. There isn't anything either of you can do for now. Why don't you go back to the quarters and I'll be along shortly.

"Can I see Patrick before we leave?" Cille pleaded.

"Make it short. He's in a lot of pain and I want to get him comfortable."

Cille rushed to his side and said, "Patrick, I'm here. Can you hear me?"

Through tears of pain, Patrick looked at her and smiled, saying, "We had a charge going and my horse hit a hole or some slick shale rock and we tumbled down the hillside. I hurt, Cille, I guess from having the wind slammed out of me when I hit the ground and I don't have much feeling in my right leg. My mount nearly landed on top of me."

With tears of anguish falling from her face, she urged, "Try to relax, sweetheart. Frank said he will be doctoring you shortly and I'll come by when I can."

Patrick smiled as they began to take him into the infirmary. The women returned to the Slaughter's quarters. This would be the beginning of a long evening. While waiting, they had a brief visit from Catherine, Rahema, Katie, Kathy and Mary. Before they departed, the commandant dropped over to visit with Cille for a moment. He later spoke with Doc Slaughter and visited briefly with

Patrick.

◇ ◇ ◇

It was days later when Doc Slaughter called Cille to the side. "There is nothing but bad news."

"Ok, Doctor, what is it you want to say? Is it about Patrick?"

"Yes and no. Word at muster is that Lieutenant Masters and Sergeant Kidding only got a slap on the wrist for their escapades in this part of the country. They were both galvanized troops assigned here, but they have been transferred to Fort Lincoln and have made some plea arrangements to ride with one of the units under the command of Colonel Sturgis. I know this isn't going to set well with Patrick. The only consolation is they have been transferred to Fort Lincoln, but as for now, they are both back to full duty."

"I'm glad neither one of them will be stationed around here. Patrick told me of the threat Masters' made. What is the rest of the bad news?"

"I can do no more for Patrick here. I recommend that you all venture to St Louis for an evaluation from a surgeon there. Maybe he can help get Patrick's back pain to where he can sit, walk and maybe someday ride again. I don't have the equipment or know-how to get the job done here."

Cille thought for a moment, then said, "If it means that he has a chance to improve, how soon will we be allowed to leave?"

"Benton Barracks has a hospital the military once used, but they are closing it down. I understand that there is a good hospital in midtown St Louis run by the Sisters of Mercy called St. John's. General Sherman has given me the go-ahead to contact a surgeon there and see if he might be able to see Patrick. I've made my recommendations to the command and I'm sure it will be just a few days before we hear from St. John's."

"Then I'll make preparations and I'll leave the paperwork to you and the Army," Cille said softly.

Several days later, word had come from St Louis that they had a doctor on staff that might be able to help with the damage Patrick had suffered. They would accept the arrangements from the military to make payment. They recommended he be transported downriver and a horse-drawn ambulance would be summoned at dockside once he arrived.

Doc Slaughter made the arrangements for two troopers that had worked with him in the infirmary to accompany Patrick, carry him to the boat and from the boat to the ambulance in St Louis. The troopers were to return to Fort Rice immediately following Patrick's transfer to the medical staff dockside.

Their easterly journey began at the docks south of the Fort Rice garrison compound at the end of August. The steamer 'Logan Fancy' was making a southerly journey to St. Louis, Missouri to pick up military supplies. As they prepared to board the steamer, the muddy waters of the Missouri River were splashing against the keel as it tied up to the dock. Although the waters were not as high as when the spring thaw took place, the waters served notice that it was rushing to the south and would carry the steamer there quickly.

When the steamer arrived in St Louis, there was the standard jostling among boats in hopes of finding the ideal mooring place dockside. When the captain of the 'Logan Fancy' tied up at one of the docks, they were all surprised to see that the horse-drawn ambulance was waiting just off the wharf area.

Patrick had his ride to the hospital. Cille, Lizzie and Sadie made arrangements for their lodging and the long wait began. There would be surgery and a few days in the hospital before Patrick would be released. He would be allowed a short period of convalescence before a follow up with the surgeon. That period of rest would allow a visit with family back East in Monroe, New York.

Through knowledgeable staff members, a route traveling by train was arranged. The Mississippi River had been recently spanned by Eads Bridge allowing rail service to those on the eastern side of the river. Arrangements had been made for the family to ride on the CP&StL, a passenger train that traveled from St Louis to Peoria and on to Chicago. From Chicago, they would transfer and ride on the New York Central Railroad until Buffalo, New York, then transfer to the BNY&E, at Buffalo, New York and the last leg of the journey was on to the Erie rail line, with a stop in Monroe, New York. Cille was so thankful that she didn't have to deal with the confusing ticket scheduling. There was just too much to deal with, as it was such a large undertaking.

Cille had sent a message by wire to her parents in Monroe giving them the time and date they were expected to arrive. The journey would be a long and arduous one for her while having to make most of the decisions for the first time in her life. Fresh out of surgery, Patrick was in a considerable amount of pain for the entire trip. The least amount of jostling made him uncomfortable. Cille had the medicine he needed to take, and she cared for him as a nurse. Lizzie tended to Sadie and watched over her while Cille was consumed with other duties.

◇ ◇ ◇

The Hodges met the train at the depot as it rolled to a stop. When the Woodburys got off the train, they were met by Cille's parents. Constance called out, "Let me get my hands on my granddaughter."

Cille, Lizzie and Sadie stepped down from the train under the watchful eye of Augustus. He called out, "Randu, give us a hand," as they assisted Patrick from the passenger train.

Patrick was given a hand from the train, assisted in getting into the carriage and escorted into the house when they arrived at the estate, where the weary travelers were made comfortable. The remainder of the family was close by to give moral as well as physical support.

Once inside, Constance took Sadie by the hand and led her to the kitchen, "Come with your Grandmother, my dear child. Let's see if we can find a cookie and a glass of milk."

They returned from the kitchen a couple of moments later. Sadie was all smiles and Constance stated, "I hope you know this child is about to be spoiled in a proper and dignified manner." Turning to Cille she said, "You have sure matured my dear. Before you went out West, you were still my Little Cille."

"Mother, I assure you I haven't changed that much. I may have changed by growing up after facing a lot of different situations."

"If you only knew how deeply I missed you and how much pleasure it gives me just having you home. And this precious bundle is going to be spoiled if I have anything to do with her."

"There is something that Patrick and I would like to share with you both," Cille said. "We're going to have another child in the months ahead."

Constance smiled, and when she spoke, her voice was at a higher octave, "Really, oh I do hope it is another girl. That way Sadie will have a sister to play with."

Sadie broke away from her grandmother long enough to be at her mother's side. She held up the last bite of cookie for her mother to taste.

Deliberately bending down and as the cookie hit her lips, she murmured, "Mmm, oh that is so good," without eating any of the cookie, she added, "You can have the rest."

As Sadie quickly pushed the remainder of the cookie into her mouth, Augustus laughed at her actions, then turned to Patrick and asked, "When do you have to see the surgeon again?"

He said, "We'll be returning to St Louis in about forty-five days to see the surgeon for a follow-up on the surgery he performed. Until then, I am to get some rest, exercise a bit, and take a handful of medicine for my discomfort."

"Great, then that gives us time to have your parents come and visit us," Augustus boasted. "It has been such a long time and I'd certainly enjoy visiting with them once more."

"That would be nice," Patrick said. "I sent word that I was having surgery but have neglected to tell them I was coming here. After the surgery, too many things happened all at once, it is almost like a blur."

Constance spoke up, "Sadie can stay close to her Grandmother during the days because I have plans for her. Lizzie will fit in and she can have her old room back, where she can assist us with caring for Sadie. Cille, you and Patrick can have the bedroom on the main level, that way he can avoid the stairs. What little belongings you brought with you should be taken to your room, until you're ready to leave.

At bedtime, Cille informed her daughter it was time to give the others a good night kiss.

Patrick received the first kiss, followed by Constance, then Sadie hesitated a bit before approaching Augustus and shyly giving him a quick short kiss. Cille took Sadie to the bedroom. She said bedtime prayers before Sadie hopped in bed and settled in between the sheets. Following the prayers and being tucked in, a bedtime story closed out the day. Cille leaned over her daughter, placed a loving kiss on her forehead, and said, "Goodnight, Dear." She made sure her daughter was asleep before joining the rest of the family.

They spent the evening catching up on all the news. Patrick rested comfortably on a sofa as they talked about a variety of things into the wee hours, bringing the family up to date. Cille helped Patrick to bed, doing her best to make him comfortable, before she returned to the sitting room to visit a bit longer with her parents. She decided not to stay up too late because she was rather tired from the long trip. When she excused herself, the house fell silent, and all knew there would be time for more visiting in the morning.

CHAPTER 22

Return to Duty at Fort Rice 1876

Augustus Hodges left the estate early venturing into town to send a wire to Joseph D. Woodbury and Mattie, inviting them down to see their son while he was recuperating from his recent surgery. The message read: Patrick and Cille arrived in Monroe yesterday. Patrick will stay here and recuperate from surgery. Come as soon as you can. No need to respond, your lodging at the estate is waiting for you. The wire was signed A. Hodges.

◇ ◇ ◇

Cille and Sadie were up early visiting with Constance while the help was preparing breakfast. Patrick had a rough night and Cille elected not to disturb him, allowing him to get some much-needed rest. In the dining area, Sadie was sandwiched between her mother and grandmother, undoubtedly the center of attention. The morning conversation was spent loving on Sadie, and it was clear from the beginning that she was going to be spoiled to an added degree.

After they finished breakfast, Sadie went into the sitting room with her grandmother while Cille checked on Patrick. As she entered the room, she smiled at her him and said, "Hello bright eyes, I love you, but boy did you have a restless night. That's why I allowed you to sleep in. How do you feel?"

"I still hurt a bit. I think I need a cup of coffee and some of that pain medicine."

She had kept the medicine away from Patrick at the request of the surgeon. She recalled his words, 'Keep the pills away from your husband because they are habit forming and too many will only cause added complications. Administer them to him as I have instructed and not a bit more.' Cille took the bottles of medicine and measured out the amount he was allowed to take. She placed them on the end of the table and said, "When you get dressed, you can visit with the others and take the medicine with your morning coffee." She was beginning to feel the pressures of not only being a mother, but the role of a wife and nurse as well. She smiled. Deep within her heart, she loved them both and felt honored to do what she could for Patrick and Sadie.

When they left the bedroom, they joined Constance and Sadie in the sitting room.

After Patrick had eaten and taken his morning dose of medicine, he made himself comfortable on a sofa, propped up with pillows. No sooner had he settled in, when Augustus returned from town. They spent the rest of the day visiting with the Hodges'.

Throughout the day, Cille would go to the bedroom and get the medicine for Patrick as she nursed him. She also checked on how her daughter was being spoiled by the happy grandmother.

◇◇◇

Two days after receiving the wire from Augustus, Joseph and Mattie Woodbury arrived in Monroe. When they arrived at the Hodges estate, it was the beginning of a festive occasion for everyone. The Woodburys were concerned for their son, but the one that received the most attention was Sadie.

As the evening hours grew late, Cille spoke up and said, "Sadie, it is time to excuse yourself and get ready for bed."

Sadie eased down off the chair she was sitting in and went about giving a kiss to everyone, the first being to her father. When it was time to kiss Joseph, she stalled a bit, possibly intimidated by his bushy sideburns, before she slowly approached him and gave him a quick kiss. She turned without haste and ran to her mother's side before they headed to the bedroom.

While Sadie and Cille were gone, Constance said, "My daughter seems to have her hands full. I'm so proud of her. It seems that she has taken all her responsibilities in stride and still manages to keep her composure."

Mattie said, "Patrick, you should feel fortunate to have the likes of Cille as your wife and mother of your lovely daughter. She is marvelous and I can certainly see why you married her. I love her for her loving ways."

Patrick didn't remark, but smiled and seemed to swell with pride, knowing both sides of the family were proud of her. He excused himself and joined his family before Cille left the bedroom.

When Cille joined the rest of the family, she sat down, smiled and said, "Well, that is done for the moment. I hope the two of them rest well." After the bedtime prayers, Sadie hopped in bed to listen to the bedtime story that Patrick had to tell. He kissed her and gingerly went to his bed. When he was settled in, she turned to see Sadie sound asleep. She kissed each, leaving soft comments for the pair before departing the bedroom."

Joseph's hand reached over and rested on Cille's shoulder as Mattie said, "We are so proud of you and we appreciate the care you have given both Patrick and little Sadie. You have such a loving touch."

Cille was flattered by the comment, and uttered, "It is my duty to the both of them. I love them and I love the both of you for saying those kind words."

They remained up late visiting and the Woodburys brought the rest of them up to date about happenings in the Boston area.

◇ ◇ ◇

The period of healing had come to an end and Patrick and the family, along with Lizzie, made ready at the train station for their return trip to St Louis. The extended family gathered on the depot platform and talked briefly before the train arrived. They shared last-minute comments before those departing stepped onto the passenger train. They exchanged parting waves through the train's closed window glass before the passenger train left the station.

◇ ◇ ◇

A long and tiresome trip, Patrick was returning to receive a check up from the surgeon at St John's in St Louis.

During the examination, the surgeon left an indelible mark on Patrick when he said, "The surgery has not mended what was broken. The fragile bone structure may not stand much more stress before complications set in. Cavalry duties are out of the question and garrison duties will be limited at best for a number of months. Extended periods of rest will be necessary to allow the bones to mend. In time some, but not all, of the pain will diminish. I will make my recommendations to your superiors."

Patrick was released from the hospital in St Louis with the understanding that he would follow a set of therapy guidelines. The surgeon had done what he could, but the injuries were too severe to correct. He was left with a debilitating limp and extended periods of sitting would only aggravate the injury, causing numbness in his lower back and right leg unless the therapy was followed properly. Aided by the limited amount of pain killing medicine he was ordered to take, Patrick understood the surgeon's concerns for his health.

◇ ◇ ◇

The following morning, they stood on the docks booking passage up the Missouri River to Fort Rice for the family and Lizzie. They would go home for now, but home would remain a question in both of their minds until his case was reviewed by General Sherman.

Patrick's career not only as a cavalry officer, but as a military officer would remain in question. Not having a say in whether or not he continued in the Army, as he wished consumed his thinking. They would return to Fort Rice and await the decision of the Army.

Cille remained at his side giving support and encouragement. "Patrick, if there is no longer a place for you in the Army, there is a whole world out there to explore. We'll have to accept the injury and deal with it in a positive manner. With God's help, we'll handle it together. Our love will see us through these difficult times. Then we'll move on and face other challenges."

◊ ◊ ◊

When the steamer 'Pioneer Lady' was making her approach to the landing at Fort Rice, Cille turned to Patrick and said, "It will be nice to be back home."

A sincere smile accompanied his replied, "My heart is here and not back East. There is something about this place, this land, that makes me feel good. If I can't stay in the Army, I don't know what I would do."

"Certainly," Cille responded, "there is something you will be able to do. Let's not borrow trouble by second guessing what the Army decision will be."

He smiled, and said, "We best get things together. We're almost there."

The steamer eased to the dock area and the Woodburys got off, along with a bundle of extra items sent with them by her parents. Lizzie took care of Sadie. Cille stood near her husband as he struggled with the walking cane. The crewmen unloaded several parcels belonging to the returning family and set them on the dock. Several troopers meeting the steamer took the belongings to the Woodbury quarters.

The women went to the quarters while Patrick made his way to the headquarters building. He did so alone, without any assistance. He was greeted by all those inside who welcomed him back to the fort. He asked, "Is there any word from the Army as to my disposition here?"

Colonel Crittenden asked inquisitively, "Not a word. What is it that you're expecting?"

"When I left the hospital in St Louis, they said they would send a report to General Sherman and a medical review board would be making a ruling on my career."

"Sometimes it takes a while for the board to be appointed, then maybe days before it is convened. It also depends on how many cases it will be reviewing," the Colonel advised. "The decision they put forth may be far from what a person is anticipating. Why are you asking?"

"It doesn't look good, according to the surgeon. I'm not sure if they will see fit to keep me in the Army or to turn me out to pasture. The surgical staff claims I'll need to keep up with some form of therapy for a spell, to see if my condition improves."

Their conversation lasted a few minutes longer, with Crittenden closing by saying, "Let me remove you from any duty and place you under Doc Slaughter's care."

Patrick returned to his quarters and spent a quiet, relaxing evening enjoying the comforts of being home. Lizzie puttered around the living quarters, keeping busy. Sadie rushed to her toys while Patrick and Cille talked of funny memorable moments they had in Monroe with their parents and reflections of the past.

"I look for Doc Slaughter and Linda to drop by later today." Patrick said. "I saw him coming from the headquarters building. I imagine he has talked with the colonel about my status."

"I would like to have tea and cookies available when they arrive," Cille responded. She turned to Lizzie and asked, "Would you bake up a batch of those cookies and have the tea water hot should we have company?"

"Sadie and Iz already gots the fixin's from the cupboard and she sayin' she gonna help," Lizzie answered.

That afternoon, true to their beliefs, Doc Slaughter and Linda dropped by their quarters and had a short visit with them. Their arrival came moments after the first batch of cookies had come from the oven.

◇ ◇ ◇

Patrick was up early and made his way out the door and to the headquarters building to visit without having to do his military duties, as Cille gave Lizzie instructions for the day. Cille anticipated that there would be several guests visit once the word got out that they were home.

Lizzie went about making additional cookies while taking care of Sadie as she darted about the living quarters sprucing up the home for any expected company. "Is ya got any preference for the cookies, or is Miss Sadie goin' ta make the decision?"

"You can make her favorite," Cille replied, "then make a couple dozen of those from your secret receipt."

"We is goin' ta make a mess of cookies, ain't that so, Sadie?"

Moments later, before the cookies were pulled from the oven, there was a knock on the door. Lizzie raced to the door to find Katie Benteen and Linda Slaughter standing with large welcome baskets in their hands. "Miz Cille, you got a mess of company waiting for ya at the door."

"Have them come in," Cille replied.

When Katie and Linda came into the sitting room, there was a three-way race to see who was going to talk first and there was no clear winner. When things settled down, they began catching up on the news from around the fort and the news from back East. There was serious talk and a light sprinkle of humor tossed in for an enjoyable chat.

As Lizzie strolled into the room, she balanced three cups and a pot of hot tea on a tray. She rushed to the kitchen and returned with two dishes full of cookies. A plate full of Sadie's favorites and a plateful of those cookies for which she refused to share the receipt with anyone.

◇ ◇ ◇

Weeks later, Patrick and his family were on their way to Bismarck, Dakota Territory to do some shopping after a stop at Fort Lincoln. Because of some of the garrison commitments at Fort Rice, and deployment of troops, Crittenden asked Patrick to deliver paperwork to Fort Lincoln. Patrick saw it as an honor to be doing something, Cille found it interesting because she would get a chance to see Libby and Lizzie was excited about seeing the maid, Mary Ann. Libby and Mary Ann hadn't seen Sadie but once after her birth, and she had grown so much over the last several months.

They traveled upriver by steamer and tied up at the docks near the south end of Fort Lincoln. When they arrived, Patrick took his time walking with the assistance of a cane. The women casually walked nearby. From the gentle slope to the grounds of the fort, they walked on the lush grass of early summer. Approaching from the water's edge, they entered the compound south of the commissary store and the headquarters building where Patrick dropped off the material with the Duty Officer. They walked across the south end of the parade field to the single row of Officer's quarters.

Midway across the parade field was the home for General Custer and his wife Libby.

While walking up the steps of the majestic two-story house that stood overlooking the large parade field, bordered by the garrison, Patrick struggled with every step. Cille was nearby to lend a hand, but Patrick's pride and her desire to preserve his dignity restricted her open assistance in public. Lizzie and Sadie made it to the door first and stood there waiting for the others to arrive.

Mary Ann came to the door before they could knock. She stood with fresh towels draped over her forearm as she said, "I seen ya's through the lace on the door. Goodness, is this house gonna be surprised. Come on in."

Mary Ann shot through the house announcing the visitors. General Custer was in his study and came to the front of the house to greet the callers. When he saw Patrick with his cane and twisted features, he paused before saying, "Come into my study, where we can visit."

Patrick headed to the study as Libby and her maid appeared in the foyer. Mary Ann said, "Lizzie bring that chil' in the kitchen, I gots a treat for her and for you too, but Iz gonna put a limit on you, eatin' my favorite cookies." Both had their favorite receipt and neither felt compelled to share it with the other.

Mrs. Custer smiled and said, "Cille, goodness, is it good to see you." As she looked at Sadie in passing, Libby proclaimed, "She sure has grown from the last time I saw her. Come into the living area and you can tell me all the news of your trip back East and when the baby is due."

Cille smiled and said, "I'm about six months along. As for the trip, it was an adventure." In detail, she talked of the stay in St Louis for Patrick's surgery, the train ride to Monroe and the visit she had back East with her parents and in-laws before they had to return to St Louis and finally, the trip upriver to Fort Rice. Libby sat back and enjoyed all that Cille was saying.

The visit was extended, but not a long one. Patrick knew that the General's time was limited. When he left the General, he stood in a doorway listening to the women talk for a moment before Cille excused herself to see to Patrick's needs. For the women, the visit was way too short, with each vowing to spend more time together the next time they had a chance to meet.

When they arrived at the headquarters building, they were informed that a settler's wagon was ready to leave. The wagon was returning to Bismarck and they could ride along. Patrick seemed to throw caution to the wind and agreed to the short trip by wagon. It was crowded on top and became most uncomfortable for Patrick. The wagon seemed to hit all the rough spots, and when it was pulled onto the raft, the jolt was nearly more than what he could stand. Nearly the same bump took place on the eastern bank. The wagon was jostled by a short drop as it left the raft and headed into the downtown section of Bismarck. Patrick made a mental note of not doing this too often, as he wasn't feeling too spry.

When they arrived in Bismarck, they could see that the largest community this far west was busy with commerce. People in the streets entertained thoughts of settling on land they could buy in choice areas and those who wanted to homestead. There was a fever among those who wanted to settle in the western part of the territory.

During their shopping, the topic came up several times in their conversation. Homesteading would be an option should the Army not find a need for him any longer.

Several hours were spent shopping, going from one store to the other. Cille suggested, "Before we leave, let's stop by one of the land offices to see what all the excitement is about."

"That certainly sounds like a good idea to me," Patrick said. "I'm rather tired going from one establishment to the other. I'm ready to make the return trip before too long."

Their last stop was at the land office. Upon entering the office, they had to wait for three other families to get their information first. When they were called upon, the land agent, J. R. Butler, painted a rosier picture of land east of the Missouri River. There was talk of even single women homesteading and making a go of it. "They served out their requirement by building on the land and by living there for five years. "Proving up" is what it's called."

"You talk of the women homesteading; how about a family?" Patrick asked.

J.R. thought for a moment and said, "Well there are two other ways. One is to be there before the land goes public, then you can file paperwork of preemption and the other is to grow timber on the land. Either way, you still have to face the government and satisfy the requirements."

Before the Woodburys were ready to leave, the land agent added his last bit of information, "If you don't want to build or serve out the required five years on the land, maybe you can find someone who will sell you their homestead and you can buy it from them and pay a small fee and own it outright. There are several options, and as a land agent here in Bismarck, I'll see that you get a choice homestead."

Patrick and Cille took some information from the land office with them to review over the coming days.

They left the land office, heading toward the docks on the Missouri River. Upon their arrival they didn't have to wait long before securing transportation down river. The steamer Little Lady would be leaving shortly on a return trip to St. Louis, Missouri.

The sun had nearly disappeared below the western horizon when the Little Lady reached the landing at Fort Rice. The Woodburys made the gradual climb from the banks of the river en route to the fort and their quarters.

Lizzie went to the kitchen and immediately went about preparing supper. Sadie was exhausted from the trip and fell asleep on the sofa. Patrick rested in a chair, exhausted from the walk up the bank with his troublesome back and continued use of a cane, which he had not yet grown accustomed to.

Cille was excited. She took all the parcels from their shopping and unwrapped each one before placing them in the house according to where they would be most useful. The new clothes were laid to one side to be washed and ironed before being hung in the closet with the other garments. She hummed while she went about the small but important chore. She had just finished when Lizzie announced, "I got fixin's on the table, if ya hungry."

CHAPTER 23

Prospects of Homesteading 1876

The prospects of preparing for the future were exciting as Patrick and Cille sat around the table during the day discussing the material about homesteading. Several days had passed since their visit to Bismarck before they received a letter from the land agent. Patrick sat across the table from Cille and read the letter aloud from the land office.

April 10, 1876, Bismarck, Dakota Territory

To: Mr. Woodbury, Fort Rice From: J. R. Butler

There is a homestead back East in Cass County that may be of interest to you. If you have about five days to spare, we can catch the eastbound Northern Pacific passenger train in Bismarck, ride to Fargo, then we'll take a buggy from there to south Cass County and inspect the 80-acre Furnberg homestead. Anne Furnberg has been widowed and is trying to make a go of it with a young child. Indications are that she may sell out rather cheaply. She first acquired the land on the 25th of May a year ago. Let me know your intentions, if interested.

Thanks, J. R. Butler

He handed the letter to Cille as she replied, "This is quite interesting. I'm so glad we stopped into his office last week."

"Maybe this is something we should look into," Patrick said, then said, "Should the Army decide to 'put me out to pasture'."

"Patrick! They certainly wouldn't treat you like an animal, after what you have done for them."

"It's a figure of speech, Cille. When they can find no use for the mounts, they turn them out to pasture. I was trying to look at the lighter side of an uncomfortable situation. I just don't believe they'll resort to shooting me."

"Let's talk of something more pleasing and meaningful," Cille replied, "like the prospects of looking into what Mr. Butler has to say."

"I hope there is something to the letter. Cille, I have fallen in love with this country. Going back East isn't what I would like to do if the Army fails to find a need for me any longer."

"You know I'll be by your side, Patrick, whatever you decide. I want to see you happy. Why not see if you can get a few days off, to make the trip? We can be prepared for whatever happens, should it come to that. Let's consider going to Bismarck and making the trip to that homestead."

"That is something I believe I'd like to do."

"I'll be by your side and we'll enjoy the trip by train. I want to see your bright side shining once again."

Patrick grimaced as he got to his feet and said, "I'll be right back. Maybe a trip like this will take my mind off the pain in the legs that the medicine doesn't seem to help."

Moments later, Cille watched as he left their quarters and headed for the Infirmary. She knew it would be some time before he would return because he enjoyed visiting with Doc and the men while catching up on the latest news.

Cille went to her desk and began answering a letter from her parents. Lizzie was in the kitchen making homemade bread and a batch of cookies for Sadie. The toddler watched her every move. The dimly-lit quarters fell into silence, interrupted only by Lizzie's occasional humming and babbled questions from an inquisitive child.

Sadie was standing in a chair pulled up to the table and couldn't resist putting her hands in the flour near the very end of the table. It wasn't long before she had treated herself to a facial.

Lizzie called out, "Miss Cille, don't ya go missin' this. Come catch a look at spooky Sadie. Your daughter don' did herself up fancy."

When Cille went into the kitchen, she stood shocked as Sadie turned toward her mother. Sadie stood with flour in her hair, on her face and hands. She paused trying to look horrified for her daughter's benefit, but couldn't help but start laughing. When she calmed down, she said, "Sadie, you look a mess, but so cute and I dearly love you." As she approached her daughter, Sadie reached out and wiped her hand down her mother's nose, causing Lizzie to laugh.

There was laughter in the kitchen and before long, flour also marked Lizzie's cheek, courtesy of the little baker. The kitchen was beginning to smell like fresh baked goods, and before long, the entire house would be filled with the pleasant odor.

The evening meal was ready to bring to the table. The household was patiently waiting for Patrick to come through the door. Time passed and Cille finally relented, "Lizzie, I think it's time for supper."

Lizzie had no more started placing food on the table, when Patrick returned from his extended stay at the infirmary and headquarters. He was far from being downhearted.

"What's the smile all about?" Cille asked.

"It's the road at the end of the month," Patrick replied.

Inquisitively, Cille asked, "What do you mean?"

"We have orders for Fort Lincoln. I'll be leaving the cavalry here and assigned to administrative duties under Colonel Samuel Sturgis. He's the garrison commander. We will leave our quarters here at Fort Rice at the end of the month."

She looked a bit relieved before remarking bluntly, "Great, you're hurt, can't ride and can only hobble. Now they want to put you behind a desk."

"I'm just being assigned there for limited administrative duties. I'll still be with the 7th," he assured her.

"If you're comfortable with that, I guess I will be also. At least they have better living conditions than what I have been putting up with here."

"I have until the end of the month to break in my replacement. Doc Slaughter will allow me to do what little duty I can perform and still remain under his care here."

Puzzled, Cille asked, "They're sure?"

"Don't question the military. I'll need to be here until the end of the month for the formal release, my last act of duty, before going upriver."

Cille held her inner joy in check as she said, "Well! The food is on the table. Now that you're back, you can say grace before we eat. But before we do, did you ask for a few days off?"

"That I did. I asked for the time off before they told me of my orders. All I have to do is let them know when we need to make the trip."

◇ ◇ ◇

The week passed so quickly, that Cille seemed to have little time to prepare for the trip. They now found themselves at the depot in Bismarck, standing on the platform waiting to board the 9 A. M. eastbound Northern Pacific passenger train to Fargo, Dakota Territory.

With a stuffed valise, J. R. Butler the land agent joined them moments before the belching cinders from the train rained down on them. They would soon be on their way.

Cille and Lizzie, with Sadie in tow, boarded the train followed by Patrick and Mr. Butler. They sat in the passenger car waiting for the conductor to arrive and punch their tickets. The women sat on one side of the aisle and the men on the other.

As Cille listened, Mr. Butler explained to Patrick the process of acquiring a homestead. The land they had planned to visit was an area a short distance from the edge of the Sheyenne River with a spring nearby. "Most of this homestead is in flax. A 39-year-old strong-willed widow with a young child is homesteading some 80 acres. Anne Furnberg lost her husband shortly after the birth of their son Christopher. She hadn't been out here long. I think she came out west from Minnesota in a covered wagon and later managed to stake her claim. She's been trying to handle it all on her own, but is falling on some tough times and needs help. She might sell the homestead just to collect some money for her time and leave the new owner to either finish out the five-year requirement in order to `prove up' or buy it outright."

With a quick interruption, Cille asked, "How did you come to find out all that information?"

Mr. Butler said, "There is talk all up and down the railroad by land agents of what is going on in order to fill new homesteads, as well as those that can't make it on the land. It's our job to place good folks upon these lands. That's how we make our money."

"Isn't there anyone nearby that can give her a hand?" Cille asked.

J. R. explained, "There is a parcel connecting it, but there is no one on it. You wouldn't qualify for homesteading it. Your husband can buy out the one parcel and homestead the other if he likes. Then again, if you don't want to do it that way, maybe your helper would like to homestead next to you."

"You mean Lizzie could acquire land through the Homestead Act and I'm not allowed to do so?"

"The law is very straightforward in that regard. If you are married, the land must be listed in the husband's name. Now there are several single women who homestead; such is the case of the one we'll visit tomorrow. And on occasion, there are black homesteaders, some men and a few single black women that think they can live on the land for five years in order to 'prove up'."

Cille bristled at being excluded by the law, her silence speaking volumes as that of a rebuffed woman.

The journey to Fargo would be through some scenic country that Cille had never seen. To her, it was quite interesting. Patrick explained to her what his job entailed when he was assigned under General Rosser a few years back, protecting the railroad workers between Fargo and the town of Bismarck on the Missouri River.

Mr. Butler, on the other hand, paid more attention to the paperwork he had brought along than the countryside passing by. From time to time, he would recant all he had told them about the land they were to visit and avoided getting too deeply involved in explaining things to Cille.

When they arrived in Fargo, they made arrangements at the local hotel for the night and for a large buggy to be available the following morning. The trip to southern Cass County would be a long, hard buggy ride.

◊ ◊ ◊

Leaving Fargo behind and riding over the rough countryside with a full stomach made everyone a bit uncomfortable. A short distance from Fargo, they spotted tarpaper shacks of homesteaders randomly dotting the terrain. Most of the shacks appeared to be abandoned, while others had evidence of occupancy. Every mile or so, the sight of a Soddy was evident. Some of the homestead land was under seed, while others reflected no work on the soil.

The buggy stopped twice for water and a bit of chat with some of the homesteaders. They were a friendly group. Upon leaving, both Patrick and Cille were impressed over the hospitality these determined homesteaders possessed.

When they arrived at the homestead of Anne Furnberg, she was in the field working the soil. Off to the side of the field and not far from her watchful eyes, was a large basket where her son Christopher played with a few homemade toys. The blanket had been placed in the shade of a large tree to provide some relief from the heat of the day.

As the wagon rolled to a stop near the field, she quit her work and shaded her eyes to focus in on the buggy that came to rest between her and the rays of the sun.

J. R. called out, "Hello Anne, we came to give you a visit."

Anne lowered her hand from her face and went to the edge of the field and got her son before she made any attempt to approach the wagon. When she arrived, she said, "Mighty nice to have someone come by for a visit. I don't have many folks stop by this time of year."

He said, "I'm Mr. Butler, land agent and this is Mr. and Mrs. Woodbury and their family. They came by to look at your homestead. I understand that you are having some problems and might want to sell your claim."

"Climb down out of that seat; I'm not going to stand here crainin' me neck just to chat."

Upon getting down from the buggy, Cille was the first to speak. "Anne, I'm Cille, this is my husband Patrick, my help Lizzie and my daughter, Sadie."

"I'm pleased to meet each of ya. Tis true, I was a thinkin' to do away with the place. You see that thar river. I jumped in on the other side almost a year ago. I latched on to a log and I swum to this side to stake my claim. I went back the same way and got my son and we rode over on a raft and I been farmin' every day. Tis rough land here, not like the rollin' hills in Norway. I felt sorry for meself and thought whats a use. Then I get letter from me sister and brother-in-law, they soon come to this country. I write and tell them to bring me nephew Ole. He can live with me and take care of Christopher. They say they come and bring Ole, so I feel better and change me sad thinkin'. They be here soon to help with the work, before they get some land of their own."

J. R. said, "But they came all this way. Can they at least look around?"

Anne looked at Cille and said, "I am so sorry you had to make such a trip. Would you come to my cabin and have some tea with me? Most times it gets quiet and lonely around here."

"I would love to, Anne," Cille replied.

The one-room tarpaper shack was home to Anne and Christopher and offered little room inside. Before long, the tea was ready and the conversation between Cille and Anne slowly came to an end.

"You see, I was married a few years back," Anne said. "We had a cabin about five miles from Fargo. We had a cow and some chickens and would sell butter and eggs in Fargo. But he died shortly after the birth of our son. I had to sell everything to give him a proper burial. The only thing left was me and me son, Christopher. I know times be hard, but I think maybe best I stay to make home for me son. I'm sorry you made such a long trip."

Cille said, "There is nothing to be sorry for. I will leave here so much richer from knowing you. I wish to know how to write to you from time to time."

Thirsting for more information, Anne asked, "When is the baby due?"

Undisturbed by the question, Cille replied, "I'm about six months along."

Mrs. Fernberg nearly pleaded, "Do keep in touch. I'd sure like to know how you're coming along."

Reassuringly, Cille said, "I promise to write you before the baby gets here."

As Anne gave her the mailing address, she promised to write as well. Everyone was in the buggy waiting for Cille to climb aboard.

After their short visit, the buggy rolled over the hill to the parcel joining Anne's homestead to the south. Patrick was uncomfortable but listened as Mr. Butler pointed out the features of the pieces of land. The stay was brief before the buggy rolled northward toward Fargo.

That evening, Mr. Butler asked Patrick about several parcels of homestead land in Cass County that he pointed out on the county map. "What options are you going to accept? I have explained several ways you might proceed."

Patrick replied, "I will not commit myself to one plan or the other at this point. I can't. I'll discuss it with my wife first, before we make any commitment. Is that acceptable?"

"Sure, sure. I'll be at your disposal when you do."

The return trip to Bismarck was more enjoyable without the pressure of homesteading.

Patrick made himself comfortable in the passenger train seat and felt the pain in his back ease up. Before long, he was enjoying the scenery as much as the rest of the family.

CHAPTER 24

Released from Military 1876

The Northern Pacific Railroad passenger train from Fargo arrived in Bismarck in the early afternoon. The belching cinders from the stack and the screeching of large locomotive wheels against the cold steel tracks brought all movement to a halt with a small jerk. Passengers jumped up, as if they wanted to be the first ones off the train, with the exception of one family.

Patrick was having problems with his back from having to sit so long. "Cille, the medicine doesn't last as long as it once did. I'll have to talk with Doc Slaughter when we get back to Fort Rice."

"It may not be the medicine," Cille added, "you can't sit in one place for an extended period of time and expect to jump up and move like you once did. I thought you might be in trouble when you didn't stretch your legs at Crystal Springs or Driscol. I believe the last time you got up and walked around was that short stop in Jamestown."

"I'll have to take this as a lesson about getting up and becoming more limber. I know now what they mean by stretching the legs. No one can do that for me, except myself."

Cille said, "I'll check with the workers at the station to see if they know when the next steamer is going down river."

After the Woodbury family had stepped down from the train, they waited on the platform while Cille went to talk with the stationmaster.

When Cille stepped into the station house, she had to wait a moment to capture the depot agent's attention. There was a message coming in on the wire and he was responding on a telegraph key. The dit-dit-dah rhythm meant little to Cille, other than the knowledge it was a telegrapher's code for communication. When he was through, he looked up and said, "What can I do for you, pretty lady?"

"My husband and I arrived on the train and we are in need of a buggy to take us to the dock. Do you know when the next boat is due going down river?"

"I know about trains, but not the boats. But I do know that there are a couple of buggies generally hanging around behind the station house that would be for hire. Maybe one of the men would know more about the boat schedule than I would."

Cille thanked the stationmaster and turned to leave. Taking her time, she marveled over the structure of the building. She thought the railroad spared no expense on a station house and compared it to the quarters at Fort Rice that she had to contend with. How different the two buildings were. Turning the corner at the far end of the station house, she saw a buggy arriving from the west. She waited a moment, and as the driver pulled his team to a stop, she asked, "Excuse me, but would you happen to know anything about the schedule of the boats going down stream?"

"Just came from the docks, Miss. There is one about to tread water coming in from the south. Ya need a ride down to the docks?"

"Yes, there are four of us and some luggage. Would you be so kind to give us a hand?"

"Don't mind if I do." He made a couple of quick loops around the break with the reins and hopped from the buggy.

Within moments, the Woodbury family was up in the buggy and headed to the docks at the river's edge. The driver was helpful in seeing that the luggage was taken to the edge of the dock for easy boarding.

Patrick appreciated the added help and gave the driver a larger than usual tip.

Looking down into his palm in surprise, the driver said, "Thanks mister, that means added milk and bread to take home tonight."

They were in luck; the Delta Blue Belle, a dingy looking sidewheeler, arrived from down river and was going to make a quick turnaround and head down stream after unloading several flats of cargo and a handful of passengers. The Woodburys were the only family boarding and the Delta Blue Belle was already ahead of their captain's schedule because of the lack of cargo to wrestle with. It wasn't long before they were leaving Bismarck behind. Riding the current on the Missouri River helped make the trip to the docks at Fort Rice a smooth and quick ride.

The docks were a welcome sight as the long journey came to an end and most everyone was ready to call it a day. When they left the boat, they made their way up the steep incline to the Fort. They were met by two troopers who carried most of their heavy bundles.

"Lizzie, take Sadie and go ahead and show them where to place the bundles. I'll stay with Patrick and give him a hand."

He whispered, "I can handle myself," not wanting to draw attention to himself.

"Sure, you can. I just wanted to be the one to keep you company on the way up. No need to leave a good man behind." She smiled and softly added, "You are a good man, so I'll stay by your side. Goodness, I came this far west to be with you, not going to abandon you now."

"I'm doing okay. I don't need you to be lifting too much and hurting the baby."

"I feel fine and the baby won't be here for another three months."

"Just the same, Dr. Slaughter said no heavy lifting."

"Yes and he also told you to get up and walk more often than you do. I can see his advice isn't being followed too closely by either of us."

Patrick smiled and allowed her to take some weight from his hands so he could handle the walking cane while balancing himself.

That evening, Patrick left their quarters to find Frank and get some much-needed medicine for his pain. Cille sat at the table discussing with Lizzie what items needed to be boxed up first in preparation for the move at the end of the month.

"Take the items we don't use that often, set them to the side and we'll box them. We'll keep out those things that we need up to the last minute."

"Iz just a smilin', cause we iz goin' to where I can visit with that sweet Mary Ann who be Libby's help."

Not wanting to discourage her, Cille said, "I'm not sure how much you'll be able to see her. I understand there is a limited amount of people that get to do any visiting at the General's house, other than on social affairs. To top that off, you're leaving Rahema behind."

"I know Mary Ann and me gets to visit a bunch. I jus' know we can see more of each other, bein' that close. No way to make excuse, you see. Iz jus' know Rahema likes ta visit more, so she be goin' about finding a way to make a trip to see Lizzy."

Cille smiled as she knew by being at Fort Lincoln, she was bound to visit with Libby more, also.

The following weeks were filled with preparations for the move and an abundance of socializing. Added visits from others at the fort were made, knowing they would be parting company and may never get to see the others again.

◇ ◇ ◇

As expected, the last day at Fort Rice was filled with excitement and fanfare on the post parade field. The day started early with the formation of troops being assembled on the field. Units included the 3rd Battalion headquarters of the 13th infantry that included companies B, E, F, G and H, as well as units of the 17th and 22nd infantry regiments and several units of the 7th cavalry. This monthly ceremony impacted Lieutenant Patrick Woodbury, the recipient of a citation for his duties above and beyond at Fort Rice while stationed there.

Unfamiliar with all the military protocol, Cille didn't watch the commotion on the parade field. She was in their quarters and figured it was just another end-of-the-month routine the post went through. For Cille, the importance of getting the last few things ready for the trip to Fort Lincoln was more important. The Army had their priorities and she had her own.

Shortly after the morning muster of troops and Officers Call, a wagon pulled up in front of the Woodbury cabin. A detail of men began loading the wagon that would make the journey some twenty-five miles north to Fort Lincoln.

Patrick would point out what items needed to be loaded next, while Cille held her breath, worried about the way some of the items were handled. It didn't take long until the wagon was lashed down and made ready for the rough ride north. The second wagon would be used for the Woodbury family to ride on along with a couple of military crates. They were escorted by a detail from one of the units of the 7th Cavalry Regiment that was stationed there in support of the infantry.

Cille enjoyed the fresh air and the prospects of arriving at Fort Lincoln before the day was out. What concerned her most was the uncomfortable shifting Patrick was making in order to find some relief from the spasms that sometimes came on while sitting in one spot too long or in an uncomfortable position for extended periods of time. She would be glad when this day was done for all concerned. It was going to be a long, rough ride.

◊ ◊ ◊

As the patrol and wagons topped the last rise, Cille could see Fort Lincoln all spread out on the west side of the Missouri River. It was on the northern side of the mouth of the Heart River. The neatly-assembled rows of white canvas tents seemed to stand out brighter as the sun was making its descent in the west. Beyond the hundreds of tents in the garrison was a commissary, the administrative headquarters and ammunition warehouse. Billeting for enlisted members of the 7th was on the eastern side of the parade field. Officers' row and housing for single and married officers and the larger house belonging to General Custer were on the western side. His house was nearly center of the parade field.

When they arrived, the patrol was notified where the Woodburys would be quartered. As the wagon rolled to a stop near a wooden walkway, Colonel Samuel D. Sturgis of the 7th Cavalry and his wife, Jerusha, welcomed them to Fort Lincoln.

After a quick introduction, Colonel Sturgis said, "Lieutenant Woodbury, you're just in time for a briefing. We'll let you get an ear full, then you can return to your quarters and finish unloading and getting your quarters in order."

Cille looked perplexed, but Jerusha said, "There is something big going on and there has been speculation for days. I believe they'll find out what the news is tonight. Cille, let the troopers lift all the belongings out of the wagon. Let's go into the quarters and you can tell them where to place the furniture while we chit chat."

"That sounds good, Jerusha," Cille said with a gasp. "I'm utterly worn out from the loading and making the trip in one day. I think I could honestly lie down on the floor and fall asleep."

"My dear, this has got to be hard on you. When is the baby due?"

"It's due sometime around the latter part of May or early June, as near as I can tell."

"Great," Jerusha said, "that will give us other women time to meet, greet and socialize, long before the baby gets here. It's about time we had some excitement around here."

"Do you know Libby?"

"Heavens, yes, we see her quite often. Whenever George is out of the house, we sometimes have a hen session at her place because it allows us more room. She is a very special gift to the rest of us here. If there is something we want but don't have, she generally gets her way, and the General sees to it that it is carried out."

In time, the quarters took on an appearance of comfort, although there were boxes and baskets of unwrapped items cluttering the floor space. The wagon was emptied and the unpacking would be left up to Cille and Lizzie. Sadie was no problem, as she fell asleep on a stuffed chair shortly after it was hauled off the wagon earlier in the evening.

Jerusha said, "Well young lady, I'll get out of your hair and head over to my quarters and have coffee ready for Samuel when the meeting is over. I'm curious what all the rumors have been leading up to. I'll drop by tomorrow with some of the girls so that you can get acquainted faster."

"Have a good evening. I sure enjoyed our talk."

"See there, the meeting must be over, I see your husband coming up the walk now. I'll rush home for now and visit with you later."

"Good night," Cille managed to say, as Jerusha headed down the wooden walk at a quickened pace, toward her quarters.

Cille remained at the doorway and welcomed Patrick as he entered the quarters. "Welcome back stranger, how did the meeting go with the General?"

"The 7th is going to head into Montana in a little more than a month. They are going to make a big push to see if they can get most of the Indians placed on reservations. There is Crazy Horse, Sitting Bull, Gaul and a few other chiefs that have big followings and force them onto a reservation. They will be taking most of the 7th out on this expedition and the men at Fort Rice will be included on this one."

"Where do you fit in on the big plans?"

"Custer has decided to have me conduct what administrative duties I can perform here on post. I will be under Colonel Samuel D. Sturgis of the 7th Cavalry. He's the Garrison Commander. I will be taking care of what little administrative duties are left behind, until the 7th returns."

"What happens with your medical treatment?"

"I'll be seeing Doc Middleton; he's the Post Surgeon. Doc Slaughter has talked about him quite a bit at Fort Rice. He speaks highly of his medical skills."

"I dearly hope he can do you some good."

"The medicine that he can dispense is here, but I'm sure any new surgery will have to be done back in St Louis. As for now, they are looking at the medicine to relieve the pain rather than any further surgery or therapy. The medical facilities are adequate here, but some consider them better at Fort Rice."

"That's not very reassuring."

Patrick said, "Most of the 7th will be leaving Fort Lincoln on the 17th of May and head into Montana in an attempt to root out the Indians and get the rebellious lot to move onto reservations. That isn't all the bad news, though." Cille looked on, not sure what to expect as he continued, "At the briefing, I ran into Lieutenant Caleb Masters. He's now riding for the 7th Cavalry, and if looks could have killed, I would have been mortally wounded at the headquarters building."

Cille said, "Maybe he'll be one of the men leaving with Custer on the 17th of May and you won't have to be concerned about him being around here with that kind of attitude."

"Time will tell on that situation. Oh, by the way, I passed Libby on my way out. She plans to have a visit with you as soon as she can. She is happy you're on post and said you two have a lot to catch up on."

◇◇◇

At Officer's Call the following month, Patrick was called into Colonel Sturgis' office and was informed, "The medical review board that was appointed by General Sherman has rendered a decision to medically retire you from active service as of the last day of May, 1876."

Still standing at attention, Patrick looked at Colonel Sturgis and said, "That limits the amount of administrative duty I'll have to do for the General, doesn't it, Sir?"

"Lieutenant, relax and have a seat. It was a good thing they found your injuries as a result of military action. There will be a small sum of money and a limited amount of medical care you will be entitled to, as long as it is related to the injury." Colonel Sturgis talked of varied subjects, mainly asking about Patrick's family. It was a good visit. The colonel learned of Lieutenant Woodbury's background and Patrick learned he would enjoy working under an understanding colonel.

When the meeting was over, Patrick thanked the Colonel and when he was excused, he went to his quarters, where he informed Cille of the Army's decision.

◇◇◇

On the 17th of May, 1876 there was a lot of fanfare as the 7th Cavalry regiment went about the morning parade activities to include the band playing the General's favorite music before the units were led into the western hillside to the west of Fort Lincoln. They had their assignments and would be gone for a month or two.

◇◇◇

It was on the 18th of May when Grace Middleton, Jerusha Sturgis, Libby Custer and Mary Ann found a reason to stop by the Woodbury quarters. They were going to see how Cille was coming along.

Lizzie opened the door and the women were made welcome.

Cille was excited and said, “Goodness how do I rate such a large calling?”

Grace spoke up, “Doc wants me to check up on you and these other ladies thought it would be a good idea to do it today.”

“Iz a knowin’ wha’ ya was about to say,” Lizzie said as she headed into the kitchen, “so Iz on me way ta fetch them cookies and I put the water on. Come on Sadie, Iz needin’ some help.”

Grace asked, “How are you feeling?”

“I’ve started having some contractions, but they don’t last long and they are an hour or so apart,” Cille said, “nothing you would call serious, yet.”

Libby laughed, “Girls, this is her second and I have a feeling there will be some squalling later in the day.”

“I’ll check with the boss,” Grace said, “I’ll be right back,” as out the door she went.

Jerusha called out behind Grace, “Have Doc tell Samuel I’ll be late for supper and that I’m here.”

Mary Ann eased around the other women and found her way to the kitchen saying, “Iz a hunch ya best get the water on, an’ get yaself ready like las’ time.”

“You gots no need to go funnin’ with me, Mary Ann! ‘Cause Iz gots my han’s full tryin’ ta get the cookies and tea ready. There no call for ya to get excited an’ scare Miss Sadie.”

“No way Lizzie,” Mary Ann shot back, “Iz jus’ sayin’ what the res’ of thems be sayin’.”

When Lizzie began delivering the cookies and tea to those in the sitting room, Grace came through the front door. In her hand was a medical satchel and in her head were the last-minute instructions from her husband.

Grace said, “Cille, Doc got a hold of Patrick and those two will try to batch it out over the supper hour at my quarters. They’ll be there if we need them.”

Cille smiled and said, “I don’t get it, I think you all are just in a hurry to … OOH! That was a big one.”

Laughter filled the quarters before Libby said, “Let’s start timing the contractions and see where we are.”

Tea and cookies came in handy while they sat around chatting about one thing and then another to pass the time. They waited on the next contraction to arrive.

Lizzie and Mary Ann managed to get supper ready and served to those gathered in for the night's activities.

Libby made sure Lizzie and Mary Ann had all of the necessary items near the bed. Cille was bound to need them later on. There was an oil cloth and ample hot water when the time came.

The garrison trumpet player was sounding taps when Cille let out a muffled call for help through clinched teeth. She was quickly moved to the bed. Moments later, the cry of a young lady named Elizabeth filled the quarters as her mother settled back to relax.

There was excitement in the Woodbury household and the women saw to it that others in the Fort knew of the happy occasion.

◇ ◇ ◇

Three days after Elizabeth came into the world, Patrick was in Bismarck to look at a house for rent. It held enough space to be adequate for a short stay. He had made arrangements with the owner and the house would be available at the end of the month.

He stopped by the land office and talked with J.R. Butler and asked him if there was any land for homesteading out west of the Bismarck area and exactly what he was looking for. He told Mr. Butler his situation and that he would be living in Bismarck until such time as a suitable homestead site could be agreed upon.

Mr. Butler said, "I'll give it my top priority and I'll let you know when I have several sites to visit in hopes they are what you're looking for."

◇ ◇ ◇

At the end of the month, with most of the 7th Regiment out west, at Officer's Call there was less fanfare as Lieutenant Woodbury was mustered out of the Army and sent into civilian life. Hours later, his personal belongings were placed on a wagon and the trip to their new residence in Bismarck was made. It was the last move that the Army would be involved with.

The owner of the house was available to show Cille and Lizzie the house before he handed the keys to Patrick. He left the family alone as they went about moving in their personal items. The troopers did most of the lifting and shifting of large furniture and boxes, placing them where directed.

There was a cordial farewell from the troopers. They wished Patrick and Cille the best before the detail boarded the wagons and returned to Fort Lincoln.

CHAPTER 25

A House on Homestead Land 1877

When they were settled into their new home, they were not expecting a young man to come knocking at their door. In his hand he held a telegram from back East, fresh from the depot telegrapher. Patrick thanked the lad and gave him some change as a tip for delivering the message before they read the telegram.

To: Patrick and Cille Woodbury

Bismarck, Dakota Territory

From: Mr. A. Hodges

Monroe, New York

Four happy grandparents - awaiting word of when you get settled into your new home - we would love to make a trip out your way if it is convenient - please respond - Mr. A. Hodges

Cille smiled at Patrick and asked, "Are we settled in enough for company?"

He looked into her eyes and said, "I believe we can make things comfortable for them if they make the trip. It would be rather nice instead of us having to go back East."

She smiled even wider and said, "The depot is too far for you to walk. I'll walk over there and send the reply this instant, if you're sure."

Patrick said, "Let's do have them come out. I know they're anxious to see Elizabeth and Sadie and I can't think of any reason to delay them from coming out this way. It is rather nice that both sides of the family want to make the trip at the same time. I'm rather tired of traveling after our last trip to St Louis."

As Cille prepared herself for the short walk, she grabbed a light shawl to place over her shoulders to protect her from the chill. She knew the grandparents were anxious to see the children, and on her way to the depot, she made up her mind on how to notify them.

On her way to the depot, she took her time, amused at the hustle and bustle of the many people as they darted from one store to the other. The community of Bismarck was full of excitement. At the far end of the street, she had a small incline to walk up, until she was on the station platform. When she entered the depot, the telegrapher asked Cille to fill out the information and she wrote:

To: Mr. & Mrs. A. Hodges

Monroe, New York

Grandfather and Grandmother Hodges - mother and father are settled in - tell Grandfather and Grandmother Woodbury to come - look forward to seeing you - please advise on when you will arrive - Sadie and Elizabeth.

She was pleased and tickled to see the expression on the telegrapher's face as to the content of the message. When Cille returned home, she told Patrick what she had done. They would wait for her parents reply.

◇ ◇ ◇

It was two weeks after Cille had sent the message that they were standing on the platform at the depot, watching the Northern Pacific passenger train slowly make its approach to the Bismarck depot.

As the train finally came to a screeching halt and the cinders that had been belched into the air had finally settled, a conductor stepped from the train placing a box down on the platform and stood by to aid those leaving the train.

Augustus was the first to step onto the platform from the train He turned, reaching up to help Constance down from the train safely. Following her was Mattie, before Joseph handed down several boxes and valises. Joseph stepped down from the train and adjusted his vest before they looked up the platform to see the welcoming party.

There were cheers of joy and a round of handshakes and hugs intermingled with conversation. The women expressed love over the children while the men looked on.

When they arrived at the house, Lizzie had made up two of the bedrooms in anticipation of the company and had a big batch of her favorite cookies available. Shortly after the guests settled into their rooms, they gathered in the sitting room to visit. Lizzie had retreated into the kitchen and was busy preparing the evening meal.

Before the evening grew late, Cille excused herself and told Sadie to bid the others good night. Sadie went from her father to her grandparents, exchanging a good night hug and kiss from each.

Cille took the children into her room, and made their beds. Elizabeth bedded down in the middle of Cille's bed and Sadie was on her smaller bed nearby. Sadie asked, "Are you going to tell me a story, tonight?"

Cille sat on the floor near Sadie's bed, and they said bed time prayers before she began a short nursery rhyme. When it had ended, she said, "I think it is time to close those beautiful eyes and go to sleep. Tomorrow will be a big day." She leaned over her daughters and gave them a good night kiss on the forehead before checking the blankets once more. When she got to her feet, she said, "I will leave the door cracked to make you comfortable," before she turned and joined the others.

The Woodbury household had their kerosene lights on late into the night, as the conversation ranged from the children to the wonderful scenery on the way from New York to Bismarck, before any of the adults were ready to call it a day.

In the following days, the visitors took a boat ride to Fort Rice to see where Patrick had been assigned at one time. They planned to go to Fort Lincoln later on before they returned to Bismarck. While at Fort Rice, they conveyed their sympathy to Colonel Crittenden' and his wife Catherine for the loss of their son, John Crittenden III, and Mary McIntosh for the loss of her husband Donald at the Little Big Horn in Montana. They made a brief stop to see Captain Benteen and his wife Katie before they visited with Kate Gibson, who was happy her husband had returned from the Little Big Horn.

Before they returned to the docks, Rahema, the Crittenden's maid, pulled Lizzie to the side for some loose chatter. "Lizzie, Iz gots a perfect man for ya."

"Ain't lookin' for no man," Lizzie shot back.

"Ya ain't gittin' any younger chil'. Goodness lest way hear me out."

"Supposed I could, what ya gonna say, sweet face."

Rahema said, "Callin' me names don't help none, but my brother come all this way from Baltimore, to visit with me for a spell. He's widowed and has two good size boys to care for."

"What!" Lizzie countered, "Ya fixin' to have me burdened with a man, that be loaded down with two overgrown younguns, do I have somethin' written on the front of my face?"

Her smile nearly busted into a laugh before Rahema said, "He jus' might be prominent, and if he is, what you gonna say about that?"

"Prominent with two hungry boys that sounds like work for me."

"Fact is he ain't prominent, but he's not as poor as I once was. He works nearly every day and so does his boys. I was hopin' ya would consider this as a favor, for someone you left behind at this fort. Can I count on my bes' friend for this one simple thing?"

Lizzie said, "Scratch down my new address in Bismarck, and have him come callin' one time. He can leave the boys behind, so Iz can get a good look at him, before there be another time."

Rahema took down the address and reassured Lizzie, "I no go pullin' no wool over your eyes, he's a good man, you'll see for yoself."

The visit between the two maids was short lived. The rest of the group was anxious to leave and go to the boat docks in hopes of catching a ride on the boat they saw coming up the Missouri channel.

Upon returning to the docks, they boarded a steamer and traveled upstream to Fort Lincoln. The boat captain said, "I'll be here for quite a while and I'll blow the whistle when I'm ready to depart."

They called on Colonel Sturgis and his wife Jerusha to convey their sympathy regarding the loss of their son James at the Little Big Horn. Before they left Fort Lincoln, they visited the Custer house where they met for a few moments with Libby and expressed their sorrow.

Their stay at Fort Lincoln was as short as the visit at Fort Rice. They hurried to the docks to catch the same boat they had ridden upriver on, as it would be going as far as Bismarck for the night.

As they made their way back to Bismarck, Matty said, "It was a beautiful trip, but one that was full of sorrow. It is so sad that there has to be such an enormous amount of loss of life in order to get the West settled."

Constance replied, "I'm so glad your Patrick didn't have to go on that assignment. I'm thankful he's here to be with Cille and the girls."

When they returned to the Woodbury house in Bismarck, the sadness of the day seemed to be forgotten. Over the course of the stay, the girls were seemingly spoiled as they went from one grandmother's lap to the other for several moments of pampering. The men were proud of the girls, but they seemed to gather near Patrick and their talk was about other things.

During their stay, nothing was mentioned of what Patrick would do for work or the prospects of homesteading. Patrick and Cille didn't volunteer any conversation on the subject.

When the time came, their parents were ready to board the Northern Pacific Railroad passenger train, and head for home, one family heading to Monroe, the other to Boston.

As they gathered on the platform, Mattie said, "Cille, your children are simply lovely. Do take care with them and thank you so much for standing by Patrick and for being such a gracious host."

Constance boasted, "Sadie is sweet and Elizabeth is sugar coated. They can come to see me anytime they get a chance."

Before long, there was only time for short hugs and kisses as the visitors were called by the conductor to board the eastbound train. Through the passenger train windows, the Woodburys could see their parents getting settled. Within moments, the train was leaving the depot and heading east.

A short time after returning to the Woodbury house, the chimes to the front door rang and Lizzie went to answer the door. To her surprise, a well-dressed man of color stood before her and asked, "May I speak to Lizzie?"

She suddenly felt uneasy, not knowing whether to invite him in or chase him off. She stepped out on the porch and said, "I'm Lizzie, Iz you related to Rahema?"

"My name is Ben-jomine, and yes she iz my sister. She asked me to call on you. I happened to be in Bismarck today and thought

I would ask you to join me for a bite to eat at the restaurant down by the docks."

"Iz got my hands full, almost ready to serve supper to the Woodburys but let me ask Miss Cille." She opened the door and left her caller standing alone on the porch.

Inside, Lizzie asked, "Miss Cille, Iz gots me a caller at the door, he bein' Rahema's brother. If it not be askin' too much, the food is on the table and…"

Cille lit up like the wick in the kerosene lantern had been rolled up. "Lizzie, I think it's great. You can invite him in at least long enough for you to freshen up and we'll make do for the evening meal. You need to get out and enjoy yourself. Now get him in here."

Lizzie smiled and turned on her heels quickly, opened the door and said, "Ben-jomine, ya can come in ta res' them weary feet and sit a spell, Iz needin' ta freshen up some before Iz feel proper to be steppin' out."

Ben-jomine entered the house, and after meeting Patrick and Cille, he had a seat in the sitting room until Lizzie came downstairs. As they left for the restaurant, Cille and Patrick looked through the lace on the front door curtain to see the happy couple headed down the street.

"I hope this is a good situation for Lizzie," Cille said.

Patrick smiled and said, "We can wish her well. I'd hate to lose her, but she has a right to a life of her own."

"Let's eat," Cille said with joy in her voice, "or do you think we should wait up for her?"

He smiled and helped Cille, while at the table, and in feeding the children.

◇ ◇ ◇

The first encounter with Ben-jomine would not be the last for Lizzie, and over the coming months, they saw each other several times. For the first time in her life, she was experiencing a wonderful feeling and planned to share some talk with Cille. Ben-jomine was welcomed into the Woodbury's house, and it seemed that Lizzie and Ben-jomine were becoming more and more devoted to each other.

When the Woodbury family had an opportunity to venture west by invitation of J. R. Butler, they jumped at the chance. There was a parcel of land east of the Little Missouri River and not too far south of a small settlement springing up that had yet to be named. Their last stop on the Northern Pacific would be after crossing the Little Missouri River to the makeshift town of Little Missouri, where most of the commerce and tent housing was available.

The entire household made the trip, including Lizzie. She would take care of the children, when Patrick and Cille had other things to tend to. When they arrived on the train in Little Missouri, they rented a carriage and Mr. J. R Butler drove them south over rolling hills, past the Custer trail ranch and the Maltese ranch. The further south they rode, the dryer the countryside looked. There was a shortage of water for most of the land. They traveled over a number of hills before they came upon a homestead where Ted and Mathilda Drake now called home. They stopped the buggy in hopes of getting some water.

Patrick called out, "Howdy mister, Patrick Woodbury and family. Thought we'd stop by and get a bit of water off of you."

"Ted Drake here and my wife Mathilda is in the house with the youngun."

"I'm no such a thing, Ted," she directed the rest of her remarks to those in the wagon; "You women get down out of that thing and come in out of the heat of the day. I have cold water inside and I just might have some cookies left over for the little ones."

Mr. Butler was looking at the map he had brought along and was pointing out about where the parcel of land was located.

"I know where you're talking about." Ted spoke up.

Patrick said, "How far away is it?"

With a chuckle in his voice, Ted said, "As near as I can tell, it will be close to 757 turns of a buckboard wheel and you'll be on a ridge overlooking the land for your new home if you go thinking of homesteading. It's just over yonder east of here a bit."

They enjoyed the visit, but the stop at the Drake's was brief and before long they were headed east to take a look at the land.

Before the day was over, Patrick had acquired an application for a section of land consisting of 640 acres and made arrangements for homesteading a quarter section or 160 acres adjoining his homestead in the name of and for Lizzie Jane Betts. They would help her improve her land so that she would have some land of her own.

The stop at the homestead site was long enough to discover that there was a source of water for the property with a creek running through one of the valleys. The property was on the northeast side of a long slope on the side of the hill. The homestead portion set aside for Lizzie was on the northern side of the creek and had fairly level land on which to build a home and have some land to put to seed. When they were satisfied with the boundaries, Patrick suggested, "I think we best head back to Little Missouri, check in on some housing for the night and finish up with the applications."

◇ ◇ ◇

When the family returned to Bismarck, they decided not to move onto the homestead until the following spring. There was the lack of shelter for the family and a house may not be put up in time for the winter months. J. B. Butler still had time to file the homestead application paperwork and then get the deeds back to Patrick and Lizzie. They would settle in and make plans for an early spring trip to the homestead where they could start early on building and furnishing the home place with the items they needed.

A delay in moving west was alright with Lizzie. She was contacted the day after returning by Ben-jomine, inviting her to enjoy a meal at the restaurant and meet his sons on the following Friday.

"Iz gonna enjoy meeting the boys. Iz hopin' they both goes to settin' a good example."

As Ben-jomine stood on the porch, he said, "We's been workin' at the new hotel from ground up. Sometimes they be tired frum unloadin' the wagons of lumber an' brick. But they plan to eat that night, make no mind if you like them or no."

"Ben-jomine, Iz gonna give them my best side," she said, "and jus' what type of work is it you do, as a number one type job?"

With smiling eyes and a smile upon his face, he said, "Me an' the boys have our own contractin' business. Rufus is fifteen and Rupert is thirteen and they both can put out a big day's work, 'cause Iz the main boss. We carpenter and lay brick and stone.

Mos' times I bid the job, an' then others I jus' do the work for wages. But it iz me and the boys, we work as a package."

Lizzie smiled and said, "Not gonna say um impressed, till Iz go layin' my eyes on your work, but so far you seem convincin'."

Ben-jomine smiled and said, "Lizzie, it will be a treat to see you Friday night. Iz it ok to come callin', about six in the evenin'?"

Lizzie responded with a big smile and a nod of her head, sending Ben-jomine into the street with a skip to his walk.

Saturday morning following breakfast, Lizzie went to Cille's side and began asking for advice. "Miss Cille," Lizzie asked, "Iz gots a problem. Iz not familiar as how to go 'bout thinkin' right."

Cille was cheerful and did her best to help Lizzie untangle her emotions. She felt privileged that Lizzie would come to her and open up as much as she had. She would not put the trust her maid had in her in jeopardy. They talked for a long time before Lizzie excused herself and went about cleaning the house, smiling and feeling more comfortable about finding someone who would listen.

◇ ◇ ◇

In November, the Woodburys made a trip to St Louis after making arrangements to see the surgeon once more. The back spasms were more severe, and through correspondence with the hospital, they felt a new technique in surgery might relieve part of the problem. There would be a chance of some relief of pain, and with new medicines, possibly something to aid in the pain killing area.

The trip to St Louis did not include Lizzie, who remained behind in Bismarck for personal reasons. Cille felt more at ease making decisions now, and the children were no problem, as they were well behaved. The hardest period of time for Cille would be when her husband was in surgery. The extended stay and waiting sometimes wore at her patience.

Patrick underwent surgery and was in the hospital for seven days in traction. When he was allowed to stand, his legs were weak. But with therapy, two days later he was discharged from the hospital with no follow up scheduled.

Nearing December, the Woodbury family made plans to visit Monroe for Christmas and visit with both sides of the family. If his parents were unable to come to Monroe, they would venture up to Boston for a few days. They left St Louis by rail over the same tracks they had previously traveled. The children were excited and looking forward to spending Christmas with those that spoiled them.

◇ ◇ ◇

Several months had passed from that day they had first ventured out to check out the homestead. They were now located on a section of land that covered nearly a square mile and adjoining them was Lizzy's quarter section of 160 acres.

When they were in Little Missouri some time back, they had run across three men looking for work. They identified themselves as Joe, Jeff and John better known as the 3-Js. They gave Patrick some local references as to their honesty and ability to get a job done, as a fair amount of the buildings had been constructed by them. They claimed they were fairly good carpenters and Patrick hired them to get the house on the homestead up before the snows of the coming winter came whistling across the plains.

The Crowfords had finished up their contract in Bismarck, moved to Little Missouri, and were deeply involved in seeing that Lizzie was cared for. One morning they came to the homestead and offered their help. Patrick had agreed to the terms and additional lumber and supplies were ordered in Little Missouri and shipped by teamsters to the homestead site.

That evening, Cille asked, "Patrick what kind of agreement did you make with the Crowfords?"

Patrick smiled and said, "They will do the stonework, oversee and do a lot of the interior carpentry of our five-bedroom home. It is to be completed first. Joe, Jeff and John will do the framing and roof along with the outbuildings. In return, all Crowfords asked was for me to furnish the building supplies for Lizzie's three-bedroom house on her homestead because they planned to do all the work. Ben-jomine offered help from the boys when we go cutting into the soil and planting a crop. The field help would be for the boy's wages."

"I feel good about this place," Cille said, "instead of just referring to it as home. I thought it would be nice to name the homestead."

Knowing his wife could get sentimental at times, he looked into her eyes, leaned over and gave her a kiss and asked, "What do you have in mind?"

"I love some of the flowers around here. How about calling it 'Prairie Rose'? That way it says something sweet about our home."

He looked into her eyes and saw how serious she was in her return gaze. Patrick smiled and said, "It is lovely. Prairie Rose it will be and I think it was sweet of you to think of such a thing. We'll have the name recorded on the deed. Mentioning sweet things, I think there is something going on across the creek. I saw Lizzie and Ben-jomine walking hand in hand across part of her land, as if they were making dirt sketches for her house."

Cille said, "Sounds like Lizzie is going to have the Crowfords close by for a spell. I wonder if she is keeping something from me?"

"I don't think they are trying to keep the relationship a secret. I believe in time, they will settle down together. That's my guess."

Numerous wagon-loads of lumber and supplies were brought up from Little Missouri. There was additional help from three new men on the job to help Joe, Jeff and John. Before long, a small-framed, two-story house consisting of three bedrooms upstairs, two downstairs, a sitting room and a kitchen-washroom attached to the side of the house came together. The sitting room was larger than normal. It led to a large porch on the eastern side of the house looking down over a long valley and the land where most of the fields would be plowed. Lizzie would have her room upstairs. Two rooms were reserved for guests, if needed, during the night. The girls shared one of the bedrooms downstairs. A small barn and corral were built before they decided to mark the quarter section with stones for Lizzie.

Over time, the Woodburys had a lop-eared mule to help pull the plow, four horses and a buckboard. Rufus and Rupert Crowford would take their turns in the field to turn the soil on both sides of the creek. Patrick had managed to walk his land, even though he had some problems with his back, as the medicine didn't hide all the pain. He had to use the cane more often lately to control his balance. Rufus managed the plow, as the mule pulled it through the soil for the first time. The furrows at the end of the day didn't look none too promising, but Rupert's cross plowing of the field seemed to bust up the clods. The field began to take on an appearance of being able to stand some seed.

They built a chicken coop, purchased some chicks and brought them out to the homestead. That same day, they bought a milk cow from their neighbors Ted and Mathilda Drake.

Although Lizzie had her own land on the adjoining section, she stayed with the Woodburys until the following summer when a small three-bedroom, living room, kitchen-wash area could be built. She had named her parcel of land 'My Place', and had it recorded on the deed. The Crowfords were on hand and it didn't take long once the supplies from Little Missouri arrived. Rufus borrowed the Woodbury mule and plow to prepare a large garden spot for Lizzie. Then she would be making the move across the creek to satisfy the term 'living on the property', a requirement to prove up on her homestead.

CHAPTER 26

Jumping the Broom 1878

With the house completed on Prairie Rose, Cille was in hopes they would be able to have a social gathering and invite the nearby neighbors over for a house warming.

After shopping in Little Missouri for some items for the farm, ranging from seed for the early spring to food for the table, Patrick began inviting those he met to come out to Prairie Rose. A planned social get-together was scheduled on a Saturday afternoon and evening at the end of the month, allowing those who traveled so far time to return home and prepare for church the following day. With the planned event, pastries, breads and of course, Lizzie's cookies would be available with water, milk, tea and coffee to drink. It was suggested that the hard stuff be kept in the buckboards and passed around among those who chose to take a nip. The social gathering was a way of getting to know their neighbors.

When the last Saturday rolled around, it was shortly after the noon meal when company started arriving at Prairie Rose for the social and housewarming. Off on the horizon, above the elevation of the house, they could see the buckboards when they first came in sight. The wagons seemed to keep coming until midafternoon. Some callers were from the Custer Trail and Maltese ranches that lay north of Prairie Rose. The mercantile owner, the hotel manager and his family ventured from as far away as Little Missouri. The butcher shop keeper, railroad workers and their wives came from a small settlement east of the Little Missouri River. Ted and Mathilda brought their daughter Gloria along to play with the girls.

Some of the men brought along their string instruments, and before long there was guitar and fiddle playing out on the front porch. Folks gathered in the yard and those in the house raised the windows so that they could hear the music. The smaller children played with toys in the girls' room, where parents could keep an eye on the younger set. The older children played in the yard. It was a great get-together and some of the women suggested they do this more often.

As the gathering ended, a string of wagons began departing Prairie Rose and heading up and over the distant horizon.

◇ ◇ ◇

When it came time for harvesting the fields, the Woodburys were surprised to see several wagons coming down the hillside loaded with men. As they pulled up into the yard, one of the men called out, "Mr. Woodbury, we're here today to get your crops in, right along with the Crowfords."

"I'm much obliged. This is something I didn't expect," Patrick answered from the porch.

One of the other men called out, "We enjoyed the social and we thought it would be the neighborly thing to do."

Patrick joined the men in the yard and they began discussing the day's work.

Cille heard part of the discussion and called out, "Lizzie, help has arrived to bring in the grain. I'll join you in the kitchen, because there are bound to be some hungry workers come mealtime."

"Lordy be," Lizzie called out, "go countin' the workers and count on three more. Ben-jomine and his boys is due out this way 'bout that time."

Calling out to Sadie, Cille said, "Sweetheart, go entertain your sister in your room, I have to help Lizzie in the kitchen."

"But I want to help," Sadie answered back.

"Not this time, Sadie, your mother needs your help with Elizabeth. Can I count on you?"

Lizzie quickly added, "I let you help me with the cookie bakin' later, if ya do as ya was tol'."

Sadie responded and said, "Ok, I play house with 'lizabeth in my bedroom."

With the children out from underfoot, Cille and Lizzie began putting together a meal to satisfy the hunger of fifteen hungry workers.

Ben-jomine and his boys showed up at Prairie Rose early in the morning. They went directly to work on the barn they had been working on for days. They wanted to have it completed before the day was out.

After the noon meal had been served up, the men went back into the fields and Ben-jomine and his boys went back to work as well. Cille and Lizzie were left with the dishes, then to immediately turn around and prepare for the evening meal. It was a day of happiness, thankfulness and a whole lot of work.

At the end of the day, the harvesting was completed on both sides of the creek and the carpentry work was done. The men were headed to their wagons to leave for their home place after eating a wonderfully-prepared evening meal. Ben-jomine stayed around to sweet talk Lizzie a bit before he took the boys and headed back to Little Missouri.

The Woodburys settled in for the evening, thankful for good neighbors. Lizzie called out, "Sadie, gets a chair and get to the counter, we gonna make some cookies. You have a choice of which one you wanna bake firs'."

In the process of making the cookies, Lizzie patted out a bit of dough and said, "Sadie, puts ya hand on top, Iz gonna shows ya a secret."

As Sadie placed her small hand on top of the dough, Lizzie took a table knife and traced around her hand and extended fingers. She took the excess dough and tossed it back with the rest of the cookie dough. While making five handprints in the cookie dough, Sadie was all eyes when they scooped them up and placed them on the cookie sheet.

Lizzie said, "When theyz done, I gets one, you gets one, and your mother, father an' sister gets whats lef'." Bright eyed, all Sadie could do was nod her head and smile.

When the handprint cookies were served up by Sadie, Cille said, "My goodness the cookie looks just…just like your hand, doesn't it?

Sadie smiled and handed the other to her father. He said, "Do I kiss the cookie hand or do I get to eat it?"

His daughter replied, "Eat it. The other one is 'lizabeth's."

Patrick smiled and said, "I think I'll bite the fingers first."

Bright eyed, Sadie looked on as she hid both of her hands behind her back, not knowing if her father was going to bite the cookie or her fingers. They all laughed at her actions.

Springtime came early and the mild winter months became a distant memory. Patrick made arrangements for lumber to be delivered across the creek to My Place, as promised. Ben-jomine, Rufus and Rupert got busy working on the frame of Lizzie's house.

When some of the work was slow enough, one of the young men harnessed up the mule that Patrick had and began plowing the fields down below the Woodbury house. When the fields had been plowed, the other would take the mule and bust sod on the opposite side of the creek for Lizzie's garden and her fields.

Making plans wasn't hard for Lizzie because she wanted to have a huge garden, as she enjoyed canning and putting up the vegetables. A large section near the house was set aside where she would have a flower garden. A sack of various flower seeds she had purchased would later bloom and give color to her side of the creek. She let the men worry about the grain for the field.

Patrick and Cille thought Lizzie might change the name of her homestead instead of calling it My Place, but it never happened and it stayed the same on the deed.

With the growth of Lizzie's garden came the hoeing and pulling of weeds. Tending the garden kept Rufus and Rupert busy along with working in the grain field.

Lizzie stayed at the Woodbury home and worked during the days, seeing to it that everyone was fed. But from time to time, she would go to the door, look across the yard full of chickens and the creek beyond to see her home rising up from the rich Dakota soil.

As Lizzie's house neared completion, there was something on her mind as she made her way back to the Woodbury house with Ben-jomine at her side. They tapped on the door and waited nervously. When Patrick opened the door, he invited them in and called out for Cille. They went to the sitting room and made themselves comfortable.

Ben-jomine cleared his throat and said, "We come ta give yas an invite and the news. I found the courage to ask Miss Lizzie to jump the broom with me and she say she would."

Cille erupted with cheer, "Great! When is the happy occasion going to take place?"

"We couldn't be happier for the both of you," Patrick said. "We accept the invitation and look forward to the happy day."

When the day came, the crops were in the fields, and the garden was doing well. Lizzie's house was completed. It stood as an empty shell for now, waiting to be filled with the love of a happy couple.

By invitation, Patrick and Cille toured the house as Mr. Crowford ushered Lizzie from room to room. When the tour was over, Ben-jomine and Lizzie stood near each other and looked at Patrick and Cille for their approval.

Cille was the first to speak, "It is beautiful. Ben-jomine you do such good work."

Patrick added, "Cille and I have discussed what we would like to do and we are asking you to accompany us into Little Missouri tomorrow so we can furnish the house as our gift before you jump the broom." Turning to Ben-jomine, he asked, "Can I count on you and your two sons for help getting the items back to the house?"

On the day following the tour of the house, the Woodburys made their trip to Little Missouri. When the shopping was completed, they made the trip back to Prairie Rose with a wagon of furniture to be off loaded across the creek.

It was near dark when the empty wagon pulled up in front of the Woodbury's and Lizzie came to the door and knocked. She had her guests with her. Cille answered the door and invited them in.

Lizzie was excited, "Iz gots all that furniture squeezed inta every room and Iz a wonderin', is I ta stay here or move to My Place?"

With great cheer in his voice, Patrick spoke up and said, "Lizzie, Cille and I have known for a long time there would come a day when you would be living in your own home. If you feel comfortable in living across the creek tonight, you may do so or you may stay here the night. Feel free to take your belongings from your room when you are ready, with our blessings."

"Your move from Prairie Rose to My Place can be done at your leisure," Cille added. "We will always hold you in our hearts and you're most welcome into our home at any time."

"You mean Iz free ta go to My Place and live there?

"That is your homestead over there," Patrick said, "and it requires you to live upon your land. If we need your help, we'll call on you and we'll pay you for your help."

They talked a bit longer before she went to her bedroom and gathered her belongings. Lizzie called down from the top of the stairs, "Ben-jomine, you and them boys can come and get what Iz got lef' in this place."

Several small pieces of furniture and personal belongings were removed from the upstairs bedroom and taken to the wagon. Lizzie stood in tears as she tried to say what was appropriate and what was in her heart at this time in her life.

Cille cupped Lizzie's face in her hands and said, "We love you and we want to see you happy. Go and enjoy."

Patrick added, "And don't forget, we're just a short distance away if you need us."

Lizzie had wanted a fall date to 'jump the broom' and it gave Cille ample time to try and contact Rahema in Fort Rice. She had written a letter and was in hopes of getting a reply. One afternoon, Ted and Mathilda brought their daughter Gloria over to play with Sadie and Elizabeth and to deliver a letter they had picked up in Little Missouri for Cille.

Mathilda said, "Cille, go ahead and read the letter. It might be something important."

Picking up the letter and opening it, Cille read the note inside. It was from Rahema. It was clear that she had had some help writing the letter and another letter was included.

The first note said: Cille, got your letter, I'll be there before they 'jump the broom'. They say I can catch the train and be in Little Missouri on 31 August. Can someone meet me when I get there? Signed Rahema

The second note was from Catherine Crittenden: My Dearest Cille, Thomas has been reassigned and we will be leaving Fort Rice in September. We are excited about accepting your invitation to visit on the first part of September. We will be escorting Rahema to the happy occasion. She will be going back East with us, as we have grown rather close and practically consider her family. We will arrive on the Northern Pacific in Little Missouri on August 31st. We look forward to the visit. Signed Catherine Crittenden.

Cille looked up and said, “We’ll have company for Lizzie’s wedding. She is going to be ‘jumping the broom’ with Ben-jomine and we hope you and Ted will accept an invitation to be here.”

Mathilda said, “We’ll be here and thank you for inviting us. I hope we can have some of the neighbors nearby join in also.

“I’ll be spreading the word,” Cille said, “and I hope you will help so that I don’t miss anyone.”

“I’m going back into Little Missouri day after tomorrow and I’ll tell as many of the folks as I can. Maybe we can have a big gathering. When is the event to take place?” Mathilda asked.

“Lizzie has it set for 2 PM on the afternoon of the first of September,” Cille replied, “and we have company coming in from Fort Rice. She is sure going to be surprised to see Rahema, and Ben-jomine is going to be surprised as well to see his sister.”

They visited and talked of the wedding, and the girls played in Sadie’s room with their dolls, while the men visited in the front yard.

Ted called out from the wagon, “Mathilda, get Gloria and hand her up here. We best be heading for home; I have milking to do.”

The day came when the neighbors came to visit and do the harvesting on both homesteads. Lizzie left her home and joined Cille in the kitchen to help prepare the meals for those working in the fields. It was a day filled with nearly the same crew showed up to do the work and at the table for a hearty meal at noon and again in the evening. The three Crowfords were missing, as they were building a house in Little Missouri. Lizzie stayed late at the Woodburys helping to clean up the house and do the dishes before she made her way back to her home across the creek.

On the 31st of August, the Woodbury family made their way to Little Missouri to do some last-minute shopping. Lizzie stayed at the house to take care of Sadie and Elizabeth, until they returned.

Patrick used a buckboard that had an added seat attached to it. When they picked up their guests at the depot, Patrick and Thomas Crittenden would sit in the front seat. Catherine and Rahema would sit in the back seat with Cille. The items they bought during the day and their guests’ luggage were placed in the back of the wagon.

The return trip was lengthy, but with the added conversation with their guests, the time seemed to pass relatively quickly. Patrick pulled the wagon up next to the front porch where the guests were invited inside.

As the visitors made themselves comfortable, Patrick took time to pull the wagon near the barn and put the mule in a stall with feed and water before returning to the house.

Upon entering the house, the Crittendens were made comfortable in the sitting room, amongst cheers from Lizzie and Rahema as they retreated into the kitchen to talk.

Rahema said, "Iz come to see my brother, and if ya jump ovah the broom with him tomorrah, I guess Iz done come ta pay ya a visit, too."

Lizzie said "You funnin' with me now. I told you long time back, Iz not lookin' for a man and two hungry boys, but I guess I was wrong 'bout that." They laughed and began kidding each other and catching up on the latest news.

After caring for the mule, Patrick returned to the house and hung up his dusty jacket before he joined his guests.

Catherine said, "Cille, this house is simply beautiful. It's a shame there aren't quarters of this nature back at Fort Rice. In fact, I haven't seen too many houses in Bismarck that would measure up to this lovely home."

"Thank you," Cille replied, "Patrick knew what he wanted and he found a crew that had it built in no time."

Thomas asked, "Is Patrick doing any better after his back surgery?"

Cille smiled and said, "Thank you for asking. He had a second surgery shortly after he got out of the Army and it seems to be helping some. He still has to use the cane, but a lot of the pain he once had is controlled now with medicine. He tries to tough it out at times, but he'll rest when he's fatigued."

When Patrick joined them, he made himself comfortable just in time to hear Lizzie say, "Iz got a tray of them cookies, if ya like." There was laughter throughout the house and the passing of cookies, while telling the latest news about Thomas' reassignment back East.

In the late hours of the day, the Crittendens were shown their room and Lizzie said, "Iz gonna take Rahema with me to My Place and she can help me in the mornin'." As they walked across the creek, their high-pitched laughter echoed down the peaceful valley.

Lizzie and Rahema arrived before the noon hour, had their meal upstairs and made last-minute preparations for the wedding. Rahema helped her get into her dress. Lizzie would remain upstairs until it was time for the bride to make her appearance out in the yard for the festive occasion. They were waiting for her crown.

Cille took a kitchen knife and called the girls outside to the flower bed where Sadie and Elizabeth helped pick out the flowers that would be made into a round wreath crown for Lizzie.

Elizabeth said, "I pick these and these." They were the yellow flowers and some prairie rose.

Sadie picked two handfuls of blue, red and multi-colored flowers, and said, "I like these, aren't they pretty?"

Cille said, "They sure are," as she cut several flower stems that could be braided and made into a small wreath that would secure the flowers that the girls had chosen. This was their special gift for Lizzie.

As they sat on the porch, the girls watched their mother make the small head wreath. The girls took turns handing her their choice of flowers as Cille asked for them.

After the floral crown was made, Cille escorted the girls upstairs. At the door of Lizzie's room, she had the girls hold the crown of flowers as she tapped on the door lightly.

When Lizzie accepted the crown of flowers, she made a fuss, "Iz declare, it be Little Elizabeth and sweet Sadie and my, my you girls do my heart happy. Lookie here Rahema, theyz done made that special crown for my head, for the jumpin' of the broom."

Both girls soaked up the praise that Lizzie would hand down to them quite often and today was no exception.

Before they left the room, Rahema handed Cille the broom that would be used in the ceremony. It was decorated with bows to reflect the cultural folk lore and the Gullah way of life.

Cille took it downstairs and placed it in her bedroom where it would be presented later as part of the ceremony.

Shortly after the noon hour, tables were placed in the yard up close to the house, to hold wedding gifts brought by the guests. A short time later, several wagons from nearly every direction began descending on Prairie Rose. They pulled up in front of the Woodbury's house and gathered in the yard. When the time came, they made a large circle.

About an hour after noon, a wagon came across the hilltop making a silly z-z pattern down the hill, letting everyone know that it was the groom being escorted and for those in the yard to get ready.

When the wedding, took place, the circle of friends gathered closer and seemed to engulf the bride and groom as the ceremony began. Rahema came from behind and placed a broom on the ground a short distance behind them. When most of the religious ceremony was completed, the bride and groom were asked to turn and face those gathered. When they did, Lizzie and Ben-jomine held on to each other's hand as they jumped across the decorated broom to finish their vows. The broom would later adorn the wall above the fireplace in their new home.

The crowd cheered and the joyful couple was well received by those gathered. The men stepped back for a moment as they went to their respective wagons and brought forth an abundance of wedding gifts. Refreshments were brought out of the Woodbury house, including an abundance of cookies and the wedding cake. There was much happiness in the yard at Prairie Rose.

As the the Crowfords opened the gifts, they pointed out each for others to see. There were quilts, pillows, a feather tic mattress, fruit trees, bushels of apples, fruit jars and canning supplies before the smaller gifts were unwrapped. A milk cow was brought from behind the house and presented to the newlyweds. One of the cultural pieces presented by Rahema was something Lizzie could use as a swing basket woven by the Gullah people in lower South Carolina. Their culture can be traced back to Sierra Leone in Africa. And there was an added special gift of several chickens and six guineas. The guinea is a bird that is prominent in West Africa and the offering reflected the Gullah culture.

The visiting continued until the evening meal. It was served outside on tables that had previously been placed in the yard. The crowd sat on their wagons to eat, or on the porch, depending on where they could find a place to sit. Shortly after the evening meal, the well wishers began heading to their own homes.

Before the sun came to rest in the West, Rufus and Rupert got into the wagon and returned to a small settlement east of Little Missouri, leaving their father to begin a new chapter in his life.

Ben-jomine took Lizzie's hand and they walked across the bridge to their home. The boys would become a part of the household, but not on this day, allowing the happy couple twenty-one night times to adjust before they would be welcome into the house.

Patrick, Cille and their guests stood in the yard to see Benjomine pick up Lizzie and carry her across the threshold. They cheered in hopes that the bride and groom could hear them from the distance. When there was no response, many of the guests continued celebrating with music and dance before the sun went down. Then they went inside the Woodbury home and continued visiting into the late hours.

◇◇◇

Two days later, the special guests returned to Little Missouri for their trip back to Fort Rice. The wait at the depot was longer than expected as the passenger train was late because of trouble further west. The Woodburys requested that the Crittendens keep in touch. And Rahema promised to keep in touch with them and with her brother and sister-in-law. When the locomotive did arrive, the guests boarded and waved from their seats near the windows, as the passenger train began leaving Little Missouri and making its way east.

◇◇◇

In the coming months, Prairie Rose would prepare for whatever the Dakota winter was going to throw at them.

In late November, on a morning that did not so much as hint at bad weather approaching, Patrick made a trip into Little Missouri for much needed supplies. By midday, the howling winds across the Dakota plains began to push a winter storm across the frozen countryside to near white-out conditions.

Neither he nor Cille had any idea this storm would be carrying such a blast of snow and making the blizzard conditions so treacherous.

On his return trip, the wind whistled and each flake of snow and frozen particle in the air stung Patrick's skin when it made contact.

He had his hat pulled low, his coat collar pulled high around his neck and a scarf up over the bridge of his nose. The gloves on his hands were nearly frozen stiff as they held onto the reins controlling the only good mule he had on the farm.

Patrick had heard if he let the mule have its head, it would eventually find home. With the conditions so bad, he had little choice but to keep the mule moving forward and hoped what he had heard was true. The storm continued with gusts of wind that rocked the small wagon as the wheels etched their way in the snow, leaving behind little evidence that anyone had traveled this part of the country. The bone-chilling weather was getting to Patrick and he was sitting in the box of the wagon beginning to shake uncontrollably. He hoped he would get home soon, or he may never get to see his Cille and the children again. He was sure some of the items under the tarp behind him had frozen, maybe a few items damaged. He had to find home soon.

Suddenly the mule stopped. Patrick raised the reins and brought them down hard across the hind quarters of the mule. It was of no use; the mule refused to budge.

Frustrated, Patrick made a couple of loose loops with the reins around the hand brake and stepped from the wagon box onto the wheel and then to the ground. He went up front to gather enough reins in an attempt to pull the mule into action. The mule's head pulled back as Patrick began to turn and face the direction of travel. While pulling on the reins, the wind had let up enough that he could see the outline of his barn before them.

His heart leaped with joy. He was home and not more than twenty feet away was the entrance to the barn. He dropped the reins and went to the barn door. The snow had drifted up around the door and he had to find a shovel in a shed nearby so that he could shovel the snow back enough to get his mule into the barn out of the elements.

The wind howled and it seemed that with every two shovels of snow pushed out of the way, there was one that filled back in from the wicked winter wind.

When he left the barn, he went directly to the house. He would have to warm up a bit before they could even get the wagon unloaded. He was cold and every move he made seemed to become more difficult than it should be. He banged on the door and called out, "Cille, open up. It's me."

As the door swung open, she cried out, "Oh, Patrick," as she helped pull him inside and closed the door behind him. "I've been so worried about you. That storm has been howling something terrible. I thought you would get here hours ago. But as time passed, I began to worry. The windows became so frosted, I couldn't see outside and when I opened the door, I couldn't even see the barn. Oh, am I glad to see you."

"Cille, I'm near frozen stiff. Help me out of these things. I need to stand by the stove and thaw out."

"I'll get a blanket to drape over your shoulders. How are your feet?"

"I don't know. I lost feeling in them some time ago and my hands are so stiff, I can hardly move my fingers."

"Move over to the stove. I have just put some more wood in it. I have it about as hot as we dare and it still doesn't seem to heat the house."

"It's bad, Cille, and we'll have to go out and get the supplies from the wagon in a little bit. I have the mule in the barn and the wagon is just outside the barn door."

Cille turned to get her coat and said, "I'll get the supplies, you get warmed up."

"No, Cille, wait just a minute or so. We'll do it together, that way it will be just the one trip and I know where I tied off the ropes so we won't have to waste time in the cold."

Moments later, they rushed from the cabin in the direction of the barn. A short time later, they returned to the interior of the house with the supplies in hand and both nearly out of breath. They had to buck snow nearly knee deep to and from the barn. Getting the supplies proved more difficult than expected, because the rope had nearly frozen beyond the point of any give to it at all.

Once inside, Patrick said, "Let's look at the mail. I saw a letter in there for you. I just stuck it between some of the packages."

Cille recognized the letters from her mother by the handwriting.

Patrick asked, "What's the news from back home?"

"Mother and Aunt Esther have been busy with socials because of the elections and Father nearly lost his seat to a fellow named Cordry Renfrow. But, when the final vote was counted, Daddy had won. Mother was pleased with that. I haven't finished the rest of the letter. I'll let you read it when I'm done."

When morning came, Patrick couldn't see out the windows because of the frost. The winter storm had passed and the winds had died down. But the amount of snow left behind was a significant gift from Mother Nature for the Dakota Territory homesteaders to deal with. He opened the front door, only to find the wind had drifted the snow almost waist deep on his front porch. He looked across the creek and could see lights in the Crowford house and smoke coming from their chimney. It looked as if they had done ok during the night. He closed the door and went to stand by the stove.

CHAPTER 27

A Change of Seasons 1879

The months of winter into January of 1879 produced an enormous amount of snow. The freezing temperatures from out of the north plagued man and animals. The temperatures fell well below freezing and the wind out of the north made it feel even colder than that. Before the yearly thaw had a chance to happen, there were four to five-foot snow drifts that blanketed the ground in some spots. The first storms of the early winter had left snow drifts as high as a man's shoulders in places. The savage winds that accompanied the snowstorms caused severe drifting and drove the temperature several degrees below freezing. When the Chinook winds blew through the area, the top of the snow became hard and crust-like, leaving part of the underlying snow in a softer powdered format.

When the time came for Patrick to make his trip to the barn, the top of the snow would hold him up for two or three steps before one of his legs would drop through the snow crust. The sudden jolt to his frame caused him to grimace as he tried to cope with what Mother Nature had thrown at him. After he had made it to the barn, he shoveled a path back to the house. The snow beneath the crust wasn't heavy, and with each scoop shoveled out of the path, it soon piled up on the leeward side of the newly-formed path.

After drinking a cup of coffee and warming up a bit near the stove, Patrick ventured to the barn where he harnessed his mule to the buckboard and made an attempt to make a new trail to the top of the ridge toward the Drake's homestead. Patrick had made several trips into Little Missouri a couple of weeks prior, stocking up on supplies and provisions for Prairie Rose and the Crowfords, but provisions were becoming scarce.

When he had dug out enough near the barn to know he could get to the ridge line, he would check in on Ted and Mathilda Drake. His mule was several hands high, and with Patrick's encouragement, the two jolted the buckboard through the snow until the trail to the top of the ridge was completed.

Ted said, "As for us, we're ok, but Gloria's been fussing and can't seem to understand why she can't visit with Sadie and Elizabeth."

"The drifts once you leave the ridgeline are piled up pretty high," Patrick replied. "My mule did all he could to get the buckboard out of the yard and to the top of this ridge."

"How are the Crowfords?" Ted inquired.

"I could see the stick and banner Ben-jomine and Lizzie had flying this morning. That is their signal that all is well across the creek. I saw lights through their windows and smoke coming from the chimney. They are doing okay. I'll be picking up some supplies for them as well for our house."

Ted and Patrick made a two-wagon journey for the first run into Little Missouri. As they ventured into Little Missouri, they could see several ranch hands working feverishly trying to break trail across the open prairie to save what was left of their herds. They were trying to get them to one central location.

Arriving in Little Missouri, they found that a lot of the goods at the mercantile were out of stock. The rail service to the community had been hampered and a lot of the goods the store depended on were held up as far away as Dickenson, several rail miles to the east.

They purchased what was needed with each homestead having to go without several items. Their stay in Little Missouri was short, so they headed for the southern hill country following the tracks they made earlier.

When they arrived at the Drake's homestead, Ted waved as Patrick continued over the ridgeline and into the next valley. The morning trail was easier to travel, but was still a task for the mule that had already put in a long day.

As Patrick pulled into the yard, Ben-jomine came out of Prairie Rose and helped unload the wagon. He and Lizzie had come over to visit with Cille while Patrick was in town.

There was evidence of a long path that Ben-jomine and his sons, Rufus and Rupert had shoveled between My Place and Prairie Rose while Patrick was gone.

With the goods unloaded and taken inside, Patrick went about taking the harness off the mule and taking him into the barn for water and an extra helping of oats. Then he shut the barn door and made his way to the house to warm up.

Before he came into the house to shed his winter coat and gloves, Cille met him at the door and wrapped her arms around him, saying, "Hello stranger, can I welcome you inside to where you can stand by my fire?"

Patrick reached out, pulled her in close, and gave her a kiss that left no doubt in her mind that he was not a stranger. He said, "You smell good."

Cille pulled away and said, "That cold weather must have played tricks with your sniffer. That is shampoo that I used on the girl's hair. Lizzie and I gave them both a bath and I had a tussle with both of them."

"Why's that?" Patrick asked.

"After drying their hair, I wanted to put their hair up in braids. Sadie was all for it, but our little Elizabeth put up such a ruckus we finally gave in to her wishes. She wanted to have her hair in a ponytail, simply because she didn't want to look like Sadie."

He laughed and said, "She's getting a personality already, isn't she?"

Cille smiled and said, "Yes, she has a stubborn streak about her. I can't imagine where she gets that from."

Given a golden opportunity Patrick took the chance to tease his wife , "It appears to resemble some of the Hodges traits."

Quick with a comeback, Cille snapped, "I ought to throw you back outside without a coat on for saying such a thing." They laughed and made their way into the sitting room.

Patrick said, "Lizzie, here is a letter for you from the land agent."

Lizzie handed Cille the letter wanting her to read it for her. It was a short note and Cille said, "The land agent recommends leaving the deed under My Place - Lizzie Jane Betts or lose all the time toward proving up. Name change to Ben-jomine Crowford on deed would require starting fresh on proving up." Cille said, "That was nice of him."

"No name change needed, Lizzie. You're lucky." Patrick replied.

"Iz gonna leave as is, cause I done gots the agent letter, say ok to do so." There was laughter at her remarks.

"How's Daddy's girls?" he asked, as they bounced into his lap. Elizabeth said, "I got my hair fixed and it flies when I do this." She shook her head from side to side to cause the ponytail to brush upon one cheek before it whipped around to touch the other.

"Daddy, I had my hair done in braids this time," Sadie said with a smile. "Lizzie said I could help her with making cookies if I sat still long enough to have my hair fixed that way."

"We done whooped up a batch didn't we, Sadie?" Lizzie bragged.

Before Sadie could answer, her father looked his daughter in the face and very seriously asked, "Can I have two of them?"

Sadie jumped down from his lap, shot into the kitchen, crawled onto the chair and retrieved two cookies for her father.

Cille was right behind her and got a cup of coffee for Patrick, knowing he needed warming up on the inside and that it would go good with the treat.

"Elizabeth not goin' ta be bribed, inta somethin' she not wantin' ta do. She had head set on a pony tail in her hair, and bribe or no, she done had to gets her way," Lizzie laughed. "But Sadie, she sho' enjoys getting' her little fingers in the dough and squeezin' and playin' with what flour iz lef' on the end of the table."

Ben-jomine chuckled, "Them iz a pair. Ya not know they be sisters from the way they look or talk. They both gave Lizzie and Miss Cille a hard time, before the hair fixin'."

"I talked with the owner of the mercantile in Little Missouri today, Ben-jomine, and they are offering a fair price for eggs this summer. They will buy as many as you can deliver."

Lizzie smiled and replied, "Iz like that, and wez gonna be gittin' into the chicken business."

With his big eyes open wide, as he shook his head slowly, Ben-jomine said, "I see where iz gots my hands full buildin' a long chicken coop for some layers this spring. With a sack of scratch not too high along with the scraps, some be free romin', theyz jus' might do good."

"Come fall we go and do some butcherin' where Rufus and Rupert can help pluckin' them pinfeathers. Jus' might soften up them rough hands." Lizzie laughed, knowing the boys would rather work with lumber, rock and mortar, than to mess with cleaning chickens.

The couples visited for a while before the Crowfords excused themselves to face the elements and make their way back to their house across the creek hidden beneath the snow that remained on the roof.

Patrick stood by the window and watched their neighbors trudge through the snow on their trip home. When they reached the lowest part of the valley before crossing the creek, the snow had drifted nearly chest high to Ben-jomine who was not a short man.

When Patrick turned to Cille, he asked, "Did Lizzie mention anything personal to you while she was here today?"

"No, but I thought her apron rested a little bit high around her waist, when she was making that last batch of cookies. She was so busy chatting with Sadie, I thought it best to let her bring up the happy news."

He turned to look into Cille's eyes, and said, "I'll have to make another run into Little Missouri before the week is out. The mercantile should have their supplies in by then, and if they do, I'll stock up for us and the Crowfords."

"They'll appreciate that," Cille replied.

"I almost forgot. When I left this morning, I stopped by Ted and Mathilda's. They're having a tussle with Gloria; she wants to come here to visit and play with the girls."

Cille said, "Maybe that can be arranged if this winter weather decides to give us a break. Maybe we can pop some popcorn or make a batch of molasses taffy. The girls might enjoy pulling the taffy until it looks like light brown glass where it breaks or then again maybe not so much pulling, so it can remain soft and chewy."

"That has been something I haven't had in a spell. I remember my mother dropping a bit in water to check the consistency before the pulling would begin." Patrick said, as thought back to when he had done some pulling and eating taffy.

They spent the rest of the evening around the stove keeping warm. When it came time for the evening meal, they gave special thanks to the Lord for the food and Patrick's safe return after venturing out into the Dakota blizzard.

◇◇◇

The spring thaw came with a trip into Little Missouri for Patrick, hoping to get the seed they needed. He would soon use his mule to plow the fields both on Prairie Rose and on My Place. With this in mind, he planned to use him sparingly to make long trips. When he was at the mercantile, he asked once again if the offer to buy fresh eggs still stood. He was assured that it did and Patrick mentioned that his neighbor would have some eggs in the future for him to bring to town.

As soon as the land on Prairie Rose was dry enough to plow, he wanted to get the seed into the ground early, in hopes of getting a jump on the pesky grasshoppers. If they got to his field and ruined it early, maybe he would have time for another planting and harvest before bad weather set in.

When Patrick went to leave the mercantile, he noticed two children sitting on the wooden walk outside the store. They held a crude handwritten sign that offered a puppy and kittens for sale, cheap. After some thought, Patrick decided that a young pup might keep stray coyotes at bay and his barking would warn them of unwanted company. Also, the kittens would be a nice surprise for the girls. He paid a fair price and the children scampered down the street with a veritable windfall of money to give their parents.

With the three additions to Prairie Rose safely secured in the buckboard, he headed home in hopes of getting there before the evening meal.

◇◇◇

As Patrick pulled the buckboard to a stop in front of the house, Cille and the girls came out to welcome him home. They exhibited a triumphant air about them, making him ask"What has been going on while I was in town?"

Elizabeth spoke through a large gap in her baby teeth, "We milked Bessie and fed the chicky, chicky, chickies."

Sadie corrected her, "We did not. Mother milked her and we watched."

"That's nice. How did this all come about?"

Cille said, "We weren't sure how late you might be and we thought it would be nice to have some of the chores done, so that you could enjoy your surprise when you get to the table."

"Surprise? Speaking of surprises, girls come with me. I have a surprise for the both of you." When he got to the back of the buckboard, he lifted out a small box, reached inside and brought out two gray tabby kittens and offered them to the girls.

It was love at first sight and the girls both hugged the kittens as they ran to their mother. Elizabeth said, "Look what I have! My own kitten."

Sadie said, "I have the other, isn't it cute?"

"They are adorable," Cille replied about the time she saw Patrick reach into another box and pull out a young German Shepherd pup. "I don't suppose that is my surprise?"

Patrick said, "No. I thought we needed a watchdog to warn us of stray coyotes and I thought it would be good for the girls as well. I didn't forget you completely," as he reached into his coat pocket and pulled out two sacks that had seeds. One was a surprise variety pack: plant them, then be surprised. The other contained seed for hollyhocks. "I was going to get some Iris bulbs, but we'll have time later for them as they get placed in the ground in the fall."

"Thanks, my love, you know how much I love flowers. You're so thoughtful."

They were all laughing as they watched him unhitch the mule and take Buster into the barn for feed and water in his stall. Before they went to the house, he unloaded the seed sacks and two sacks of scratch for the chickens and placed them inside the barn.

On the way to the house, Patrick unloaded the box of food items and placed it inside on the kitchen counter. Cille's cheerful voice said, "Sit at the table and the girls will get the surprises after they put the kittens down and wash their hands."

Moments later, the girls came to the kitchen where their mother took them to the pantry door. They chimed, "Close your eyes, Daddy." Within moments, the surprise was placed on the table.

Elizabeth said, "You can look now."

He opened his eyes and in the middle of the table were two special cupcakes with individualized decorations on them and his favorite, a chocolate cake. Cille clarified, “I baked the cake.”

Elizabeth said, “I made this one just for you.”

Sadie added, “I made this one special for you. Do you like the decorations we put on them?”

“I love them. My goodness what did I do to deserve such a surprise as this when I came home?”

It was all summed up when Elizabeth explained, “We love you, Daddy.”

As Cille got out a fresh glass of milk for the girls and a cup of coffee for Patrick and herself, there was laughter in the kitchen. They sat at the table where the girls had cake and he had two cups of coffee and a slice of cake. “I’ll save the cupcakes for after supper.”

There was still frosting on the girl’s faces when there was a tap on the door. Patrick answered it and welcomed Ben-jomine and Lizzie into the house.

Ben-jomine waited until they were all seated before he said, “Wez here ta let ya know the good news. Go ahead Lizzie, tell ‘em.”

Lizzie held on to her husband’s hand and said, “Wez gonna have a baby.” Her emotions nearly got the best of her, she was so happy.

Cille nearly leaped to her feet from the sofa, but managed to restrain herself, “Great, when’s the happy occasion going to take place?”

She replied, “Near as Iz can tell, it be ‘bout June.”

Ben-jomine smiled widely and looked at Patrick as he asked, “Congratulations, what are you both hoping for?”

“Bes’ be a girl, Lizzie already feels outnumbered, even if she rules most of the goin’ ons, below the roofline.”

Although the visit was brief, the Crowfords stayed long enough to have cake and coffee before they went back across the creek.

After the evening chores had been completed and the evening meal dishes were put away, they settled in the sitting room. Patrick read a lengthy nursery story to the girls, then came the bedtime prayers before they were ushered off to bed. The rest of the late hours were shared with talk of how they were so lucky and the love they had for each other. They went to bed early.

The house was quiet during the night, but there was a knock on the door early in the morning. When Patrick answered the door, he saw Rufus bright eyed and smiling before he said, “Iz gots ta borrow your mule, hitch the plow and get him down in your fields. Papa say it needin’ done, before we can borrow the mule to do Lizzie’s garden.”

He gave Rufus a hand with hitching the plow. Patrick asked, “How are Ben-jomine and Lizzie these days?”

Rufus looked as if he was keeping a secret, “Theyz slow getting’ up in the mornin’, but theyz doin’ what theyz suppose to. Pappy and Rupert started on the chicken coop and Iz been tol’ ta get ta plowin’.”

Patrick watched as Rufus took the mule to the field and began breaking sod for another year of planting. Both men were smiling as if they saw humor in the other’s actions.

By the end of the week, the soil had been plowed and the fields were under seed. Patrick stood back and looked at the field, knowing his back and hip would have given him problems if he tried to do that amount of work himself. He was thankful for the Crowford boys as they worked in his fields on an alternating basis, and when they didn’t, they worked for their father doing what needed done on their homestead. There would be times during the summer when the boys would be doing building work in Little Missouri. They were good at carpentry and stonework, almost as good as their father.

◊ ◊ ◊

With the beginning of summer, the flowers around Prairie Rose and on Lizzie’s homestead were in abundance. Cille took the girls into the kitchen, and said, “Today, we are going to do something special for the table.”

Sadie asked, “What is it, Mother?”

Elizabeth said, “I want to know, too.”

“We are going to go out and tidy up the flowerbeds and pull a few weeds. Then we are going to cut some flowers and make a special bouquet to decorate the center of the table.”

The girls learned a bit more about weeding as they were corrected by their mother, "That was a flower not a weed, Sadie. Elizabeth, don't walk on the flowers, please. Stand out here and reach in to pull the weeds." It became a learning process, one that was enjoyable for Cille.

Excited about making the bouquet, the girls worked well together but were soon tired of thinning the flower beds and pulling what few weeds were crowding the plants. In the end, they created a wonderful arrangement for the middle of the table. With that task complete, Cille went about preparing the evening meal.

Sadie and Elizabeth were sitting on the porch holding their kittens up close to their shoulders, when the Drake's buckboard came to a stop in the middle of the yard.

Patrick called out from the barn and Ted headed in that direction. Cille called out from the front door and Mathilda and Gloria headed toward the house. Gloria stopped to visit with the girls on the porch.

The two women stopped near the door as Mathilda asked, "Cille, we have to go into Little Missouri tomorrow and might have to make a run to Dickenson before the day is out. We may not get back to the homestead until late tomorrow night. Is there a chance Gloria can spend the night, and if it is too awful late when we get back, maybe tomorrow night?"

"You just leave Gloria here and she can play with the girls," Cille replied with a smile. "I understand; she has wanted to come over and my girls have asked often of her."

The Drakes stayed for the evening meal and Mathilda commented, "My goodness, what a beautiful idea; flowers for the middle of the table."

Cille replied, "Sadie and Elizabeth picked them out today and that is the arrangement we came up with, isn't that so girls?"

Elizabeth said, "I picked out the pretty yellow flowers and Sadie did the rest."

"I got most of the flowers," Sadie replied, "but it was Mother that fixed them in the jar and tied the ribbon on them."

Mathilda added, "They are simply beautiful. This gives me an idea for Gloria and me when we get back."

As the special visit came to an end, the dishes were cleared from the table and washed before the Drakes returned to their homestead, leaving behind their daughter, Gloria. The girls had gotten down from the table and were playing house in Sadie's room.

Gloria's overnight visit was what the children needed. Before bed, they ate a small bowl of popcorn and said their prayers.

In the morning, they talked of making molasses taffy if they were good girls. They played well during the morning, and following the noon meal, Cille went to the kitchen to prepare the ingredients for the taffy.

When the molasses mixture needed to be pulled, Cille called the girls to the table. She gave each of them a small amount of taffy. She showed them how they had to pull the mixture apart and how to fold it and pull again. "Let me see your hands, and I will put a bit of butter on them first."

Gloria got the giggles. She began pulling the taffy, as if it was a game. "This is fun," she said, as her hands became a little sticky.

Elizabeth and Sadie laughed and chuckled as they went about pulling the pieces of taffy they were given.

It wasn't long before the strength of their little arms seemed to play out and Cille sensed it was time put an end to the taffy pulling. It was going to be soft taffy at its best. She took several pinches and made small helpings from the taffy that the children had pulled while the children washed the butter and some stickiness off their little hands.

Cille said, "Girls, if you watch, I will show you what this taffy looks like when you pull it longer than you have." She continued pulling until the molasses became a clear brown glassy finish, and before long it became stiff and brittle. "See it is almost as clear as brown glass."

The children took a short nap in the afternoon as Cille prepared for the late arrival of the Drakes. As the evening wore on, she turned to Patrick and said, "I don't believe they are going to make it tonight. I think I'll tuck the children in bed." She took them into the bedroom and read a story to the three of them, then prayers and told Gloria that if her parents came during the night, she would be sure to wake her.

Returning to Patrick's side, she said, "What a beautiful day. Gloria is sure well-mannered and the girls played well together. Boy, did we ever have fun with the taffy!"

Patrick smiled and said, "The taffy was sweet, but not as sweet as my lovely wife whom I have the pleasure of looking into her beautiful eyes this late at night."

She nuzzled into his shoulder and said, "I take it you're trying to sweet-talk me."

He smiled and replied, "You could say that." They settled in for the night. It was calm and the winds had left Prairie Rose alone for a spell allowing the German Shepherd to rest on the porch near the door. There was a stillness and peace in the small valley.

◇ ◇ ◇

When the dog began barking, there was a frantic rap on the door. Patrick rushed to the door and called out, "Who is it?"

"Rupert. Iz a needin' help!"

As Patrick opened the door, he said, "Come on in, what seems to be the problem?"

"It not be me, it be Lizzie, she screechin' big time and howlin' for help. We go to calm her, then she shout she not need no help from any man no mo'. She snap, jus' get Miss Cille, she know what to do."

Cille joined the men at the door and asked, "Is she about ready to have the baby?"

"One minute she done do ok, then she go hurtin' and moanin' about a hurt sayin', Ooh dat hurt! Then she grabs hol' her big tummy like this." He demonstrated for the Woodburys.

"Patrick watch the girls, I'm on my way to help, Lizzie. If I don't miss my guess, I'd say she has gone into labor and is about ready to have her baby. I'll send word back by one of the men." Cille rushed out the door and made her way to the Crowfords.

The front door was wide open and Ben-jomine was standing on the porch waiting for Cille to enter the house. "How is Lizzie?" Cille managed to say.

"Tiz my Lizzie, she sittin' at the table fussin'," Ben-jomine answered, apparently wounded by some of the comments Lizzie had directed his way.

"Greetings, Lizzie," Cille asked, "what is going on?"

Lizzie replied, "Iz a crampin' big time, and the men in the

house are lost for comfort words, so Iz jus' send for ya."

"How long ago did you have a cramp?"

She thought for a spell and said "Iz not pay any attention to no clock, jus' the pain." Then there was a pain and Lizzie's eyes seemed to shoot fire, "There it go again. Ben-Jomine cause fo' paining me!"

"Lizzie, we'll start from now counting the contractions and timing them," Cille said. "When they start getting close, we'll go from there. Just try to make yourself comfortable and we'll see if that baby is about to come into this world."

Cille got up from the table and put a pot of water on to heat up. She asked, "Lizzie do you have extra towels and an oil tablecloth we could use?"

"Theyz in the cabinet in the hall and the tablecloth is ovah in that drawer."

With the supplies close at hand, she sat down to talk with Lizzie and assure her that it would all end well. Several minutes lapsed and then Lizzie had another cramp.

"The timing of the contractions is fairly close," Cille commented. "Ben-jomine, go to the house and take Rufus with you. Have Patrick get the mule saddled and send Rufus to the Drakes to deliver this note." She found some paper and scratched out, 'Mathilda, if you and Ted can come, we need your help right away. Lizzie is about to have her baby. Gloria can bed down with the girls and the men might enjoy Ted's company. Signed Cille'

No need to be told the second time, the men shot from the house. Cille took one of the beds and placed the oil cloth across the mattress and placed the towels on a dresser nearby. She made sure they had plenty of light in the room and brought in two extra kerosene lamps.

There were several more contractions before Cille heard a commotion across the creek. She could see that Mathilda was on her way. Lizzy continued placing the blame for her pain on poor ol' Ben-jomine.

When Mathilda entered Lizzie's home, there was cheers and laughter from the three of them until Lizzie had another cramp.

A short time later, they helped Lizzie on the bed, and propped up with several pillows, and the waiting began. Cille and Mathilda took turns reassuring Lizzie that it would be over before too long.

The birthing process began and all went well before a little baby boy entered the world raising a fuss from the time he grabbed his first lung full of air. Cille told Lizzie, “Look here, you have a baby boy.”

Mathilda gasped, “Cille, help me, we have another!” The baby boy was placed on a towel and quickly covered with another towel as she turned to give Mathilda a hand. A little girl came into the world raising more noise than her brother had.

Cille said, “Goodness Lizzie, you have twins!” With mother and children doing fine, they helped Lizzie get cleaned up before they had the men come back to the house.

With a voice bigger than all of outdoors, Mathilda went to the porch and yelled out, “The babies are here! It’s twins! Come on over!”

Ted and Patrick awoke the girls, got them dressed and joined the others across the creek at the Crowfords.

Ben-jomine arrived and went directly to his Lizzie. Upon seeing the twins, he said, “Iz a lovin’ ya Lizzie, youz one sweet woman.”

“Oh Ben-jomine ya iz my main man, iz forgiven ya fo causin’ the pain and look what we done did and done, we gots us twins.”

With curiosity, Ben asked, “What say we go namin’ ‘em.”

Lizzie smiled, and proudly said, “Iz gonna be mos’ happy ifin we go callin’ the boy Benji after his father.”

“Sweetnin’,” Ben-jomine said, “ifin that be the case, Iz gots ta name this little darling, Nizzie after her mother. Ifin we go fixin’ names that stick, is they stuck?”

With a smile on her face, Lizzie managed to say, “Theyz stuck!”

Laughter abounded throughout the house and everyone got the chance to see the twins up close.

There was happiness in the valley and before long, there was silence at both houses: the Woodburys with guests and the Crowfords with twins. They all settled in for the night and once again, a peaceful quiet settled throughout the small valley.

Morning came and shortly after breakfast, Sadie, Elizabeth and Gloria carried three fresh-cut flower bouquets across the creek to the happy mother and her babies.

CHAPTER 28

Fall Harvest and Hunting 1879

When the fall months became full with the social and farming calendars running close together, the harvesting crew appeared once again at Prairie Rose and My Place, where there was much work to be done. Cille was so thankful Lizzie was up and about and ready to help with the cooking. In the bedroom, Sadie and Elizabeth proudly watched over Benji and Nizzy.

While Patrick had help in harvesting his fields of grain, he told the lead man, "I appreciate what you men have done. We feel obligated to share some of the profit with the crew from our last year's crop on both homesteads."

He replied, "Our work is extended to those in need. It is our understanding that you have back problems, preventing you from harvesting the grain on your own and the parcel across the creek was no problem. It is our way of helping out good neighbors."

Patrick smiled and said, "With the work your crew did last year, I made a good profit and being a good neighbor in return, we would like to see that the men get a share of the bonus we enjoyed in our harvest last year."

The foreman said, "That is mighty kind of you and the Crowfords. I'm sure the men will appreciate the added money as well. You're a mighty fine man Mr. Woodbury and we're thankful for the Crowfords as well. We're just glad to help out when we can."

After the harvesting crew was fed at noon and in the evening, they began to prepare for yet another homesteader's place in the morning, further evidence that folks in these parts of Dakota enjoyed helping others in need.

Ben-jomine had Rufus and Rupert help bring in the produce from the garden and collect the eggs that were so plentiful. This year, an extra amount of produce would be held back at My Place for additional canning. The abundance of good vegetables was set aside to make the trip to Little Missouri for the grocer at the mercantile.

Along with harvesting the garden came the chore of butchering chickens. It was a lengthy process and the Crowford men did this chore a distance from the house so that the smell wouldn't upset the new mother. Ben-jomine said, "Rupert you fix a wire snare to do the catchin' of them chickens. Rufus you go get the ax and get ready at the choppin' block. Iz gonna get the hot water, in two metal buckets."

They would process ten birds at a time. When the chickens lost their heads, they flopped around in the yard for a spell. Then, held by the feet, the carcass was dipped into the first batch of hot water. Next came the feather plucking. Most of the feathers were intended to be discarded in an empty scratch feed sack, what few missed the sack would be gathered up later. Then another dip into the hot water, to help remove the rest of the feathers. As the chickens were dipped, the pin feathers were meticulously removed. With the feathers gone, the bird was then cleaned. The heart, liver and gizzards were separated and placed in packets for the butcher in Little Missouri. There would be freshly butchered chicken and fresh eggs along with the produce to take to town the following day. When the day was done, there were a total of fifty chickens freshly butchered.

Ben-jomine said, "Iz proud of you boys, that be one good day's work. I'll take care of the meat, yaz needin' ta take the feathers a good distance from the house, and burn 'em, and the buckets that were used for dipping, dump em on the ground, a long, long way from the house."

Rupert said, "Iz gots the feathers. Rufus you be the bigger, so ya can handle the buckets of water."

Rufus retorted, "Iz gots them, jus' 'cause you be the puny one."

◇ ◇ ◇

Prairie Rose became the focal point for some of the social events, and on the first of September, they held another. Several families from as far away as Little Missouri and Mandan made the trip. There were two couples that ventured out as far away as from Dickenson. One of the couples was the Swavinguns. Bjorn originally came from Canada, and at one time was a trapper. Later on, he was a scout for the Army on a part time basis. They were instantly a likeable pair, not only to the Woodburys, but to those gathered at the social. Bjorn was Scandinavian by ancestry, but claimed Canada as his homeland until he moved to Dickenson. His wife Uvonnie was a blond with rosy cheeks and a French-Canadian accent. She was very personable and had the women at the social laughing from one moment to the next.

The other couple was Hank and Arlene Boyer, close friends of the Swavinguns. Although the Boyers had a hint of a French accent, they were easy to understand and hailed from Bangor, Maine, where their family was in the fishing business. Upon moving out west, they established a mercantile in Dickenson.

Cille said, "Mathilda would you give me a hand and help introduce Uvonnie and Arlene to the rest of our guests and please bring others to my attention, if they are new to the social?"

Mathilda smiled and said, "This is going to be fun. Come on Uvonnie and Arlene, let's get acquainted." They went about the crowd visiting and having fun, while Cille and Lizzie checked on things in the kitchen and on the younger set.

Bjorn was dressed in trapper's attire and had a handful of men cornered in the middle of the yard chatting on his trapping days. Ted and Patrick were among those left spellbound. "Ya vant to be careful ven ya go after a bear. Some don't vant ya to be in their space, if they have cubs." He was a talker and when he knew he had their attention, he seemed to stretch the truth.

One of the ranch hands from the Maltese asked Patrick, "You wouldn't be interested in two fine saddle horses, would you?"

Patrick said, "I very well might be. Tell me about them."

He went on to explain, "I have had this pair for over a year, after I broke 'em in. They are about as docile as any spunky four-year olds can be. They're gentle but have a lot of heart. I'd like them to go as a pair and I'd be willing to throw in the saddle and bridle for both."

"That sounds like a mighty fine offer." Patrick said, "what are you asking for them?"

"I'd like to get a fair offer. You'll just have to see them to appreciate what they're like. I gone and met this young lady in Dickenson and I popped the question last week. She accepted, after telling me I had to give up my cowboy way of life to keep her."

"Congratulations, "Patrick conveyed, "When's the happy occasion?"

"Not for a couple of months. So, if you'd like to take a look at the pair, just swing by the Maltese and I'll show them to you."

"I'll make it a point to drop by later next week. I'll have to make a run for supplies to Little Missouri and I'll stop in on the way back. It will be sometime in the afternoon, does that sound ok?"

With an appreciative smile, the ranch hand said, "I'll be looking for ya. I know you'll be pleasantly surprised."

A smaller group of men listened to Hank Boyer and the tale of his fishing experiences, "We went by boat from Bangor, Maine down the Renobscot River to the bay of the same name, fishing and checking out lobster traps. Sometimes we would put in at Belfast or Camden, depending on the roughness of the water. When we had a big catch, we would venture back to Bangor and sell our catch to the market vendors on the docks. My father started the trade and owned his boat. As a boy, I worked with him when I wasn't in school."

One of the men asked, "Lobsters ya say, just how good eating are they?"

"Hank smiled and said, "The vendors paid a good price for them, because the restaurants in town served them up to the higher class. If they are prepared right, they are a delicacy and mighty tasty dipped in hot butter."

"Not seen the like of such around these parts," the man replied.

Boyer agreed, "Neither have I. They are generally served up shortly after the catch. I'd say shipping them this far might be out of the question."

When the music began, the visiting and story-telling ended and some of the wives called out to their husbands for some attention.

Musical ranch hands from the Maltese Ranch furnished most of the music. They were a lively group with guitars, fiddles and banjos and one of the ranch hands had a melodious voice, as he sang. There was pickin' and grinnin', dancin' and prancin', along with a gentleman that called the square dance. The dancing was held a short distance from the tables of food because of the amount of anticipated dust the crowd would be kicking up.

A few couples waltzed. Teenage boys got up the courage to ask some of the shy farm girls to be their dance partner. Many joined hands and sashayed around the yard during the square dancing. Some of the girls flirted and cast coy glances to get the boys' attention. As they paired off, the boys got busy getting punch and cake or a piece of pie for their date. The girls enjoyed the attention.

The smaller children were busy playing hide and seek, running around with a piece of chicken or cake in their hands.

A few of the smaller boys played "Kick the Can" to see who could kick it the furthest and off toward the barn, there were boys who were trying to walk on stilts and some of the girls played hoop 'n' tee.

Rufus and Rupert sat on the porch politely listening to Ben-jomine talking with Vandi Tutu, a new arrival to Dakota from the small settlement east of Little Missouri. His wife Hawa was inside helping Lizzie and Cille. Vandi was an older, soft-spoken gentleman, "Iz gots my roots as far back as Sierra Leone in Africa. Iz come from the village of Kisi, that make me a geezee."

Ben-jomine and his boys listened as the older gent talk of his Gullah heritage. "In Kisi, we used Krio when we talk." He used a few Krio phrases; no one listening responed. "I met Hawa when the slave ship put us off in South Carolina. We were sent to the same plantation house, and when we could, we 'jumped the broom'. When we could go our own way, we come to this land, Lordy Iz don't know why, but here we iz."

"Thank you for the Shukublay," Ben-jomine said, with a nod and a smile.

Vandi said, "It be Hawa that make the basket. Some say it is a handsome basket, like the Sierra Leone Shukublay, it is our gift to another who enjoys our culture."

Sadie, Elizabeth and Gloria played house in Sadie's room and kept a close eye on Benji and Nizzie. Lizzie was helping Cille in the kitchen with the new neighbor, Hawa, as they tried to coordinate the festivities. Hawa was preparing a Gullah rice dish to share with all of the other food.

The social event was the largest they had had so far at Prairie Rose and everyone seemed to enjoy themselves. There was an abundance of food and all in attendance enjoyed a taste of the many diverse dishes from many different backgrounds. In the waning hours of the day, all of the guests made their way home or returned to Little Missouri for lodging. Bjorn and Uvonnie remained at Prairie Rose as guests of the Woodburys. The other couple from Dickenson, Hank and Arlene Boyer, would spend the night with Ted and Mathilda Drake.

◇ ◇ ◇

A day after the social, the Woodburys and Drakes took their guests out hunting. Lizzie agreed to watch the children while they were gone. Not far from the homesteads to the south was a grassy flat land where they took shotguns and harvested several prairie chickens and pheasants

Cille had a shotgun and was in front of the others when a ring-necked pheasant made a commotion as it took flight. She raised the shotgun and pulled the trigger; with a bang the bird fell to the ground.

"I'm impressed, where did you learn how to shoot like that?" Bjorn said.

"Years ago, some of the troopers took us women out on a hunt, while the men were doing their duties. I very much enjoyed learning the process." Bjorn was impressed with her ability. She said she was willing to learn all that she could. He teased and said, "How about learning how to track birds and animals as well as man." She took him up on the offer.

Bjorn showed the women how to identify tracks and how to tell how old they might be. The men tagged along and learned something as well. They paid particular attention to how the soil drifts and the small grasses break while a track is made. Before he concluded, he also showed them how a person could make tracks and camouflage them to make them look older than they were. Bjorn enjoyed sharing the tricks of his trade in great detail. He said, "I can tell ven there be prairie chickens nearby or pheasants in the vicinity, ya just vant ta look close at the ground."

When the sun passed the high point, they were getting into an area where the prairie chickens were in abundance. Everyone took a turn and harvested several birds collectively. After a good day enjoying the hunt, they ventured back to Prairie Rose.

The following day, the men ventured further to the east on the southern side of the South Heart River on an antelope hunt. They took their long-range rifles and did their best to shoot a few pronghorn antelope. Patrick drove a buckboard to bring the larger game back and to pick up a load of wood to use later in the winter months. Only a few trees dotted the land making the hunt for wood a challenge and consequently, the hunt for antelope. They found a few trees that had fallen over time. They were dry and easy to handle, so they tossed the wood onto the back of the buckboard.

It was near noon when off in the distance they could see several head of antelope grazing at a leisurely pace. They traveled as close as they could with the buckboard, then got down from the wagon to set up their cross sticks for a distant shot. Bjorn said, "We need to take aim and shoot almost as one, then reload and fire as quickly as possible if we have time."

Ted was on the far left and would shoot an antelope on that side of the small herd. Hank was next to him and would aim for one closer to the middle and Patrick was next to Hank and would shoot a bit to the right of center. Bjorn would shoot to the right side of the herd. When they were ready, Bjorn said, "Now!" as four rifles roared. They quickly reloaded and tried for their second shot before the antelope were too far away. They were lucky there were seven antelope on the ground. Not one of the men would admit they had failed to get their second pronghorn. There was comradery between the hunters as they field dressed the antelope on the open prairie. There would be meat to take back to Prairie Rose and later to Dickenson. When they returned, they would cut the meat into pieces and wrap it in waxed butcher paper to be properly cooled in the icehouse until the next morning.

◇ ◇ ◇

When morning came, Patrick helped Bjorn pack his belongings into the small carriage he had used to make the trip from Little Missouri. Cille assisted Uvonnie, and between the four of them, the meat and eggs were loaded with care. They placed the meat on a small block of ice to keep it cold enough to make the trip in the back of the Woodberry's buckboard.

Ben-jomine and Lizzie received a good supply of meat in exchange for several dozen eggs from their bountiful poultry business. Lizzie agreed to keep Sadie and Elizabeth until the Woodburys returned from Little Missouri.

With Patrick's buckboard full of wild meat and an abundance of eggs, he planned to take the same amount to the Drakes and unload Ted's share when they arrived.

After leaving the yard, they ventured to the top of the ridge on their way to the Drake Homestead. Ted and Mathilda were happy to receive their share of antelope meat and eggs delivered to their home.

They were in time for a taste of prairie chicken Mathilda had just removed from the oven. She had prepared it to show Arlene Boyer how to make the one-piece meal. Along with the bird cut up into small pieces, she had added vegetables hidden beneath a golden-brown crust. Each had a helping, along with a cup of coffee. Patrick agreed to pick up some staples for the Drakes.

After the short visit, they prepared the wagons for their trip to Little Missouri, before their guests made their train trip east to Dickenson. The Woodburys would accompany the visitors as far as Little Missouri, since they had to get a supply of staples for Prairie Rose, the Crowfords and the Drakes.

The Woodburys accompanied the Swavinguns and the Boyers with their buggies following each other. It was a long and bumpy ride, but before long, the three wagons rolled into the streets of Little Missouri. Patrick reined up his wagon as the Swavinguns reined up on the left side of his wagon and the Boyers pulled up on the right, ready to return their buggies.

"Let's not become strangers. We enjoyed having you and you're both welcome back any time," Patrick reassured them.

Cille spoke up and said, "Uvonnie and Arlene, I'm counting on the both of you to come back soon. I've simply enjoyed having you both out at Prairie Rose."

Arlene said, "Hank moves when Hank wants to, but I'm sure he enjoyed the trip. We'll be back, when? That is the question." Then she laughed knowing he had heard her make the remark. "Yah," Uvonnie replied, "Bjorn he be back, that be for sure. He might vant to track himself back out this vay, jus' to say he done some different trackin'." She laughed as she elbowed him in the ribs.

Hank and Bjorn claimed their share of the meat and eggs from Patrick's wagon at the train depot before they departed. They promised to visit in the coming months. Each family felt they had found friendship between each family, by having something in common, as living on the open prairie.

◇◇◇

With a wagonload of staples on their return trip to Prairie Rose, they stopped off at the Maltese ranch to visit with the ranch hand and to see the saddle horses he had offered at the social.

True to the ranch hand's word, Patrick was indeed very pleased with the horses. The young ranch hand sold the pair and they were tied to the back of the buckboard as the Woodburys made their trip back to Prairie Rose.

Cille looked over at her husband and said, "I dearly love that Palomino. I think he's a dandy."

He looked at her and said, "I assume that is your pick?"

She scooted closer to him on the buckboard seat and turned to look into his face up close, "That would be nice of you if it was." She wrinkled up her nose and planted a kiss on his cheek.

Patrick fell into deliberate silence for a moment before saying, "He's yours. I'll take the roan."

Excited, Cille quickly wrapped her arms around Patrick, gave him a hug and planted another kiss upon his cheek. She nearly knocked him off balance in the seat. They laughed and continued their trip back to the Drakes and then on to Prairie Rose.

When they pulled the wagon into the yard, the girls were at the Crowfords. Cille made a trip to the Crowfords for the girls, while Patrick tended to the chores. The children were busy, off from the porch sweeping the yard with their small homemade brooms. When Cille approached them, Elizabeth said, "We wanted the yard to be clean for Lizzie and the babies before you came home." They laughed as Lizzie heard the comment from the porch and Cille from ground level.

Sadie looked up at her mother and said, "We got to help Rupert bring in a bunch of eggs from their long hen house. It was fun."

Cille told Lizzie, "Tell the boys Patrick is back and we bought some supplies for your household."

Lizzie called out, "Rufus and Rupert, get across the creek and fetch what they done brought back."

Cille visited for a moment with Lizzie and then said, "Girls, it's time to thank Lizzie for watching you and we're going to have to go home."

CHAPTER 29

The Death of Patrick Woodbury 1882

Patrick had made his early spring run to Little Missouri to get seed for the field and feed for the chickens and livestock. When he returned home, he was distant and quiet as though something had happened in town.

Cille knew there was something bothering him, and after the evening meal and tucking the children in bed, she asked, "Patrick, what is it that's bothering you?"

"I nearly bumped into Caleb Masters and Joe Kidding in Little Missouri. I came around a row of tents onto Main Street as they were stepping up on the walkway before going into the saloon. I don't know if they saw me as I passed by or not. I've had a funny feeling about this all day."

"I'd hate to think," Cille said softly, "that after all this time, they are still holding you responsible for them being caught doing what they shouldn't have been doing in the first place. I hope it was just a passing thing."

He said, "Cille, Caleb made the threat back then and I didn't take it lightly. I wouldn't put anything past him. If he would play footsies with hostile Indians, he just might pack a grudge a long way. When he was at Fort Rice, he was an ex-rebel that swore allegiance to the union and agreed not to fight the Army but fight against the Indians. He's what they labeled a galvanized troop and I think Kidding was of the same background."

She replied, "Let's not try to borrow trouble and hope that it was just a quirky chance meeting in town."

"Well just the same, you asked and I told you. I did not plan to share those unpleasant memories with you."

"Patrick, that's why we're together," Cille said lovingly. "We share and try to comfort each other. I know our marriage is strong enough to withstand talking about some of the discomforts of life."

"We can agree on that part," Patrick said, "I was just hoping never to relive those unpleasant memories."

"I'm here for you my dear and I know you would be there for me. That is what's comforting."

They changed the subject and talked of other important things that concerned Prairie Rose.

Early in the morning, Rufus came over and harnessed the mule to the plow to start work in the field. Patrick joined him in the yard and said, "I'll be right down to talk with you."

Patrick returned to the house, picked up his Spencer rifle and a pocket of ammunition and ventured to the field below the house.

Rufus looked on in disbelief as he watched Patrick come to the field with the rifle. His wide eyes showed concern as he asked, "What goin' on Mr. Woodbury? Iz here to work, but ya spoofin' me."

He said, "It isn't you Rufus. I just thought I would bring it along in case we have unwanted company out this way."

With a big smile on his face, Rufus replied, "Iz glad ya say what ya did. Now Iz can go about plowin' the field, knowing you iz the one in control."

"I would like you to take Buster and do the first plowing in this direction," Patrick added, as he pointed north and south, "That way we can retain some of the moisture for the field a little bit better before we go cross plowing and planting seed." Patrick watched as Rufus began plowing. He remained at the edge of the field with his rifle for a long time before returning to the house.

Bothered by his unusual behavior, Cille watched Patrick as he ventured into the field below the house, before she went to the barn to help with the chores.

Before they enjoyed the noon meal, Patrick placed the Spencer back on the hooks above the door, took the ammunition from his pocket and placed them back in their usual place. She thought maybe he felt better now. They sat at the dinner table with the girls, he said grace before enjoying the meal and seemingly brushed aside the odd encounter the day before.

◇◇◇

Cille was exhausted and managed to stay near the house during the afternoon. She did not venture into the fields with Patrick, as he supervised one of the Crowford boys. Being by his side for so many years, she knew something was bothering him. He hardly spoke the entire morning. Each time she looked at him, he was deep in thought and had a worried look on his face. Could the near encounter be bothering him or was there something else?

She was concerned about how Patrick felt. He didn't appear sick, but during lunch he broke his silence and said, "I just don't feel quite right, just as if something is going to happen. I just don't know, but I feel it in my gut."

Patrick went about doing outside work while Cille tended to the chores in the house. The girls were underfoot and she had to tend to the cooking on the stove. She laid Elizabeth down for her afternoon nap and had Sadie lay down with her until her sister had fallen asleep. Then she was allowed to get up.

Wanting to surprise Patrick when he came in from working in the field, she prepared a surprise for supper. Maybe his favorite meal would cheer him up.

When Patrick left to work outside after lunch, she went to the barnyard searching for one of the roosters that had been unruly with the girls on occasion. She fixed a wire snare and before long, had the rooster by the legs. It didn't take her long to take him around the side of the barn where the bird lost its head on the chopping block.

Returning to the house, she went about cleaning and butchering the rooster. When she had it cut up, she placed the pieces in a pan of cold water to wash it thoroughly before she went about boiling the meat in a small pan of water.

While Cille was preparing the chicken, Sadie came from the bedroom where Elizabeth lay sleeping. "Can I help you now, Mommy?"

"You can watch if you like. I'm making some chicken and dumplings special for your father."

"Good, I like them too, Mommy."

"I know you do. There will be plenty to go around. I got rid of that old rooster that was bothering you and your sister."

"I'm glad. He sure done pecked and scared Elizabeth a lot yesterday."

Cille placed the cut-up rooster into a pan of water and brought it to a boil. She checked the meat and when it was tender, she pulled the meat from the pan. When the meat began to cool, she separated it from the bone. She left the liquid in the pan, which made excellent chicken broth. After separating the meat from the bone, she made small chunks of the meat and returned it to the pan. At the table, she poured two cups of broth in a bowl, added an egg, a dash of salt, pepper and a bit of baking powder and began thickening it with flour. When the mixture became thick, she took a spoonful of the flower mixture and dropped it into the chicken broth on the stove. After a few more spoon-dropped dumplings, she scraped the remaining bit of batter from the bowl for the last dumpling. From experience, Cille knew when the dumplings puffed up, they were about ready. Before long, the chicken and dumplings were ready for the table.

Cille spent the remainder of the afternoon preparing the meal, waiting for Elizabeth to wake from her nap and Patrick to come in from the field. Elizabeth didn't sleep long and was soon up playing with a corn husk doll that Mathilda had made for her last birthday.

With the workday completed, Patrick returned from the field. He put up Buster before he came into the house. Dusting himself off before entering the door, he called out, "Cille, it's about as dusty out there as I have seen it. I sure hope we get some rain before long."

"Supper is about ready. Soon as you get washed up, we'll eat."

"Something sure smells good," Patrick replied, as he brushed a few times at the dust on the sleeves of his shirt.

"Sadie, wash up, get those hands clean, then you can help set the table," Cille said. "When you're through, help get your sister washed up for supper."

After the blessing, Patrick said, "Cille, my goodness, you sure know how to spoil a fella. Chicken and dumplings, the way to a man's heart."

"You work hard, and at lunch you weren't yourself, so I decided you needed a bit of cheering up."

"I'll take that any day of the week. Which one of the hens bit the dust?"

"Wasn't a hen this time. That old rooster that kept chasing and pecking the girls had pushed me too far."

"Cille, I was beginning to believe he was the one responsible for keeping the bull snakes from the hen house. Maybe that is what made him so mean."

"Well! I'm not going to let no rooster peck on a snake and then come pecking on my girls. I don't care what he did. If I had known, he would have been served up long before this."

Laughter filled the house as they passed the food around the table and enjoyed the meal.

When the supper meal was over, Cille asked, "Still got that funny feeling in your gut?"

"Sweetheart, I just have a feeling something is bound to happen. Don't ask me what, but I've had these feelings off and on since I had the near run-in in Little Missouri."

She asked, "Maybe we can put it to rest for a while and let's enjoy the rest of the evening together?"

He replied, "You're right, now is not the time to discuss it in front of the girls."

Sadie and Elizabeth crawled up on the sofa next to their father and had him read them a story.

Several of the nursery rhymes were short, so Patrick chose a long story out of the Mother Goose book and before long, the girls were looking sleepy.

After the children were asleep, the tired parents settled in for some leisurely conversation. Each had picked up a book they were reading and would stop and make a comment to each other every three or four pages. It was a quiet time and they both enjoyed this time where they felt most together, doing what they enjoyed. The coal oil lamp on the table provided light for both of them.

They were nearing the time to close their books and call it a day when there were two short barks from Duke outside, followed by a knock on their door. Patrick rose to his feet and called out, "Who is it?"

"It's me Pat, glad you're still up," was the answer from the night.

Without thinking, Patrick opened the door, and when he did, the thunderous roar of two shotguns ripped into the night. Patrick was thrown back into the house with his chest and abdomen ripped open.

Cille screamed at the horror playing out before her. She knew any instant they would come into the house and do the same to her and her girls. Panic and fear filled her instantly. She wondered why Duke hadn't put up a larger ruckus, until after the shooting, then knew that he was a friendly pet and socialized with many of the guests that came to Prairie Rose.

From the darkness that surrounded the house, she heard a voice call out, "Get that dog away from me! Ouch!" as he swung at the angry shepherd. "Mount up and let's get the blazes out of here, Sergeant."

In the dark of night, she heard two horses ride from Prairie Rose as she rushed to Patrick's side. Elizabeth and Sadie were sitting up in bed screaming, terrified. But Cille knew immediately that Patrick was dead and any words of comfort were lost in her throat. As she heard the girls screaming and crying, the only thought that kept playing through her mind was that they should not see their father in this condition. She tugged hard at the large throw rug on the floor, upsetting two chairs, and draped it over her husband.

She went to her daughters to hold them and tried to calm them down. Panic was setting in. She said, "Sadie, get the both of you dressed, quickly." She ran across the house, grabbed the rifle above the door and some ammunition from the drawer. She returned to the bedside to help the girls and then ushered them quickly out the door on their way past the barn. When her eyes cleared, she made their way across the creek to the Crowfords, where she left her girls without much explanation.

Arriving at the barn, she quickly harnessed the mule to the wagon and made her way out of the barn, rushing toward Ted and Mathilda's farm. She raised the reins and whipped the mule at a run most of the distance.

The wagon rolled into Ted and Mathilda's yard and she pulled hard on the reins. Their dog was barking and putting up a fuss as Ted stepped through the door of his cabin with a rifle in his hands.

Realizing something was wrong when he heard Cille yelling at the mule. He called out, "What is going on out here?"

Through a sobbing, screeching voice, she called out, "Ted, they shot him, they shot him."

He ran to the wagon as Mathilda appeared in the doorway. He reached up and held out his hand to assist Cille to the ground.

"They shot who and when did it happen?"

"Patrick! My god they shot Patrick and just rode away. Just a little bit ago." She sobbed as the pain and anguish tore through her body. She managed to cry out, "Sadie and Elizabeth are at the Crowfords," as Ted helped guide her into the house.

When they were inside, they sat Cille in a chair at the head of the table and offered her a cup of coffee. Ted and Mathilda did their best to calm her down, in hopes that their conversation wouldn't disturb their daughter Gloria.

"Ted, they shot him without warning. They knocked on the door and when Patrick answered it, there were two blasts. It tore him to pieces. All I could do was lay a rug and a blanket over his body and get the girls out of there. Oh my, it was terrible! He never had a chance!"

"Who did it, Cille, who did it?"

Amid sobs and pain that gripped her, nearly causing her to double over, she cried, "He never hurt anyone, why my Patrick, he was a good man?"

"Here take some of this coffee and we'll put another pot on, won't we Mathilda?" as he looked at his wife.

Gloria awakened with all the commotion. Mathilda came over to Cille's side and said, "Don't drink that icky stuff, it's as old as yesterday's dishwater. Let me make you a fresh batch."

"Cille, I'll take the wagon of yours back and do what I can at the house." Ted said as he got into the rest of his clothing.

"Be careful when you get into the buckboard, I have the rifle up there some place."

◇ ◇ ◇

It seemed like hours before Ted returned to his farm. When he arrived, Gloria was back asleep and Mathilda had managed to calm Cille to the point where she could talk without sobbing and having wrenching contractions. When he pulled into the yard, he whistled loudly and called out, “Mathilda, I’m home. I’ll put the mule up before I come in.”

When he stepped through the door, his expression exhibited the gruesome scene he had witnessed. He looked at Mathilda and said, “She can’t go back there for a few days.”

“How bad is it?” Mathilda asked.

He grimaced, and shook his head in the negative. “I’ll make the arrangements for you, Cille. I’ll have to go into Little Missouri to get a coffin. Do you want him buried on the farm?”

Cille raised her head and said, “Ted, I would rather have him buried in the cemetery outside of Little Missouri. If it would be on the farm, it would be too close for the girls. I think Elizabeth is too young to understand, but Sadie would.”

“I’ll head over there in the morning. I need to get a couple of hours’ shut eye, before I conquer another full day.”

She said, “You two have been very good for us, but I can’t stay here long. There are chores and things to do at home and I need to check in on the girls at the Crowfords.”

Ted looked into Cille’s reddened eyes and said, “There has to be time enough for someone to go in and clean before you go inside your house. I’ll try to get some help, but until that is done, you’ll have to stay here. Why not get the girls and then come back here where they can play with Gloria and not be close enough to see what is going on?”

Mathilda said, “Cille, you must understand and know you’re not putting us out none. We both know if things would have happened in reverse it would be me at your place. That’s what friends are for.”

“Oh, by the way,” Ted said, “I found the rifle in the buckboard. It wasn’t loaded and I didn’t find any extra shells around the seat or on the floor of the box.”

Looking dumbfounded, Cille said, “I guess I just panicked and grabbed.” Then she thought for a moment and said, “No, I have the cartridges in my pocket.”

“Makes no difference now,” he said, “Under the circumstances I may have done the same thing.”

Upon her return to Prairie Rose, Cille went to the Crowfords, got the girls and made the return trip to the Drakes.

When the Woodbury wagon was gone, Ted went to the Crowfords and explained his situation. Within moments, the entire Crowford family was at Prairie Rose helping Ted clean the house.

Ted did his best to get the house clean. They burned the blanket and large rug, and mopped the floor several times with hot water and lye soap.

Ben-jomine and Lizzie did their share of work while tears rolled down their faces. Rufus and Rupert did what they could and remained somber while taking in all the details before them. It was a sad chore that had to be done.

◊ ◊ ◊

Patrick Woodbury was buried at the cemetery in Little Missouri at a graveyard ceremony attended by numerous friends of the family. There was no time to prepare for other services. The military outposts were too far away to request military honors at the cemetery and there was no guarantee that they could provide men to carry out this request. There also was not even enough time to notify many distant friends or family from back East of Patrick's burial, on this hot, dusty dismal day.

A procession followed the black funeral wagon carrying the undertaker, the pastor and Patrick's body. The first wagon was for Cille and the girls. The second was for Ben-jomine, Lizzie, Rufus and Rupert Crowford. The third carried Ted, Mathilda and little Gloria Drake. The fourth wagon carried the Bentleys, a couple from the mercantile dry goods store, in Little Missouri. Other wagons from Little Missouri followed and joined others that had gone directly to the cemetery.

Filling in as pallbearers were Ben-jomine, Rufus, Rupert, Ted, Roger and the preacher. They placed the casket on slats of lumber across the opening, then the pastor took up his position at the head of the open grave.

Cille stepped up near the clergy and the brief service began. She held on to her daughtersas they shared the grief of losing a husband and father. Others gathered nearby and wept openly as well.

Several waves of ominous clouds raced from horizon to horizon pushed on by a blistering hot wind. The sun beat down with merciless heat, scorching the dry countryside. Yellow prairie grass and sage remained a tinderbox ready to catch fire. Strong gusts of wind forced the tall grass to ripple and make waves across the landscape. Spears from the short yellow cheat grass broke loose and became airborne. They joined the sand and dusty grit stirred up from the parched soil. It swirled and whipped across the open plains causing a temporary dust storm. Whirling particles brought sharp stings to the face and hands of those gathered out in the open.

Cille's tiny frame collapsed and she fell to her knees on the soft mound of Dakota clay. Her hands began shaking, the clinched fists slowly opened and her fingers stiffened, the palms opened with fingers extended, before they gripped into the freshly turned soil. She raised her head to the heavens in defiance and stared directly into the storm and sun. Her chestnut red hair, usually well brushed, was ratty, unkempt and whipped back on her shoulders by the wind. Her complexion, long damaged by too many hours toiling in the hot sun, had lost its softness. Her eyes squinted while she stared, as if to conceal and hold back the color. The hurt she endured forced a steady stream of pain and anguish-laden tears across her sun burnt face.

"Why! Oh why, tell me why!" she screamed, "Why my Patrick, why my Patrick, why?"

Sadie and Elizabeth were weeping and seeing their mother crying added to their pain.

The family's pain was too much for the other mourners to endure as some began sniffling, crying and weeping aloud.

With the final words from the clergy, the mourners each took a small handful of dirt and were about to drop it on the coffin that now rested within the grave.

Cille cried out for all to hear, "He was a good man who doesn't deserve to have dirt thrown at him, not when he was alive and not now. But, I won't say that about the people who did this to him. I hope they get the same treatment or worse. I would love to be there and see it."

"Why! Oh why, tell me why!" she screamed, "Why my Patrick, why my Patrick, why?"

Cille sobbed openly and without shame

"Why! Oh, tell me why!" preceded the internal eruption of pain and emotion causing uncontrolled shaking. Her body wrenched and suddenly seemed to wilt as her face fell from the skyward glare and her forehead smashed into the darkened soil in front of her knees.

Two men stepped forward, each placing a hand on her shoulder, and in an attempt to help Cille to stand, they removed her from the internment site.

Their attempt was met with weighted resistance. With patience, they pulled her away from the grave. Her hands held on to part of the prairie soil. The two girls remained close to their mother.

Once away from the mound of dirt and turned in the opposite direction, she began to relax and stand. She remained under the control of the two men, who tried to comfort her. For those who attended the burial, there was an unusual sadness brought on by the brutal savagery of living on the western plains.

With one last outburst, she harshly screeched, “Why?” Then with her explosive temper, she flung both of her hands full of dirt to the ground and shouted, “They’ll pay for this, I swear it. As long as I have a breath in my body, I’ll hunt them down, every one of them.” With that said, she broke down sobbing, gathered her two daughters and they left the cemetery.

One of the women stepped into the funeral buggy and helped Cille and the children up into the seat. She softly held Cille, giving her comfort and allowing her to cry without stopping her.

At the head of the grave, the reverend from Little Missouri completed the grave side ceremony and stepped back. He bent at the waist and picked up some soil. He stood straight for a moment, remembering Cille’s comments, before allowing a bit of the soil to slide between his fingers, then raised his hands to his lips. His words seemed to get lost in the big gust of wind that stirred up the loose dry soil.

An elderly lady draped in black stepped forward. In her arms, she supported a large collection of prairie roses. She divided the flowers and placed half of them on the casket, reserving the other half for the grave marker later.

When the service ended, those gathered to show their respect began to depart the lonely cemetery. Three of the black canopy-draped buggies began the trip back to town. Eight men remained behind and began the task of filling in the grave.

The Drakes had stepped into their wagon. Ted dismounted and approached Cille’s wagon before he remarked, “We have a couple of onlookers. Anyone you know?"

Cille strained her eyes trying to figure out who it might be. She recognized the horses as military mounts. She began to shake, as she paid particular attention and memorized every detail of the horses. She wanted to burn the images of the horses in her mind.

"Who is it, Cille?" Ted asked.

"I don't know. I don't know who they are." She stared as her memory replayed Patrick's concern.

Mathilda cried out, "Cille, for heaven's sake, tell us."

She still shook, still remembering the knock on the door and the blast. Then she recalled hearing the words, "Let's mount up and get the blazes out of here, Sergeant."

Ted commanded, "Who are they!"

She seemed to come to her senses and looked into Ted's face, "I don't know. I really don't know." She had an idea who it might be, but she didn't want to put Ted and Mathilda in danger.

Mathilda asked, "Did they have anything to do with Patrick's death?"

"I don't know. I just don't know."

There was no need to continue the questioning under the current circumstances. Ted and Mathilda both knew that and showing compassion now was more important than pressing for information. Ted said, "Cille, you and Patrick have been the best neighbors we have ever had. Just because he is gone, don't shut us out. We want to be there to help. All you have to do is ask."

Mathilda placed her hand on Cille's knee, "You're like a sister to me. I love you and I feel part of your hurt. Please let us help, when you're ready."

With sadness in her eyes, Cille looked down from the wagon as the tears rolled off her face. "I love you too and I'll be in touch. I just need some time for now."

With frustration and doubts, Ted said, "We all need to do some shopping, as do the Crowfords. I don't like what I see, so we're not going home unless we all travel together." Cille nodded and Benjomine, close enough to hear the comment, nodded his head as well.

Ted and Mathilda headed back to their wagon. He felt uneasy with the onlookers nearby and loaded his rifle to have it ready near his leg, should he need it. They would follow the funeral buggies back to Little Missouri.

Cille rode from the Little Missouri cemetery in the funeral buggy to the livery, where she would get her wagon and head toward the Mercantile before she went home.

When they arrived at the livery she said, "Girls let me get you both in the buckboard." Before she stepped up into the buckboard, a man's voice called out, "Ms. Woodbury."

She stepped back and stood near her wagon momentarily while three wagons belonging to the Bentleys, the Drakes and the Crowfords passed on their way toward the mercantile store. As she turned, she saw Russell Coby, the self-appointed town marshal for Little Missouri. He was leaning up against the smithy shed and his right boot was propped up against a stump that supported a large anvil. "Girls, get in the wagon," she told her children, as she turned to address the self-appointed lawman, "What is it, marshal?"

"I'm rightly sorry to hear about your Patrick. Why didn't you report it to me? I had to hear of your troubles second hand."

Cille stood rigid, her tear-streaked face became flushed and her eyes narrowed, "When my husband was gunned down, you didn't do a thing to help. Was it out of your jurisdiction?"

"Now look here!" he said defensively. "Your husband's death is under investigation."

"A whole lot of good that will do, we both know that! Who is going to investigate what! I know it would take three, maybe four days, for a courier to make it to Fort Lincoln or Rice, and if the commander is so inclined, he may send a detachment. By the time they got here, a good ten days would have passed."

Russell said, "No woman in her right mind should be living out yonder with kids, especially when she ain't got no man. You should move to town, where it is safer. I'd look after you."

"Marshal, my husband cut that farm out of this forsaken land by using what few tools he could get his hands on. He put his heart into it. I'd rather be horse whipped in front of a crowd, than let his dream die by throwing up my arms and moving into town."

"Just the same, you ought not to stay out there without a man."

Offended by his remarks, she replied, "Well for your information, there isn't anyone good enough to take his place!"

"Now don't be so headstrong to think you ought to go back out there after what has happened."

"I am, because that's where I call home. I plan to get some things together and get on doing what needs to be done."

He replied, "What kind of work needs doing out there?"

"Man's work and justice! Apparently, it's something you don't know the first thing about."

"Now Ms. Cille, don't you go about taking the law into your own hands. If you do, I may have to come a calling."

"You do just that! It best be in an official capacity, 'cause your hide is no more welcome than the smell of a stinking skunk."

"Look, Cille, our talk isn't getting either of us nowhere. I need you to stop by the office right soon and make out a report of death."

She stood her ground, hands resting on her hips. "There isn't a thing to report. It's a waste of good time. You won't do anything about it, so it's left up to me. If you'll get out of my way, I have things to tend to."

He shrugged his shoulders and said, "Okay, I'm not standing in your way. But mind you, don't step across the line. The Army and I have responsibilities and we'll carry them out."

"I'm sure you will," she snapped. "If I do cross the line, you'll be the first to know. I'll toss the evidence smack at your office door." She got onto the buckboard with the girls, left the livery and headed for the mercantile.

Pulling up in front of the dry goods store, Cille said "Sadie, watch over Elizabeth for a couple of moments. I'll be in this store and come right back, okay?" Lifting her dress slightly with both hands, she stepped up onto the wooden walkway.

The door to the store was left standing open to allow a breeze to enter. Walking to the counter where Roger Bentley, the owner, was counting on his fingers trying to balance the books, she said, "I want the best and longest-range buffalo gun you have."

Shocked by her comment, Roger asked, "Cille, what in the world are you going to do with such a thing? Hunting buffalo isn't a sport for such a lady as you."

Cille bit her lip to fight back the tears as she searched for the words she needed to say. She knew what she wanted to do with the heavy, high caliber gun, but only replied, "I don't need any of them culprits messing with what crops I have left."

Roger agreed, "That's for sure. I ain't seen it so hot as it has been. Most folks face the same problem. But this here long-range cannon ain't no toy," as he picked up the rifle and patted the stock. "I reckon it packs a bigger recoil than the likes of which you might be able to handle."

"Makes me no mind. I can pick myself up and dust myself off, just as long as I can hit what I'm aiming at."

Roger slowly said, "Well, if you're sure."

"I am and give me plenty of cartridges too, while you're at it," Cille quipped, holding back the bitterness she felt. "I'll be doing some serious practicing."

"If you get a big bull, are you in need of a knife to skin it?"

She was ready to say no, but suddenly changed her mind. "Do you have a good sharp one that keeps a good edge? And I need a small bag of licorice for my girls."

Roger picked up a large knife, its blade hidden within a heavy scabbard, "Let's look at this one." He pulled the knife out of the leather casing for her inspection and offered it to her handle first.

Holding the knife in her left-hand, blade up, she gingerly touched the finely-honed edge. Roger went about getting the licorice.

Audrey Bentley stepped into the front of the store in time to hear Cille say, "I'll take it, put it with the rest."

In astonishment, Audrey raised her voice, "Roger!" Then, turning to Cille, she added, "My dear child, I hope this is not what I'm thinking you're about to do."

Cille turned to face the older Audrey, one of her closest and dearest friends. She said, "It is and I aim to use them."

As she quickly walked across the floor, Audrey wrapped her arms around Cille. "Honey I understand your anger but let the marshal and the Army pursue the matter. They're more experienced in these matters, and they handle weapons like that," as she pointed to the buffalo gun resting on the counter.

"Look, Audrey, the marshal here in Little Missouri will only help men if it benefits him. As for a woman, he has other ideas. Right now, he thinks I got what was coming to me for living out there. He's not about to take my side and go up against another man with a gun. He isn't that kind of lawman. Some of the Army units that are around here are so corrupt. That's part of the reason why Patrick had to leave the military. He caught Lieutenant Caleb

Masters and Sergeant Joe Kidding illegally dealing and trading with the Indians. I don't know how they got away with it, but the commander at Fort Lincoln seemed to think they were all right and my husband was a trouble maker. Somehow, they twisted the truth. Patrick was a good man and they literally forced him out of the Army after his injury. He liked this area so much he took up farming. They gunned him down; I know they did, simply because he knew too much."

In a motherly tone, Audrey spoke up saying, "Now, now honey, you're just bitter from your grief."

"You bet I'm bitter!" Cille shot back. "They'll pay for what they have done!"

"My goodness child, no one can go it alone against trained men and those savages. "Well," she scoffed, "you don't even know the first thing about it."

Pushing Audrey back gently, Cille reached over the counter and patted the high-powered rifle. "I may not be a match up close, but let them get in my sights and we'll see."

"That's no way to talk, Cille!" Audrey was in shock.

"It is when there's nothing left," Cille softly said. "Patrick and those girls were my reason for living and putting up with this place. Patrick's killers took him away from us. I know who they are, and I swear, I'll get every one of them or die trying."

Roger cleared his throat and reached out to retrieve the buffalo gun saying, "Maybe Audrey is right, Cille."

"Don't make me go elsewhere, Roger! You know I'll get one here today or someplace else tomorrow. You two have been close friends of the family and I hope we can stay that way."

Audrey spoke up, "Honey we are and we're here to help you."

She broke in, "If you want to help me, please let me do this my way. I ask you not to stand in my way. Let me get the supplies I need to get this thing over with."

Moments later Cille walked out of the store. Audrey stayed behind standing in the doorway, while Roger carried the heavier bundles to the wagon. Cille stepped into the wagon and held out her hand as Roger lifted the bundle and then handed her the buffalo gun. Roger spoke first, "Cille, me and Audrey are here day or night if you need us. If you get in a fix and can't make it in, but can send a message, you just let us know."

“Thanks, Roger. I don’t want you two to get into trouble. Please don’t volunteer any information to the Army or the law.”

Roger smiled, patted her hand and said, “Take care of yourself my friend.”

Cille rode off with a quick glance to the doorway where Audrey stood. Each exchanged a a slight wave of the hands. She rode from Little Missouri in the direction of her farm as the girls enjoyed their treat.

◇◇◇

The Drakes followed Cille’s wagon until she turned east toward Prairie Rose. The Crowford wagon that had been following dropped in behind Cille’s wagon before they topped the ridge and rolled out of sight. Ted and Mathilda headed for their farm, each hoping Cille would call on them in the days ahead.

By the time Cille had arrived back on Prairie Rose, the sky had cleared and the wind had settled down. She would be the only one staying in the house as she had made arrangements with the Crowfords for the girls to stay there temporarily. She walked the girls over to the Crowfords before she returned to Prairie Rose to do chores before nightfall.

CHAPTER 30

The Kidnapping of Sadie and Elizabeth 1882

Two weeks after Patrick's funeral, the crops in the field began to show growth. However, the prospects for rain were scarce, at best.

Elizabeth and Sadie remained at the Crowfords while the interior of the house at Prairie Rose was under repair from the shotgun blast that had peppered the wall.

When the Crowford boys moved to Little Missouri they were hired to work on the De Mores family home east of the river. They would be gone for several weeks, allowing the girls to use one of the spare bedrooms at My Place.

Ben-jomine traveled to Littler Missouri to buy the materials needed to make the repairs at Prairie Rose. While Ben-jomine worked on the interior, Cille did the outside chores, including milking of the cow, collecting eggs and feeding the chickens and livestock.

While Ben-jomine made the repairs inside, the girls visited the yard of their home. It was a quiet day, not overly hot. A pleasant stillness seemed to rest in the valley that Cille called Prairie Rose. The girls had a flower garden that needed tending to so they were having fun taking care of their flowers. When they finished caring for their flowerbed, they planned to take some freshly cut flowers to Lizzie as a centerpiece for the table. Cille allowed Sadie to use her good scissors to carefully cut the flower stems.

"I want to have these in with the other flowers," Elizabeth said. "I think they are pretty; I like yellow."

Sadie replied, "We don't need a lot of them because those flowers are bigger than these."

Little sister complained, "How many are you going to let me take to Lizzie?"

"Pick just three," Sadie said, "and then we can use these others to fill in."

"I want this one and them two," Elizabeth harped, "And I get to hold the jar until you put the rest of the flowers in it."

Cille was nearby doing most of the weeding of the bed. She looked at the girls saying, "Sadie you two make up your minds and I'll be right back. I'm going to the spring to get some fresh water."

Duke trotted alongside Cille, on her journey to the creek.

◇ ◇ ◇

Lizzie was out in the back portion of their yard at My Place and had a blanket on the ground for Benji and Nizzie to keep an eye on them while she cultivated her garden. She had managed to work up a sweat. She looked up in time to see Benji with a handful of dirt and a grasshopper as he lifted them to his mouth. She hollered, "Benji, not no need to be puttin' that nasty ol' thin' in yo' mouth."

He saw his mother coming and paused just long enough for Lizzie to remove the prairie critter from his grasp.

She unclenched his little fist, the dirt fell to the blanket and the grasshopper leaped to safety. She lifted Benji and moved him more into the center of the blanket. Nizzie fussed a bit wanting to be picked up as well.While cleaning Benji's hands, there was a thunderous noise. Several drunken Indians came riding into her garden. They rode into the middle of the chickens in the yard in front of her house as fast as they could ride.

The Guinea hens immediately began making a fuss. Two Indian ponies reared and the riders lost their position. They were unceremoniously dumped in the yard in the middle of the racket. The horses didn't run very far and the Indians were able to make a running stagger to get back onboard and head off the property. Two of the Indians in the lead managed to grab a chicken on the ride through.

The Indians cut across the creek onto the property of Prairie Rose. They caught Sadie and Elizabeth on their way back to see Lizzie on their return trip to the Crowfords. The sisters were in their own little world, talking, as Sadie carried the jar in her hands that held the shorter flowers. Elizabeth was saying, "I will hold on to the yellow flowers until we see Benji and Nizzie's mother."

The Indians rode swiftly through the Prairie Rose yard and grabbed the girls before the rest of them rode off through the grain field. The girls didn't hear in time to react.

Cille screamed when she saw the girls held like rag dolls. Left afoot near the bottom land, without a weapon, all she could do was scream and cry out for her girls. Duke raced after the Indians as she ran to the house. Before she got to the porch, Ben-jomine was stepped through the door with Patrick's rifle, trying to get it loaded.

When Cille got to the porch, she took the rifle cartridges and loaded swiftly, but when she turned, the Indians were nearly out of sight. Agony set in, and she cringed and sobbed as she sat on the porch, stunned at what had just happened.

Turning to Ben-jomine, Cille said, "I have to saddle my horse and get my girls back. I'll chase them down and get them."

Ben-jomine said, "Iz got the rifle in my hands now, and you iz in no shape to give chase to no Indians."

"But they're my girls and the savages have them, can't you see that!" Cille screamed.

"Yes 'um Miss Cille, I seez that, an' I seez ya goin' out not fixed to do nothin' but get killed and that no do them girls no bit a good."

She stood shocked, defiant and mystified that Ben-jomine would talk to her that way. She broke into tears and sobbed, "But they're my girls, all I have left. I am their mother and I have to do something to get them back. I just can't stay here and do nothing! I won't!"

He looked into Cille's face, "Iz not goin' ta stop ya Miss Cille. But Iz not goin' ta let you leave Prairie Rose without the fixin's to knock dust out of a blanket."

"What does a blanket have to do with it?" Cille shot back.

"Iz glad ya askin'," Ben-jomine added, "'cause Iz gonna tell ya this much: think of what ya have to do firs'. Gits yaself fixed for the fight, an' then do jus' what ya gotta do. Iz willin' ta help ya get ready for whatever, Miss Cille, but Iz askin' ya to think of best way to get them girls back. It be too late to ride out all shook-up and unready to do."

With a look in the direction the Indians had gone, Cille saw Duke returning to Prairie Rose.

There was a long pause before Cille said, "Okay Ben-jomine, I understand. I'll get things packed, but I'm leaving first thing in the morning.

"Now Lizzie's got lunch fixed and we'z gonna go to the house, and eat. We can talk about what ya have to do and I help all I know."

Holding her head high with unbending pride and through tears of anguish, she said, "Thanks for the shake-up. Maybe I needed that."

Her neighbor said, "Come with me and let's see what Lizzie has in the pot." They walked across the yard, across the creek and into the Crowford house for the noon meal.

Lizzie was about as mad as anyone could be and she was ready to voice her disgust about the Indians to the first person to listen to her. When she found out the Indians had kidnapped Sadie and Elizabeth, she was silent. A cry from deep within crowded her voice as she said, "Oh, Miss Cille, Iz sorry, I not know."

"Can I ask that you do the chores on Prairie Rose," Cille asked, "for a couple of days, until I come back? The cow will need milking, the chickens tended to and the rest of the stock fed and watered. Don't worry about the crops in the field."

Ben-jomine said, "Iz gonna take care of it. You jus' take care of Miss Cille and Iz hopin' them girls comes back with you."

◇ ◇ ◇

Cille went back to Prairie Rose after lunch and prepared for the early morning departure. To familiarize herself with the new rifle and the others, she spent part of the afternoon doing some serious target shooting in the valley below the house. As she kept shooting, she thought of the day when Bjorn tried to teach her how to track. She mentally reviewed all he had said and hoped that she remembered how to do the tracking, because her precious daughters depended on her.

She grabbed the buffalo gun, Patrick's rifle and a large amount of ammo. As she cut across the yard and down a narrow-beaten path near the creek bottom, she could hear a stray meadowlark calling for a mate, her cow off in the distance and the racket set up by a small flock of magpies.

She spent the rest of the day sending thunderous volleys down the small valley. When the shooting started, the birds left, resulting in a deadly quiet between rounds. The weight of the buffalo gun was more than a match for Cille. She rested the heavy barrel on a jagged stump of dead cedar that had been struck by lightning. By comparison, Patrick's rifle was lighter, and easier to handle.

With each round, she took careful aim at a target. She wanted to know the guns and understand where her shot would land. With the second round fired, she misjudged the kick. Her thumb rested across the stock and banged into her cheekbone. She grimaced and reloaded. The next round, she kept her thumb to the side and rolled with the punch. The rest of the day progressed, with Cille being amazed at the distance each shot would carry. She was even more surprised at the accuracy of her shots when she concentrated. Within a short time, the air filled with the smell of gunpowder. After firing a few rounds, she adjusted the long rear sight and fired at another target further down the sloping valley. With each setting on the rear sight, she made a mental note where each shot fell.

Ending her practice, she cradled the heavy guns in her arms and headed up the narrow path. She could feel the bruising caused from the kick. Her right shoulder beneath her calico dress was tender, making her right arm feel heavy and nearly useless. Her cheekbone was swollen and the side of her face felt puffy and tender.

Upon returning to the house, she placed the heavy weapons on the table. She went to the far corner of the room and knelt in front of a chest. When she lifted the lid to the heavy trunk, the hinges squeaked. She shuffled the contents until she had found what she wanted, taking pride and care with each item.

The first to be removed was her husband's cavalry saber and sheath. She placed it on the floor, between her knees and the chest. Then she removed the military revolver and gun belt. These she placed near her right side. In the corner of the chest, under folded clothing, she found a box of cartridges and a single adjustable field telescope. She turned and pointed it across the room, adjusting it to her sight. She thought how beneficial it would have been to her when she was shooting. She laid the shells and the scope next to the revolver.

Two bright objects in the corner of the trunk caught her eye. She reached for them and pulled out two academy insignias given to her husband the day he graduated from the academy at West Point. Her eyes filled with tears while she held them next to her bosom. She wept and called out his name, "Pat, oh Patrick." The tears flowed for a moment, before she placed the emblems aside on the floor. Her hands were shaking and the buildup of emotions was nearly ready to overcome her.

She reached into the chest once more and removed two handmade dresses belonging to Sadie and Elizabeth. She slowly closed the lid to the chest and got to her feet. The items she removed from the chest were placed in the seat of a chair at the table. She removed her black dress from the chest and loosely draped it over the back of a chair.

After standing, she wrapped her husband's gun belt around her waist. The last hole in the belt didn't come close to fitting. She walked over to the edge of the small iron stove near a small chest where an occasional block of ice was stored. She took the ice pick and punched two holes in the leather belt with the aid of the edge of the stove. She tried the belt on once more and was satisfied when the revolver felt comfortable on her hip.

Upon hearing an approaching wagon, she went to the door when it pulled into the yard. Opening the door, she could see Ted and Mathilda Drake.

Ted yelled from the wagon seat, "Thought we would stop by to see if you're all right."

Mathilda jumped down from the wagon holding a small basket in her hand. "Cille, this isn't much, but we thought a bit of food would do you some good. We both figured you wasn't eating right today and we heard a thunderous amount of shooting over this way."

Cille couldn't speak clearly and cried out, "They rode in here and kidnapped my girls."

Ted said, "Who did what?"

"There was about a dozen Indians," Cille said, agonizingly, "They wreaked havoc in the Crowfords yard, then came across the creek, swooped up Sadie and Elizabeth from the yard, and cut a trail through the grain field."

Mathilda asked, "When did this happen?"

"They were here about noon," Cille said, "Ben-jomine stopped me from saddling up right away and going after them."

"Glad to hear that," Ted said, "you're no match for them, Cille."

"I am, too!" Cille shot back," I'm not going out ill prepared, as I could have. That was me practicing and getting a handle on that buffalo gun. I'm leaving as soon as I can in the morning."

"Cille, my goodness young lady," Mathilda pleaded. "I know your pain must be running wild, but listen to us. This is no way to go about trying to get your girls back. You're just one person. Please don't go out. Ted will get some others to go and give chase to see if he can get them back, won't you Ted?"

"Give me a day," Ted said, "and I'll have a handful of riders to go with me and we'll do our best to bring the girls back."

With pleading eyes, Cille looked at them and said, "Ted, you have a wife and child to take care of. I can't ask that of you. I have nothing to remain here for. Patrick is gone and now they have taken away all that I live for. It is my fight and I'm ready to leave in the morning, so please don't stop me from what I have to do."

"But Cille…" Ted began before she stopped him.

"I've got to do this, can't you see," Cille said, "it's my girls, and if I can't bring them back alive, I still plan on bringing them back one way or the other. They'll pay for what they have put the girls through and what they have put me through. Please just let me do this my way and allow me to go with your blessings and prayers."

The Drakes stood silent with sympathy in their hearts as they nodded. Mathilda said, "Our prayers will be said and our love goes with you. Please be careful and return to us. We'll hope and pray that the girls will be with you."

Ted reached out and pulled Cille close for a reassuring hug, and whispered, "Take care, my friend."

Mathilda wrapped her arms around Cille and whispered, "You're like a sister to me and I mean that. I'd hate to lose a sister, so please don't take chances. My heart goes out to you; I'll be praying."

Cille looked at the both of them and said, "You both have been such good neighbors. I'll be back or die trying to get my girls. I do love the both of you."

He looked at his wife and said, "Woman, it's time we get along. There isn't much daylight left and I have chores.

The wagon pulled from the yard and Cille went to the barn to care for her horse Dublin, Pat's horse Champ and the mule Buster. Before leaving the barn, she took several cans of chicken feed and scattered it around in the barn. She went to the coop, opened the door and left ample feed for the layers. When she walked back toward the house from the barn, she tossed the can aside and picked up the saddlebag. She carried it in one hand and in the other, the basket the Drakes had left behind.

When she stepped into the house, she dropped the saddlebag on the floor and placed the basket on the table. She lit the oil lamp before replacing the dingy globe. The interior of the house came into full view from the light. She sat at the end of the table and ate from the basket Mathilda had given her.

Fighting back tears of mixed emotion and bitterness, she began to prepare for the next day. She pulled her black dress from the back of the chair and folded it neatly, placing it at the corner of the table. She took the small dresses and placed them on the black dress, not knowing if she would be dressing her girl's bodies later. She held on to the military academy emblems for a moment before resting them on the dresses. With the string that bound her earlier purchase, she tied the bundle together after one last fold. The remaining string she poked with her finger into the folds. Cille was careful to make sure the tightly tied bundle would fit into one of the saddlebags.

She went about collecting dry food items, filling a canteen and preparing a bed roll. She set aside a pair of pants, a blouse and a jacket for her ride. When she felt ready for the next day, she blew out the light and went to bed.

CHAPTER 31

The Ride Out Alone 1882

The night was short lived and Cille awoke to see the dawn give first light to the narrow valley. Gone was the security of having a family that until recently was growing together. The warmth of Patrick's body next to her was gone as were the early morning cries from Sadie or Elizabeth, complaining the other had stolen more blanket than she should have during the night.

Wasting no time gathering her belongings, she crawled into a pair of buckskin-colored trousers, a faded yellow blouse and a thin buckskin jacket. One change of clothing is all she allowed; a small bed roll wrapped around the change of clothing. The saddlebag became her traveling dresser and chest one side containing her black dress of mourning, the dresses belonging to her daughters and Patrick's US military academy insignias, and in the other, a supply of ammunition. A draw string sack containing food and utensils lay on the floor near the door. The two canteens banged together giving off a hollow shallow sound before she started filling each with water using the dipper in the kitchen. What water missed the throat of the canteen, it spilled into a shallow pan resting on the right side of the stove. Taking her time, she filled each canteen to overflowing. Trying to remember all she had to do, she realized that her horse would need water before they left the farm and Duke would need to be fed. She rested her husband's rifle, military saber and telescopic field glass on the table near the buffalo gun and the large knife she had purchased. She placed her husband's gun belt around her waist. She drew it up tight, catching the tongue of the buckle in one of the holes she had punched with an ice pick.

She went to the icebox for a quick drink of milk, but this only brought out the lack of attention to detail in her life. Without ice, in the wooden box, the milk had curdled and was rancid, disquieting her senses when she opened the lid. She quickly closed the box in disgust and despair. Fishing around inside the basket Ted and Mathilda had left Cille tried to balance a dipper of water in one hand in an attempt to satisfy her thirst and without spilling some down her front. She grabbed at one of the larger pieces of bread fried in grease and lightly sprinkled with sugar. She smiled thinking of Mrs. Drake, knowing her dear friend and neighbor had spent a lot of time in front of a hot stove to make the tasty treat, remembering Mathilda had called the bread dough-bra-gots. After finishing what was left in the basket, she washed it down with a swallow of the remaining water from the dipper.

Stepping from the house, she set out a pan of food for Duke before their long journey. She slowly closed the door then made her way to the barn. What few chickens that remained loose had taken up refuge in the barn claiming the oat bin or hay trough where nesting was good. They chose whatever rafter they could flutter to in an attempt to stay free of the marauding coyotes. They always came calling late in the night. When she opened the door, the hens fluttered from their perches and onto the ground, loose feathers, dirt and grit filled the air. The squawking clatter got on Cille's raw nerves . She was definitely unprepared for the racket that filled the empty barn and the early morning hours suddenly lost the quiet peaceful tranquility within the small valley.

Going about the chores of saddling Dublin, she thought of what lay ahead. Her thoughts wandered from past events to visions of future encounters. When the horse was prepared to ride, she collected the reins in her hand and led the horse to the woodpile near the door of the woodshed.

She took the saddle bags first, and with the assistance of an old stump, she stepped up and tossed them across the back of the saddle leaving enough leather strapping to tie down her bed roll. The bedroll was larger than expected with her change of clothing rolled up inside; there was just enough leather to secure the bedroll. Returning to the house, she picked up the saber, Patrick's rifle and the buffalo gun in its sheath. The saber she dangled from the saddle horn, resting on the left side of her mount. The buffalo gun rested on the right side of her mount, with the butt of the stock sticking up near the saddlebag. Pat's military carbine rested in a sheath beneath the right stirrup.

Returning to the house once more, she took the skinning knife, placed it on the pistol belt and carried it on her left side. The field glass she stuck between the gun belt and her body. She picked up the large drawstring sack of goods and utensils. It was heavier than she thought. Tugging at the sack, with a struggle, she managed to get it near the stump. The sack was placed on the right side of the mount and then drawn up close to the saddle horn resting on top of the lariat. Half out of breath, she returned to the house, collected a swig of water from the dipper, reached over onto the table and grabbed the two canteens. She looped the canteens straps over the saddle horn and allowed them to dangle on the left side of her mount.

Taking the reins, she led her horse to the nearby creek for a drink of water. Considering her first course of action, she decided on following the hoof prints the Indian ponies had left the day before. She knew they were old and possibly of no help, but then again, they would give her a sense of direction for her to work from. She also realized the weather may have erased some of the trail, but she had to try. She took Duke to the field and talked to him as if he could listen, pointed in the direction the Indians had ridden. The German Shepherd seemingly understood every word. He sensed that they were going after the girls and he was ready.

Cille led Dublin to the old stump once more, where she could use the block of wood to help her get into the saddle.

Before swinging up, she said, "Dublin, let's see if there is room enough for me up there." She swung into the saddle and headed out across the countryside. The tracks marked a trail that headed southeast from Prairie Rose. Duke took the lead and at times was a good distance ahead before he would turn around and wait. It wasn't long before the tracks were lost because of the wind filling them in with dust and loose soil. She couldn't make out the tracks, but Duke was wise and kept his nose close to the ground, sniffing out a scent. Following the same general direction, they picked up some tracks at the base of some rim rock. Those few tracks also seemed to disappear thanks to Mother Nature, but Duke moved forward.

At the crest of each hill, she would pull up her mount. Taking the telescopic field glass in hand, she scoured the harsh landscape. For a time, she felt she was the only moving part on the countryside.

Using the field glass, she picked out her route from the crest of one hill to the valley floor and up the side of yet another hill. Parts of the valley floor were filled with dirt canyons of varied depths. At times, the going was slow and arduous. Duke slowed and eventually moved forward, as if knowing something she didn't.

It was near dusk when she reached the crest of a high ridge. From where she sat, she could see for miles. Searching the countryside bluffs, hillsides and the distant flatland, she could see a cavalry unit on patrol. It was too far for gunshot to get their attention and too far to reach before nightfall. The rest of the countryside lay still with a few birds chirping and the hawks circling high overhead and off in the distance.

Riding a short distance near some rim rock, she came upon a large overhang. She pulled up when Duke turned and barked. When she got down from the saddle, she looked at the markings in the soil. The Indians had stopped there for a spell. She looked at Duke as he whined while sniffing near an area that showed markings of her children. In the dust, she could tell that their hands and feet had been bound. She was angry at what she saw, but so proud of Duke for leading her here and finding this spot. They made a cold camp for the first night.

The following morning, she scanned the rugged terrain once more trying to plan a path through the choppy dirt canyons. Satisfied with the new course Duke seemed to lead her on, they descended from the high crest.

Near midday, after riding out of a deep dirt ravine, fear gripped her. She reined up quickly, seeing Duke hover close to the ground, as if telling her something. She dismounted quickly, realizing there was scarcely enough prairie grass and dry twigs to conceal her presence.

A large group of Indians rode by at a high gallop. Her first impression was that the group was being chased down by the unit of the 7th cavalry.

When the dust settled around her, she stood up on a mound of dirt to see if there were additional riders. There were none, so she mounted being very cautious as she and Duke pressed on.

At the top of the next ridge, she discovered why the Indians were travelling at top speed. They were riding hard to join others and engage a small immigrant wagon train off in the distance. From her vantage point, she could see three large groups of Indians converging on a small group of wagons. Viewing the clash, she could see Indians fall long before the shot could be heard. It didn't take long for the Indians to converge and wipe out the small group of travelers.

All the Indians stayed around the battle site for a short time rummaging through some of the immigrant's belongings before they slowly rode off with their dead and wounded.

The detail in the telescope was unclear as Cille strained to see more. All she could see was the scattered wagons and bodies on the landscape. Dead horses, as well as men, dotted the small patch of open ground.

She turned her mount and continued her course away from the nest of Indians. She rode into the dirt canyon and travelled for some distance before finding a cut in the high banks that would allow her mount to carry her from the dust-sunken pit.

Finding herself out in the open, she feared being spotted before she would have a chance to find cover. Her mount was snorting and breathing hard, but responded when she quickened the pace. Few trees dotted the landscape and she was fortunate to find a small clump of cedar near the crest of a ridge.

Her fears were reduced when she scoured the countryside from which she had just traveled. She was not being followed. Taking time to clear her mind and gather her thoughts, she dismounted for a spell to give Dublin a much-needed break.

For the next few days, Cille rode the countryside searching for answers. Duke was doing his best and at times, she wondered if he had lost their trail. How was she ever going to accomplish what she had set out to do? At one point, she was almost discovered by the Indians, adding another obstacle to her seemingly impossible journey. She realized that she must not only be the hunter, but avoid being the hunted.

The irony was not lost on her that she was asking a dog to lead her to the Indians, yet she hadn't seen any trail where she could use her knowledge that Bjorn had taught her.

It was late one afternoon on the fourth day out, halfway between Black Butte to the east and the Cannonball River to the southwest. Cille rode atop a ridge, concealed herself near two trees and a scanty patch of brush. She took the field glass and began her systematic sweep of the rugged terrain.

Suddenly through the glass, she saw eleven Indian ponies, two belonging to the 7th cavalry and a wagon drawn by a team of horses. At the rear of the wagon stood eleven Indians, a lieutenant, a sergeant, a civilian and her two daughters.

Several of the Indians were mistreating an Indian woman. They were offering her up in trade to the white men for additional booze, beyond what the small bundle of pelts had drawn and trying to barter a price for the two children.

A filthy whiskey peddler appeared to be the most interested in the woman, but it was unclear what his intentions were for her daughters as he helped two of the Indians tie the Indian maiden down near the rear of the wagon. The woman was kicking and screaming before one of the Indians cuffed her hard across the face. She fell to the ground silent. They finished binding her arms and legs.

Blood pumping with resentment and anger, Cille hated seeing this form of treatment. She clinched her teeth so tightly, her face began to shake as she tried to control her temper. She raised the glass to get a clear focus in her mind of the Indian ponies and their markings. She focused in on each Indian, trying to collect facial features and dress, anything that would identify them later on.

The drinking began at the end of the wagon. Fur pelts were stacked next to the barrels of booze. Cille figured the Indians must have bought the fire water in exchange for the furs and possibly the woman and her girls.

Cille studied the lieutenant and the sergeant very closely, including their mounts. She searched her mind trying to remember who had threatened her husband. The names would not come to her.

While studying the civilians, Cille wasted little time. They would get their medicine, if she had to chase their wagons down to get them. She would first pursue the lieutenant, her primary target.

As the drinking began in earnest, Cille continued studying each person in detail. Seeing enough, she dismounted. She took the sack of utensils and canteens from the saddle horn and dropped them to the ground. She pulled the heavy buffalo gun from its sheath. Reaching into the saddlebag she collected extra cartridges.

Resting the heavy gun on the lower limb of a tree, she looked down the lengthy barrel. It was a long shot at best. Adjusting the rear sight and estimating her distance, she took aim. She waited too long to pull the trigger, causing her eyes to become blurry.

Raising her head from the stock, she wiped her eyes. She looked down the barrel and lined up the sight on the lieutenant. She pulled the trigger. The high-powdered gun roared, rocking her backwards. The shot fell short and she quickly adjusted the back sight. Confusion had broken loose at the small gathering, as each raced for their horses. The civilian jumped up onto the wagon seat, frantically whipping the reins, leaving the Indian woman bound in the dirt and the girls behind.

Cille, overcome with fear and disappointment, became angry and tried for the lieutenant once more. He had made it to the saddle of his mount. Taking quick aim, she pulled the trigger once more. The gun rocked her back hard, as she saw the lieutenant blown from his horse.

In disbelief, the sergeant once mounted, dismounted, seeing the lieutenant fall. Then he suddenly mounted and rode away at a high gallop. The drunken Indians were physically slow in mounting. They seemed disoriented, wondering which way to ride.

When the Trader's wagon, moved away, Cille reloaded and fired at the civilian. She missed the man, but hit one of the horses. It fell and the other horse was thrown to the ground as the wagon upended, also tossing the civilian to the ground.

The Indians grabbed the young girls and rode down the valley. Cille quickly reloaded and mounted Dublin. She dug her heels in and he responded galloping, along the near smooth crest of the hill. Her horse was slowly gaining on the Indians. She remained on the hill, parallel with the sobering ten.

From the valley below, Cille rode with the evening sun behind her. Her rich chestnut red hair bounced in the air. From where the Indians were, her hair looked as if it was on fire. This struck fear into the scampering Indians, and they suddenly changed direction riding for cover in a dirt canyon. She could see her girls held by the Indians as they raced toward the ravine.

Cille gave pursuit, but before she could gain enough ground to consider another shot, they disappeared into the canyon. She was as wild as a cat in a frenzy after her prey, but aware of any impending danger.

Riding up to the mouth of the ravine, Cille threw caution to the wind and rode inside. The darkness of the deep shadows enveloped her. She rode a short distance further before pulling her mount to a stop.

Before leaving the ravine, she suddenly caught sight of one of the Indians riding his pony up the steep loose soil.

Dismounting, she rested the barrel of the heavy buffalo gun on a large boulder. After a quick sight adjustment, she aimed and fired. The kick brought excruciating pain to her shoulder. The pain jerked tears loose, but not before seeing the Indian blown from his horse. His body tumbled down the steep embankment.

Lifting the buffalo gun, she felt the painful bruise on her right shoulder. She placed the heavy gun back into the sheath.

Being careful when she mounted, the pain was tolerable. She pulled the revolver from its holster, took the reins in her left hand and rode forward cautiously with her right arm resting in her lap.

She rode up to the Indian, making sure he was dead. Dismounting, she removed the lariat from the saddle after she holstered the revolver. She made a loop, working it around the Indian's feet. Then she heard her Elizabeth crying, "Mommy, Mommy!"

Cille turned the lariat loose, mounted, pulled Patrick's revolver and slowly moved forward through the dirt canyon with Duke in the lead. Suddenly Duke raced from sight. As she rounded the corner of a large boulder and fallen tree, she saw Duke sitting near Elizabeth as she stood near the large dirt bank.

After holstering the revolver, she dismounted and cradled her youngest daughter to her breast saying, "My Elizabeth, my sweet, sweet child, I love you dearly." Then Cille lifted her daughter onto the saddle, suddenly realizing she should have had Champ along for her girl to ride.

When she was on top of Dublin, Elizabeth said, "Sadie! I hear Sadie, Mommy."

Duke suddenly disappeared from her sight. She drew the revolver once more for immediate response, in case she needed to defend herself and her daughter. As she led the horse through the dirt canyon, she was worried that Elizabeth was sitting too high if there was an ambush. Just then, she heard her oldest daughter crying. Moments later, she found Duke sitting next to Sadie as she hugged his neck. The scampering Indians had thrown her to the ground in their attempt to get out of the dirt canyon in a hurry.

Placing the revolver in the holster, Cille reached down and hugged Sadie saying, "Oh, am I glad to see you. I love you, my sweet bundle. Goodness, it's good to see the both of you again."

Lifting Sadie up into the saddle behind her sister, Cille led the horse back to where the first dead Indian was. Looking above the canyon wall as they began leaving the ravine, she could see one of the Indians on the ridge line. She gathered Patrick's carbine and took aim, not knowing if her shot would be true because it was a long shot and uphill. She carefully calculated her shot, breathed slowly, held it and then pulled the trigger. To her surprise, the Indian fell from his pony.

While leading her horse back to where the first Indian was, she looped the lariat rope around the saddle horn only to hear Elizabeth say, "Mommy, he was mean to me. I don't like him."

"He won't bother you any longer, sweetheart," Cille replied and pulled the Indian to the area where the second Indian had fallen.

She was afoot for now, but she had her daughters riding high as she walked up the ridge.

When her mother was securing the second dead Indian, Sadie said, "This one hurt my arms, Mommy, when he tied me up at night."

"Well, he isn't going to hurt you after today, I took care of that," her mother replied.

Elizabeth said, "Mommy, I'm really hungry."

The voice of her older sister replied, "They didn't let us have much food. I'm more thirsty than hungry."

Thinking of what added problems she now faced, Cille recalled what little provisions she had left in the bag that rested across the valley, where she had dropped it before she went shooting. Benjomine's words about going out unprepared rang in her ears. Cille said, "I know girls, I'll try to get you something to eat and drink in a short while, okay?" Neither girl answered but looked on to see their mother approaching the Indian.

After taking a couple of loops from around the saddle horn, Cille led Dublin off the ridge dragging both Indians.

Upon pulling her mount up near the broken trader's wagon, she could see one horse was dead, but the other had managed to stand with part of the harness still wrapped around its neck. The civilian must have broken his neck, when he was suddenly thrown over the horses and plowed into the ground. Cille bent over and removed the loop from the Indians.

Cille led Dublin in the direction of where the lieutenant had fallen. The lariat trailed behind her horse making small puffs of dust. The lieutenant's mount had not run far and was about twenty yards away, as if he was ground hitched.

She wanted to see if she could get to the mount. She walked slowly, leading her horse as her two daughters rode in the saddle. As they approached the military mount, Cille was able to gather in the reins without the horse shying from her. She led both horses back to where the lieutenant lay upon the ground.

Seeing the Indian pony, she realized the woman was still bound and left on the ground. She walked up to the Indian pony slowly, hoping that it would not bolt and run from the area. She reached out and pulled in the reins as the pony raised its head and snorted. With each little movement she made, it sent sharp pains about her shoulder as a reminder she was not left unscathed by the confrontation.

Not wanting to attract attention, the Indian girl remained still on her back, her head turned away from them. Cille walked over to where the woman was tied on the ground. She approached slowly keeping the reins of the Indian pony in her hand. Cille offered a friendly smile as the woman rolled to show her face and stared back with tears in her eyes. She had been savagely beaten and the marks on her wrists and legs showed no mercy when they bound her.

Pulling the large knife from its sheath, Cille ran the blade between the woman's outstretched arms. When she held the knife still, the Indian woman slowly pulled her hands back and forth allowing the blade to sever the thin leather strips.

Cille handed the reins of the Indian pony to the woman before she bent to cut the leather that tied her legs at the ankles.

The Indian woman slowly got to her feet and saw Cille slide the long knife back into its sheath. She stood for a moment rubbing her wrists unsure of what would happen next. "My name Tans-A-Hide. Where are the other whites?"

"My name is Cille and I came to save my two daughters," as she pointed to the pair sitting in the saddle. "There are no others that ride with me." There was no reason to stand around and try to talk. She led both horses over to where the lieutenant was. Tans-A-Hide followed on foot, leading her pony.

When they arrived, Cille could see the lieutenant wasn't a pretty sight. The shot had caught him between the shoulder blades and most of his chest was blown out the front of his shirt.

Cille tossed Lieutenant Master's hat on her saddle horn. Tans-A-Hide looked on, not realizing the reason for Cille's anger and actions. She pulled Masters back to the wagon in the same way as she did the Indian. Tans-A-Hide mounted her pony and followed a short distance behind the lieutenant's dragging body. With slack in the lariat, Cille removed the loops from around the saddle horn and dropped it. She secured the reins of the horses to part of the broken wagon.

"Girls, I'll get you both down from the saddle for now," as Cille turned and got them down off Dublin. As best she could, she said, "Tans-A-Hide, remain here with my daughters and my dog." Tans-A-Hide looked puzzled, but dismounted and made no effort to follow her.

She got into the saddle and rode Dublin to the top of the ridge. Upon her arrival at the crest of the hill, she picked up her canteens, the large bag with utensils and very little food. Before she returned to the trader's wagon, she rode far enough north to see what general direction the sergeant had ridden. She was satisfied that it was due north, and over time, he would be around Dickenson. She returned to the wagon where she dismounted.

While Cille was gone to the ridge, Tans-A-Hide went about freeing the horse from the harness and equipment that held it captive to the broken wagon. She secured the horse next to her Indian pony.

All sorts of reason and logic seemed to leave Cille as she worked herself into a state of frustration. Various emotions drove her to the brink of being overwhelmed.

Cille took the canteens and saw to it that her daughters had a drink, then turned to Tans-A-Hide offering her one of the canteens. She knew her children were hungry and she had little food left in her sack. She frantically looked through the remains of the trader's wagon and found some bread, a jar of molasses and several pieces of jerky. With that and what she had in her sack, they had a meager amount to eat for one or two days. They ate and offered Tans-A-Hide some of the food. She knew that it was nearly four days' ride before she would be home. Her first thought was to return the same route and try to see if there was any food left where the immigrant train was stopped by so many Indians.

Duke found several pieces of meat that had been thrown from the wagon and was enjoying the scraps.

"Girls, I want you both to stay here by the broken wagon, while I take care of some things nearby. Keep Duke close by. He sure missed the both of you."

There was little daylight left and she had to work fast. Tans-A-Hide looked on for a while before she dismounted and helped as much as she could with what was to be done.

Taking the hats of the white men, Cille stuffed them into the bag. She removed the feathers that were attached to the Indian's hair and tossed them into the bag.

Then she went about stripping each body to the waist, leaving only the trousers and loin cloth. Tans-A-Hide helped as the clothing was removed. The belongings were crammed into the bag, including boots and two pairs of moccasins.

With scraps from the broken wagon, she sat each dead body up so that their feet came together where she placed a broken whiskey jug at their feet. She was exhausted working with one good hand and arm, the other exhibiting sharp pain with excessive use. She hoped she hadn't broken a bone and was only badly bruised.

Making arm motions and some verbal commands, Cille asked Tans-A-Hide for help. They braced each body up in a sitting position and their right arm braced so that the hand could hold a message for all who passed by to see. In the civilian's hand, she tied a strip from the black dress she wore at funerals. In the lieutenant's hand, she tied a strip of black cloth holding her husband's military academy insignia awarded to him at West Point the day he graduated. Cille shed bitter tears, and through her anger and determination for justice helped her prepare the deadly message. In the Indian's hand, she tied a black strip of cloth and two strips of a calico dress belonging to each one of her girl's dresses she had removed from the chest at home.

Satisfied with how she had arranged the four, she was ready to leave. She had the girls ride in the saddle on Dublin. She quickly gathered her remaining belongings, tied them on the lieutenant's horse and mounted up.

Tans-A-Hide stood looking up at Cille. When she turned to get a last look at the four, she let out an Indian scream, ran to one of the dead Indians and struck him in the face violently. In doing so, she knocked him from the sitting position. She looked at Cille and nodded her approval, as if to say she vented her frustrations, too. Then she sat him up and propped his arm the way it was before her outburst. She went to her pony and mounted. She rode over to the horse from the booze wagon and tied a lead rope around the horse's head.

The sun was beginning to fade from sight and Cille wanted to put at least some distance to the west between her and the four dead men before they settled in for the night.

They hadn't ridden far when they were forced to pull up for the night. The sky was filled with heavy dark clouds and the girls huddled closely, sharing each other's warmth beneath what bedding they had. Tans-A-Hide was left to manage on her own.

CHAPTER 32

Discovered by Indians 1882

Cille didn't remove anything from Dublin or the military mount, for fear of not being able to put it back on their mounts in the morning. The reins were loosely wrapped around a nearby limb of a cedar bush. She leaned up against a large clump of dirt and huddled her girls in close. She held her husband's revolver in her hand throughout the night.

She was exhausted. The pain in her right shoulder had let up some, but the fear of not totally trusting Tans-A-Hide kept her from falling asleep. After all, she had her daughters with her and their safety was foremost in her mind.

Tans-A-Hide bedded down close by and from time to time would raise her head to check on Cille. There was an uneasy trust that kept Cille or Tans-A-Hide from getting a good night's sleep.

Cille knew that once anyone discovered the four dead men, she would become very unpopular in these parts.

With the first hint of light, they mounted and began a slow pace back to the land Cille was more familiar with. She had no idea how far Tans-A-Hide would ride along with her before she would go her own way. She could only guess their journey was two- or three-days' ride.

The length of the day was rough on Cille and Tans-A-Hide, as neither had too much sleep. Cille's shoulder gave her trouble during the day with a throbbing, deep ache. While they rode, she held Dublin's reins up close, as her girls were too young to ride alone. Tans-A-Hide was riding half asleep, with the lead rope of the trader's horse across her leg and tied off on the saddle horn.

As the sun was beginning its final descent, they saw the charred frame of a burned out one-room cabin in the distance. Pulling the field glass out, Cille could see what appeared to be an abandoned homestead site. There was a partially torn down shed that would give some protection during the night, for all of them and the horses.

It was a slow and arduous trip down the long sloping hillside and across the valley before they reached the abandoned structure. It was evident that the property had been abandoned for several years. The shed was perfect for their concealment.

For a sixth night, Dublin remained with the saddle and equipment on his back. Cille released the sack of provisions and they went about getting something to eat. All four had eaten very little since early morning. Cille's guarded trust softened and the women found peace between each other. Unsure why Tans-A-Hide continued to tag along, she realized she was also in fear of being discovered by the wrong people. Cille leaned up against one corner of the shed and quickly succumbed to sleep brought on by total exhaustion.

◇ ◇ ◇

The day was well underway and suddenly they were not alone. Cille was startled awake by Dublin shifting his weight and Tans-A-Hide's soft hand across her mouth.

Looking through the slats in the shed, fear struck her heart. Cille tried to keep Duke still as Tans-A Hide and Cille went to the girls, woke them and placed their hands over their mouths before they could make a sound. On the hill immediately on the other side of the burnt cabin, a band of twenty-seven Indians were riding in a line about three quarters of the way up the hill, parallel with the horizon. They were staying out of the skyline riding slow and their approach to the cabin and barn was cautious.

Cille swallowed hard and pulled the revolver from the holster.

A soft hand rested on the hand that held the revolver and Cille looked up into Tans-A-Hide's face. She was shaking her head and motioning for her to be still and quiet.

Without warning Tans-A- Hide screamed, grabbed the reins of her pony and left the protection of the shed. She was tugging at the reins as she ran in the direction of the advancing party of Indians.

In an attempt to hush the girls into silence, Cille held them close as they all cowered to the ground, peering through the slats, unsure if Tans-A-Hide would turn their budding friendship against them.

When Tans-A-Hide approached, the leader reined up. She spoke to him in Lakota. "I have been beaten. There were others who took me from the river five days ago and they tried to sell me to the whites for fire water. There were shots fired and some of them were killed. I get away and ride here to hide and rest. I am happy to see you."

"Our chief is angry," Stone-Fist said. "He sent us out to find you. I say I will go. You are to be my bride; my head get angry and my heart weighed heavy. Where had they taken you?"

"I can take you to where I last saw them." Tans-A-Hide said.

Stone-Fist grunted, "We cannot find them if you stay on the ground talking."

One of the young braves had dismounted and was walking toward the shed. Tans-A-Hide cried out in her native tongue to stop his advancement as she rushed to place her body between the youth and the shed. In her attempt to conceal Cille, she had exposed her by trying to avert the bloodshed of one of her own and possibly the woman who saved her.

"You tell us of one thing yet you act another," Stone-Fist yelled out. "I demand you tell me at once, what is going on?" His arms waved in the air as he directed the rest of his party to take up a defensive posture around the shed.

Out of frustration, Tans-A-Hide cried out in a pleading voice, "I will show you, but listen to what I say."

"Tell me now!" Stone-Fist demanded as he grew angry.

"There is but one other and her children in the shed with their horses. The white woman is the one that saved me from the whites and those of our kind who have bad blood and will do anything for fire water."

Angry, Stone-Fist leaped from his pony and stood before Tans-A-Hide, "You want to bear me a son, yet you hold your tongue and try to hide the truth. You anger me!"

"She is a white woman who saved me from being spoiled by the white men," Tans-A-Hide pleaded. "I was bound and tossed to the ground. This white woman saved me and I owe her. She has shared her food and water with me, also. She says she rides with no other whites. She rides alone."

With a bitter face, Stone-Fist stared at his bride-to-be and angrily demanded, "You get her and bring her before me now!"

Tans-A-Hide turned and rushed into the shed. She looked at Cille and approached slowly. She softly rested her hand on Cille's gun hand and shook her head. With passion in her eyes, she looked into the eyes of a white woman who was in fear of what was going to happen to her and her girls.

When they left the shed, Tans-A-Hide pulled the reins of the trader's horse. Cille held the reins of Dublin and the army horse as the girls walked next to their mother. Duke walked next to the girls. They stopped before Stone-Fist, who motioned for others to search the shed.

"Why you ride on the grass land that is not yours?" Stone Fist demanded as he added, "Tans-A-Hide say you Rides-Alone."

Cille tried to gather her thoughts and expressed them quickly, without anger, to the strong figure of a man that stood before her. "I had," and she began using her hands, "a husband who was killed by blue coats and my two small girls were taken from my home by Indians that drink fire water. Two of your kind are dead and I have killed one of the blue coats and a trader that took pelts for fire water. He was going to take in trade Tans-A-Hide and my daughters. I am so angry! I will hunt down the rest that have done me wrong."

Stone-Fist scoffed, "You think you can do that? You not as big as Tans-A-Hide, she knows what best be left for men, like me and my brothers." He swung his arms around to include the other braves that rode with him. "See, you already hurt."

Cille swallowed hard and said, "I have nothing to live for, other than my daughters, and to satisfy my anger. I will hunt them down or die. They have done me wrong."

"I see mark on horse that says you have long knife's horse," Stone-Fist grumbled. "I do not understand."

"It was an army horse at one time. I killed the long knife that rode this horse; now it is mine." Cille replied.

The expression on Stone-Fist's face changed very little as he asked, "Then you hunt the white soldier for what they do?"

"There were two blue coats I hunt!" she held up two fingers for emphasis, hand shaking. "One is dead, I have one more to hunt and

I will see him dead!"

Tans-A-Hide blurted out, "I tell you, what she say, is truth. She has shirt from blue coat in here." She pointed to the bag where Cille had stuffed part of the dead man's clothing.

Stone-Fist helped take the bag from the saddle horn. When she opened it, Tans-A-Hide pulled out lieutenant Master's shirt. They examined the holes in the blood-stained shirt closely.

"What with other horse?" Stone-Face demanded.

Tans-A-Hide said, "Was part of a wagon team, it belong to the trader's wagon. Rides-Alone use big gun to stop trader. One horse fell dead; this horse I take."

Stone-Fist returned the shirt to the bag and secured it to the saddle. Cille said nothing, watching. Suddenly, Stone-Face waved his arms and shouted, "You go!" Tans-A-Hide gave her and the girls a hand in getting into the saddle before Stone-Fist said, "Rides-Alone you go, Tans-A-Hide will show me where we pick up the trail of those who took her from our village."

Tans-A-Hide mounted her pony and pulled the lead rope of the trader's horse, as they rode off in the direction of the dead still sitting on the ground.

Relieved that she and the girls could move on, she followed the road leading from the property. It was nearly hidden, but Cille figured it had to lead to civilization. The day was hot and the going appeared slow. The only time she pulled her mount up was when there was water. The terrain she was riding had very little of that.

◇ ◇ ◇

Near mid-day and a long ride away from where they were discovered, Cille knew they were short of food and sought out the immigrant wagon train that she saw days earlier. When she topped the ridge, she saw the remains in the valley below. Not being sure of how safe it was to go into the open, she spent a long time looking through the spyglass for any signs of danger.

When she felt it was safe, they rode directly to the wagons. Not prepared to see so many dead still on the ground, Cille focused on the task at hand and searched for food quickly, looked through the remaining wagons. There was bread and cured meat from the barrel at the side of the wagon and an ample supply of water to fill the canteens. In one wagon she saw two quilts and took them for the girls to use at night.

If she had time, she would try to bury those left on the ground by placing a tarp over them along with a small layer of dirt and rock. She didn't know how safe she was out in the open and again took the telescope to closely examine distant landscape for any signs of danger.

Panic set in and Cille knew she must hurry. She was ill prepared for what she saw through the telescope. To the east riding her way were sixteen Indians and coming in a hurry.

With the swing of the canteens, the loops over the saddle horn, the food items haphazardly shoved into the sack near her girls' feet and the quilts loosely draped over the front of the saddle, she swung into the saddle. They headed for a ravine a short distance away, as fast as they could ride.

Dropping into the ravine, they rode for a distance around the face of the hill that came out near the top. Without revealing their position, she used the telescope to see if she was in for a fight.

To her surprise, among the Indians were the same she was looking for and behind them was a unit of the 7th Cavalry closing in on them. The chase was short lived in the valley. When the Indians were captured, Cille thought she could forget about them, as they would be taken from here and placed on a reservation some distance away.

But in her mind Cille knew there was still one more out there. Not an Indian, but a yellow belly bluecoat named Sergeant Joe Kidding.

The military unit was close enough to see the immigrant wagon train and they rode in that direction. She could see where some of the troopers were detailed to dig appropriate graves for those who were killed.

Thoughts of being discovered by the military unit sent chills throughout her tiny frame. She had killed a lieutenant and was now in possession of his mount, an army horse. She had to find a way to put some ground between them and quickly.

Cille gathered the reins in and said, "Girls, hang on tight. We are going to have to ride a little bit fast for a while." They left the far side of the hill and headed for the next set of hills a short distance away, Duke trotted alongside of Dublin, as if that is where he needed to be.

When evening fell, they were under a bluff where Cille could clearly see the vast open terrain. They were not followed and she began to feel a a little more at ease. She helped the girls down from Dublin and they made a cold camp once more.

Sadie said, "I'll pull the bread apart for you and I will help Elizabeth get ready to eat."

"I might be smaller than you, but I don't need your help, do I, Mommy?" Elizabeth spoke in her defense.

Frustrated from all that happened during the day, she was not prepared to listen to any squabbling. But it also occurred to her that it was nice to hear her daughter's voices once more. "Please don't fuss girls. I will try to get us home by tomorrow."

When the sun set beyond the distant hills, the light of day faded fast as they settled in for another night. In the vast open spaces on the Dakota prairie, they huddled in a cluster near each other. Elizabeth curled up in the log cabin design quilt they acquired from the ill-fated immigrant wagon train. Sadie found warmth wrapped up in her quilt of a nine-patch design. Cille had the wool blanket from her bedroll. Duke took charge of security for the night.

◇◇◇

It was the day after her rescue by Stone-Fist that Tans-A-Hide directed the twenty-seven warriors to the site where a white woman named Rides-Alone had saved her from being soiled and forced into slavery.

As they rode up to the site of the killing, scavenger birds flew away from the dead bodies. Still sitting in an upright position, parts of the bodies had already been pecked at by the birds

Stone-Fist and Tans-a-Hide dismounted and she showed her husband-to-be where she was bound and where the drinking took place.

"Where did Rides-Alone shoot from?" he asked.

She pointed to the top of the ridge some distance away. "She first showed her anger from the tall tree. Two times her gun roared in anger. Then one of the bluecoats felt the anger. The whiskey peddler felt the anger from the same area, as he rode away to hide. The anger only talked one time to claim him. She followed our kind that does bad things into one of the canyons across small valley. Rides-Alone rides without fear. She followed and come out of canyon after fire stick barks anger two more times. She saved her children and brought back these two," as she pointed to the dead Indians.

When they approached the site of the four dead, Tans-A-Hide stood behind lieutenant Caleb Master's body and said, "This man and one other bluecoat bring this man," as she stepped behind the whiskey peddler. As she stepped behind the dead Indian, she said, "This is the one who was with the others when they took me from the village. He put marks upon my face with his angry fist." Without another word she doubled up her fist and struck the side of the dead Indian's head. He fell over from his sitting position. "He and this other were the ones that take Rides-Alone children from her home."

All the others in the party sat upon their horses watching Tans-A-Hide vent her anger as she propped the body back into a sitting position. She said, "Here look at these," as she pointed to the torn remnants of clothing dangling from each dead man's fist. "Rides-Alone is angry, leaves message. Those who have done her wrong will sit in death as these do. I see her anger, but up close, I see a heart that hurts in her eyes. She say she do others same way or die. They make big mistake, when they killed her husband and took her family and brought her to anger."

"Not only will she be hunted by those she seeks to find, but the long knives and the white man's law will seek her out also," Stone-Fist said. "As she rides upon this land with her anger, she will carry name Rides-Alone. She will be known by no other name among our people. We must not forget the one with dancing red hair and the sight of the dead man's horse she rides upon."

Stone-Fist and Tans-A-Hide mounted their ponies and the group headed toward the trail as it pointed from the canyon.

◇ ◇ ◇

It was near nightfall on the following day when she spotted a cabin and some outbuildings through the glass, still too far away to identify. She thought she recognized the area, but each hill seemed to blend into another meaningless and unrecognizable mound of dark soil. As the sun set, she wasn't sure how far off the cabin was.

As nightime fell, she and the girls continued their ride toward the cabin. The moon was out and the landscape was lightly highlighted. Dublin was tired, but headstrong and sensed the correct path he had to follow. At times, he was pulling forward on the reins as she held them in check. The military mount was tired as well and stumbled at one point snapping Cille out of a sleepy daze. Still, they continued down the growth-covered old trail.

The sound of a barking dog brought a weary smile to her face. They were getting near the cabin. She was beginning to feel better.

Suddenly a voice yelled out, "You in the night, who are you?"

"Hello, it's me, Cille and my two daughters." Her voice didn't carry too well.

"What in blue blazes! Are you a woman?"

"Last time I checked, I was. It's Cille."

"Girl, get over here, Mathilda has been worried sick about you."

She and the girls dismounted and followed Ted into the cabin. Mathilda was in a corner hovering with a revolver in her hand. "Ted, you liked to scare the tar out of me for taking such a long…" Seeing Cille, she screamed, "My goodness, my sister, am I glad to see you. Sadie and Elizabeth, oh, it's good to see you children as well." She turned and woke up Gloria, so that they could visit. She ran to Cille to give her a hug.

When she did, Cille cried out in pain, "Oh no, Mathilda no. Oh, it's my shoulder."

"My goodness, Ted, she's hurt."

"Honey, sit down over here."

"That buffalo gun did a number on me," Cille explained. "I think I'm badly bruised or I've busted something."

"Come over here and sit on the edge of the bed," Mathilda said. "Let me take a good look at it."

Cille got up from the chair and sat on the edge of the bed.

Mathilda pulled a faded blanket across a piece of thin wire, giving them some privacy. She removed Cille's blouse and uttered, "Oh mercy!"

"How bad is it?" Ted inquired.

"It is swollen bad!" Mathilda replied. "Goodness that's the ugliest purple and green I've ever seen."

Ted said, "I'll take care of your horses and see that they have feed and water."

"Would you please?" Cille pleaded. "That saddle has been on their backs for several days." When he left, she turned to Mathilda and said, "While he's gone, can the girls and I wash up a bit?"

"I should say so." Mathilda rushed to get a pan of water, wash cloth and towel. "We'll get your clothing set aside for the wash tomorrow. I have something around here you can wear until I wash your clothes and I'm sure we can find something for the girls as well."

"Thanks, Mathilda," Cille said.

Mathilda took the clothing, opened the cabin door and tossed them near her washing tub on the porch outside the cabin.

Within a short time, Cille and the girls had sponged off and all were in some soft, clean clothing. She allowed Mathilda to tend to her shoulder as best she could.

They joined Ted at the table where there was fresh milk and a homemade sandwich for the three of them. Ted and Mathilda's daughter Gloria was awake and full of questions for the younger set. Ted and Mathilda decided that Gloria would sleep between them the rest of the night and Cille and the girls would sleep in Gloria's bed.

◇◇◇

Two days later, Cille spoke to the Drakes, "I am beholden to both of you, but I must go to Prairie Rose to take care of what is needed there."

"You and the girls are most welcome to stay here for a bit longer," Mathilda said, "Your ordeal had to be draining."

Cille said, "You have truly treated me like a sister, but I do have to be getting along. I thank the both of you for all that you have given us. You're immensely appreciated."

Ted replied, "If it is help with the stock or in the field you need, just say the word. I'll try to make some time available to help out."

"Goodness sakes, Ted," Cille responded, "You have your hands full here on your own homestead. I asked the Crowfords to look in on things. Ben-jomine has been taking care of the chores, and if he had to, I imagine he called on his sons to help."

"Just the same, Cille," Ted added, "Don't hesitate to call on us if there is a need."

The departure from the Drake homestead was a solemn affair for the girls. As Sadie and Elizabeth sat on Dublin, Sadie called down, "Gloria, someday can we play house again. It was fun.".

Gloria replied, "Come back and play with me. I don't have anyone to play with."

Elizabeth looked down from the saddle and said, "Gloria, if Sadie can't come maybe, I could. I like playing with you because you play fair."

Cille swung into the saddle on the army mount and they waved goodbye As she took Dublin's reins in one hand and her own in the other, they began their short journey to Prairie Rose.

◇◇◇

When Cille and the girls rode into Prairie Rose, Ben-jomine was closing the barn door after doing some of the early morning chores. He looked up and said, "Goodness Miss Cille, Iz sure glad ya gots Sadie and Elizabeth with ya. Lizzie iz sure gonna be happy ta see ya's back. Let's go cross the creek and let her know ya iz here."

"Ben-jomine, I need to keep this mount under cover," Cille said, "and I'll get Dublin in the corral before we go."

"Iz gonna give ya a hand, then we go see Lizzie." Ben-jomine said, "Come on girls, let me gets yas down from up yonder."

Lizzie was excited when they came through the door, "Lordy, Iz glad ta see the whole lot of yas. Iz been prayin' that I see the day, when yas all come back to the valley."

They hugged and as they embraced, Lizzie added, "Iz glad ya gots them girls back. I knew ya left here with a broken heart that could only be mended with havin' back the two gems that light up your world."

"I'm glad, also," Cille said. "I hope, I never have to go through that experience again, and I certainly wouldn't want either of them to go through what they endured, either."

"What's for lunch?" Ben-jomine asked.

"The corn breads in-zee oven and Iz got soup in the pot." Lizzie replied. "Ya all gonna have a bite with us in a bit, ain't ya Miss Cille?"

"Thank you, Lizzie. I have some talking to do with the both of you after we eat."

After eating, the girls played on the floor with Benji and Nizzie while Cille and the Crowfords gathered on the porch for a short talk. The weather was warm and Lizzie's garden showed great promise. Ben-jomine collapsed in a rocker that had seen better days and barely rocked as he prepared to listen. Lizzie and Cille sat in old weather beaten straight-back chairs that had long lost their usefulness at the dinner table.

Cille said, "I hate to impose more that I have, but there is something I have to do and I would appreciate your help."

Lizzie said, "What is it Miss Cille, no chore too great that we-uns can't help with, ain't that so Ben-jomine?"

"We owe a heap of helpin' to ya Miss Cille. What iz it need done?"

"I'd like the girls to remain here instead of at Prairie Rose. I need to make a trip to Little Missouri in a couple of weeks, then I need to make a trip to Dickenson. I'll be gone for several days. Can I have you look after the girls and tend to the chores until I get a few things taken care of?"

Ben-jomine looked at Lizzie and almost in unison they said, "Wez can do that for ya."

"I need to visit Patrick's grave at the cemetery," Cille said softly, "and get some supplies, see the law in Little Missouri before I make a trip to Dickenson. I'll be back after going to Little Missouri, but the trip to Dickenson will take some time. I need to see the land agent to get Prairie Rose legal and in my name. I want to visit with Bjorn and Uvonnie Swavingun for a few other details."

"Them girls can stay right here," Lizzie replied. "Theyz a big help with the twins and me. And Ben-jomine gonna help watch over em, you jus' go and do what ya have ta. We see ya when ya gets back."

The visit with the Crowfords lasted into the night. When Cille had tucked in her girls, she explained that she would be gone for a day, but she would be back to see them. Then she went to Prairie

Rose for the night. She would use the time to take care of the bruise to her shoulder and think over of what she would do in Little Missouri, when the time came.

During the days, Cille took care of cleaning the house and household chores inside the house. Ben-jomine was a fine carpenter and the walls no longer showed any sign of what had happened to Patrick that fateful night. But being a typical man, Ben-jomine didn't remove the dust and sawdust left behind in the work area. Nevertheless, she was thankful for his work and wouldn't get upset over a chore that took little time to correct.

From early morning until near noon, Ben-jomine would visit Prairie Rose to do the chores outside and on occasion his boys Rufus and Rupert would visit and help out.

◇◇◇

The day before Cille planned to visit Little Missouri, she had supper at the Crowfords. The two boys had visited that afternoon. Rufus said, "Miss Cille, wez been workin' on the De Mores house and it be a big house. Me and Rupert been talkin' with the main man Marcus. He say, he iz buildin' the town to name it after his wife, her name iz Medora. He say, he wants to meet with ya, when his Medora comes to their new house."

"What on earth for?" Cille asked.

"Iz gots no idea. Marcus iz a funny man, he say, he iz French, whatever that mean."

They all laughed at their conversation about the Frenchman and enjoyed the evening.

◇◇◇

Cille was up early and left Prairie Rose shortly after breakfast. She had a long ride ahead of her and wanted to make it to Little Missouri before sundown.

Her purpose for visiting Little Missouri was three-fold. First, she would go to the dry goods store to stock up on supplies and buy some ammunition. Second, she wanted to stop by the cemetery to visit Patrick's grave and spend a few precious moments of reflection. The third was to make a call on the law, such as it was. The town was considered a wide open, anything goes, cluster of a few buildings and several tents. If one brushed up against the law elsewhere, it made little difference, as long as the local law was observed. The local law overlooked any of those passing through who may have had a “colorful past”.

Over the last few days, Cille’s shoulder had healed. Ted and Mathilda had done their best to see that she got some much-needed rest and that she mended properly. They had taken her in for a couple of nights over the last week and had checked on her progress at Prairie Rose. She appreciated their concern, but they couldn’t take away the pangs in her heart to see that justice was administered her way.

It was near noon when she pulled up Dublin on the eastern bluff looking down on the narrow waters of the river. On the opposite bank, the seedy town lay tranquil in the midday heat. Cille lightly dug her heels in and leaned back in the saddle as Dublin moved down the steep embankment. At the base of the sandstone bluff, a sand bar and boulders stretched out into the shallow waters. Cille noted that the river was extremely shallow as her boots in the stirrups stayed well above the slow-moving stream. It would soon begin to limit river commerce if it dropped much further.

Riding up a dirt bank, she approached the outskirts of Little Missouri. Four more large tents and one cabin had joined the small town that was so dependent on the shipment of goods down-river to other markets.

Swinging from the saddle in front of the trading post, she was hassled by two burly, unshaven, odor reeking men bearing ill manners. Nothing but river scum, she thought. “Hey, Ward, this here filly is just what I need to keep me company going downriver. Ya betcha, I de sure enjoy the ride,” then he laughed.

“Shucks, Eddie, you’d no more pay attention to what you should be doing and run her aground at the first bend.”

When Cille walked by, she gave them both a disdainful look and went into the trading post. Eddie laughed and snorted before spitting out a mouthful of tobacco juice. “Ain’t no problem being run aground with that kind of woman. Fact is, it might be enjoyable.”

While inside the mercantile getting her supplies, she assessed the potentially dangerous situation outside and wanted to be prepared for any altercation. She reached down and folded the leather flap of her holster back, so that it rested between her body and the gun belt. If she had to use force, she didn't want anything to be in the way.

About the time she had her supplies on the counter, Audrey entered the store, "Cille it's good to see you. Has Roger told you the news?"

"What news?" Cille asked.

Audrey replied, "We're selling the mercantile and moving across the river come summer. They're building a new town called Medora. We made arrangements to have our store built on the main street and should be moved in about May or June."

"I'm happy for the both of you. It'll save me having to make the trip way over here just to get supplies."

Not intending to leave the store for a while, Cille enjoyed the short conversation with the Bentleys before she ventured into the street to face the unkempt pair.

When Cille left the mercantile, the two men stood near the hitching rail, where she had left Dublin. Ward said, "Here she comes now, Eddie." Both men began stroking their bushy beards and itching to pursue an acquaintance.

As natural as can be, Cille set her supplies on the ground in an attempt to show she was unconcerned. Giving the appearance of ignoring the pair, she suddenly drew her husband's revolver, as quick as any man would in a gun fight. She rolled the chamber on her left arm from elbow to wrist, as if to check the cylinders, before returning the revolver to the holster, about as fast as she had pulled iron. She stood her ground and looked directly at the two river rats.

Ward stopped stroking his beard and turned to walk off. Eddie stopped mid-stroke and slowly scratched a spot. He twisted his jaw, moving the wad of chew in his mouth, then joined Ward and they walked off.

Cille picked up her supplies, tied them to the saddle horn and mounted Dublin. Riding past the dejected pair, she heard Eddie say, "Well, Ward, I think she's meaner than any wild cat I'd ever care to mess with."

She rode through the streets and into the countryside to the cemetery. Dismounting, she walked over to Patrick's grave site.

Standing in silence, she looked at the crudely made wooden marker before she knelt down holding on with both hands before her forehead came in contact with the wood. A steady stream of tears traveled down her face. No sound, just an abundance of tears as she knelt for the longest time. She brought her hands to her mouth and kissed her fingers before her hands touched the mound of soil marking her husband's grave.

She said, "Patrick, if you only knew how much I miss you. I'd give anything to have you back. They stole you from me. I'll hunt them till their dying day. I got Caleb Masters and you were right. I caught him and Sergeant Joe Kidding with a booze peddler dealing with some renegades. But there will come a time I'll get Joe Kidding, too. I was able to see the renegades that kidnapped Sadie and Elizabeth and rode rampant across Prairie Rose. I shot the two that plucked them up from the yard. Thank goodness the girls were not badly hurt. They were dusty and hungry when I found them, but they're near home now and staying with the Crowfords for a spell. We saw the others getting rounded up by the Army. Now there is only one left for me to hunt down and I'll do it." She stayed a while longer before returning to her horse.

Before leaving the cemetery, she removed some items from a sack. There were a few articles she had belonging lieutenant to Caleb Masters, the peddler and the two Indians. She laid them on the ground. She took out her black dress, tore off four short strips and tied them to each wad of clothing. Placing the items near the saddle horn, she swung into the saddle and headed for town once more.

Pulling up in front of the marshal's law office, she called out, "Russell Coby! Hey, you in the office? Russell!"

The door opened and two men stepped outside: Russell Coby, the self-appointed town marshal and Sid Butler a self-appointed judge. Cille noted that both men were unarmed. "Well, Ms. Cille," Russell said as a smile filled his face. "Mighty pleased to see you come to your senses."

"I didn't come back to be sweet talked. I left here a while back to do a job." She tossed the belongings at his feet. "Here's what's left of the four of them. Their bodies can be found south of White Butte before you get to the 'Y' of Cedar Creek."

Coby stood with a gaping mouth as he stared at the four bundles. Looking up he said, "Cille, I can't let you get away with this. It's not right, you go dumping the remains at my feet this-a-way. I don't like it none, the Honorable Judge Butler here don't like it either and the Army sure as thunder won't take this very easy."

"You can't stop me!" She dug her heels into her mount and rode Dublin at a high gallop out of town.

Russell whirled around, raced into his office to get his gun and returned outside. Cille had already disappeared over the edge of the riverbank and was out of sight. "She's in trouble now!" he scoffed, turning to kick at the four bundles of evidence inside his office.

Sid said, "Marshal Coby, she will need to be brought before me and I'll put a stop to that hateful attitude."

Returning to the east bank, she headed toward Prairie Rose. Although rested from her stay at Ted and Mathilda's, she felt the urge to stop by Prairie Rose to visit the children once more before she left for Dickenson. She knew the marshal would most likely be making a house call.

CHAPTER 33

Dickenson, Dakota Territory 1882

Cille arrived in Dickenson after riding over forty miles. Unsure how to look up the Swavinguns, she stopped by the train depot and asked the telegrapher. He said, "Young lady, they are on the eastern outskirts of the town. You just go down Main Street, and when you see a gray two-story house on the north side of the street with a white picket fence, that will be where Bjorn and Uvonnie live. You can't miss the place. There is a large gray barn out in back resting on about forty acres."

When she arrived at the Swavinguns, Uvonnie met her at the door, "Come in Cille, we heard the terrible news about Patrick. I'm so sorry we couldn't come. We were in Canada and found out about his death three days after his funeral."

They both sat in the sitting room and Cille began explaining her troubles. When Bjorn came in from his chores, he said, "Ms. Cille, it is a great honor that you have made us a visit. We're both sorry to hear about your Patrick."

"That hasn't been all my problems," Cille replied. "About two weeks after we buried him, a handful of drunken Indians rode rampage across the farm and kidnapped my daughters."

Uvonnie gasped, "They did what?! Oh, Bjorn did you hear that? I'm at a loss for words."

Bjorn said, "How long ago did this happen?"

"It's okay really, I just…"

"What?" Bjorn snapped, "I can't believe my ears." His wife seemingly pulled back in shock.

"No, it is alright," Cille said, "let me explain. They took the girls and the following day, I took Duke our German Shepherd with me and found them. I happened to shoot a lieutenant from the Army, a whiskey peddler, and the two Indians that snatched my girls, but the rest of the Indians and a blue-coat got away. The girls are safe now with my neighbors, the Crowfords, and the Army has captured the rest of the Indians that were in the group."

"That is good," Bjorn said. "What is it that we can help you with?"

"Well, there is one more that I need to even the score with. He is a sergeant in the Army named Joe Kidding."

Uvonnie spoke up, "Cille, do you know what you're asking my Bjorn to do? Go against the Army, men he has worked for on occasion."

"No, I'm not asking for his help directly. I'm here to see if he could refresh my memory on the tracking skills he once taught me. I'll do the tracking. When Kidding left the site where I shot the four, he headed this direction. His tracks indicated that he was coming this way. Then when I find him, I plan to drop him. You see, the lieutenant and the sergeant were arch enemies of Patrick's while he was at Fort Rice. And they are the two I found with the whiskey peddler."

"But sweetheart, you have two beautiful girls at home waiting for you." Uvonnie pleaded, "You can't do all this by yourself."

"Maybe not, "Cille answered, "but that is why I'm here. I need a few pointers to tip the scales in my favor before the showdown."

"How long ago did the shooting take place?" He asked.

"Most of this took place about four weeks ago, why?"

"Well," Bjorn said, "The rate of travel and the weather may hamper any tracking, but if he has come this direction, my advice is this: Don't spook the game in the bush."

Cille was confused, "What do you mean by that?"

"He sometimes talks in riddles and rambles on, but somewhere down the road, he'll make his point." Uvonnie was quick to reply.

"If Sergeant Kidding has ridden his horse into this town," Bjorn said, "That is okay with us. But if he knows you're tracking him, he may panic and skip the country. He may find out later, when you spook him, you'll be prepared for his actions."

"I'm here to learn Bjorn and right now you're confusing me."

"All will come together in time. Uvonnie and I will show you some of the things you need to know and I assure you they will help."

They talked at length in the house before they found themselves between the barn and the house. Bjorn had taken a broom from the porch and was sweeping a large section of the yard. He asked Cille to get her horse and told Uvonnie to saddle up. He did so as well.

While they were in the yard, Bjorn said "Cille, you and Uvonnie ride next to me across the yard." When they had, they dismounted. Bjorn took Cille into the area he had swept that now had the horses' hoof prints. "Look at the prints while I go get our work horse."

Cille looked at the prints in the dirt, and when Bjorn brought the work horse out, he rode it across the yard and hopped down to join the women on the ground. He said, "Look at the prints at a walk. Pay particular attention by looking at the shoe prints and those imprints of a heavier horse than yours. The army horses are generally heavier and with a man on top, the prints are etched deeper into the soil. Now we move over a bit and again, we will trot our horses across the yard. Then we will get down and read the shoe marks once more including the prints made by the work horse. When that is done, we will gallop across the yard and study the markings once again. We will walk about in the yard and not disturb the prints so that you may go back and study them again."

"Be careful, Bjorn sometimes tries to trick people, as if it is a game with him," Uvonnie warned. "He has been a tracker for a long time and sometimes he might forget you are just learning."

When they began studying the prints, Cille said, "I can see the difference. The ones we rode at a walk, the prints are not as etched in the ground. Those at a trot gouged deeper into the ground and at a gallop, the shoes bit even further into the ground and tossed back a bit of soil."

Bjorn thought the yard training was going well, so he suggested, "Let us take our horses out to the pasture, where there is uneven ground, ground cover, rocks and dirt along with a few twigs and then you can see the difference the hoof prints make." They rode in a line much as they did in the yard, and in one section, Bjorn had the horses cross paths riding on top of the other prints and generally disrupting the pattern any of the other horses had made.

The riding and reading tracks went on for the rest of the afternoon. When they returned to the house, the Swavinguns insisted that Cille spend the evening. True to nature, the weather changed and got colder during the night.

The heavens to the east were a bright mixture of pink and blue when morning came. Bjorn said, "Let's go out and look at the tracks we made yesterday. Study them at length and learn from what you see. While you slept last night, Uvonnie and I made another row of tracks. After you have studied the ones we made together, I want you to tell me if I was riding Uvonnie's horse and if it was me or Uvonnie riding the work horse by looking at the prints. There just might be a scant difference.

There was laughter and at times mistakes in interpreting the prints, but in the end Cille said, "I never realized there was so much to this. Thanks, I have learned a lot."

Uvonnie said, "He has enjoyed himself sharing the trade he knows so well and I have enjoyed your company as well."

"Yah," Bjorn said with a smile on his face. "I have had fun, I hope I have made this task a bit more pleasurable by showing the funny side of a Swavingun." They all laughed and enjoyed a bit of levity for a change.

Morning had long passed and they made their way back into the house for a bite to eat. Bjorn said, "Cille, after lunch, let us all three ride through the streets of Dickenson to see if you can find the Army horse that Sergeant Kidding was riding. If you find it today, there will not be a confrontation. Remember: don't spook the game in the bush, there will be time to flush him out later."

Cille couldn't believe that he was serious about her not confronting Kidding if she saw his horse. That was almost asking too much. Then she realized that she had to keep her friends out of the fight. She had asked for their help and she would have to honor their wishes for now.

When they saddled up for the ride through Dickenson, Bjorn said, "Cille, I must insist that you leave your guns here at the house. We are just going to take a leisurely ride to gather information, if it is out there. You must learn to control the situation. By learning that, you will be in control. Remember what I say on this day, and from now until the day you meet the sergeant on your terms, always be in control."

She agreed, "I find it hard to agree with you Bjorn, but I did ask for your help and I appreciate what the both of you are doing."

◇◇◇

They made their ride through the streets of Dickenson at a slow and leisurely pace. For the most part, there wasn't anything out of the ordinary as they rode up and down the streets north and south. Taking the streets east and west, they began in the residential part of town and worked toward the business district.

As they drew close to one of the saloons in the main part of the business area of Dickenson, Cille inhaled deeply and Uvonni said, "What is it, Cille?"

"That's his horse," she responded, as she reflected back on her previous assumption, "I knew he headed this way."

Bjorn was quick to reply, "You girls keep riding down the street, I want to check something out. Keep the same pattern and I'll join up with the both of you later." He reined his horse in at the same rail that the military mount was hitched.

When he dismounted, he deliberately smoothed out some of the soil near the hind quarter with his soft moccasin boots without being overly obvious about what he was doing. The military mount moved its hind quarters over so that Bjorn could make a couple more swipes with his smooth leather boots.

He tied his horse to the hitching rail and went into the saloon. There was a handful of people drinking. One of them was in uniform and wore sergeant stripes. Bjorn said, "I need a quick shot and I'll be on me way." He tossed his coins on the bar.

A barkeep set the shot glass down and poured it to the rim. While waiting for the barkeep, he overheard the sergeant say, "I have got to go to Little Missouri. I've got some chores there and need to collect my pay. I'll be back this way in about a week, then I'll pay you back for the short loan."

With a quick drink, Bjorn made short work of the shot of whiskey, then casually left the saloon.

At the hitching rail, he backed his horse out and in doing so, smoothed over more of the dirt in the street near the military mount. He swung into the saddle and went to find the women.

Moments later, when he rode up next to the women, Uvonnie

asked, “And what was that all about?”

“The horse belongs to the sergeant, I’m sure,” Bjorn said with confidence. “He’s at the saloon and I believe he’ll be leaving before too long. Let’s turn up here and we’ll take a distant gander to see if he has left yet.”

“And if he has, what in the world are your intentions, my dear husband?”

“I plan to show Cille the hoof prints of his mount, that’s all.” Bjorn replied.

Uvonnie asked, “Are you getting involved?”

Cille broke in, “No, Bjorn I can’t let you get involved. This is my problem and my fight. Please let me handle it my way. I owe it to Patrick; I made a promise.”

“I’m not getting involved in your fight, Cille. I’m going to show you a mark or so in the street that’s all. What you see, you need to memorize and keep in that pretty little head of yours. You asked me to show you something about tracking and that is what me intend to do. Nothing more, is that okay with the both of you?” He chuckled, amused at their concerns.

Both women became quite for the moment as they continued their ride. When they crossed the street a block away, they looked and saw Kidding mounting up. Bjorn said, “We’ll ride a couple blocks up and cut across, then go back and take a look.”

Their leisurely ride became somewhat tense with each person not sure exactly what was going to happen next.

When they rode past the saloon, they went to the hitching rail beyond where the military mount had been. Uvonnie stayed with her horse as Bjorn and Cille dismounted and walked one hitching rail away.

Bjorn said, “Just as I thought, the mount moved back over where I had smoothed out the ground with me foot. Cille, look at the shoe print on the front hoof and, this is interesting, look at the back hoof on the right side.”

She leaned over to see exactly what he was talking about. He continued, “The branch of the shoe is off to the side a tad, and for some odd reason, the toe of the shoe is smaller than the others. The forward part of the toe shows the shoe is a mismatch and the hoof hasn’t been trimmed down as it should be. Look, you can see the outline of the hoof beyond the branches of the shoe. I’d say the right shoe has been replaced in a hurry, because it is not a perfect match. The others seem to be a set. In the trade, it is called a cold shoe because it was not heated and adjusted to fit the hoof. A good farrier would have at least heated the shoe to fit by using a puller and spreader along with taking care of the hoof's rough edges with a rasp to keep it from being injured."

Cille looked on and tried to commit all she saw and heard to memory. "All that from a hoof print, Bjorn? That is interesting, isn't it?"

He looked up at her and said, "There is the marks you need to keep in mind. He shouldn't be too hard to follow. Now let's get out of here." As he stood, he scuffed the area to remove some of the prints in case someone saw them looking at the marks in the soil. They walked to their horses and mounted up.

From the saddle she said, "I see the land office is across the street. I'll need to visit with them before I return to Prairie Rose."

They returned to the Swavinguns where they put up the horses. Upon leaving the barn, Bjorn and Uvonnie joined hands as they walked to the house. They went to the kitchen table inside the house to enjoy a cup of coffee.

It was near dusk when Uvonnie said, "You're spending the night again with us, I hope, because we sure have enjoyed your visit."

She said, "I'll have to leave first thing in the morning. I need to stop by the land office and then make my ride to Prairie Rose. I have to get back to see my daughters. I miss them and I know they miss me. I'll have to make it up to them someday."

Bjorn spoke up, "Cille, I nearly forgot to mention, when I was in the saloon the sergeant mentioned that he was headed to Little Missouri to do something, then he was going to be heading back this way to pay off a loan."

She smiled at Bjorn and said, "You let him get a jump on me, didn't you?"

"There is no time like tomorrow to learn the tracking. If he has gone to Little Missouri, he'll be there before you get your start. Don't rush things. Go home, check on the girls. There will be time in the months ahead to do what you have set out to do. Just remember to be in control and don't flush him out until you're good and ready."

Uvonnie said, "I wish you would find it in your heart to let someone else do what needs to be done. It's not something us women should have to do."

With sympathetic eyes, Cille said, "I made a promise to Patrick that I would hunt them down and I intend to keep that promise. I won't rest until I have done what I have set out to do. I hope you understand."

"I understand your anger," she said, "I just don't want to see you hurt."

Cille smiled and said, "That is why I came all this way to ask for some help. I know I can't do it without being prepared. I have learned a lot in these last two days. I didn't realize there was so much to tracking. I'll say this much: I'll try to be careful, and I thank you both for your concern."

Bjorn said, "When you get home, practice on the rifles and with the revolver until you feel you can use them as an extension of your arm. When you have to use them, it will be like pointing a finger at what you want to hit when you pull the trigger. Learn to use them as well as how to track. Commit to memory and rely on your reflexes. That is where your confidence will come from, when you control the setting. Our love will be with you as you go out to fulfill that promise."

There was silence for a moment, then Cille said, "I love you both for the help you have given me. I'll keep in touch once this matter is behind me."

◊ ◊ ◊

The morning was quiet at the breakfast table, the sendoff was reserved. Cille knew she had to stop by the land office before she headed out of Dickenson on her way home.

When she arrived at the land office, she gathered the paperwork from her saddle bag and went into the office. She had to get Prairie Rose in her name and make arrangements for the transfer of the homestead at a later date. Her visit was quick, and in minutes, she found herself in the saddle leaving Dickenson.

She was a short distance out of town, when she got down from the saddle and looked for the odd hoof print. It didn't take long and she was soon on his trail, even if it was a day late. She would follow the trail, learning as she went. When Dublin had carried her near the Little Missouri River, she would head south to Prairie Rose, take some much-appreciated advice and use it. Right now, she wanted to see her daughters and hold them close letting them know that she loved them.

When she arrived in the makeshift town, it was under serious construction and located east of the Little Missouri River. She ran into Rufus and Rupert in front of the newly-opened Bentley mercantile. Rufus said, "Miss Cille, Wez been workin' for De Mores, and he come in town to get some supplies. He's wantin' to meet with ya, if ya gots a bit of time."

Cille said, "I don't have a lot of time. I plan to ride out to Prairie Rose and get there before it gets dark."

Rupert said, "It not take no time, he's in the mercantile, and oh no he not, here he comes."

A well-dressed aristocratic looking gentleman stepped up near the boys. Rufus began to speak as correctly as he could trying to make the proper introduction, "Mr. De Mores, this here be Mrs. Woodbury, the one wez been tellin' ya about." The other gentleman standing with De Mores was not introduced.

"I must say, I am deeply honored to meet you Mrs. Woodbury. The stories I hear about you have caused me to look forward to meeting you and it is certainly my pleasure," as he gracefully tipped his hat.

"Nice to meet you, also," Cille replied, "these young men have spoken about you and the magnificent house they are building."

"The chateau is for my adorable wife Medora. She should be coming this way before long. I would feel honored if you would come by the chateau when she arrives. I have had the pleasure of telling her about you and she is looking forward to meeting you."

"Thank you very much for the invitation. I will be looking forward to meeting her."

De Mores said, "If I may, let me introduce my dear friend Mr. Arthur T. Packard. He is the editor of the paper over in Little Missouri."

Mr. Packard nodded politely and said, "Mrs. Woodbury, it is indeed a pleasure to meet you. I look forward to seeing you in the near future. I would like to do an article about you in my issue of the Bad Lands Cow Boy sometime in the near future, if I could persuade you. Most folks just call me A.T."

Overwhelmed by the offer, she said, "I, I'm not sure at the moment. I'd have to think about it first. Right now, I'm heading out to Prairie Rose and I'd like to get there before dark."

A.T. said, "I do understand. Perhaps at a later date?"

In a French cavalier style, De Mores said, "The honor is ours and we shall not detain you from your chosen duties. Do have a pleasant day. Medora and I look forward to seeing you shortly after she arrives. Have a pleasant day," as he gestured once more in a gentlemanly fashion.

Cille was impressed by their behavior, smiled and replied, "My pleasure, gentlemen. Rufus and Rupert, I'll see the both of you out yonder if you're going to be visiting your folks in the coming days." With that, she went into the mercantile and purchased some licorice for the children before she made her ride out of town.

When she entered, she saw Audrey Bentley and said, "Audrey what an improvement over your building in Little Missouri. Congratulations on your move. I need some licorice and I'd like to have some ammunition for the buffalo gun, my carbine and for this here revolver."

"What on earth are you going to be shooting at?" Audrey asked.

"I plan to do some target shooting," Cille replied, "more for pleasure than anything else. I'm challenging myself to become proficient with the lot and a mess of cartridges ought to do the trick. The licorice is for my girls and Lizzie's Benji and Nizzie."

Audrey went about filling the order and asked, "How have things been going for you these days?"

Knowing Mrs. Bentley was digging for information and would put up a fuss if she really knew why she was buying the ammunition, she replied, "I'm just taking it one day at a time. Life has been rather tiring, that's for sure." She neglected to mention the girls' kidnapping, the chore she faced getting them back or the trip to Dickenson. The less she said, the less word spread of her troubles and intentions.

Mrs. Bentley smiled and said, "I should know. This move and handling all the stock has kept us rather busy. I'm just thankful we don't have to move it again."

Cille paid the bill, took the two sacks containing her order and left the store. She was happy that she was going to be riding south to Prairie Rose to see her daughters, Sadie and Elizabeth.

◇◇◇

When she arrived at My Place, Lizzie was in the garden hoeing the tomato patch and Sadie and Elizabeth were playing with Benji and Nizzie at the far side of the garden.

As she reined up, the girls let out a squeal and came running. Cille had no sooner landed on the ground, when her two daughters hugged her around the waist.

"Goodness, I sure have missed you girls."

Sadie, said, "We missed you a lot. We had fun with Nizzie and Benji and Lizzie showed us how to bake her kind of cookies."

Elizabeth chimed in, "Mommy, I bet I missed you more than Sadie. Can we go home and sleep in our own bedrooms? I miss being there. I like it here, but most of my dolls and toys are in my bedroom, and I like to play house with them.

Her question hit home and caught Cille unexpectedly, "I believe it is time we do that." She turned to Lizzie and said, "I thank you for all you have done. I need to be with my girls for now and show them I care."

Lizzie smiled and said, "Theyz no trouble. Theyz been helpin' me a heap with Benji and Nizzie. Iz do understand what ya sayin'. I go fetch the things theyz a needin'."

"Where is Ben-jomine? I didn't see him when I rode up."

"He been doin' some hammerin' in your barn all day. Gots no idea what for, but he be makin' a bunch of noise."

"Before I forget, I have some licorice for all the children," Cille replied. They gathered around her as she handed out the licorice.

Moments later, Cille and the girls headed across the creek to Prairie Rose. As they passed, Ben-jomine was coming out of the barn saying, "Miss Cille, Iz glad yas back."

"Glad to be back," Cille replied, "Lizzie said you have been doing some work in the barn, today."

"Yes um, Buster that crazy ol' mule ya gots, done kicked the stall all the way to the ground las' night, when Iz go puttin' him up. He's one stubborn mule and mean at times. Iz gots it fixed now and Iz headin' home to get some food to satisfy ol' Ben-jomine."

Cille said, "I won't detain you. I'll drop over tomorrow to talk a spell."

He waved over his head as he headed home. Cille and the girls went into their home for the first time as a family in over a month. They were home, they had more love to share and they were going to fix supper together. After they ate, Cille sat down with her daughters where she could read them a story before they went to bed. Before she tucked the girls in for the night, they said bedtime prayers and expressed gratitude to the Lord for his love and the love they shared together as a family. It felt good to be back home on Prairie Rose.

CHAPTER 34

Medora Von Huffman - Marques De Mores Arrives 1883

When the winds of winter and the spring thaw had passed, it was time to go into the fields and prepare the ground for seed. The Crowford boys, Rufus and Rupert, were on hand to do the manual work in preparation for planting. Buster the mule had acquired an attitude over the winter months, becoming unpredictable in his response at times. But with patience, and a little bit of understanding, the boys managed to get Buster to cooperate.

Cille waited until the fields were planted before she called them to the house at Prairie Rose and said, "Rufus and Rupert, your work in the fields has been greatly appreciated. We had a good crop last year and the price we received from the grain was good. Here is a portion of the profit. I hope you both will take it for your work, along with my deepest gratitude."

Rufus looked at the amount and his eyes became bright, "Iz much obliged Miss Cille. This be way beyond what wez even hoping to get paid. Iz thanks ya."

Rupert said, "Miss Cille, Iz gonna work for ya any time ya want. This bein' a heap more than Iz gonna charge anyone else. Iz thank ya from the bottom of the heart. There be but one other favor Iz askin'. Can we two use Buster to bust the sod on My Place?"

"Yes, you may," Cille said. "Anytime you need Buster to do the plowing, he's available to either of you. I am grateful for the work the both of you have done over the years. I felt it was only fitting that you received more than just for your labor alone."

With the crops in the field, and a handful of chores, Cille felt that she and the girls would be able to handle most of them. She knew that if the boys were not available, she could call on Benjomine, if help was needed with the harder chores.

After the Crowford boys left for My Place, she said, "Girls let's get started on your flower gardens." They were up against the house and a small patch out beyond the clothesline. She had purchased two small sacks of flower seed from the mercantile, special for her two gardeners.

When the girls were outside, Cille kept a rifle close by for their protection. She felt that if there was a next time, she may not be so lucky to have her girls return. She lived with that fear in her heart.

"Little sister, I'm going to let you choose which flower bed you want this year," Sadie said, "because I had my choice last year."

Elizabeth smiled and said, "I want the ones next to the porch on both sides of the steps. You can have the one by the side of the house and out by the clothesline."

The girls squatted down with small hand tools and smoothed their garden after their mother had stirred up the soil in each bed. Cille came along and drew a line in each bed and the girls took the seed and listened to instructions before going about casting the seed in the line of dirt. They were careful about pulling the soil over the seeds before sprinkling water on the flower beds.

They had grown tired in the afternoon and took a short nap. Cille had the German Shepherd, Duke stay at the front porch to guard the house while she took the rifle and revolver to the valley and did some target practice. She was beginning to understand each weapon and her accuracy improved over time. Her thoughts went back to Bjorn Swavingun, understanding his advice on becoming familiar with each gun until it was almost natural. Her practice was short because she wanted to return to the house and prepare the kitchen for making cookies when the girls got up from their nap.

When the girls awoke, they went into the kitchen and before long there was flour on the counter, in the pans, a mixture of cookie dough between them and two cookie sheets. Elizabeth saw some flour close to Sadie and said, "Look here." As Sadie turned to look, Elizabeth slapped her hand down hard in the small amount of flour causing it to billow up and over her sister's dress.

Sadie, not to be outdone, quickly placed both hands in the flour and came down the sides of her sister's face, before Cille said,

"Now girls, is that any way to act?"

Both of the girls looked at her and, almost in unison, apologized for their actions to her, but not to each other. They looked at each other and began laughing.

There was a commotion in the yard and Cille went to the door to see the Drake's wagon had pulled to a stop. They were coming across the yard, each parent holding on to their daughter's hand.

"Goodness, it's good to see you," Cille cried out. "Come on in. The girls have a mess of cookies going and I'll get the coffee on."

With the cookies in the oven, the girls took Gloria into Sadie's room where they began playing house with the dolls. Cille placed the second cookie sheet in the oven and quickly prepared the coffee.

Ted and Mathilda took a seat at the kitchen table while Cille got the cups from the cupboard. Ted spoke first, "We heard some shooting over this direction a bit ago, so I thought we best check things out."

"I've just been doing a bit of target shooting. Hard telling when I might have to use such skills." She didn't comment further.

Mathilda said, "There are a few of the neighbors across the hills that want to have a small get together for the children, one of them is a former teacher. They also thought maybe a church service could be held on Sundays, if they could find a parson to come out this way."

"I'm glad to hear about the teacher. Who is she and how far from here do they live?"

"If I'm not mistaken, there be about five families that are trying to make a go of it about five miles southeast of us." Mathilda explained. "They're in an area where it might be hard going, unless they have some rains during the summer."

"I wouldn't want to farm that area," Ted said. "I have a rough enough time on what ground I bust up each summer, but that land out there isn't what I'd call a good choice to try to prove up on. We finally have the land for our own, now. Last month, the land agent came out and we have proven up; got the deed to the place now."

Cille said, "I guess this fall, I'll have the land agent out here to check things out. I had the homestead put in my name last fall, when I was in Dickenson. I thought he might let me have it then but changed his mind and said I'd have almost a year left to prove up."

"Shoot, they don't do much when they come out," Ted replied. "They take a look to see that you have a house and crops in the field. Cille, it's just a formality to them when they see a place like what you have here."

"I hope that is all it takes," Cille said. "I would hate to lose it after what Patrick put into this land and the amount of work the Crowford boys have put out."

Mathilda asked, "Lizzie and that man of her's will be proving up about the same time, won't they?"

"We got the homesteads at the same time. I guess the land agent will get the both of us the same day," Cille replied.

Ted said, "Cille, you and the Crowfords don't have a thing to worry about. I wouldn't fret about it none."

The cookies were ready to come out of the oven and the coffee was hot. When Cille collected the cookies off the hot cookie sheets, she called out, "Girls, there is cookies and milk in the kitchen. Best come get the cookies while they're hot."

As the leisurely visit came to an end, Ted said, "Well woman, I think we best be heading home. I have chores to do."

Moments later, the Drake wagon was pulling out of the yard while Cille and the girls were headed to the hen house to feed the chickens and collect the eggs. Next, they would go to the barn to feed the stock and milk the cow before taking the milk and eggs to the house. When the chores were done, they headed to the house and prepared the evening meal.

◇◇◇

It was near noon on the following day when a wagon pulled by a classy pair of horses made its way down the hillside in the direction of Prairie Rose.

Cille and the girls were in the yard when it pulled to a stop. From where she stood in the yard, she looked up into the plush driver's seat. Marquis de Mores held the reins and next to him was A.T. Packard. She called out, "Greetings, what brings the two of you out this way?"

Marquis de Mores said, "The trip was my idea. A.T. came along to see what was south of the chateau. Rufus and Rupert Crowford gave me directions to this place. My desire was to tell you my wife Medora will be coming out this way early spring. I have told her about you and your escapades and she wants to meet you as soon as she arrives. She has been intrigued about your situation and we're inviting you to the chateau when she arrives. I certainly hope you will honor us with your company."

Cille said, "I'd love to. Would the two of you like to hop down and come in out of the heat of the day?"

"Ah, what an invitation," De Mores quipped, "how could one refuse such a beautiful gesture? But my dear young lady, we cannot stay long."

"Girls, run ahead and get the cookies out. We'll have them along with cold milk or coffee," Cille requested. She informed the company saying, "The Crowfords are right across the creek. Lizzie and Ben-jomine have two small children, twins named Benji and Nizzie, and Rufus and Rupert are Ben-jomine's children from a previous marriage. They have certainly helped me out from time to time. They are mighty good neighbors."

De Mores said, "The Crowford boys have an eye and hands for building and the chateau stands as proof of their ability."

When they were at the table, A.T. spoke up and asked, "Mrs. Woodbury, I'd still like to write an article about you in the Bad Lands Cow Boy. Have you made a decision yet?"

"Please call me Cille. I feel more comfortable with that. It's ok to be formal in a formal setting, but for now, Cille would be just fine. Your answer is no. I would prefer not to be used in an article. You see, I'm not the most welcome person in Little Missouri according to the law they have there."

A.T. returned, "Cille it shall be. I may have my newspaper office there, but I do not necessarily condone what goes on beyond the walls of my newspaper office. If your answer is no to an article, would you entertain an offer of me writing a book on your life?"

She looked at him and smiled. "I would have to think on that as well."

"I'll take that as a maybe and not a definite no and a not-so-definite yes."

"I think your coffee is getting cold," she told him as she offered to fill his cup. There was laughter and the subject for the time being was dropped.

The visit was short lived, and before long the men excused themselves. They made their way to the wagon and were soon headed up over the hill, on their way back to the chateau and the town of Little Missouri.

◇◇◇

It was early April when word had reached Prairie Rose that there was going to be a lot of fanfare in Medora. Marquis de Mores had let it be known that his wife Medora, for whom the town was named, would be arriving on the Northern Pacific passenger train in the afternoon.

Cille had deliberately waited until the following day of her arrival before she would call on Medora.

Most of the community was on hand at the depot to welcome Medora on the day she arrived on the train. There was a carriage waiting for her and the Marquis de Mores was in charge of seeing that she had the grandest of tours throughout the streets of the small town he had named after her. After all, it was her money that started the town and the refrigerator business that stored meats before they were shipped back East to his contacts. It was his intention to make Medora the biggest meat packing industry in the West. The ride up and down the streets was done before the carriage made the short trek to the bluff above the community where the chateau was waiting for her.

With the bulk of the well-wishers left behind in town, she was greeted upon their arrival by a small group of well-wishers and hired help on the porch of the chateau. Medora was introduced and spoke briefly with each one, before she entered the majestic chateau that her husband had built for her.

◇◇◇

Cille left the children with Lizzie and made her way to Medora on Dublin. When she arrived in the community, she headed to the bluff overlooking the town and to a majestic home called the chateau.

When she arrived, she had no sooner dismounted when Marquis de Mores came through the door and said, “Cille, I know you have ridden a great distance. Please come inside. My lovely wife Medora will be so excited.”

She followed him through the chateau until they arrived in the sitting room, where he softly announced, “My dear, this is Mrs. Woodbury; she prefers to be called Cille. She is the one I have told you about.”

Medora got to her feet and met them halfway across the room.

“Welcome to this part of Dakota,” Cille said, “I hope you enjoy it as much as I do.”

“Please come over here to the sofa,” Medora replied, “and sit with me while we’ll have tea and some sweets. I am so pleased to meet you. My husband has told me so much about you and the excitement that surrounds you.”

“I’m not so sure about all the excitement, but I have been kept rather busy trying to survive.”

Looking a bit tired from her lengthy trip, Medora smiled and said, “He looks at you as if you are the Western day Joan of Arc.”

“I’m flattered that I am admired in that high regard.” Cille replied. “I’m a widow trying to make do on a homestead south of here while I raise two lovely daughters.

While waiting for the tea to be served, their conversation began as if they had known each other for a long time. Medora was so easy to talk to and Cille didn’t mind the dozens of questions she asked. She found her to be very Victorian, where Cille seemed to miss that portion of her life. She felt she had grown rather rough around the edges over time on the prairie.

Medora said, “I was a Von Huffman before I married. I remained behind for a time while my husband ventured here after his time in the French military. He found the west challenging and wanted to build a home for me and build his meat packing empire.”

“The chateau is lovely and the town is what is needed on this side of the Little Missouri”, Cille said. “The town across the river is rather rough and has a lot of lawlessness; not a place for the softer set.”

“I have noticed a change in the lifestyles,” Medora confirmed, "as I rode across the country. When I got off the ship in New York, the dress and manners of the men and women were proper and resembled those in France, but as I rode further west, the behavior changed."

Cille mentioned, "I was born and raised in the community of Monroe, a short distance from New York. My parents sent me to Paris for finishing school, a couple of years before my debutante. I married a soldier who was later stationed out here in the Dakota Territory. He became injured and later we homesteaded before his death. That is why I am living in this part of the country."

"Oh Paris, how I enjoyed the times I spent there," Medora commented. "It is such a small world. I was raised in Europe and spent a lot of my time in France. I travel all this distance only to find that the woman my husband admires has been to France."

"I remember some of Paris," Cille added, "but most of the time I was chaperoned and my contact with anyone outside the school were very limited."

The visit ended with Medora insisting, "Cille, I look forward to seeing you as often as you can come by. It makes no difference if it is for a leisurely chat or a quick refuse in a time of need. If that is the case, tie up your horse at the bottom of the bluff. There is a path near the cottonwoods that will lead to the back door of the chateau."

Cille said, "Thanks Medora, I may take you up on both in the future if I need to. I have so enjoyed the visit. Should you talk your husband into bringing you south as far as Prairie Rose, I would be most happy to have you visit and meet my daughters."

Medora said, "I would like that and I may ask him to take me out that way."

"There is a bit of riding I have to do in order to get back to Prairie Rose." She excused herself and went to mount up.

As she mounted Dublin, Cille rode down off the bluff into the town and planned to ride south at a quickened pace in order to get home in time to do the chores, after picking up a treat for the children.

◇ ◇ ◇

Cille picked up the girls from the Crowfords and walked to her home at Prairie Rose. The girls bounded into the house before her, but when she stepped inside, a cold chill and a quick flashback of Patrick mortally wounded and laying on the floor with the far wall bloody and peppered with shot flashed through her mind. It was only momentary, but it felt real to her. She stepped through the door and went to the kitchen to see what they could have for the evening meal. Ben-jomine had the girls accompany him earlier and they had done the chores for her.

When the dishes had been cleared from the table and cleaned, she sat the girls down and read them two stories. The girls said their bedtime prayers before they were ushered off to their bedrooms and tucked in for the night.

◇◇◇

The yearly harvest took place and Cille felt lucky to have so many close friends. The Drakes and the Crowford family showed up at Prairie Rose to help feed the workers in the field. When the crops were done, they would take the grains to market for her and she would get paperwork later concerning the market value and a bank draft for the crops.

While the crew was on Prairie Rose, there was the noon meal and the evening meal provided before they headed out to harvest another homesteader's crops. Cille would see to it that the foreman was paid ample funds to divide among the crew as well for the work they had done.

When the harvesting crew left for another homestead, the nearby neighbors stayed to visit for most of the evening. Ted had gone home to do his chores early and returned to pick up Mathilda and Gloria, who had visited after the harvesters had left. Ben-jomine and the boys took care of Cille's chores and those of his own. This allowed Lizzie to help out with serving and cleaning up after the evening meal. It was a full day with a lot accomplished.

CHAPTER 35

The Killing of Joe Kidding 1884

It was a beautiful day, with the crops in the field, their heads breaking through the ground showing that the seed had germinated and that there would be a harvest in the fall if all went well. The sun was out to warm the landscape and the heavens were clear making this an ideal day to enjoy nature at its best.

Marquis de Mores and his wife Medora were joined by A.T. Packard as they rode in a buggy from the chateau to Prairie Rose.

Cille saw the prestigious carriage from a distance and knew who was calling. She was happy that she had asked Lizzie to make a batch of her famous cookies so that she may have them on hand should company arrive.

When the carriage pulled to a stop, she was in the yard to greet them. “It is an honor to see that you have come this far to visit me on Prairie Rose.” The company began to get out of the carriage. “Welcome and let’s go into the sitting room, where we can enjoy refreshments and pastries.”

Medora said, “It is beautiful out this way. I can certainly see why you love it here.”

Cille replied, “Thank you, this is where I call home.”

When they entered the house, after became seated in the sitting room, Sadie and Elizabeth came in from their bedrooms. Cille said, “Come here girls, I would like you to meet Mr. A.T. Packard and this gentleman is Marques de Mores with his wife Medora. This is the lovely lady I was telling you about.” Turning her attention she said, “Medora, this is my oldest daughter, Sadie and my youngest, Elizabeth.” As they were introduced by their mother, they curtsied, as they were previously instructed.

"I'm very pleased to meet the both of you," Medora replied. Turning to Cille, she said, "and their manners are a reflection of their proper upbringing."

"Girls, would you join me in the kitchen," Cille requested, "where I can furnish the coffee and you may help me by delivering the pastries to our guests."

Moments later, the coffee was delivered along with the trays of cookies. The girls excused themselves properly and went into the kitchen where they enjoyed cookies and milk.

With an honored guest at her side, the visit in the house was short lived before Cille gave Medora a tour of the homestead. A look over the fields, the chicken coop from a distance, and a tour into the barn was brief. She looked at her guest and said, "All this will be in my name whenever the land agent visits and we can show that we have improved the land over the last five years."

Marquis de Mores and A.T. Packard followed behind taking in all the information but allowing Medora to be the main guest as Cille pointed out all that was on Prairie Rose.

The Marquis and A.T entered into the conversation often, and before long, the honored guests excused themselves for the long drive back to the chateau.

Before leaving, Medora said, "Cille, I do so much want you to visit at your leisure or when you visit the town of Medora. I have enjoyed your hospitality and remember our conversation about coming by if you need immediate refuge."

"You're so kind," Cille replied. "I'll keep in touch and thanks for the visit today. I speak on behalf of myself and the girls. We have enjoyed your calling."

As the carriage was making its way to the top of the hill, another buggy with a top was coming down the hill. Cille stayed in outside and was surprised when the buggy rolled to a stop in the yard.

A tall middle-aged gaunt gentleman got out of the buggy and said, "I'm looking for a Mrs. Woodbury, might you, be she?"

"I am and with whom am I speaking?" Cille asked in return.

"Jefferson Marley, the deputy land agent for the area. I see that there is little I need to report on your homestead. If I may look around just briefly, I'll be on my way. I assume the homestead across the creek is that of a Lizzie Jane Betts who later married a Crowford?"

"You have my permission to have a look," Cille replied with a smile, "And yes, that is the Crowfords across the way. They are home, and I'm sure Lizzie will allow you to look around. Ben-jomine is the man of the house over there."

Following a brief tour of Prairie Rose, he said, "Mrs. Woodbury, I need your signature on a couple of these forms and I'll be on my way to the Crowfords. You will have your deed to the homestead recorded and available for you in about two weeks in the Dickenson Land Office."

"If the Crowfords have proven up according to your requirements," Cille asked, "would I be able to pick up their deed as well, when I make the trip, or are they going to have to make the trip themselves?"

Mr. Marley said, "I will need to have their permission for such a transaction."

"I'll accompany you across the creek, and if their word today is enough, will that be sufficient?"

"It will and I will make a note of it on the papers they sign."

They went to My Place and before long, the Deputy Land Agent was on his way back to Medora before he made his return trip to Dickenson.

Ben-Jomine and Lizzie were happy as Cille congratulated them on proving up. It was a day to celebrate before she left for Prairie Rose.

◇ ◇ ◇

Two weeks had passed and the girls were being watched by the Crowfords, while Cille made her way to Dickenson to get a copy of the deeds.

Upon leaving the land office, she was putting the deeds in the saddle bag when she looked across the street and saw Sergeant Joe Kidding swing into the saddle. She jumped from behind Dublin and went to draw, but the flap was in her way. She quickly tucked the flap between the beltline and her body. He caught her actions and knew he was in trouble, because he whirled his mount into an alley as fast as he could go. She muttered, "Bjorn wouldn't be happy; she spooked the bird."

Cille returned to Dublin's side and secured the deeds before she mounted. She was no fool. She knew going into the alley was a way of being set up on the other end. She rode a block west and then came down the street on the opposite side of the block riding slow. She was cautious and began to glance down at the ground. Sure as thunder, in the street she spotted the right rear hoof print. The shoe hadn't been changed in all this time.

The prints headed out of town in the direction of Medora. Not far from Dickenson, the tracks made a sharp turn to the south into some rugged terrain. He was either heading to another location or trying to wind up behind her. She took a slow approach following the tracks.

◇◇◇

Cille was exhausted and her tiny frame slouched in the saddle as she rode. She guided her horse down the dusty street in the direction of the Medora livery. The tracks were gone, missing among numerous other riders and wagon tracks. Maybe she could pick them up on the other side of town. The past weeks had been an empty, agonizing effort, riding up one hill only to go down the other side. She traveled through arroyos, ravines, small ditches, canyons, gullies, washes and across dry creek beds. He had done his best to lose her in the rugged terrain. The going was rough at times for Cille and her mount. Dublin needed a rest and she would visit the Bentleys to make arrangements for some much-needed supplies before aimlessly riding out of town on her way back to Prairie Rose. Maybe she could pick up some clues as to what her next move would be by rumors in town.

As the hunter, she was never willing to quit her pursuit as the fervor of her anger still raged within her. At times, an uneasy feeling would creep over her, as though she was being watched or followed. Her movements had to be clear and calculated. They brought out a savagery in one who only a short time ago was content doing chores and standing up for the man she loved. Not one waking moment was spent underestimating her adversaries. She knew her enemy was crafty. She had to learn more each day if she was to survive and fulfill her promise to Patrick. Pushing herself hard and fast, knowing the difficulties of completing the task she had set forth, she pressed on supported only by loving memories of her late husband. She was aware of her weaknesses. After all, she was a woman out of her element and traveling in a savage land. Yet she drew her strength from within, determined to right a wrong.

Most of her essential provisions were running mighty low. She needed to stop in and see Audrey and Roger Bentley for supplies. While she was there, she would try to get some much-needed rest while visiting with her friends. But first, she had to see the smithy at the livery, check Dublin's shoes and provide care for him. Cille fully realized that her safety, her life, depended on Dublin. Cutting corners where his care and wellbeing were concerned was not an option.

Riding down the quiet street, raucous noise from the saloon got her attention. Someone was having a howling good party and several cowboys were whooping it up. She could see A.T. Packard, Little Missouri's editor, on the boardwalk with his printer's pipe in hand about the same time he recognized her. He tipped his hat and she responded by smiling and saying, "A.T."

Suddenly, she reined up, staring at a horse at the hitching rail. Her blood surged through her body, seemingly spreading new rejuvenated life. She held out a hand, as if to stop Packard. She did not have to search her memory long to recognize that particular horse. She realized her efforts in the hunt had paid off. The excitement of the moment filled her with an awakening spirit, where she could fulfill her vengeance or die trying. She felt deep-rooted bitterness surface, with a need to be soothed.

A.T. stood watching, seeing her pull back on the reins as the horse walked backwards. She motioned for him to join her in the street, "What is it, Cille?"

Wasting no time while dismounting, she met him on the ground. She replied with almost a whistle through her teeth, "I found me a killer."

"What?"

Pointing to the horse tied at the rail, she spoke, as the pain and anguish boiled within her tiny frame. "That mount belongs to the killer I'm looking for."

With astonishment, A.T. could only reply, "But that's a cavalry mount."

"Yes, I know and the rider is none other than a culprit named Sergeant Joe Kidding."

The Editor responded, "So what if it is? What do you plan to do?"

"Simple, I'm going to kill him!"

A.T. said, "Cille, you've been in the sun too long."

"Maybe so, but I'm going to need your help."

"Help you do what, kill the man?"

"No, I'm not asking that, but I am asking you for a favor." She reached into the saddlebag, pulled out her tattered black dress and fished for her late husband's military academy insignia. Gritting her teeth, she savagely grabbed at the material, ripped a strip of black cloth from the dress and pinned the emblem on it. Holding it out, she softly asked, "A.T. can you take this inside the saloon for me and call out his name? When he answers, dangle this in front of him and let him know he has an invitation to step outside."

"You're loco!"

"Maybe, but I'm also serious."

Reluctantly, A.T. held out his hand and took the black ribbon. "You're sure?"

"Yes, I am, and don't stand too close to him when he comes out. I just might get trigger happy."

Packard looked into her face. Her eyes had narrowed and her jaw was set and a sense of determination marked her presence. He cocked an eyebrow, nodded his head slightly, and said, "Luck be with you, Cille. I hope you make it so that I might get a chance to write that book."

Cille softly whispered, "Do this for me A.T. and I just might say yes on the book." She saw him turn and walk toward the saloon, as if he hadn't heard her soft comment.

She dropped the reins of her horse to ground hitch him and took up a position in the street, off of the boardwalk, on the side opposite side the saloon. She folded the flap of the military holster back to where it rested between the belt and her body.

Traffic on the street suddenly came to a halt, sensing an impending shootout. The Marquis de Mores was in a buggy with his wife Medora and they had a front row view of the fight from their carriage. He was excited over what he was seeing, while Medora was reserved, concerned for Cille's health.

◇◇◇

As A.T. had pushed open the batwings, he stepped inside and with a booming voice called out, "Kidding! Sergeant Joe Kidding!"

There was an unusual silence that grew from the crowd, where plain talk could be heard and understood. He called out once more, "Kidding!"

A tall broad-shouldered trooper turned around to face the editor. "It better be urgent; I don't like your tone. No man yells at me in that tone of voice and gets away with it, unless it's downright important."

The saloon took on an eerie quiet. A.T. seemed to chuckle, as if enjoying himself, "Oh, it is." He held out the black ribbon, as it draped over his index finger, held stiff by the weight of the insignia.

Kidding stood with his back to the bar, as Packard walked forward, intentionally slow. The hush of the crowd grew as those gathered began to wonder what was going to happen next. Kidding's eyes narrowed in on the black ribbon and insignia. He appeared lost for words as his face took on a bewildered expression. He had seen the likes of the black ribbon and insignia before on the day Lieutenant Caleb Masters was blown to bits. He had returned to the scene to see how the others were arranged. Not only were they dead, but they were posed in such a way as to pass on a haunting image, one that he had carried for some time.

In a tone hard and penetrating, A.T. said, "The lady's name is Cille. She is calling you a killer and she sent me in here with this invitation. She is calling you out." He held the ribbon up close to Joe Kidding's face.

The sergeant reached out, snatched the ribbon and tossed it to the floor. "That no good sod buster's wife has gone too far. I'm tired of her dogging me here and there. She has no call for what she is doing. She has been dogging my trail all the way from Dickenson. Is she hiding and planning to ambush me or out in the open?"

Packard began to feel an enjoyment fill his body, to see the large-framed trooper begin to melt like candle wax being left too close to a hot stove. He smiled and spoke softly, “I don’t believe she feels it is necessary to hide in ambush. She is confident and is out in the street waiting for you. I’m going to step outside and let her know the invitation has been extended. Finish the drink you paid for and I’ll let her know you’ll be out shortly.”

A hint of uncontrollable panic briefly crossed the trooper’s face. He stood motionless as A.T. turned to walk out the door.

Various sounds from chairs scooting backwards from the tables filled the saloon, as cowboys and troopers scampered to the saloon window to see what would surely happen in the street.

Standing broad shouldered, not wanting to show he was intimidated, Kidding turned, grabbed his beer and finished it without bringing the mug down from his lips. He turned to face the door. His friend, Corporal Hendricks, walked with him as far as the door and said, “I thought you said you lost her on the trail.”

◇◇◇

From the far side of the street where traffic had stopped, Deputy Sheriff Henry Harmon suddenly appeared and said, “Mrs. Woodbury, if this is a shootout, I can’t let you go through with it.”

Cille said, “Sheriff, he killed my husband out at Prairie Rose by gunning him down with a shot gun. I have tracked him here and I plan to take care of business.”

“I can’t let you do that! I’m the law in this town and I can’t let you do that, Cille! I’m telling you, I’ll arrest you if you draw leather. I mean it!”

“Where were you when my Patrick was gunned down?” Cille spoke sharply.

“I was in Mandan enforcing the law,” Harmon explained. “Now I am here in Medora and I’m telling you there is no gun play.”

“You can’t stop what is going to happen,” Cille responded, “I have already sent an invitation into the saloon for Sergeant Joe Kidding to step outside and he knows who sent the invitation.”

Harmon spoke with authority, “If he comes through the batwings, Cille, he’ll have to answer to me. You’re out of it and I am saying this for the last time: there will be no gun play on your part. I'll take care of the situation, understood?" He kept walking toward Cille until he was close enough to have the batwings of the saloon in front of him.

"But I have tracked him here," Cille cried out, "and he deserves to get what's coming to him."

"Cille, you have two fine children at home. I understand what you have gone through, what you did on the open prairie is understandable. Any mother would have done nearly the same. But this is different; this is in town. I represent the law, and I am here to handle this matter. Don't cross me and the duties I have sworn to uphold!"

She stood her ground for a long moment, then said, "I sure hope you can handle it, Sheriff, because I'm sure we don't have much time to discuss it further."

A.T. suddenly stepped outside and was holding one of the swinging doors open. He basked in the knowledge that the tiny Cille had such a profound impact, obviously striking a raw nerve, on the likes of a large trooper. And he was allowed up front, where the action would be, to witness something exciting first hand. He thought 'What a story line'. Then he saw Deputy Harmon standing near Cille.

Both troopers stepped through the door. Corporal Hendricks took up a position on the opposite side of the entrance, but allowed the louvered door to swing back into position. It made several awkward squeaks before becoming motionless. Kidding stood on the walkway for a moment until he was clear where Cille was standing, his right hand dangled at his side as his fist opened and closed several times. Then he saw the deputy standing near her.

The sheriff spoke up, "Sergeant Joe Kidding, you'll have to answer to me, now. I understand, you were in a party that gunned down Mr. Woodbury."

Kidding, failed to respond, stepped down from the walkway into the street and with fluid motion, pulled the revolver from his holster as he dove for the protection of the watering trough.

Cille suddenly felt nervous, but was ready to respond when Harmon pulled iron and fired. She felt her nerves jump when the round fired, and then she saw the sheriff return the revolver to its leather resting place. He was quick and confident of his shot.

Packard heard the pull of leather and automatically swung the three-foot printer's pipe he held. It ripped into Hendricks's forehead as the Army revolver fired into the walkway. The trooper fell forward on the walkway, dead. Sheriff Harmon looked up to see the trooper crumble. Cille walked across the street to see Kidding up close. He was face down in the dirt and motionless. She looked up at Packard as the anger within her subsided, only to hear him say, "You're both nuts!" Looking at Harmon he said, "Why in the world did you put that fool thing away when you did?"

"I only needed one shot," he replied.

A.T. looked at Cille and said, "You never fail to amaze me. Didn't you see his partner getting ready to pull iron on the both of you?"

Her lips turned into a smile before she answered. "Oh, come on, A.T., you know I didn't have an argument with the man. I just figured you were closer and wanted to write a book, so I let you do the gentlemanly thing that needed to be done to protect us. And from the looks of things, you did quite well. I'm impressed."

People from inside the saloon filled the street along with those already outside in the open. Endless chatter about what had happened was almost deafening. Someone shouted, "He shot him right in the head."

As Cille looked up at A.T., she commented, "That's where you shoot snakes, isn't it?"

Packard stepped down from the walkway to join them, "You're mighty sure of your shot, sheriff."

"That I am," then he remarked, "But as for you A.T., you're brutal as all get out."

"You're pretty sure of your shot," Cille responded, "but what would have happened if his friend would have ducked?"

Harmon smiled more openly and said, "I didn't miss and he didn't duck."

The saloonkeeper came through the door and down off the walkway. He held out the black ribbon and emblem. "I think this belongs to someone out here." Cille held out her hand and took the ribbon. The barkeep turned and went back inside.

As Cille picked up the reins of her horse she heard the sheriff say, "A. T., how did you get involved in this affair?

"I saw Cille earlier and she called that trooper a killer, then I notified him in the saloon. When he stepped into the street, he went for iron. You shot him. From where I stood, he drew first. You can tell your brother G.W. back in Mandan that's how I saw it and I think you're a Jim Dandy of a lawman."

"Why did the young trooper interfere?" Harmon asked.

"Near as I can tell," Packard replied, "they were drinking at the bar together when I went in. All I did was extend the invitation and came out. I was on one side of the door and that trooper stood on the other side. When his buddy was dropped, you had already holstered your iron when he started to draw down on the both of you. I slapped him in the head after he had cleared leather. His shot went into the walk."

The sheriff looked at Cille and A.T. saying, "You two are collecting one heck of a bad reputation. Cille, you have so much hatred built up, folks in these parts will be glad to see you get rid of it. I hope this is the end of it, for your sake. As for you, A.T. that printer's pipe ain't always going to be the answer to settling things. Now you two get out of my sight for a spell."

Cille spoke up, "Oh, Mr. Harmon, take this black ribbon and my husband's insignia and give it to the undertaker. I want it buried with this one," pointing to Sergeant Kidding. "When he wakes up in the hereafter, I want him to know my husband and I send our regards."

Reluctantly, the lawman took the strip of black that held the insignia. "Now you two get out of my sight! Somehow, I'll try to convince the Army that they had it coming and I'll have to make arrangements for them to come and get their horses."

"Oh, by the way, Sheriff," Cille added, "when you get in touch with the Army, tell them I have a military mount out at Prairie Rose that belongs to them. And when you get a chance to share the news with the constable and the judge in Little Missouri, tell them the last trooper bit the dust. He seems to have a keen interest in what I'm doing, especially if someone comes up dead."

Harmon raised his head shaking it slightly saying, "You're pushing it, Cille."

Packard turned to her and asked, "Where to, Cille?"

"To the livery I guess. I was headed in that direction, when I got side-tracked. I take it I'll be escorted in that direction?"

"Well, Cille, I see it's clear we're not wanted around here, so

I'm fixing to do just that."

On their way to the livery, Marquis de Mores and his wife Medora rode by in their carriage, smiling and waving at them in passing.

She collected the reins and walked down the middle of the street toward the livery. A.T. asked, "Cille I would be most obliged if you would allow me to write about your life out here in the west. I find you extremely interesting."

Her emotions were getting the best of her as tears filled her eyes for what she had gone through. All of the bad times had finally come to an abrupt halt and she overwhelmingly realized how deeply her anger had affected her. She answered, "I don't like what I have become since Patrick's death. There isn't a thing in my life worth writing about."

"I find that hard to believe. I would like to write the book about you and how life has dealt you a difficult set of circumstances. I want to show how you responded to life, living out here on the open prairie. I might even write a comment in the Bad Lands Cow Boy about what happened around here today, something exciting to keep the circulation up, but not near as in-depth as I want to write on you."

"Why do you want to write about me?"

"I've been thinking of writing a book and having it published back East. It will be a true story that will let others know what it's like for a woman to survive out here."

Cille thought on the idea for a few moments, then said, "A.T., I appreciate what you did for me today. I'll consent to you doing the book, but first give me a bit of time to adjust. I need some rest and a little time to return to the person I was before. I've shamefully neglected my children and friends too long. There will be a time when we can get together and start the book. I'll let you know when I'm ready."

When they arrived at the livery, she left instructions with the smithy to check Dublin's hooves and shoes to insure they were healthy and fit properly and to see that he had an extra special order of oats as well as a good rub down. She would be back later to pay her bill. Then A.T. and Cille left the livery on their way to the dry goods store.

As they stepped into the store, they could see Roger was busy behind the counter and Audrey was in the back getting material for one of the customers. Cille went about getting what she needed as she walked around the small store. A.T. tagged along quietly, not making any conversation.

Before she was ready to leave, Cille said, "I need to get my horse, then I'll stop by to get these items. I have got to get back to Prairie Rose today."

Cille left the store and headed to the livery while A.T. excused himself and said he was riding to the chateau to do some visiting. She bid him farewell and continued on her journey.

After getting Dublin and a good report from the smithy, she returned to the store and picked up a large sack of licorice to go along with the other items. She then made her way to Prairie Rose to deliver a deed to the Crowfords and an added treat for the children.

On her way out of Medora, she was beginning to feel some of the anger in her life slipping away. In the days ahead, she would visit Patrick's grave and let him know what she had done. But for now she wanted to see her daughters and try to make up for lost time.

◇ ◇ ◇

Upon her arrival, Cille rode into the barn at Prairie Rose where she took care of Dublin before making her way to the Crowfords to pick up the girls. Ben-jomine had done the chores early and the girls had been fed. When she tapped on the door, there was such joy throughout My Place. Sadie and Elizabeth were happy their mother was back, they could sleep in their own beds and they had their licorice. Benji and Nizzie were also happy as they ate their licorice in silence.

Lizzie and Ben-jomine stood with their arms interlocked and she held out the unfolded deed as they looked on, proud beyond words. They had traveled west with the Woodburys, trusting their word. They worked hard over the years and now the proof was unfolded in Ben-jomine's hand; a deed for the land they worked on so hard. They had proven up. Now they were not only tenants on a piece of land, they were the outright owners. They looked into each other's eyes, and Lizzie said, "Ben-jomine, Iz glad you iz mine. Look what we gone and did."

Ben-jomine looked into Lizzie's eyes to see that they were tearing up. "Not no need to go cryin', but the proof was in the makin' a long time ago. You had My Place, then you had me jump the broom, to say welcome to My Place, now wez got the deed to say it belongs to no one else cause its Our Place now."

Lizzie turned to Cille and asked, "Did ya gets your deed, too?"

Cille smiled and said, "I have the deed at the house and I'm so glad for all of us. It has been a struggle from the beginning and I want to thank the both of you for all the help you have given me over the years to help me prove up. It is a good feeling, isn't it?"

She visited with the Crowfords for a short time before calling to the girls saying, "It's time to go home." When she uttered the words 'go home,' they had a wonderful sound to them.

When Cille and the girls crossed the creek on their way home, she thought of her plans to go to Little Missouri in the morning to see Patrick's grave. They had passed a milestone.

CHAPTER 36

When the Military Came Calling 1885

It was early in the morning when Cille said, "Girls, I think it would be nice if we pick some Prairie Roses and a selection of flowers from your flowerbeds to take to your father's grave today. I'll do the dishes first, then we'll go out and pick the flowers we want.

Elizabeth said, "I get to take a whole bunch, because I love my Daddy."

Sadie asked, "Are we going to collect the Prairie Roses first or the ones from our flower gardens?"

Their mother said, "When the dishes are done, I will give each of you a quart jar so you can pick a few flowers from your beds. I'll trim them before we put some water in the jar, so they will look nice for several days. We will do the same trimming and watering with the Prairie Roses. Then we'll hitch up Buster and make a trip to the Little Missouri cemetery where we will place them on your father's grave. We'll stay in the town of Medora where we can do some shopping and come home tomorrow."

When the dishes were dried and placed in the cabinet, Cille got a pair of scissors, two quart jars and some ribbon. Sadie carefully chose the flowers she wanted to place on her father's grave. She said, "I bet Daddy will like these. I think the bluebells and these daisies will look really nice."

Not to be outdone, Elizabeth chose the flowers from her beds near the front porch. She pointed to the iris and said, "I want those. They are special because Daddy is special. After Cille had cut the irises and placed them in the jar her daughter was holding, they went into the house where she tied a bow around each jar.

Cille gathered up three more quart jars, before they stepped outside. They walked up the hillside and picked a number of Prairie Roses. When they were trimmed and placed in the jars, they returned to the house where colorful bows were added. With the dipper, she gave each jar a measured amount of water. They left the flowers on the table for the moment before going to the barn and harnessing Buster to the wagon. Cille picked up a wooden egg crate and placed it in the back. When they returned to the house, they took a towel to support the jars in the crate and placed it on a folded quilt in the back of the buckboard. Cille placed a small spade in the wagon so that they could partially bury the jars in the ground at the cemetery.

Moments later, they were on their way to Little Missouri. It would be a long trip, nearly twenty miles, from the homestead to the town of Medora, then about two miles to the west. The cemetery was located on the western bank of the Little Missouri River, a short distance from the town.

It was the latter part of the afternoon when they arrived at the cemetery. Their visit across the river went largely unnoticed. Cille set the buckboard brake and set about getting their flowers from the back of the wagon.

Elizabeth said, "I want to carry my flowers."

Sadie replied, "I'll carry mine and I'll help with the spade. You can carry all the Prairie Roses," as she looked into her mother's eyes.

Cille warned, "Be careful where you walk girls. It isn't nice to walk on someone else's grave. Follow me and I'll show you where we will put the flowers."

When they arrived at Patrick's grave, Cille set the flowers down and used the spade to remove some of the weeds that had grown near the headstone. Then she dug a hole for the five jars. She turned to her daughters and said, "How do we want the flowers arranged?" She placed the jars in the opening and asked, "Do we want all Prairie Roses in the center and your flowers on the sides or do you think this way would be better?" She arranged the Prairie Roses on the outside with one jar separating the girls' selection.

Sadie and Elizabeth looked at the arrangements and both agreed that the Prairie Roses needed to be separated by their flowers. When the jars were in place, Cille said, "Girls I think it is time to say something to your father if you wish. Let's kneel down over here and say what we would like."

Elizabeth said, "Do you want me to say it out loud?"

"If you wish," her mother responded.

With a voice much louder than what her mother anticipated, Elizabeth belted out, "I miss you Daddy and I miss you bigger than the tallest flower I brought today. Now I got a big hole in my flowerbed at home, but that is ok with me. I got the good ones that the grasshoppers didn't bite on. I love you and I wish you were here to read me a bedtime story."

Sadie had her turn and said, "My dearest Papa, I miss you every day. Sometimes I cry a lot because you are not here, but Lizzie says your spirit is in the air circling around where we live. I look up when I am sad, but I don't see you. I love you and miss you more than all the flowers on the hillside. I hope you like the flowers I picked and those that Elizabeth picked and the ones Mama picked. I love you, Papa.

Cille was momentarily choked up before she added, "Patrick, my heart is heavy-laden with grief. I made a promise a long time ago and justice has been served. But while I harbored so much anger, I'm afraid I didn't do justice to the girls. For that, I am so deeply sorry. I miss you something fierce and the days that have passed have been agonizing to deal with. Now that there is no longer a reason to seek vengeance, I pray that I can get on with living and do the best for the girls. They have been so good, and I love them for how they have responded. You have touched my life in so many wonderful ways. I miss that and the wonderful love you showered over me. We have proven up; Prairie Rose is ours, and justice has been served. I'll do my very best to see that the girls are brought up right. I love you, Patrick so very, very much." With that, she kissed her fingertips and touched the headstone. She got to her feet and they made their way back to the wagon.

When they left the cemetery at Little Missouri, they returned to the town of Medora and found a room at the hotel before they went about town shopping. The girls were excited to be with their mother on this day, especially shopping. A short time later, they ate their evening meal at a rooming house before returning to the hotel and saying their bedtime prayers before bed.

◇◇◇

When Cille and her girls rode over the crest of the hill in their wagon, they began the gentle descent down the hillside into Prairie Rose. Cille could see there was a rider some distance to her rear that was gaining on them. They would make it home a few minutes before he showed up. As of now, she had no idea who the rider could be.

Cille pulled the wagon to a stop in front of the house and told the girls, "Quickly, get inside." She followed them, and when she stepped inside, she grabbed the revolver in its holster, wrapped the belt around her and grabbed the telescope. When she stepped into the doorway, she took the scope and saw the deputy from Little Missouri coming to pay her a visit. She called out "You girls stay inside!"

She went outside and stood by the wagon as Russell Coby, Marshal of Little Missouri, reined in his mount a short distance from the wagon. "Cille, I come to pay you a visit."

"Is it official or of a personal nature, Marshal?"

"Well," Russell said, "I guess you could say it's a little bit of both, depending if you're cooperative."

"What is the official business, first?" Cille asked.

"I didn't get a nasty bundle dropped at my office door like you did some time back, but I see you caused another trooper to bite the dust."

"He had it coming," Cille replied, "but I wasn't the one that put him down."

Coby spoke in a cocky fashion, "Makes me no mind if the trooper bit off more than he could chew, as long as you can become friendly. A woman like you needs a man around to see that things are run right. I kinde thought, I just might be that kind of fella to do just that."

Unwilling to put up with his behavior, Cille snapped, "I have no use for a man of your caliber, end of conversation. I suggest you rein that horse around and get off Prairie Rose right quick. You're out of your jurisdiction and way out of line."

"Now look, Cille," the marshal returned, "If I catch you in Little Missouri, I'll arrest you and have you pulled before Judge Sid Butler for your behavior by tossing spoiled evidence at my doorstep. And I have half a notion to turn you in to the Army and let them know where you hang your sun bonnet."

"Marshal, you'd have to catch me first and I don't think you're that swift." Cille spouted. "You're both self-appointed into your positions and the general public knows it. You're both lucky the real law hasn't cracked down on the both of you. As for turning me into the Army, that fits your character. I would expect nothing less." She had enough, stepped away from the wagon and took up a stance.

Coby looked down from the saddle and saw that he had pushed her too far. "Now Cille, you know you have me at a disadvantage sitting here like this, but if I had my feet on the ground, that would be a different story."

Cille failed to smile, but said, "If your feet hit the ground any time soon, you won't be riding out of Prairie Rose."

"You'll pay for this, Cille, I promise you that," as he reined his horse around and left the yard in a gallop.

◊ ◊ ◊

A week had passed when Cille looked up on the hillside to see a lone rider coming down the hill. She waited in the yard to see a military officer rein up his horse and ask, "By chance, is this Prairie Rose and might you be Mrs. Woodbury?"

"That it is. I'm Cille. What brings you out this way?"

"I'm Major Mark Collins. I have the responsibility of investigating some matters out this way and I need to talk with you, if I may."

"If it is short, you can say what you want from the saddle. If not, hop down and I'll get the coffee on. We can talk in the kitchen."

When they entered the house, Cille called out, "Girls, we have company. Please do not disturb us for a few minutes and go play in your rooms."

With coffee and some fresh pastries on the table, Cille got right to the point. "Major, what is it I can help you with?"

Mark asked, "I understand a Lieutenant Caleb Masters and a

Sergeant Joe Kidding entered your life at one time. I would like you to tell me, in your own words, what transpired without me having to ask a bunch of questions. In fairness, I will say that the Indian agent, Leonard Goddard, who watches over the Standing Rock Indian Reservation south of Fort Rice, reported a story to the Army. There seems to be a brave named Stone-Fist and a maiden named Tans-A-Hide that tell a story about someone called Rides-Alone. I have also received word from Deputy Sheriff Henry Harmon how the death of Kidding came about and that his mount and Corporal Hendricks' mount were in the town of Medora, awaiting transfer back to the Army. He also stated you told him you had a military mount here on Prairie Rose. And I might add there was a strange complaint from the marshal at Little Missouri about your behavior. I'm here to listen to what you have to say, and if you have the mount, I will give you a receipt for it and take it with me as I leave here today."

"Let me put the coffee pot in the middle of the table where we can fill up without being distracted," Cille suggested. She began her story back at Fort Rice, to the time when Hendricks and Kidding saw Patrick in Little Missouri ending with the night they killed Patrick. She included the day the Indians kidnapped the girls, her discovery near Black Butte and her actions. She mentioned the Army patrol that captured the rest of the raiding Indians and her struggle to track Kidding down. She made mention of A.T. Packard and Deputy Harmon's actions. The major took many notes while she talked.

When she finished, Major Collins said, "Mrs. Woodbury, I hope I can put your mind at ease. Lieutenant Caleb Masters and Sergeant Joe Kidding were prisoners of war during the civil war. They became galvanized troops by taking an oath to fight the Indians and not fight against the union. The incident at Fort Rice was swept aside because of the Indian campaign going on at the time. However, they were charged with rape at Fort Lincoln and they deserted before they could be taken into custody. They sealed their own fate and were charged with desertion, on top of other charges, and marked as wanted dead or alive by the Army. I am so sorry that your husband Lieutenant retired, Patrick Woodbury was killed by them and because of their actions. You see, I was a captain years ago and I rode alongside your husband from Yankton to Fort

Rice. I knew him well. The information I have heard here today will be entered in the files when I get back to the garrison. I will see to it that you receive written documentation from the Territorial General exonerating you of any wrongdoing in the deaths of Lieutenant Caleb Masters and Sergeant Joe Kidding. I would keep that information handy in the event local authorities question you about their deaths."

Cille said, "I'm so thankful that this whole mess is behind me."

"Mrs. Woodbury, there aren't enough words to express my sympathy for what you have gone through. I sincerely hope you know how sorry I am to hear of what happened."

"Thank you," was all Cille could say.

"I thank you for your hospitality, your testimony, and if I could get the mount, I'll be on my way."

After they had walked to the barn, Major Collins checked the horse over, looked inside its upper lip for a tattooed number, wrote it on a receipt and handed it to Cille. "I must be on my way. I wish the very best for you and your daughters. Good day."

Cille watched as he rode up the hillside on his way back to Medora and on to his military post. She was relieved to get things settled with the Army. Now all she had to do was wait for the letter from them.

◇◇◇

A month later, Ted Drake had made a run into Medora and returned with a letter from the Army for Cille. When he returned home, he picked up Mathilda and Gloria and rode to Prairie Rose to deliver the letter.

As the Drake's wagon pulled into the yard at Prairie Rose and they hopped down from the buckboard, Cille had just finished some chores in the barn. She called out, "It's nice to have company. I'll be up to the house in a minute. Go on in and I'll see you there."

When Cille came through the door, the Drakes were in the sitting room and Gloria had gone to play with Elizabeth and Sadie. Ted said, "I picked up the mail when I was in Medora. You have just the one letter from the Army post marked Bismarck.

She took it and opened it in front of the Drakes. "Well, I'll be. Major Collins lived up to his word. He has included a short letter, I'll read it later, along with a certificate of exoneration for the deaths of Lieutenant Caleb Masters, Mr. Orson Pegley, two unnamed Indians in about the spring of 1882 near Black Butte and the Cannonball River, Dakota Territory and the deaths of Sergeant Joe Kidding and Corporal Jacob Hendricks in the summer of 1883 in the town of Medora, Dakota Territory." She folded the material and placed it back in the envelope.

Mathilda said, "I take it, it was good news. I'm not sure what that big word means."

"The paperwork clears me of any wrongdoing in the deaths of those I faced in order to get my girls back." Cille said. "I guess they felt I was justified in doing what I did at the time."

Ted said, "Not too many men would have done what you did and very few women. I'm glad for Sadie and Elizabeth's sake you had the grit to do it and I'm glad the Army sees fit not to charge you on anything and have cleared your name."

"It's good news, none the less, and I thank you for picking up the mail," Cille said softly.

"Now that the news in the letter is behind us, let's enjoy some coffee and I have some homemade bread fresh from yesterday. I'll get the butter and honey and we'll enjoy it while it lasts." Turning her attention to the girls, she called out, "Sadie come in here and pour the milk for you girls and we'll have a snack.

The Drakes stayed to visit longer than usual. It was a leisurely chat and they seemed to enjoy each other's company. They drank one pot of coffee and had started a second pot before Ted even hinted of heading back home.

All three of the girls enjoyed their snack and were back in Elizabeth's room playing house with her dolls. They played well together and seemed to enjoy the extended stay.

When the time came, the Drakes got up into their wagon and headed home, allowing Cille and the girls enough daylight to do the chores.

They gathered eggs in the chicken coop and fed the chickens before heading to the barn to do the milking.

"Here chicky, chicky," Elizabeth called out as she took her small hands and grabbed some chopped corn and grit, while tossing it about in the chicken yard. The hens seemed to flock around her wanting to be the first to eat the feed.

When they met in the barn, there were two bowls to fill as Cille milked the cow. One was for Duke t and the other for their two cats that stayed near the barn and were good mousers.

Elizabeth paid more attention to the dog and cats, while Sadie got busy getting hay for the cow, Buster the mule, Dublin and Champ.

After they finished the chores in the barn, they went to the house where Cille put up the milk and prepared the evening meal.

After putting away the clean dinner dishes, it was story time and the girls curled up on the sofa on each side of their mother while she read to them. When the girls were tired, they said their bedtime prayers and were tucked in for the night.

Upon returning to the sofa, Cille opened the letter she had received earlier in the day. She read it before referring to the legal form, it read:

Dear Mrs. Woodbury,

I have finished my investigative work and presented my findings to the Post Judge Advocate General for their approval before it was sent up the chain of command. I am pleased to forward you the official notice of exoneration and to inform you that the command accepted my findings and agreed with my recommendations. I express my deep sympathy for the loss of your husband Lieutenant Patrick Woodbury with whom I had the pleasure of riding while assigned to the 7th Cavalry Regiment. I enjoyed my brief stay at Prairie Rose and commend you for being a gracious hostess under stressful circumstances. I wish you the very best while raising your two wonderful daughters.

Respectfully,
Major Mark Collins

Cille picked up the official form and read it once more before putting both back in the envelope and taking them to her bedroom, where she placed it in her dresser. She returned to the kitchen where she wrote a letter to her parents inviting them to visit Dakota and for a lengthy stay at Prairie Rose. She snuffed the lights before retiring to bed after a rather long day.

CHAPTER 37

I Love You Both with All My Heart 1886

With spring planting behind them, the stubble heads began to break through the sod in the field. It was an indication that all would go well, provided there was enough rain to keep the field strong enough to outlive the plight of the grasshoppers. Cille hoped that this would be another bumper year for the crops. A light breeze moved out of the west bringing with it the sweet scent of the Prairie Roses that grew so abundantly on the hillside. The sky was a powder blue without a hint of a cloud and the temperatures were mild for a late spring day.

Cille had consented for the girls to stay overnight with the Drakes for Gloria's birthday. With the girls gone overnight, Cille prepared to ride into Medora. Ted brought his wagon over early to get the girls and Cille took the opportunity to saddle Dublin for her trip. She stopped by the Crowfords, told them of her planned trip to Medora and asked them to tend to the chores for the day, because she would be back the next day in the afternoon. She also told them that while there, she would get the mail for the Drakes and the Crowfords.

When she arrived in Medora, she went directly to the post office and picked up the mail. The Drakes and Crowfords had several letters and she found one for her.

The letter from her parents was a notice that they had received her letter in the fall and would be making the trip to Medora on the Northern Pacific passenger train. They were making arrangements for the trip and asked if the 15th of July would be a good day for their arrival. They would wait for her reply before making definite plans.

She went directly to the depot and had the telegrapher send a wire to her parents confirming the arrival date and that she would meet them in Medora at the train station. She sent an additional wire to the Swavinguns in Dickenson telling them of a social she would be hosting at Prairie Rose on the 16th of July and asked if they could also invite Arlene and Hank Boyer. She had no idea if Lizzie and Ben-jomine kept in contact with Vandi and Hawa Tutu in Medora. She would have to ask them if they had, and if so, see that they were invited to return to Prairie Rose. The obligation of inviting would fall on her shoulders now. Patrick had taken care of that when he was alive, but things had changed. She felt a new sense of responsibility in seeing that the social event was a success and invited a host of others.

With her business done at the depot, she rode Dublin to the cemetery at Little Missouri and visited Patrick's grave for a few minutes before she rode into town.

The streets were quiet with most of the noise coming from the saloon. She reined up at the editorial office and went inside. A.T. was busy at his printing press after working on several editorial pieces. He looked up and said, "I'll be a few more minutes, then I'll be right with you."

Cille watched with interest as he went about getting his paper put to press. The smell of printers' ink tickled her nose and she nearly sneezed. She waited with inquisitive eyes, watching a man go about his business like a fine oiled machine. Moments later A.T. whipped off his ink-stained apron, came from behind the printing press and said, "What may I have the pleasure of helping you with today?"

She said, "I have made the trip to let you know we can start on the book whenever you like. I'm limited on the days I can come to town and thought you might like to get started."

Packard went to his desk and pulled out a new ledger where he could make notes in a separate binder. "Nothing like the present", he commented.

"I don't have a lot of time today," Cille remarked, "but where do you want to start?"

He said, "Let's start by sitting over here and I'll jot down notes as you talk. Why not start back with your parents, where you were born and where you spent your youth."

A chronology of Cille's life began to unfold and A.T. scratched in the ledger as quickly as she spoke. His head was down as he wrote and he seldom raised his head to look at her, as she expounded on her youth. When she felt she had stayed long enough for the day, she said, "A.T., I believe that will have to do until next time. I want to stop off at the chateau and see the de Mores family before I go to the boarding house for the night.

I'll be riding out early in the morning. I thought, I would let you know that my parents will arrive from back East on the 15th of July and I plan to have a social at Prairie Rose on the 16th. I hope you can make it. Should you have some spare time on your agenda, you're invited out to Prairie Rose. We might be able to spend more time discussing what little bit of interest there is in my past."

A.T. smiled and said, "I'll scratch it on my social calendar right now and you can expect to see me sometime in the near future."

As Cille swung into the saddle, she saw Marshal Russell Coby as he mounted his steed in hopes of catching her before she got out of town.

Cille was quick when she left, encouraging Dublin into a fast gallop. They rode out of the dusty town racing for the Little Missouri River. Cille rode upstream on the western bank to an area she could quickly ride across in the shallow water and through a narrow ravine on the opposite side.

When she got to the top of the ridge, she made a quick turn to the north and headed for some dense brush. She looked back over her shoulder to see the lawman ride to the south figuring she was headed for Prairie Rose.

Riding deeper through the brush, she came out on a small knoll where she looked south to see Russell Coby standing in the saddle stirrups, trying to figure out where she had gone.

While on the knoll, she waited until she could see Coby make his dejected return to the banks of the Little Missouri River and head back to town.

She saw him ride up on the far banks of the river before she turned Dublin to the north. She rode to the bottom of the ridge beneath the chateau, and tethered her horse. Climbing the steep bank, she came to the back door of the chateau, where she knocked lightly.

Medora happened to be walking near the door when she heard

the tapping. When she opened the door, she called out, “Come in quickly,” and closed the door hurriedly. “Are you being chased?”

Cille said with a smile on her face, “With some free time on my hands, I was over with A.T. Packard. We were talking about the book he wants to write about me. When I left, Marshal Coby decided he wanted to give me a bad time. I rode out of town so fast, when he tried to follow, I gave him the slip south of here.”

Medora looked at Cille and said, “You’re a sly one. I bet he thought you were headed home. Nice thinking.”

“I came by today to invite you out to Prairie Rose on the 16th of July. My parents are going to be arriving from back East the day before and I plan to have a social. I’d love to have you come visit and meet some of the folks around here. I hadn’t planned on having to shake the law from across the river before I dropped by.”

“The 16th of July seems like a good day for me. I’ll have to see what my husband’s plans are for that day before I can say for sure.”

“We have plenty of time and I’ll keep in touch with you, when I can,” Cille said. “I can’t stay but just a few moments, as I plan to go into town, eat at the boarding house and get a room for the night. I’ll be heading back to Prairie Rose in the morning.”

“I’m inviting you to join us for the evening meal,” Medora said softly, “and you can stay the night as our guest. I’d dearly love to visit with you where we can get to know each other better. We can talk of Paris and some of the finer things we have in common.”

“My intended visit was to invite you to Prairie Rose. I didn’t come by to eat and stay here…”

“Please,” Medora de Mores requested, “it would do us both good to sit and relax while we talk of pleasant happenings.”

“Thank you and I accept, if it is no trouble. I need to tend to my horse first. I have him tethered to a tree below the bluff.”

“I’ll go with you,” Medora said, “and we can chat as you bring your horse up here and put it in the corral with the other horses for the night.”

When they descended the bluff on the steep trail, they giggled and talked as if they were two young ladies without worries having a good time.

With the long walk around the bluff, they climbed back to the top of the ridge at their leisure. Cille put Dublin up for the night, after removing the saddle and bridle.

During the meal, they discussed the social and the de Mores family agreed to be there. Cille said, "It will give you both a taste of what a social is like when held at Prairie Rose."

The Marquis said, "We sat and watched you in the street a short time back. I must say, you're a lady of steel and you have impressed me with the way you stand for what you believe in. I have not misjudged you when I compare you to a brave woman from my home country."

Cille knew he was referring to his comparison of her as a western day Joan of Arc. It embarrassed her a bit and her cheeks felt flush. She said, "I hope I don't falter from the high status at which you place me."

"Ah, but you have not, and the other day we had a great view of you in the streets, facing a foe with your strong heart, showing the authorities you were committed to seeing justice served, either by the law or by your hand." He smiled and said, "Ah, but it is you who has set out to show others that you have no fear when there is a wrong that needs to be made right."

They talked at length at the table, well after the meal was complete. Eventually, Cille and Medora removed themselves from the dinner table and went into her study. They visited deep into the night. In the late hours, Cille retired to her guest room, where she looked forward to getting a good night's sleep.

In the morning, breakfast was on the table when she descended the stairs. Medora said, "I would be rather embarrassed if I sent you on your way without hot meal."

They visited briefly before Medora said, "I will be leaving Medora and the chateau behind and will be going to New York this fall. We may be returning to France at that time."

"I hope that we will keep in contact over the many miles that will separate us," Cille replied. "I have truly enjoyed visiting with you."

"Your address is one of my prized possessions," Medora said, "and when I am in New York or in France," Medora said with a smile, "I shall write and share my address with you. We have shared an abundance of talk regarding our travels and similarities. I too have enjoyed having you here at the chateau and visiting with you at Prairie Rose."

When their visit ended, Cille excused herself, went to the corral and saddled Dublin and eventually headed for Prairie Rose.

Arriving at home, Cille went directly to Prairie Rose, hitched Buster to the wagon and made the short run to the Drakes to pick up the girls. She gave the Drakes their mail,and after a short visit, she told the girls to get in the wagon for their short ride up and over the hill.

When they returned home, Cille put Buster back in his stall and took care of Dublin before putting the saddle and bridle away. Then she called out to the girls, "Let's go see Lizzie, I have some mail for them."

When they arrived at My Place, Cille handed the mail to Lizzie and said, "I have licorice for the children." They quickly gathered around as Sadie, Elizabeth, Benji and Nizzie held out their hands for the candy. When they had their licorice, they bounded off to play.

Lizzie said, "Theyz sure candy happy, and Iz thankin' ya for pickin' up the mail for us. Ben-jomine says the trip that distance, iz of no use, for the amount of stuff we getz sent this way."

Cille laughed, "No it isn't and I agree with him. But when we pick up the mail for a handful of folks, it saves the others from having to make the long trip."

"Wez got problems in the hen yard, Cille. Wez gots us another rooster and the one has no use for him and the hens thinks he's the bes' strutter in the yard. It makes ol' red mean. Does ya need a rooster in your yard, or Iz gonna have ta choose and have a mess of dumplin's?"

"Now Lizzie, I'll take the old rooster to spare his life if you need. I'm sure he'll get along with the mess of hens I have and I don't think the rooster we have would mind." They laughed and before Cille returned to Prairie Rose, Ben-jomine fixed a snatcher wire to catch the old red rooster. He put him in a Croker sack, ready for when she headed home.

◇◇◇

On July 14th, Cille surprised her daughters. "Today you will clean your rooms early and move your toys and clothing into my room. We will be having company tomorrow and guests staying with us on the following day. As soon as you have done that, we will hitch Buster to the wagon, ride into Medora and stay the night."

Elizabeth asked, "Who is the company, Mommy?"

Sadie smiled and said, "We'll clean our rooms, even if you tell us ahead of time. "Please tell us."

"We will be meeting the train in the morning and your grandfather and grandmother will be coming for a short visit."

Still curious, Elizabeth asked, "Then who are the guests?"

"We will be having a social here at Prairie Rose and a lot of folks will be coming. I have invited the Marquise de Mores and Medora, A.T. Packard the editor, several people from around here and as far away as Dickenson. One of the rooms will be set aside for one of the important guests, if they decide to stay the night."

◇◇◇

They made the long trip to Medora and looked forward to staying at the boarding house. The next morning they stood on the platform outside the depot watching for the billowing smoke to the east that would signify that the Northern Pacific passenger train was coming down the tracks.

One of the railroad workers waiting for the train said, "You can hear the train a coming miles off, if you listen to the rail."

Filled with enthusiasm, the girls were excited about the prospect of hearing the train coming before they could see the smoke, as the worker asked Cille, "May I show the girls?"

Cille nodded and the worker went to one of the depot wagons that had a clean tarp on it and borrowed it for a couple of moments. He laid the tarp down on the gravel and ties that were beneath the rail. He demonstrated by placing his ear on the rail. "You listen and pretty soon you can hear the train a coming."

Sadie and Elizabeth looked at their mother with uncertain eyes and she returned a nod. They both stepped onto the tarp, got down on their knees and placed their ear on the rail. With bright eyes, they lifted their heads and said in unison, "I can hear something funny."

The worker had them join their mother, he retrieved the tarp and put it back on the wagon. As they looked down the track to the east, they could see the faint hint of smoke. The girls were nearly jumping up and down, knowing they had heard the train coming. Now they could see the smoke and knew that their grandparents would soon be getting off the train.

As the train pulled into the depot, ashes and cinders filled the air and the huge metal wheels screeched against the rails as steam belched from the locomotive. Before long, the train had come to a stop. The first group of people getting off the train were workers and it seemed the last ones off were Augustus and Constance. Augustus turned and gave the conductor a hand in helping his wife to the platform. A railroad worker remained behind and handed down the suitcases and boxes belonging to the Hodges.

As soon as Constance had reached solid ground, the girls raced into their grandparents' arms while Cille looked on.

Moments later, Cille collected a kiss and hugs from her parents. She was surprised at how much they had aged. Her mother's mobility had slowed and she was taking measured steps to control her balance. Her father, was beginning to lean forward as he used a stylish walking stick to assist with his leg strength. He had lost some weight and it showed in his legs when the wind blew against his pants.

They went to the baggage section of the depot to retrieve two huge boxes they had shipped. Along with the suitcases and boxes they carried into the passenger car, they tipped a young man for loading the items in the wagon. Her parents sat in the wagon seat with her, while the girls made themselves comfortable in the back of the buckboard. They left Medora and made their way back to Prairie Rose.

When they arrived at the house, Cille's parents and Elizabeth went inside and waited in the sitting room. Cille and Sadie collected the eggs and fed the chickens, went to the barn and fed the animals and milked the cow. They secured the barn before Cille carried the milk to the house. When they arrived, Sadie went to the sitting room to visit with her grandparents.

Cille went to the kitchen to begin preparing the evening meal. Within moments, Constance was at her side, helping to put the salad and main course together. Cille called out, "Elizabeth, come set the table, please. Your sister spared you helping with the chores."

Elizabeth came into the kitchen and began setting the table. Her grandmother was surprised to see her youngest granddaughter place a formal setting at the table.

Her mother said, "Cille, I'm mighty proud of what Elizabeth is doing. I see that you have taught her well."

"They have their chores around the house," Cille replied. "Sometimes there's a fuss when one thinks she is doing more than the other, but I'm lucky they do quite well. They pay more attention to detail if they think someone is watching."

After the dishes were put away, they spent more time visiting. Augustus and Constance brought gifts to hand out. There was something special for each of them. At bedtime, Cille read a short story to the girls and asked them to tuck themselves in after they kissed and hugged their grandparents goodnight. Cille said, "I'll come in and make sure you're covered properly. You can say your prayers then; just remember on what side of the bed you're sleeping on and save room for me.

When the children were in the bedroom, Augustus said, "Cille, your mother and I have been thinking about the estate and we are asking you to consider leaving your home here and returning to Monroe with the girls. I know you have put your heart into what you have here, but hear us out. The estate will be yours in time and we realize our health isn't the best. I think it is more than what you have here. I know the ties you have here are strong and I know your decision won't come easy. We ask that you think about the prospects for a time and see if that isn't better for you than trying to make a go of it year by year, working the soil as you have."

Constance didn't allow her daughter to answer, before she said, "I love you and I love my two granddaughters. I can't always be making a trip this far to spoil the three of you. If you were back in Monroe, the girls would have a chance to go to a finishing school and be prepared to face the world."

Cille smiled and said, "Let me check on the girls, they need to say their prayers. I'll be right back."

When she returned, she continued, "I love you both with all my heart. I know your intentions are good, and although I can't say

I'm surprised the subject came up, I don't have a good answer for you yet. Patrick is buried out here, we have recently proven up and the land is now mine."

Augustus said, "Cille, we don't expect an answer right away. We wanted you to know about our health concerns, the estate and have you thinking of your options in life later on."

She assured them, "I know where your hearts are, and I promise you this much: I will give it some very serious thought. I loved Patrick and this land. We worked well together for a long time. He was taken from me and I had to work hard to keep the dream alive that we both shared. Now that the land is mine, I still see the hardships I will face. I need some time to figure out what I will do. The girls are my top priority. Let me have a bit of time to rationally plan for the years ahead. I love you both and I plan to make the best decisions for my girls. Let's put the topic to rest for a day or so and enjoy each other's company."

Reaching over and touching her daughter's arm, Constance said, "That was the sweetest thing I think I have ever heard you say. You're right. We're here to enjoy each day with you and the girls."

They ended their discussion for the night, as they had to get up early in the morning and make arrangements for the social. It would be a day of fun and meeting with old friends. It would also show her parents that there were good folks in the Dakotas and they could get together once in a while and really have fun.

It was near mid-day when a host of wagons came over the horizon and descended on Prairie Rose. Ranch hands from the Maltese Ranch provided the music along with another band from the Elk Ranch that filled in when there was a break in the action. The yard in front of the house all the way to the barn was filled with folks from across the Dakotas. A few ventured from Wibaux and Hodges, including a couple from Miles City, Montana that came in to meet Rufus and Rupert's parents. The Swavinguns and Boyers made it in from Dickenson and the Marquis de Mores, his wife and A.T. Packard came by for a visit.

Constance was pleased to meet Medora and felt that her Victorian ways were a good influence on her daughter. They visited at length and Augustus enjoyed the French-style flare of the Marquis.

Constance cornered Medora in the sitting room and struck up a lengthy conversation whilte Cille checked on her guests often. The Marquis, his wife and A.T. left for their chateau at nearly dusk, as they would have a long ride in the dark before they reached their destination.

Bjorn and Uvonnie Swavingun would lodge at Prairie Rose and the Boyers would return to the Drakes when the party ended. There were new faces and old friends that greeted one another and had a good time. The music was to their liking and they danced in the yard until it was too dark to do so.

All the children had fun, playing with their dolls and small toys, while those older got acquainted with the opposite sex and shared fun during a variety of games, the last one being an extended game of hide and seek.

When the day came to an end, all those who came ate well, enjoyed refreshments and had a good time socializing. Most left wishing that the social was held more often.

As the evening hours put an end to the day's festivities, Constance said, "I can't remember when I have had so much fun. I have certainly enjoyed meeting a host of people."

Lizzie and Ben-jomine had stayed late to help with the cleanup before they went to My Place with several guests that would stay at their house.

Uvonnie and Bjorn Swavingun stayed in the sitting room visiting with Constance and Augustus. There was laughter and much story telling. The grandparents had one of the children's rooms and the other went to the Swavingun's. Sadie and Elizabeth turned in early and were sprawled out on Cille's bed when she came to bed. It had been a wonderful day.

◇ ◇ ◇

The visit from the Hodges lasted nearly a week, before the joyful time came to an end. Now they had to make the long trip into Medora to catch the train. The wagon left Prairie Rose early in the morning and Buster seemed to take his time taking them to their destination.

When they arrived at the depot, the train was crossing the Little Missouri River on the trestle and getting ready to come into Medora. The visit on the station platform was short-lived, and before long, they were exchanging hugs and kisses before their final goodbyes.

Augustus said, “I love you, Cille. Please give some thought to what we talked about.”

“I will, Daddy, I promise,” Cille assured him.

Constance said, “Cille I have enjoyed myself beyond words. I can see why you love this place, but please consider coming back to Monroe. I will understand your decision if it is to the contrary. I love you.”

While Cille hugged her mother and gave her a kiss, she said in her mother’s ear, “I love you and I promise I will give it some thoughtful consideration.”

The time to board the train had come, and Cille and the girls stayed on the platform to watch Augustus and Constance walk down the small aisle within the train coach and take a seat near a window where they could wave their goodbyes as the train began leaving the station.

Cille had tears in her eyes as she saw her parents fade from sight. Sadie and Elizabeth waved their hands and threw their grandparents kisses until the train was too far down the track.

They returned to the wagon and Cille later pulled it to a stop at the boarding house. They went in to register for a room for the night. It had been a long day and they would do their shopping in the morning before returning to Prairie Rose.

CHAPTER 38

Leaving Dakota 1887

The meetings with Arthur T. Packard resumed anew as soon as the snow began to leave the Dakota plains. When he visited Cille at Prairie Rose, he brought his ledger along and added to the material he had already collected. He said, "Cille, I have already started the book with the early chapters bringing out your childhood and covering your schooling before you met Patrick. We covered that material last fall when you came to the office."

"When do I get to read what you have written?" Cille asked with a smile.

"I'll let you read the entire text," A.T. said, "when I have the first draft completed. Then we can go over the content and add or delete any of the material as we see fit."

Their visits were usually short, with A.T. heading back to his paper to get the next edition put to print. Cille understood that the book came second to his newspaper. His paper was dedicated to the cattle industry and his mission was to publish the best paper he could. Most of his time was spent gathering information for the paper and keeping up circulation.

◇◇◇

Cille gave a considerable amount of thought to what she and her parents had talked about. She weighed life back in Monroe for her and the girls versus life on Prairie Rose. She loved Patrick and the girls loved their father. Leaving would be heart wrenching for the three of them. She would make her decision based on what would be best for the children.

As spring planting season approached, Cille worried who would work the fields for another years crops. This was one compelling reason returning to Monroe. The Crowford boys had been so reliable over the previous years but now lived in Montana as building contractors. She realized that Ben-jomine and Lizzie were in the same situation, so she gathered the girls and went across the creek to My Place for a visit.

Upon their arrival Cille asked, "What are we going to do for some help in taking care of the fields this year?"

Ben-jomine said, "Them boy's iz buildin' up a storm where they iz. Iz done talked to the both of them and theyz gots three friends out near Sentinel Butte, that say they can lend a hand this year, but maybe not next. Rufus say the three iz ta come this way next week. I reckon we iz gonna have to wait that long to see if they show."

The thought of having to wait on hired hands that long was a concern. There was little she could do but wait out the week and, in the meantime, try to find other help. She visited with the Crowfords for a spell allowing her girls to play with Benji and Nizzie.

When morning came, Cille had the girls do their chores quickly while she hitched Buster to the wagon. They were going to Medora for supplies and some added shopping. Elizabeth said, "I take care of the chicky, chickies, I let Sadie do the work in the barn."

"She can handle the eggs and the chicken feed," Sadie said, "because she isn't big enough to handle the pitchfork and the hay."

Cille smiled as her girls seemed to rationalize and point out their differences. She asked, "Would the two of you like to get a collection of flowers together to place on your father's grave today?"

Sadie was the first to respond, "I have several I could put in a jar."

Elizabeth said, "How many jars of flowers are we going to take this time, Mommy?"

"Just the one," Cille said, "you'll have to share the space in the jar."

"I'm glad you said it loud enough for Sadie to hear. Now she knows that I get half of the jar for my best flowers." She looked at her sister as if she might have to defend herself over the flower jar issue. Sadie only smiled at her younger sister's behavior.

With the morning chores done, they quickly prepared themselves for the long ride and were soon on their way out of Prairie Rose and on their way to town.

◊ ◊ ◊

Upon their arrival in Medora, they started with a visit to the mercantile. Cille asked, "Roger, have you or Audrey any idea who I might hire to do some work in the fields?"

Roger stopped scratching some figures in the store ledger long enough to say, "Can't say as I have heard anyone looking for work. Why don't you write a note that help is needed and what for. I'll put the information in the window next to the door and maybe someone will come inside and ask. That way we can send them your direction."

"Thank you, Roger," Cille said and began writing out what she thought would get some attention: 'Help wanted, spring planting duties, good wages. Inquire within for work at Prairie Rose'.

She handed the note to Mr. Bentley and said, "I thank you in advance." He took the note and immediately placed it in the window facing the street.

A short distance from the mercantile, they registered for the night at a boarding house and enjoyed their noon meal.

Moments after eating, the girls raced outside to the buckboard where Sadie quickly grabbed the flower jar and held it tight. She anticipated an argument from her younger sister as they waited for their mother.

Elizabeth quickly chose to sit in the middle of the seat next to her mother so Sadie had to sit on the outside.

Cille hopped onto the buckboard, picked up the reins and prodded Buster into action. A short time later, they reached the Little Missouri River where she stopped Buster. She got down from the wagon, took the flowers from Sadie and poured out the warming water and replaced it with cool water from the river.

When she returned, she handed the jar of flowers back to Sadie and hopped onboard. It didn't take long for the wagon to reach the cemetery.

To avoid any argument, Cille said, "Sadie hand me the jar of flowers. You both can have a couple of moments to say some words your father. Then we'll remove the old jars and replace them with the new flower jars. We will remove the wilted flowers before we leave. I will have a private moment with your father before we go back into town."

When the girls had their turn near the headstone, they helped remove the jars of old flowers and pulled weeds before they took the old flowers and jars to the wagon. This allowed their mother a few precious moments alone at Patrick's grave.

As they made their way back to Medora, Cille was pleased to see that the girls were happy. It was a beautiful day with the sun moments away setting in the western sky. They felt a sense of accomplishment in caring for Patrick's grave because they loved and missed him deeply, but no one complained.

Before returning to the boarding house, Cille took the wagon to the depot, where she talked with the telegrapher. "I'd like some information about the train to Dickenson that returns the next day."

Unsure of himself, the ticket agent looked up and asked, "For you or all three of you?"

"It will be the three of us," Cille replied. "We will be going there and returning the next day. I have some business to tend to and I was in hopes that the train schedule would give me the time to get it done before we return."

"Just when are you three planning to take the trip?"

Cille said, "We may not leave for a couple of months, but I wanted to get the information ahead of time so we could do some planning."

"I see," the telegrapher softly replied. He went about figuring out the schedule, the cost of the tickets and wrote the information down for Cille. "This is as close as I can come to a schedule right now and I wrote the cost at the end of the note. Best check in with us a bit before you plan to leave, that way I can give you a more definitive time schedule and price."

The girls asked about the possibility of riding on the train and had many questions about when and why. They spent a bit of the day buying new clothes for the girls. Cille felt the girls had earned a couple of outfits each and she wanted them to feel good about doing the shopping. She wanted them to enjoy the day before they headed back to Prairie Rose. That evening they ran into A.T. Packard and he stopped by the boarding house for a few moments to chat and gather additional information for the book. The visit was short, before he was on his way working on another story line.

There was no response to the help wanted note at the mercantile, but the following week, three young men, none over the age of seventeen, came to My Place and talked with Ben-jomine. They had been sent out to do some work Rufus said was available.

After arrangements had been made for their stay, Ben-jomine took them to Prairie Rose, introduced them to Buster and got them started on the field below the Woodbury home.

Cille and Ben-jomine were pleased to see the three young men taking the mule to the field to get the job done. Over the next few days, the fields on both places had been plowed and the seed had been planted.

When the three went to leave Prairie Rose, Cille could hear one of them say, "I bet Ma and Pa will be surprised to see how much in wages we made."

◊ ◊ ◊

Over the past few weeks, Cille had been pondering what she would do with Prairie Rose. When the three young workers had left, she knew her answer. After the evening meal, she called Sadie and Elizabeth to the table to have a discussion before story time. She said, "Girls, how would you like to take that train ride to Dickenson in a few days?"

Elizabeth said, "I'm ready to go now. I don't know about Sadie, but I'll go. I want to ride on the train, just like Granddad and Grandma did last year."

Sadie shook her head, turned to her mother and said, "When are we going?"

"I think the first part of next week would be a good time. We'll drive Buster and leave him at the livery in Medora. We'll take the train and when we come back, we'll get Buster and come home."

The girls asked several questions before Elizabeth said, "I'm getting tired. Are you going to read us a story before we have to say our prayers and go to bed?"

"Go to the sofa," Cille replied. "I'll get the book and read until you feel your eyes can't stay open any longer. Then it is prayer time and into bed for the both of you."

◇◇◇

As the train rolled to a stop in Dickenson on the first leg of their journey, the girls were excited. As they stepped down from the train, they were met by Uvonnie and Bjorn Swavingun.

Uvonnie said, "We got your telegram earlier and you're going to stay at the house for the night."

"We can stop by the land office on the way to the house and you can get done what you need;" Bjorn said, "then we'll head to the house and visit."

Bjorn pulled the wagon to a stop in front of the Land Office and Cille went inside to do what she had set out to do.

When Cille returned to the wagon, she had a packet in her hand. She said, "That was quick. Those folks inside sure know how to handle business."

They headed to the Swavinguns house and went inside to visit. Uvonnie had already done some baking and there were pastries for all.

While they sat around laughing and reminiscing over times past, the girls played outside. Bjorn teased Cille about her tracking ability and she countered by claiming he withheld information. Uvonnie said, "We sure enjoyed the social last year. We met some new friends and lost contact with some. We sure miss those that are gone."

Cille said, "The reason I made the trip is to make arrangements. When my parents were here, they pointed out that they were not getting any younger. They want me to return to Monroe. I have taken a long time to give it some thought and I have decided to go back East."

Bjorn asked, "Is it a for sure thing and you'll be gone for good, or are you going for a short visit?"

"I'll be going back there for good," Cille said softly. "I struggled with the decision, from leaving Patrick buried out this way, to the property I now own. I had a hard time getting help to put in the crops this year and I think it will be best for the girls in the long term. They don't know my intentions yet."

Uvonnie asked, "When are you planning to leave?"

"I'd like to get the crops harvested first," Cille replied, "and maybe leave about the first of November. That way we can be home for Thanksgiving."

Bjorn asked, "Is there anything we can do for you before you leave?"

Cille said, "No, I'll make do. I will keep in touch before I leave and I'd like to keep in touch over the years."

"We will certainly do that," Uvonnie added, "won't we Bjorn?" He agreed, as they gradually began talking of other things.

The women helped each other with the evening meal. To their surprise, after eating, the girls asked to do the dishes while they visited. They talked late and were rather tired when they retired for the day.

It was shortly after breakfast when the Swavinguns saw Cille and the girls off at the Dickenson train depot. It was a rather sad departure for Cille and Uvonnie. They had grown close over the years and both were uncertain if they would get to visit each other before the first of November. Bjorn stood by hiding his inner feelings. The girls were a bundle of energy and both were filled with excitement.

Rarely was the train on time, but today was an exception and before long, they were climbing aboard and waving out the window at their friends as the train began to move.

After the train had arrived in Medora, Cille and the girls walked to the livery. When the smithy finished harnessing Buster, the Woodburys were on their way back to Prairie Rose.

◇ ◇ ◇

When the harvesting crew visited Prairie Rose, there was a bumper crop in the field. The crew had done their work and when the day came to an end, Cille paid a bonus to each of them beyond their usual wages. She said, "I have been so honored over the years to have such good dear friends that have responded and helped me care for this piece of land. I have struggled in my mind and have come to the conclusion that it is time for me to move on. We will be leaving Prairie Rose in November and extend our heartfelt thanks for all of you for your generosity over the years. I wish each and every one of you and your families the very best." Moments later, the harvesting crew was up and over the hilltop on their way to yet another field to harvest.

The day after the harvest, Cille got the girls up early for a trip to Medora. Cille's first stop was at the depot where she picked up her train schedule and paid for their tickets. She sent a wire to her parents in Monroe telling them she would be leaving on the 1st of November by train and should be home several days later if all went as planned.

When they made arrangements at the boarding house, A.T. saw the familiar wagon in town and went into the boarding house to see the three of them, enjoying a piece of homemade bread with butter and honey.

He joined them for a few moments saying, "Cille, I have completed the first draft of the book. I'll drop by later with a copy and let you read it before you give your approval. Then I will make the final draft to send off to the publisher."

Cille said, "I look forward to reading it. Will I be able to recognize myself in the book or have you done a lot of embellishing?"

He replied, "I have had the pleasure of writing a book that has a lot of heart in it. I hope you agree with what I have written. You are a magnificent lady and have fared well in a harsh land. I look forward to your comments."

They visited shortly and later in the evening, A.T. brought a copy of his writing to the boarding house for her to read at her leisure. The evening was spent shopping and retiring early for their trip back to Prairie Rose the next day.

It was nearly two weeks after the harvest when she had invited the Crowfords to her home for the evening meal. When she returned to her home, she went to her dresser where the Dakota Land Office folder was and filled out most of the information on the deed for Prairie Rose.

When the Crowfords showed up, everyone was in a jovial

mood. The evening meal was served and when it was over, Sadie and Elizabeth took care of the dishes before they had Benji and Nizzie join them in the bedroom to play with their toys.

Cille asked Ben-jomine and Lizzie to remain at the table. She went into her bedroom and returned with the large packet from the Land Office. As she rejoined them, she said, "Ben-jomine I have appreciated your help, along with Rufus and Rupert over the years. Without the kindness you have shown, I don't believe Prairie Rose would have prospered. Lizzie, you have been a part of my life for so many years, I can't thank you enough for all you have done. You're amazing."

The Crowfords smiled and Lizzie said, "Wez jus' part of the family that made the trip this far. Wez had ta stick together like burnt grease in a skillet to make it. I thank you for bringin' me out this way and the help ta gets My Place."

"You and Patrick done gave us a boost when we needed one," Ben-jomine added, "and now My Place has become Our Place."

"My Patrick is gone and my parents are in poor health," Cille spoke softly. "They have asked me to consider returning to Monroe. The harvest is in and I have decided to take the girls from Prairie Rose on the first of November and return to the home I spent my youth in."

They looked on, surprised with the news of her leaving. Then Cille said, "I have made out most of the information on the deed and I will need the both of you to sign in several places. I am leaving the entire property of Prairie Rose to the both of you."

"But this is your place," Lizzie said, as she broke down in tears. "Prairie Rose belongs to you."

"Lizzie, Prairie Rose is a part of my life. I am giving it to the both of you as my way of saying thank you for all you have done over the years. I certainly can't take it with me and I can't possibly return each year to plant the crops and see that it is taken care of. I know you will work the land and keep things up. It is my gift to the both of you for those many years of help."

"Iz overwhelmed, Cille," Ben-jomine said. "Iz gots ta ask, Iz ya feelin' sick, 'cause this is one big way ta say, I'm leavin' and here take what's left."

"No, I'm not sick. The prospect of returning to Monroe has been on my mind for several months. We had a hard time getting help this year to break ground and I am thinking of the girls and their needs. They will later be going to a finishing school, and while I am in Monroe, I can take care of my parents. Please, take Prairie Rose with my blessings. I know Patrick would have wished the same."

The paperwork was filled out and sent to Dickenson for final action. Then a deed for Prairie Rose would be returned to the Crowfords.

◇◇◇

Days before leaving, a choice of what personal and household items that would be returning to Monroe were laid out. There were the two special quilts that kept the girls warm during the night on their return from being kidnapped. Duke would accompany them to Monroe, as he was instrumental in finding the girls in the hostile land. He would remain a part of the family. The copy of A.T. Packard's manuscript about her life was returned to him, with her approval. Items that were once Patrick's were boxed and ready for shipment with them. Most of what was at Prairie Rose would remain behind for the new owners.

◇◇◇

On the 1st of November, several boxes and crates were off loaded from the wagon and placed on the station platform. The Crowfords were saddened to see them leave. A.T. Packard surprised Cille as he had bought a ticket and was going to be leaving on the same train. An apprentice would maintain the editorial office until he returned.

People in Medora spread rumors about Cille and A.T. leaving on the same train. The Crowfords would return to their new land and A.T. would ride the train to Minneapolis and St Paul before he got off. Cille and the girls would remain on the train, switching lines, until they arrived at the depot in Monroe, New York. A.T. would return to Medora some two weeks later amidst rumors about him and Cille. He never bothered to change their minds.

CHAPTER 39

A Return to Dakota 1887-1897

Cille Woodbury and her children boarded the Northern Pacific Railway passenger train and left Medora, Dakota Territory on November 1, 1887. They had many transfers to different rail lines before their return to Monroe, New York. At the depot, they were met by her aging parents with their carriage driver, Randu. When they arrived at the estate, Cille was surprised to see that Albon the servant was still with the family.

◇◇◇

When Thanksgiving Day was upon the Hodges household, there was much to reflect upon. For the Hodges, it was the presence of their daughter and grandchildren that they were most thankful for.

As for Cille, it was being home where she could enjoy the presence of her parents, caring for them where she could. Time had been unkind to both of her parents, as they seemed to have grown weary over the years. What they had missed most was being with and seeing their granddaughters grow up. They were pleased to see the girls were entering the age of responsibility properly.

They celebrated Thanksgiving with all the preparations before the meal. Augustus prayed a lengthy prayer of thankfulness, a prayer that resonated in the hearts of all at the table. It was a time of religious reflection and a deep understanding of thankfulness for family. It was a beautiful day and there was love in all hearts within the Hodges household.

◇◇◇

Cille reflected back on Prairie Rose when the area was a territory. On November 2, 1889, she was aware that the land of the Dakotas had been approved for statehood. She wondered how the laws of the land would affect those on the prairie compared to those who lived in town.

She hoped that law and order would prevail, and the ruthlessness of years gone by would soon become a distant memory for those who chose to live there. In the short time that she was gone, she wondered what changes had taken place. Maybe someday she would return to see for herself.

◇◇◇

During the month of June 1893 at the West Point Chapel, there was a double wedding. The happiness of seeing Sadie and Elizabeth getting married brought back reflective memories for Cille as she knew what the girls would be facing. Maybe not the same set of circumstances, but she was familiar with the role of an army officer's wife. They had gone to Paris for their finishing schooling, had their debutante and had soon found the loves of their lives. Ironically for Cille, she was introduced to two cadets from West Point who were not shy about proposing to her daughters. She could only wish them the best and hope that their hardships over time would be few. Now they were standing before the clergy surrounded by a host of friends and family wishing them well as the ceremony began.

It was a beautiful wedding, one that was polished with all the military fanfare and color. The sisters looked at each other as they were about to make their commitment and smiled. After the wedding, when they were turned to be introduced to those gathered, they glanced at each other once more smiling with much love in their hearts. They had grown close over the years and both realized they may not see each other for a while as their husbands were assigned to their military duties.

Sadie became Mrs. Adam Westbrook and Elizabeth became Mrs. Thomas Jacobson, both men lieutenants. The Westbrooks would see London, England as their first assignment and the Jacobsons would see Naples, Italy. They would be leaving for their assignments within the month.

As the festivities came to an end, Cille kissed her two daughters and their husbands good-bye. She was happy for them, but deep down, her heart ached.

The journey back to the Hodges estate was rather quiet as her parents were tired. Lizzie, who had journeyed from Dakota for the wedding, spoke once in a while, but was deep in thought reflecting back on those she had left behind. It would be a long ride home for her.

◊ ◊ ◊

In the fall of that same year, Constance called out to Cille in a shrill voice, as Augustus had not responded to her attempts to wake him. "Cille, my goodness Cille, come quickly I need your help!"

Coming face to face with the emotional sadness of her father's passing was hard for Cille. She tried to cope with his loss and her mother's emotions as well. It was a sad time.

One month later, Constance did not respond when Cille went to check on her. She found that her mother had drawn her last breath sometime during the night.

Two funerals in one month for both parents hurt Cille deeply. She knew her parents were failing, but to lose both of them this close together shook her emotions and she could not stop crying for a long time. Over time, she took comfort in knowing they were not hurting anymore. She had returned to the estate at their request and she was so glad they had spent extra time together and had many good times before the end. Reflecting on those happy times helped her cope with her sorrow.

◊ ◊ ◊

Cille lived a quiet secluded lifestyle for a time before some of the local married women began inviting her to small socials. She smiled knowing that the socials around Monroe were nothing compared to those she had hosted at Prairie Rose, but she enjoyed spending time with others. The wives were not intimidated with her being a widow and accepted her with open arms. The stories she had to tell kept most of them spellbound with wonderment.

◇ ◇ ◇

One morning three years later, Cille received a letter from Rahema, her long-lost friend. The letter read:

April 14, 1896

Dear Mrs. Woodbury,

In Boston; I will be heading to New York next week. Lizzie wrote and wants to tell you Ben-jomine is seriously ill and near death. I will be going to Medora by train on the 7th of June. Not sure if you want to go that far. If you can, I would like to have you ride with me. Write me if you can go.

Rahema

Cille thought for a long time and these words began to form in her mind;

PRAIRIE ROSE

"THERE'S A HOUSE UPON DAKOTA SOIL
EACH ROOM I KNOW BY HEART,
WHERE THE FIELDS OF GRAIN WITHOUT SPRING RAIN
I SAW THEIR STRUGGLING START,
WHERE PATRICK AND I SHARED OUR DREAMS
AND THE FOND MEMORIES THAT WE MADE,
OUR DAUGHTERS GREW UP, WITH MANNERS SO REFINED
TENDING TO FLOWER BEDS BY THE PORCH AND CLOTHESLINE,
THERE WAS A HOUSE THAT BECAME OUR HOME
WHERE TRAGEDY STRUCK AND LEFT ME ALONE,
MY HEART YEARNS TO RETURN AT LEAST ONCE MORE
TO THAT SPECIAL PLACE THAT PATRICK CHOSE,
A LOVING LAND CALLED ..... PRAIRIE ROSE."

Sadie and Elizabeth had returned to New York together and stopped by the estate in Monroe to surprise their mother for her birthday. When they did, they were surprised by the news of Lizzie and Ben-jomine and that their mother was planning to visit the Crowfords in Dakota.

"Do you think we can delay our return trip to Europe, Elizabeth?" Sadie asked. "Maybe we can visit with mother while she goes to North Dakota. We could place flowers on Daddy's grave while we're there and be with mother until she gets back home."

"Let's send a telegram to our husbands letting them know what the circumstances are here and maybe we'll get their approval," Elizabeth replied.

"Goodness dear sister, I think you have your husband wrapped around your little finger like I have mine. We'll ask, but I know we'll be going."

They made a quick trip to the train depot, where the telegrapher sent a message via the Trans-Atlantic wire to their husbands. They figured they should get an answer within two or three days. To their surprise, they received a reply the following day. They both wished the girls well on the trip and asked to be informed when they were back in Monroe and ready to return overseas.

"Mother," Sadie announced, "Elizabeth and I are going to make the trip with you as we celebrate your birthday. We think it would give us the time we'd like to visit with you. We figured you both might need some added company."

Elizabeth asked, "When will we be going out west?"

Cille gasped and said, "You two sure know how to get at your mother's heart. I'll get in touch with Rahema and let her know that we are ready to go out West when she gets here. She plans to go by train on June 7th from either New York or Monroe."

The girls stayed at the estate, visiting with their mother, while they waited for Rahema to write or show up.

◇◇◇

Three days later, Rahema came by the estate. They would all leave the following day on the passenger train, making their journey into North Dakota. When they got to Medora, they would rent a carriage and ride out to Prairie Rose unless the Crowfords met them with transportation.

Recently Rahema had become concerned because Lizzie didn't write of good news and she was concerned about her brother. When they left the Monroe depot on the train, the telegrapher had already sent a wire to Medora to be delivered to Prairie Rose and My Place, telling the Crowfords they were on their way, who all was coming and the time they would be arriving in Medora.

During the train ride from Monroe to Dakota Territory, there was time for all to reminisce over past events. Sadie said, "Mother, do you remember Madame de Mores?

Cille said, "Yes I do. We were dear friends when we lived in the Dakotas and I hear from Medora maybe once or twice a year."

Sadie added, "When I was in Finishing School in Paris, I had some time to spare and visited her. She is one gracious lady. She had me write to you about all the fun things available in Paris. If I'm not mistaken, she said her husband Marquis de Mores returned to the town of Medora, North Dakota in the spring of 1889 and did some hunting while he was there."

"I still have both of your letters from those days," Cille replied with a smile. "I seem to recall she had mentioned it. At the time, I was surprised that she was not with him."

Elizabeth said, "I visited her when I was there also. I can remember the great time we had, touring Paris and being entertained at her home."

The girls talked of their experiences in England and Italy and their trip back to Monroe for their mother's birthday.

Rahema and Cille talked of their time at Fort Rice, where the girls were born and how Lizzie got to meet Ben-jomine. The girls listened with interest, as the discussion went into such great detail. They talked of when Rahema arrived at Fort Rice as a laundry lady and later became a maid for the Garrison Commander Colonel Thomas L. Crittenden and his wife Catherine.

Cille asked, "Rahema, the last time you visited was when Ben-jomine and Lizzie 'jumped the broom'. You left the Dakotas with the Crittendens; what has happened to them?"

Theyz always movin'. The Army sends the colonel here and then theyz a sendin' him there, and the misses sometimes could not keep up with the many moves. They bought a small house near Augusta, Georgia, where she could be near her sister. Iz was released from my duties and given a chunk of change, 'nuff to buy a small house in the country near Boston. They treat me alright, when I worked for them and when they let me go.

Intrigued by many stories they were hearing for the first time about Cille and Rahema, the girls listened intently, captivated by all the details.

◊ ◊ ◊

There were many changes in the rail linesbefore they finally stepped on the Northern Pacific Railway passenger train in Minneapolis and St. Paul. The train cut across the northern tier of states and made its way past Fargo and Dickenson before the stop in Medora.

Cille wondered if the Northern Pacific was able to reach the Pacific Ocean area. It may be interesting to make a trip in that direction. It would certainly be different.

When they arrived in Medora, there was no one to meet them. Rahema and Sadie remained on the station platform, while Cille and Elizabeth went to the stable and rented a large wagon.

Upon their return to the depot, they loaded the luggage on the wagon then went to the mercantile and bought a container for some flowers. On their way out of town, they picked wildflowers and placed them in the container along with enough water from the Little Missouri River to keep the flowers from wilting for a few days. They stopped by the Little Missouri Cemetery, and as they approached Patrick's grave, a hush fell over them as each paid their respects. They staid longer than they expected, but each felt the need to pause and reflect back on the days when Patrick was an important and loving part of their lives.

◊ ◊ ◊

It was late in the evening when the wagon began its downhill descent onto Prairie Rose and the land near My Place. There was no response to anyone at Prairie Rose, so the group walked across the creek to My Place. When they arrived, Lizzie was in the garden hoeing the weeds out of the tomato rows. When she looked up, she cried out with a high squeal, "Iz either goin' blind from workin' in the sun or Iz seein' gracious company. Lets me get my feet untangled from the weeds, and Iz gonna be right with the whole lot of you."

"Lizzie, you ain't changed a bit!" Rahema cried out. "I thought my brother would have tamed that high-pitched Gullah voice of yours by now."

Lizzie smiled and said "Iz gonna take care of your sass in a bit. Miss Cille, Iz been missin' ya a whole lot since ya left, and my goodness don't tell my soul, this is Sadie and Elizabeth, all grown up and older from the last Iz laid eyes on ya both. Get over here the whole lot of ya, so that I can give ya each a hug."

Rahema snapped back, "Why should I go givin' ya a hug. Ya ain't shaken half the garden dirt from your front yet, Lizzie."

"Careful girl, you jus' might be the first one I wrap my arms around." Much laughter erupted and the hugging began in earnest.

Sadie asked, "Where are Benji and Nizzie?"

"Theyz both over in the las' field workin' way down in the valley. Theyz gonna be up for the fixin's, when the sun go droppin' out of the sky. Come into the house the whole lot of ya, ol' Ben-jomine is gonna be mighty surprised, when he lays his ol' tired eyes on yas.

When they went into the house, Ben-jomine was propped up in a rocker with pillows stuffed around his skeletal frame. He was weak and had lost a considerable amount of weight. His voice was labored as he called out, "Rahema, my sister you not changed one bit, but Iz afraid Iz done caught the rattles, and I took to being weak as some of the coffee Lizzie tries to fix. Give me a peck and a hug, Iz needin' some spoiling."

"What ya iz needin' is another dose of that medicine, ya slept through the first batch this mornin'." Lizzie quipped.

After Rahema had gotten out of his field of vision, he called out, "Miss Cille, Iz glad you gots out this far one more time, and iz good to see you, and oh my, my it be Sadie and Elizabeth, ya both growed up a bunch. Last time Iz laid eyes on ya, ya was both a bit smaller. Iz would have gots to my feet, but my legs don't do so good."

Cille and the girls went to Ben-jomine and gave him a light hug, before Lizzie said, "Grab ya a seat where ya can and we can go to catchin' up on gossip and half-truths." She looked at Rahema and said, “Iz knowin’ where the half-truths are comin’ from.”

Ben-jomine said through labored breathing, “Iz thought them Indians say you Rides-Alone. Now you show up on our doorstep with a whole lot of others.” He laughed and coughed a couple of times, then added, “Cille, it be good to see ya, but ya not young as ya once was, iz you?”

With a smile Cille replied, “Ben-jomine that was a few years back.”

“She not look angry as she once was, now does she?” Lizzie questioned. “Cille no longer Rides-Alone ‘cause she with family.”

The visiting was jovial and in time, Benji and Nizzie came through the door, and there was a joyous reunion of friends and family.

Upon completion of the evening meal and the dishes were cleaned up, Ben-jomine had his rocker moved close to the kitchen table where they could all enjoy sitting and visiting. They talked about all kinds of things until late in the night. Lizzie said, “Rahema you can sleep here on My Place and Cille, the door is open on Prairie Rose. Benji has put a fire in the stove and Nizzie has your rooms ready. When yas get up in the mornin’ jus’ come a runnin’ cause Iz gonna have breakfas’ waiting on the table.”

◇ ◇ ◇

Morning came with a pounding on the door at Prairie Rose. It was Rahema, and as Cille opened the door, she cried out, “Cille, Ben-jomine not answer the call this mornin’ and when Lizzie went to tend to him, he was gone. He was sleepin’ with a big smile on his face, when his number come up. He left happy.”

After recovering from the bad news, Cille and the girls got ready and accompanied Rahema back to My Place where there were tears and sadness from Lizzie and her children. Cille and the girls lent a hand and made breakfast so that the rest could eat.

Shortly after breakfast, Benji hitched the animals to the wagon and made the long trip to Medora carrying Ben-jomine’s body in the back of the family carriage.

◇ ◇ ◇

When they arrived in Medora, they took Ben-jomine to the undertaker's office and made arrangements for his funeral the following day. The graveside service would be in Little Missouri Cemetery. They went to the depot and sent a wire to Dickenson where Rufus and Rupert and their families lived. They would be there for the services as well.

◇ ◇ ◇

Following the services, Benji and Nizzie returned to My Place to tend to the crops, while Lizzie made the trip by train to Dickenson with the rest of the guests and family. When in Dickenson, she would visit the Land Office to make arrangements to have the property listed in her name on the deeds.

On the train, Cille suggested, "Lizzie, when you go to the land office, you might make arrangements for the property to be placed in your children's names, should something happen to you. You're welcome to return to Monroe and live at the estate with me. Sadie and Elizabeth will be returning to Europe once we get back to New York."

Rahema said, "Lizzie, I could come by once in a while and visit with you if you did that."

Rufus and Rupert's families made room for them while they were in Dickenson. They had to go to work the following day and Rahema, Cille and the girls accompanied Lizzie to the Land Office.

When they left the office, all the paperwork reflected that if Lizzie decided to leave Dakota and move back East, all she would have to do was sign her name in several places and have it witnessed by a local official. At that point, the deed would be ready to send to the Land Office. The new deed would reflect that the land would go to Rufus, Rupert, Benji and Nizzie.

They stayed in Dickenson for two days before the return trip to Medora and the long ride out to My Place and Prairie Rose.

After Cille and the girls had been there for the week, she said, "Lizzie, I must travel back to Monroe with the girls. They will be leaving for Europe shortly after we get back. I look forward to your letters and let me know if you decide to come and live in Monroe. I'd truly love to have you come back home."

Lizzie said, "Iz not gonna leave with ya, but Iz gonna think of what you say, and Iz gonna write ya when Iz ready."

Cille replied, "That would be fine, I understand."

Rahema spoke up, "I'm gonna stay with Lizzie for a spell, 'til she get use to being without my brother. I think she will need me here for a time, if it be okay with Lizzie and the three of you?"

A few days later, the carriage made its trip to Medora where Cille and the girls boarded the Northern Pacific Railway passenger train and made their way back to Monroe after several transfers of rail lines. The return trip was a leisurely one, spent with Cille and the girls chatting and enjoying each other's company. The scenery was nice but the visiting was what all three needed.

Upon their arrival in Monroe, New York, all three got off the train and spent the night at the estate. Before they left the train depot, the girls sent a telegram to their husbands to let them know when they would be leaving New York and about when they would arrive in England. The girls would leave for Europe two days from then.

When they arrived at the estate, there were several letters waiting for them. One of them that caught Cille's eye was a letter from her friend Medora. Cille read the letter aloud and was shocked to find that Marquis de Mores was killed in Northern Africa and his body was being returned to Cannes, France for burial. All three were stunned and saddened by the news.

Sadie looked at Elizabeth and said, "When we get to England, I believe we should make a short trip to France to call upon Medora and convey our condolences."

Elizabeth agreed, "If you hadn't suggested it, I was going to."

Cille said, "I'll send a wire tomorrow and convey our sympathy. She is such a lovely lady, and his death probably came as a shock to her. I wonder if she has anyone close, to give her comfort."

"We'll keep in touch with her, if she doesn't," Sadie said. "We'll see to that, won't we, Sister?"

"I'm sure we can keep in touch from time to time as our husbands go about their duties. I know there are times when I have ample time to do as I please and it would be nice to call on her."

The remaining time together, they went into Monroe and did some shopping before the girls packed their luggage and went to the train station and headed to New York City. From there, they would make arrangements to board a ship to England.

◇ ◇ ◇

Nearly a month had passed since leaving Dakota, when Cille received a letter from Lizzie. She mentioned that she was giving the land to her children and would be arriving on the train with Rahema in a few days. Rahema would be going all the way into New York City and not getting off the train as she went about returning home. Lizzie wrote that it would be good to be back in Monroe.

Six days later, Cille was at the Monroe train depot waiting for the passenger train to come to a complete stop. When it did, she saw her lifelong friend get off the train. She had a few items in her hands and claim stubs for some luggage, which was being offloaded from the baggage car. They greeted each other with hugs and tears of happiness, before claiming Lizzie's luggage.

Cille said, "I'm so glad to see you, how was your trip?"

Lizzie replied, "It be a long one for sure and Iz jus' glad to see you Cille, and this much of Monroe, too."

When they returned to the estate, Cille saw to it that Lizzie got settled in and they enjoyed the rest of the evening reminiscing over some of the things in life that they had shared together.

◇ ◇ ◇

Days later, they went into Monroe to do some shopping. They marveled over the changes that had taken place since they had left so many years ago. One thing that shocked them was the 1894 Velo, a self-propelled gas operated four-wheel motor car. Cille looked on in interest as Lizzie said, "Iz not sure if Iz gonna be getting' up in one of them seats no time soon."

Laughing at the sight of some of the changes, Cille said,

"Things have certainly changed, haven't they?"

Later that day, they sat in the gazebo in the center of the garden at the estate, and reminisced over the years they had been away from Monroe. They were surrounded by many extended flower beds on the back side of the estate. While looking back over times gone by, they enjoyed hot tea and a fresh batch of homemade sugar cookies, Lizzie's special sugar cookies.

Cille had found a reason to share part of the estate with Lizzie as they grew older. They had shared a lifestyle when they were out west, where they both had lost their husbands. They had a lot in common because they had both proven up on a homestead land that they chose to leave behind.

There was a pause in their conversation and it was obvious that Lizzie was deep in thought. Before she looked Cille straight in the face, she said, "Iz been thinkin' hard 'bout something and Iz needin' it wrote down." She held out a piece of paper and a pencil in Cille's direction. "Iz decided to share my secret cookie recipe with my best friend. You gets the secret firs' then we can share it with Sadie, Elizabeth, Nizzie, Benji, Rufus and Rupert. That be about the las' thing Iz gonna be able to pass along." Lizzie looked at Cille and added, "Iz here now and you have no cause to go off and rides alone any longer, 'cause Iz goin' to be right by your side."

Cille took the paper and pencil from her friend's dark hand that showed signs of heavy labor over the years. She began writing down the long-kept secret as Lizzie spoke softly and in detail. When Lizzie had finished, she sat back and smiled, as if relieved.

With sincerity, Cille said, "Thank you Lizzie, it is very nice that you decided to share this treasure with me, after all these years." They shared a laugh over the secret they shared.

The two old friends smiled at each other in hopes of sharing many tomorrows together.

THE END

The author and his wife wish to extend a word of thanks for reading this book. We hope you enjoyed the story that was written in the winds of Dakota, as we heard it. We would like to pass on Lizzie's secret recipe in hopes that you may enjoy the cookies with a cup of tea.

LIZZIE'S SECRET COOKIE RECIPE

The cookie it be crisp, that way lots of them important folks can hold it in their fingers, while enjoying tea.

Ya needin' these to make the cookie, and know when to add each item:

1 cup of butter – best if it is soft butter, homemade butter even better.

2 cups of sugar – store bought type called granulated.

3 eggs – best if they iz henhouse fresh- (4th egg separate, after dough is chilled, use to brush beaten white on the cookie.)

4 cups of flour – it best be sifted first, if not, not the same cookie.

1 teaspoon of baking powder.

1 teaspoon of vanilla, almond or lemon for flavoring - only one choice.

Cream the butter – smash and whip the soft butter to make it smooth, slowly add sugar and then add the beaten egg yokes- bes' be separate from the whites first. You mess this up, you mess up the cookie.

Then you fold in stiffly beaten egg whites and flavoring- takes more than one bowl to make these cookies. Blend thoroughly and chill.

Roll on lightly floured board, cut, and brush cookie with beaten egg white. Not only iz my cookie gonna look good, it taste good too.

Decorate cookie with jus' one of these: chopped nuts, raisins, shredded coconut, crushed hard candy or leave as is. Never make same way each time- that way fancy folks not figure out secret from the taste.

Bake in oven until light brown – takes 8 to 10 minutes.

It has been determined an oven of 375F should do the cookie good.

ABOUT THE AUTHOR

Larry Ludwig was born and raised in Montana, enlisted in the US Navy for a period of four years in 1956. He was assigned to the USS Cimarron AO-22 a fleet oiler, that operated in the pacific theatre. After leaving the Navy, he enlisted in the US Army, and remained there for sixteen years. His assignments ranged from stateside duty as a military policeman, those duties were in the lower forty-eight and Alaska. As a recruiter and career counselor, he had assignments in California and in Korea near the demilitarized zone. He retired after serving twenty years of active military service, and moved to Springfield, Missouri. He continued his education at Southwest Missouri State University, later renamed Missouri State. He holds a BS in Communications and BAs in English and Writing. He lives in Marionville, Missouri. He has three children from a previous marriage and enjoys nine grandchildren and three great grandchildren. His additional writings are *A Box of Rocks A Pair of Boots, Duke 8F15, and The Waiting*. More coming soon.

Made in the USA
Middletown, DE
04 January 2022

57649547R00205